BLUE HELL AND ALIEN FIRE

BLUE HELL AND ALIEN FIRE

MIDDANG3ARD™ BOOK FOUR

RAMY VANCE
MICHAEL ANDERLE

LMBPN

DISRUPTIVE IMAGINATION®

THE BLUE HELL AND ALIEN FIRE TEAM

Thanks to the JIT Readers

Diane L. Smith
Deb Mader
Dave Hicks
Kelly O'Donnell
Jeff Eaton

If I've missed anyone, please let me know!

Editor
The Skyhunter Editing Team

Copyright © 2019 by Ramy Vance & Michael Anderle
Cover Art by Jake @ J Caleb Design
http://jcalebdesign.com / jcalebdesign@gmail.com
Cover copyright © LMBPN Publishing
A Michael Anderle Production

LMBPN Publishing
PMB 196, 2540 South Maryland Pkwy
Las Vegas, NV 89109

First US Edition, December 2019
Version 1.01, January 2020
ISBN (ebook) 978-1-64202-670-2
ISBN (paperback) 978-1-64202-671-9

DEDICATION

*This book is dedicated to the Michael Anderle and Mundanes!
Thank you for helping me build a universe!*

—Ramy Vance

*To Family, Friends and
Those Who Love
to Read.
May We All Enjoy Grace
to Live the Life We Are
Called.*

— Michael

1

Few people ever ventured to the island.

The Mundanes had heard the legends before doing so, and they went anyway.

We're such fools, Suzuki thought when he woke up to find that he was incapable of moving. It took him a bit of squirming before he realized why.

There were rumors that the island was home to creatures of immense ferocity. Panthers the size of houses prowling through the dark, snakes that could wrap around an entire tree and pull it up by its roots. As far as the Mundanes were concerned, the creatures sounded like a petting zoo compared to everything else they had fought in Middang3ard so far.

In the past few months, they had battled orcs, dragons, a cave full of Christmas-themed monsters, techno-organic aliens, and demons, so he figured they could handle whatever the Island threw at them.

Given the position he was in, he wasn't so sure anymore.

Suzuki couldn't even turn his head.

It was as if his entire body had gone numb. The most he could move were his eyes and, even then, he felt like they were heavy and impossible to keep open.

And to think that a few hours ago, the Mundanes had enjoyed a ride on a rickety schooner with battered sails that miraculously caught the wind as they sailed to the Island.

When the Mundanes arrived, Stew was the first off the schooner, as usual. He didn't bother helping to anchor the boat. The man child was a walking pile of muscles, which had grown more defined since he came to Middang3ard.

He hardly wore any armor, his chest painted with charmed warpaint, a chain mail kilt covering his waist, swords, daggers, and battle-axes hanging from his back and waist. He was covered in scars, both from acne and battle. Thankfully, his acne had been clearing up over the last few months. A large scar ran from the top of his head to his chin, and it stood in violent contrast to the sheer enormity of his adolescent smile.

Stew splashed in the water, throwing his hands toward the sky as he fell backward into a crashing wave. "Dudes, this island is fucking *sick*!" Stew shouted. "Why did no one tell us about this before?"

Sandy waved her hand over in Stew's direction, causing a larger wave to rise and pound Stew into the shore. When Stew looked in her direction, she pretended not to see him as she magicked the heavy anchor off the schooner, dropping it into the water. She jumped off the boat and floated above the water's surface until she got to the shore.

Sandy looked slightly out of place in the small island paradise. Since coming to Middang3ard, she had not developed a definitive style, outside of her finely tailored MERC robes. Those looked like a cross between military garb and a high fashion concept suit.

That had changed over the last few weeks. Sandy had become obsessed with elvish fashion, specifically, high elvish funeral fashion. Her face was brilliantly made up with stark black makeup and lipstick, each stroke composed of a prayer to the elvish god of death. Instead of her usual MERC robes, she had opted for a rigid, formal three-piece robe-suit, tailored with the finest elvish silk, and a crisp burgundy tie. Seeing her smile or giggle was always shocking, even though it happened frequently.

Sandy glanced at Beth and Suzuki, who were still standing on the schooner. "Aren't you guys coming?"

Beth tentatively peered over the rail, looking a little worried as the sea's waves rocked the schooner back and forth. "I don't know how to swim," Beth admitted. "I hadn't really thought this far ahead."

Sandy smiled far too sweetly to be the epitome of high-fashion elf gothic. She extended her hand, and a delicate wand of black bone (in keeping with her recent color scheme) appeared between her fingers. She waved the wand, and Beth vanished from the schooner and appeared beside Sandy. "I've been working on short-distance transportation," Sandy said.

Beth was off-balance from the sudden transportation, and she teetered back and forth before falling on her ass. Unlike most MERCs, she refused to wear a uniform. She also refused to wear military-issue armor. Instead, she wore a ragtag ensemble of practical armor, function over fashion. Her hair was shaved nearly to her scalp, and she continuously scratched it. Scars covered her hands.

After she got back up, she scrolled through her HUD, tossed her armor into her inventory, and selected in a flattering, one-piece vintage bathing suit. Her back, arms, and neck were also covered in scars and burns.

Sandy took in Beth's bathing suit, envious in the way only friends can be when they see someone they care about looking that good. "Damn, Beth, when the hell did you go shopping?" Sandy asked. "Never pegged you for a thrift-store chic kinda gal."

Beth did her best 1940s pin-up pose, only to quickly lose her balance and fall again. She pulled a large-brimmed hat and sunglasses out of her HUD and sat down on the shore. "Yeah, I was going for Audrey," she said as she pointed at her hair. "You know, get the whole look going, but I totally fucked it up. Still looks cute, though."

Suzuki admired Beth from afar, trying to wrap his mind around the fact he was dating her. They'd spent so long as online friends that the revelation she was in love with him still felt too good to be true.

He knew it wasn't a dream when she turned and waved at him to join them.

Suzuki leapt off the boat into the water. When he'd first come to Middang3ard, he'd had a little bit of nerd-pudge. He'd burned that off over the last month of adventuring. Now he was a tanned and toned version of himself that could have easily been one of his old VR avatars. He wore fairly light leather MERC armor, the standard look of a fighter or warrior, with the addition of several enhanced items and charms he had picked up along the way. Nothing flashy, but if you were to look closely, you would see that even his basic leather armor had been enchanted with a high degree of skill.

It gave the exact impression Suzuki wanted. Unassuming.

No one would ever believe he was a walking powerhouse of well-thought-out tactical enhancements.

It didn't take Suzuki long to reach the shore. He sat next to Beth and took her hand in his. The sun was at the perfect angle to brighten the sky but not blind them. The wind smelled great, and he felt like he could have sat there on the beach with his party all day.

That was the last moment of comfort the Mundanes would share on the Island for some time. Everything was very quickly about to go to shit.

Whatever happened, happened fast—so fast, he didn't realize he'd been knocked unconscious until he woke up numb and unable to move.

A voice beside Suzuki roused his attention. He tried to focus on it, but his head was very fuzzy. It felt like he had just woken up from a particularly long night of drinking.

Yet he knew he hadn't. And he hadn't been out long since it was still daylight. In fact, the sun was beating down on him, and he desperately wanted something to drink, his mouth was so dry.

The voice beside him was still talking. He blocked everything out and focused on the voice, on what it was saying. At first, it sounded as if it were an entirely different language. Gradually the words started to make an impression. It was definitely English.

It was Beth's voice. What she was saying didn't make any sense, though. Then a few words got Suzuki's attention, and the rest of the words eventually caught up. "We've been drugged," Beth said.

Well, that explains why nothing fucking makes sense right now, Suzuki thought. The last few hours were a black spot. The last thing he could remember was getting off the boat and holding Beth's hand. Whatever had happened to get him drying out and unable to move under the cruelly hot sun had been forgotten in a drug haze. "Do you know how?" Suzuki asked.

As Beth spoke, Suzuki tried to turn his head to face her. Whatever had been passed to Suzuki and Beth wasn't responsible for Suzuki being unable to move. He couldn't see, but he could feel. Something was pushing down on him. Or, to be more specific, many little things were pressing down on him. It felt like he was trapped under piano wire.

Beth was still talking, and Suzuki was having a hard time following. The closer attention he paid, the easier it was to string meaning out of the odd jumble of consonants and vowels. "We've been Gullivered." Beth sighed. "Like, the whole fucking nine yards. Although, I don't remember reading anything about him being drugged. He just fell asleep. Something came and got us. Don't know how it happened or when, but it couldn't have been too long after we got here."

"So, some kind of indigenous people group captured us?"

"Yeah, you could say that. I don't know why you *would* say it like that, but sure. That's exactly what I think happened."

Suzuki strained his muscles, thinking he could just explode his bindings. It didn't happen, though. He was just as stuck as before. "Fuck." He groaned. "How the hell did Gulliver get out of this?"

Beth laughed. She still seemed to be in a fairly good mood for someone who was tied up and defenseless. "You know, I haven't read that since high school. I have no idea how the fuck he got out of it."

"Are Sandy and Stew here too?"

"No. I've been calling for them for a while but I haven't heard anything. Honestly, I wouldn't be surprised if they slipped off to fuck, and that's how we got ambushed. We should have left them to go fuck. Then we wouldn't have to wait for them to come save us. We'd already have bailed them out of this."

"I told you, outdoor sex kinda freaks me out. Instant anxiety."

"And like I told you, we're gonna work on it. We're gonna fuck on top of a mountain while goats and other woodland creatures take notes."

"First, we gotta get out of this."

Beth sighed, and Suzuki could hear her struggling. He put all his strength into slightly turning his head in Beth's direction. He was able to move a couple of centimeters, which was enough to let him see Beth. She was wearing her armor, which was good. That meant there was a chance they had gotten captured after all the Mundanes had gotten tired of being at the beach. Still, that didn't give Suzuki any more clues to what could have happened for them both to have been captured. That wasn't the reason Suzuki had turned to face Beth, though. Truthfully, he just wanted to look at her. He wasn't disappointed. Beth was staring back at him, smiling. "You really take me on the shittiest adventures," she teased.

Suzuki couldn't help but laugh as he squirmed under the piano wire. "Would you prefer to be rotting in an orc dungeon?" he asked.

"Nah. Your company is greatly preferred. So, this Milos... are his quests usually this shitty?"

Suzuki thought about it for a couple of seconds. "You know, I was originally going to say no," Suzuki started. "But now that I think about it, Milos only sends us to do bullshit. If I hadn't thought it was a good idea to get some ambrosia to cheer everyone up, I wouldn't have bothered. Now I can see why Milos didn't come to this beautiful tropical isle himself. Figures there would be shit here that wanted us dead. I say we tie him up when we get back and see how he likes it."

Beth raised one of her eyebrows as she licked her lips. "Oh, now you want to tie up our boss?" she asked. "You just keep getting kinkier."

"Just wait until I get some ambrosia in me."

"Can't wait to see what we can get in me."

Suzuki was trying to think of something to say in reply when he heard leaves moving.

A lot of them.

Something in the forest was heading in their direction. Suzuki strained his eyes, trying to focus past Beth. Out of the corner of one, he saw something rustling near the foot of the trees that surrounded them. A blue man with a slightly protruding belly stepped out. He was no taller than seven inches, and he wore a red cap. He would have been adorable if he hadn't been holding an axe and chewing on what looked like a miniature chicken head.

More blue men exited the surrounding trees. Beth's eyes popped wide open when she saw who was responsible for their capture. "Are you fucking kidding me?" she asked. "Did we get captured by Smurfs?"

Suzuki cleared his throat theatrically before Beth's glare made him stop taking himself so seriously. "Uh, I was just going to say that they're probably not called Smurfs here," Suzuki explained. "Writers and television were seeding the idea of Smurfs for the collective consciousness of viewers, so their real names are probably lost. Also, I'm pretty sure 'Smurfs' is copyrighted."

"What the hell do you propose we call them?"

"I don't know. I've never named anything before. 'Smuggles?'"

Beth laughed, and Suzuki's heart soared. He lived for that laugh. He'd die for it, too.

"Fine, 'Smuggles,' it is."

Five Smuggles walked into Suzuki's field of vision. They crossed their arms as they looked Suzuki up and down, talking to each other in a language he couldn't understand. It was filled with sharp consonants, and inflection seemed to be a large part of conveying meaning.

That and gesturing.

"Hey, Fred," Suzuki said, searching for his familiar within him. As hard as he searched, he couldn't find the imp.

Suzuki groaned. "Beth. Can you connect with your familiar?"

Beth pursed her lip as she searched within herself. "No," she finally said. "It's like they're not there. What's going on?"

Suzuki shrugged. Well, shrugged as much as his bonds allowed him to. "My best guess is that while we're tied up, they're magically bound and gagged." He couldn't help but laugh at the thought of the imp being gagged. Finally, there was a force on Middang3ard that could shut Fred up.

He looked at their approaching captors. From what Suzuki could gather, it seemed like they were preparing to skewer him. For what reason, he did not know. *Might as well see if I can ask*, he thought.

Suzuki wiggled as much as he could to catch the Smuggle's attention. "Excuse me," Suzuki started. "I don't mean to interrupt your...uh...meeting. But now that I have your attention, I want to ask you if you could possibly release us?"

One of the Smuggles took a step closer to Suzuki, his eyes narrowing with suspicion. "You talk loud. Too big. Quiet your voice," the Smuggle said.

Suzuki would have jumped for joy if he had not been so tightly bound. "Wonderful," he whispered. "You understand me. So, what do you say? Would you set us free?"

The Smuggle shook his head as he stroked his chin. "Nope. You sacrifice. We haven't had a big one in a while. You two will bring the blonde one much joy. She will overflow with happiness."

"Maybe you could sacrifice something else. Like an animal or something?"

The Smuggle's eyes went wide with disbelief. "How dare you?" he shouted, stomping his foot. "We sacrifice *you*. Now, silence. We must cover you with the sacred honey."

Three Smuggles stepped closer, each of them holding a bucket. They started to cover Suzuki's face with sweet-smelling honey, which made Suzuki's face tingle. Obviously, he would have preferred to live, but as far as human sacrifices went, this one could have been going a lot worse.

Suzuki still hadn't accepted his fate. He thought that maybe there was still a chance he could talk his way out of this. "So, what are you putting on my face?" Suzuki asked. "It smells pretty good."

One of the Smuggles looked up, his face grim and serious. "Ritual love juice," he answered. "Collected from strongest men. Stored for months."

"Oh. Well, it smells great."

"We know."

Across from the Smuggles, Beth laughed. "That is so gross." She giggled. "Death by Smuggle jizz. Who would have thought?"

A voice came from the jungle. "Death by badass ass-kicking is more like it!" it shouted.

Suzuki wished he could have turned and seen where it was coming from.

He already knew who was crashing through the jungle.

Only Stew would have bothered to give away his position and the element of surprise. Suzuki wished his head wasn't tied so tightly, so he could adequately roll his eyes and plant his face between his palms.

This was the end. This was how they were all going to die.

Stew leapt out of the jungle and landed in the clearing the Smuggles had made. He was wielding two hand axes, and he raised them above his head, ready to chop down whatever was in front of him. The size of the Smuggles was enough to make him hesitate for a moment, though. "Wait, *those* are what captured you guys?" Stew asked incredulously. "Little fucking blue men?" Stew leaned forward and kicked one of the Smuggles, sending him flying into the jungle. "You might as well have gotten caught by fucking Beanie Babies."

A few of the Smuggles went screaming into the woods, holding their caps as they ran, looking as if they had encountered madness. Stew was obviously getting off on it, hamming it up and pretending to be a monster of Godzilla-level destruction.

The few Smuggles who remained pulled their weapons. Stew couldn't help but laugh when he saw them preparing to attack. "You guys gotta be kidding me." Stew sighed as he gazed at the small blue men. "Don't know when to quit, do you?"

Something in the jungle clicked—the sound of machinery. Stew looked over his shoulder as a bolt was fired. The bolt came in low, close to the ground. It struck Stew in the leg and nearly tore through his ankle. Stew screamed in pain as he toppled over and landed next to Suzuki. The Smuggles jumped onto his body, prodding him with their weapons. Stew squirmed as the Smuggles who had run into the forest returned, carrying ropes and netting. Despite Stew's strength, the Smuggles were fast and efficient. They tied Stew down within a matter of seconds.

Once Stew was secured, the Smuggles backed away and looked at their work. "Very good," one of the Smuggles said to another. "Fast, good work. He will make good sacrifice as well. Cover him in love honey!"

The Smuggles leapt and laughed with joy as they went to the forest for more honey. They returned almost immediately and got to the task of covering Stew with it. "Are you fucking kidding me?" Stew shouted. "Are you rubbing Smurf cum all over me?"

Suzuki wiggled and squirmed until he was able to turn his head to face Stew. "We're calling them 'Smuggles,' and yeah, that's exactly what they're doing. Trust me, it's not nearly as bad as you think."

"I don't care if it smells heavenly. On principle, I ain't letting no one rub their love juice on me unless it's Sandy's idea, or they happen to be extremely hot."

"Uh, thanks for the info, dude."

Stew strained against his bonds and sighed exasperatedly. He looked like a giant child throwing a tantrum. "This sucks, dude," Stew whined. "This is what we get for helping people! That's why it's better to be a wolf than a hawk."

"You do realize that wolves are pack animals who help each other and a hawk is a solitary hunter with no flock?"

A rock hit the back of Suzuki's head. He turned around to see where it had come from.

Beth had managed to get one of her hands free. She smiled and shushed him as she continued to try to free herself.

On the other side of Suzuki, Stew was still complaining. "This ambrosia better be fucking choice," he moaned. "I am not going to suffer this indignation for some weird-tasting mushroom just because José used to like it a lot."

Suzuki interrupted Stew's rant. "Hey, quick question. How the hell did we get separated?"

"Oh, that? I slipped you and Beth one of those magical beetles Chip sent us with. Figured it would loosen you up. Then you went running into the woods. Me and Sandy didn't bother going after you because we thought y'all were trying to get your fuck on. Next time I'll know better than to let you two wander off without a chaperone."

"A, thanks for drugging us, asshole. B, shit, those things must have been strong."

"Last time me and Sandy took 'em, we danced on top of the Red Lion for a whole night. It was pretty sick. That was why I was down with getting the ambrosia. I figured if Chip and Diana were into it, it was probably going to slap pretty damn hard. Didn't know it would involve Smurf rip-offs, though. Could have done without the Smuggles."

Suzuki did his best to nod. "Where the hell is Sandy?"

"She thought it would be better to launch separate

attacks. I wasn't listening. I had been licking a beetle for a while."

Suzuki groaned. "Remind me not to try any shit Diana or Chip give me outside a relatively safe environment."

"Eh, we should be good. Sandy will be here any minute. Although, she was sucking on a beetle as well…"

There was a crash from the right, and trees exploded, and leaves went flying. Sandy stepped into the clearing. She clasped a red amulet that hung from her neck and levitated a few inches off the ground. Her skin turned ashen-white and flaked off. The ash revolved around her and transformed into a loose gray-black cloak, her body now nothing more than bones. A horrifying mask covered her face, eyes wide and mouth drawn up in a perpetual sneer. "Who are my enemies?" Sandy shouted. "Who has made a compact with death this day?"

Sandy looked around the clearing. There was no one other than the three Mundanes. She touched back down on the ground. Suzuki assumed that if he could see her face, it would have been very disappointed. "Aw, shit," she muttered. "I thought I was going to get to kill something. How the hell did this happen to you guys?"

Sandy floated over to Beth and knelt beside her. Before she could take hold of any of the bindings, a Smuggle stepped out from behind Beth's head. Sandy yelped as she fell back—an interesting sight, a pile of floating bones squealing with surprise and falling on its ass.

The Smuggle pulled out a knife and approached Sandy cautiously as she sat up. "These are what fucking did you in?" Sandy asked, her voice mocking.

Stew shouted from beside Suzuki, "Babe, be careful! Those fuckers are crafty."

Sandy stood and pointed at the Smuggle. "You will release my friends or face the consequences."

The Smuggle smiled and threw its knife at Sandy, who waved her hand, obliterating the weapon easily. She drew her bone wand and cast a fireball that sent the Smuggle flying. "That was hardly what I was hoping for," Sandy said as she leaned over.

A shout came from the clearing. The Smuggle was back. It now levitated a few feet off the ground and was chanting softly. A ring of fireballs conjured around the Smuggle as he opened his eyes and smiled viciously. He pointed at Sandy, and one of the fireballs flew toward her.

Sandy stepped to the side to avoid the fireball. Another one came flying at her, and she slashed through it with her wand before firing a streak of lightning. The Smuggle moved the fireballs into the path of the lightning, destroying it.

As Sandy and the Smuggle dueled, more Smuggles came out of the jungle. There were at least ten of them, and they all had floating magical fireballs surrounding them. Sandy didn't notice them until they blasted her from the back. She fell over, knocked out, her body and clothes returning to normal. The Smuggles acted fast and covered her body with ropes and a net.

All four of the Mundanes lay on the jungle floor, bound. They were silent for a few moments. Suzuki had really been expecting Sandy to get them out of the situation. He hadn't said it to Stew, but he'd come to see Sandy as the second in command. She was as levelheaded as Suzuki and was the powerhouse of the Mundanes. Everyone pulled their weight, but Sandy's single-minded focus on acquiring knowledge raised her into the realm of cosmic badass. Suzuki wouldn't have been surprised if she was inducted into a pantheon of gods by the time they were done with sorting out the Dark One's invasion.

The Dark One. He had only been a boogeyman to Suzuki for a few months, but all that changed after Suzuki saw the bizarre, faceless being hell-bent on bending dimensions to his will. Suzuki had been having nightmares about the Dark One since they finally looked each other in the figurative eyes.

Sandy groaned as she started to wake up. "What the fuck happened?"

Stew laughed riotously, far too carefree for the situation they were in. "You just got knocked the fuck out."

"No more the fuck than you."

"Babe, I didn't black out."

"At least I had to be hit hard enough to go down." Sandy scoffed. "What did you do, roll over and give them a nice view before they tied you up?"

"Babe, that's *your* view. I would never."

Beth imitated Stew's and Sandy's flirting in her worst baby voice, drawing each word out in the most cringe-worthy way. After she had gotten everyone's attention, she asked, "What's the plan for getting out of here? Or are you planning on waiting until I break out?"

Stew laughed, as good-natured as before. "You think you're going to be the one who busts us out of here and saves the day?" he asked. "Obviously, you need to start going on more quests with us. I'm the hero of the Mundanes. You can ask anyone. I've pulled us out of more jams than anyone else."

Suzuki wished he could have shaken his head. Stew was still so damn full of himself. At least it was worth a good laugh.

The Smuggles were making their way out of the jungle. There were more of them than before.

Nearly sixty.

They surrounded the Mundanes, chanting and humming under their breath. They were wearing a variety of head-dresses and beautiful, colorful robes.

Suzuki stared at the Smuggle closest to him, a pot-bellied little guy holding a ceremonial knife. The Smuggle was swaying as if he were listening to music and hummed softly. "At least we get to die being a part of something bigger than us," Suzuki offered. "A sacrifice is kinda cool."

There was a loud boom, and the Smuggles stopped their humming and chanting. Suzuki wished more than anything that he could sit up. Curiosity was killing him. Whatever the sound was, the Smuggles hadn't been expecting it. "Oi! Hold onto your knickers for a second," a familiar voice shouted.

It was Chip, the eccentric Chipmaster of the Red Lion. The Mundanes had been desperate for someone to upgrade their HUDs for them. Over the course of the last few months, they had become closer than friends.

At first glance, Chip looked to be a regular half-human, half-elfish gearhead, but, as the Mundanes had only recently found out, Chip's technological proclivities were a result of her being an android creation of the Dark One. She'd been put through the wringer during their last mission when she'd had her will taken and been forced to kill José, the former leader of her party. Most days, she kept to her room. Suzuki was surprised to hear her voice, let alone on a tropical island.

"Yes, yes, please hold on!" said another voice Suzuki assumed was Diana with Chip. She was also a member of Chip's party, the Horsemen, although it was hardly a party anymore with only two people. Diana was their mage. She was known throughout all Middang3ard as a fierce warrior and a baffling academic with a penchant for eating bugs that had *interesting* effects. Even though she was much more approachable than Chip, she was the Horseman Suzuki knew the least about. It was as if she had shrouded herself in mystery. She was so mysterious, you didn't even know she was mysterious.

Chip and Diana stumbled into the clearing. The Smuggles halted everything and stared up at the human and the android. Before the Smuggles could attack, Diana knelt and produced a vial filled with gold and pink glitter from her robes. "We noticed you were so kind as to find our friends for us," she said. "As a reward, we'd like to offer you this glitter."

The eyes of the Smuggles sparkled as brightly as the vial of glitter. They crowded around Diana as she handed them the vial, which was roughly the same height as they were.

A Smuggle with a long white beard and scars covering his face walked up to the one holding the vial and examined it. "Nice sparkle," he said as he appraised the glitter vial. "Enough for whole tribe. Nice sparkle, indeed. Catches sun just right. Beautiful vial. Worth the lives of your friends. You may take them."

Diana bowed low and smiled. The white-bearded Smuggle held out his hand, and Diana took it and kissed it lightly. Then she and Chip undid the Mundanes' bindings and helped them to their feet.

Suzuki looked down at the Smuggles. Their attitude toward the Mundanes seemed to have changed completely. One of the Smuggles came up and kicked Suzuki's foot to get his attention. Suzuki took a knee so he could talk to the Smuggle. "Sorry about the killing you try," the Smuggle said. "We sacrifice most off-islanders. Most off-islanders try to burn our village. Take us and make us live in clear cages. Our apologies. You do not seem like the ones who take us to cages. They never bring us glitter. They not even bother learning we like glitter."

Suzuki shrugged and smiled as he extended his hand to the Smuggle. "No problem," Suzuki said. "Everyone makes mistakes. Just glad my friends showed up before you guys finished the ritual and everything. Although it did sound pretty interesting."

The Smuggle held up his hands as he grinned. "Hold thought. Be right back," he exclaimed. The Smuggle ran over to the Smuggle with the white beard, and they chattered with each other excitedly. Then the Smuggle came back to Suzuki and kicked Suzuki's foot again. "We would like to invite you to the ritual," the Smuggle said. "Big feast afterward. For apologies."

"That sounds great! I'd love to go."

Diana and Chip sauntered over to the Mundanes. "Looks like you four could still do with a lot of mentoring," Diana said. "Here I thought there was finally a party to rival the Horsemen in their heyday, and you got captured on your first easy quest."

Sandy crossed her arms and pouted. "Okay, you didn't see those guys," Sandy disagreed. "They were packing serious firepower."

Chip threw her arms around Sandy's shoulder and laughed. It sounded hollow and less full of life than before. "Oh, she's just yanking your tailfeathers," Chip said. "Diana knows all about the inflated power of these wee shits. That was why we came when we heard Milos sent you on a little fetchy-fetch quest. Figured you might want a hand or two before you lost all of yours."

Diana nodded in agreement as she watched the Smuggles preparing for their ritual. "Yeah, I made sure to grab some glitter for the occasion. Smuggles love glitter," she explained. "I was lucky enough to be able to spend some time with them a few years ago and do some research on their tribal and ritual magic. Fascinating people. I won't lie, I'm very glad you four got captured. I don't think the Smuggles would have invited us to their ritual without feeling extremely contrite, and I've always wanted to see one of these up close. I've heard they're fascinating. And a little inappropriate, as well."

Chip glanced at the Smuggles, then pulled a small bag out of her pocket. She opened the bag and showed the contents to the Mundanes. The bag was full of multicolored beetles. "Anyone wanna get wacky and go stargazing?" she asked.

The Mundanes sighed. "Sure," Sandy said as she grabbed a beetle and tossed it in her mouth. "This is kind of a vacation, right?"

The ritual started a little past midnight. It took place in the clearing the Mundanes had been captured in.

Not that one would have recognized it as such. The clearing looked completely different than it had earlier. Small huts had been built, and a throne occupied the middle. The Mundanes were told where to sit and encouraged to be quiet and watch. What took place was worth remembering.

Diana was the most excited about the ritual. She had a notebook and pen out and was already taking notes. The rest of the Mundanes were also excited, but they had no idea what to expect. Everyone had encouraged Stew to keep his mouth shut during the ritual. Offending natives who had just extended the olive branch of peace sounded like a terrible idea.

A horn cut through the silence of the night. Once the horn quieted, the Smuggles came out of the jungle wearing white loincloths and white hats and lined up in two queues. They carried torches and chanted softly. Some Smuggles danced around the queues, throwing glitter into the air or at the chanters. Finally, the chanting Smuggles surrounded the throne. More Smuggles came from the woods, each of them carrying boards, nails, and hammers. They began the task of building a hut around the throne. The chanters continued to sing somberly as the other Smuggles worked. Once the hut was built, the builder Smuggles mingled with the chanters.

The Smuggle with the long white beard stood before the throne. He covered himself in glitter, took off his cap and tore it in two, and unleashed a wounded scream. He continued to scream as he spoke in his language, beating his chest savagely as the Smuggles around him chanted loudly. Then he knocked on the door of the hut. The Smuggles stopped chanting, and a hush hung over the clearing.

The door of the hut opened, and a female Smuggle stepped into the clearing. She had luscious blonde hair and bright green eyes. The old Smuggle bowed low before reaching into his pocket and covering the green-eyed Smuggle woman with glitter. She sneezed, and glitter flew everywhere. Once the glitter settled, the Smuggle woman took the old Smuggle's hand and took him into the room. She shut the door.

The Mundanes exchanged looks as the rest of the Smuggles chanted quietly. As the old Smuggle and the green-eyed Smuggle smuggled, some of the other blue folks began to prepare plates of food. It took more than a handful to bring plates to the Mundanes, but they managed. The plates were filled with exotic fruits and vegetables and a pile of sweet-smelling meat. Diana conversed quietly with one of the Smuggles and explained to the Mundanes as they were eating. Finally, the elder Smuggle exited the throne-hut. He bowed to the Smuggle who approached the throne-hut door. The ritual continued.

Diana excitedly whispered to Chip and a few Smuggles who were not partaking in the ritual. Suzuki wondered what they were talking about. Granted, the ritual wasn't quite what he was expecting, but it was interesting to see the culture that had inspired one of his beloved childhood cartoons.

Stew leaned over to Suzuki and prodded him in the side. "Hey, dude," he whispered. "Guess that answers the age-old question about Smurf orgies, doesn't it?"

Suzuki sighed and held his finger over his lips. "This isn't the time, Stew. This is a sacred tradition we're watching. You should be respectful."

Sandy nodded, agreeing with Suzuki. "Yeah, Stew, don't be an ass," she hissed.

Beth glared at Stew. "Yeah, douchenozzle, shut it," she said as she munched on a piece of fruit.

The night air was full of the sounds of smuggling.

Stew sighed and leaned back as he chewed on a bite of the dessert. "Whatever, dudes," he grumbled. "First time we see a little blue gangbang, everybody acts like we're in church or something."

No one bothered responding. The Mundanes sat in silent reverence for the ancient tradition of the Smuggles. After the ritual was over, the Smuggles raised their hands to the sky and cheered. The blonde, green-eyed Smuggle exited the throne room. She seemed more than a little tired and was helped to walk out to the jungle. The rest of the Smuggles quietly took apart the throne-hut and made their way into the night. Before long, the Mundanes and the Horsemen were alone in the clearing. Chip and Diana had already started to set up camp. "The Smuggle chief offered us a chance to sleep in the ritual space," Diana said. "It's a very high honor. Practically adopting us into the tribe."

The Mundanes began pitching their tents. Stew was still complaining about everyone being so serious. "I'm just saying it's funny," Stew muttered.

Sandy had already finished and was sitting by a small campfire, reading. "There is nothing funny about ritualistic sex magic, Stew," Sandy said. "It's one of the oldest forms of magic, and you shouldn't poke fun at it. They could use it to curse you."

Stew stopped what he was doing, interested. "Are you serious?" he asked.

Sandy lazily flipped through her book. "Yep. Nasty curses, too. You ready to hit the hay?"

"Yep. 'Bout ready to pass out."

"Don't pass out too fast. We're not just going to sleep after watching a ritualistic orgy. You obviously don't know who you're dating."

Stew nearly jumped into the air with joy before blushing bright red as the Mundanes and the Horsemen stared at him. "Uh, night guys," he stammered as he rushed into the tent.

Sandy closed her book and vanished it, then stretched and yawned. As she walked toward her tent, she said, "Don't forget your sound-dampening spells. From what Diana said, the Smuggles are *very* light sleepers. Night, losers."

That left Suzuki and Beth as the only ones still awake.

Suzuki looked at Beth, who was cleaning her sword. She seemed about to pass out. "You ready to hit the hay?" he asked.

Beth sleepily smiled as she stood up and sheathed her sword. "Thought you would never ask, Suzy," she said as she walked over him and draped her arms around his shoulders. "We've got some smuggling to do."

2

The Mundanes and the Horsemen rose a little after the dawn. As usual, Diana was up first. She put together a fire and started boiling water for breakfast. By the time Suzuki got out of bed, Diana had nearly finished cooking. Suzuki, still trying to shake off the cobwebs from sleep, sat down without saying anything. Diana handed him a cup of coffee, and they drank by the fire.

Suzuki would never be able to express to Diana how much he appreciated her early rising. They had been on a few small quests together since the Battle of the Viceroy, and Suzuki had grown to depend on having a cup of coffee before he was expected to be talkative. Plus, he really enjoyed being able to sit and take in the locale before the campground became a boisterous place. Once the rest of the Mundanes woke up, especially Beth and Stew, the campsite would devolve to laughter and shit-talking. Not that Suzuki had a problem with it. Just nice to be quiet sometimes.

After Suzuki finished his coffee, he dug into the bacon and eggs Diana had whipped up. The eggs were a Middang3ard twist. Diana explained to Suzuki as he ate that the eggs had come from a small ranch back on the mainland. A friend of Wendy's, the owner of the Red Lion, had managed to procure them. The eggs provided a health buff for a little over twenty-four hours. Whenever Diana could, she got some of those eggs for the road.

The two adventurers discussed the Smuggle ritual they had been allowed to observe. One of the things Suzuki was beginning to really appreciate about Diana was her curiosity about the world around her. Most of the MERCs Suzuki knew were, for good reason, very concerned with the task of taking down the Dark One. The threat of his invasion hung over everyone's head. Diana was different, though. She seemed to care a lot about Middang3ard. It was hard to imagine Diana having grown up on Earth. She often spoke of the different realms she had spent time in. It made Suzuki wonder just how long she had been serving with MERC.

Finally, the rest of the Mundanes filtered out of their tents.

Chip's hair was a mess, a tangle that hung over her face. She sat down amid a heap of mutterings and groans as she searched for the coffee. Sandy was the complete opposite. Her makeup was already expertly done, and she grabbed a plate of breakfast with the bright-eyed smile of one who's either been up for a while or who has an infinite love for mornings. Stew looked pretty indifferent to being awake. He took a plate for himself and practically inhaled it. Then he opened his HUD and scrolled through his inventory to grab the ingredients for a meal. It had become standard policy for Stew to cook his own second breakfast. The boy could eat.

Beth took a seat next to Suzuki, and he leaned over to kiss her on the cheek.

She made a fake gagging sound and smiled before clasping his hand and squeezing it tightly. Then she knocked Stew over, who was kneeling, inspecting his pot of boiling water. "You better watch your ass, Stew," Beth joked. "If you lose your balance that easily, you might be easier to decapitate than you think."

Stew dusted himself off as he stood up. "Unless someone attacks us while I'm painstakingly trying to provide for my fellow party members, I think I'll be fine," he retorted.

"Dude," Suzuki grumbled, "you know you're going to eat all of that yourself and not even offer us any."

"It's the thought that counts. And maybe if you guys didn't take so long to eat, you could get down on my grub. You'd think you guys were dining at a four-star restaurant instead of roughing it in the jungle."

Sandy conjured a book and pulled a nearby rock closer so she could prop her feet up on it. "Some of us like to taste the food we're eating," she joked.

Stew held his hand to heart and feigned a look of shock. "Me? Not taste food? How dare you insult my palate!"

They talked a little longer while Chip and Stew finished eating. Suzuki smiled through nearly the entire meal. It was moments like this when he just wanted to sit and observe. The journey through Middang3ard had at various times been harrowing and blissful. These were his friends, his party. These were the people he would die for. Hopefully not anytime soon, but it was a good thing to keep in mind when you were constantly risking your life.

Stew swallowed the last of his food and started breaking down his part of the campsite. "So, when are we going to go find this mushroom?"

As usual, Suzuki was the one who had to correct Stew.

"It's not a mushroom," he explained. "Ambrosia is a rare fungus that can be processed into an even rarer alcoholic drink."

"Ambrosia's the stuff the Greek gods were supposed to have eaten, right? Made them immortal or something like that?"

Beth looked impressed. "Wow, Stew. I didn't know you knew anything about Greek history."

"You're not the only one who grew up watching TV, you know. Some things just click, I guess."

Suzuki headed over to his tent and began tearing it down. "Well, real ambrosia doesn't make anyone immortal or give them superpowers. But Chip said it was José's favorite drink, so we're getting it for the Lion. I'm tired of seeing everyone moping around. It's about time we celebrated José and, uh, moved on."

Across the campsite, Chip glanced at Suzuki, quick, to the point, and fleeting. Chip returned to her work, and Suzuki turned back to his tent. Part of him was glad Chip had come on the quest. She had been holed up in her room, torturing herself for her role in José's death for far too long. The other part of Suzuki thought it was too early for Chip to be doing anything remotely related to José, but Chip was an adult, and a veteran MERC. If anyone knew how to handle grief, it was her.

Sandy had already finished putting away her tent. She was going through her HUD inventory as she paced around the camp, anxious to get going. "So, what's the game plan?"

Diana and Suzuki convened in the middle of the clearing. Sandy's agitation was understandable. It was time to get moving. Suzuki pulled out his reference picture of the ambrosia fungus. It looked like a red, flattened honeycomb with feelers stretching out of its hexagonal structure. He handed the picture to Diana. "This look about right?"

Diana took the picture and looked it over. "Yep, that's what we're looking for," she replied. "I'll assume Milos didn't tell you anything about the jungle."

"He said finding the ambrosia would be easy enough."

Chip chuckled as she walked over and joined the group of MERCs. "Sounds like exactly the daft line the shyster would pass along to you. This jungle is leagues from easy-peasy. Otherwise, the little fucker would have come here himself."

Suzuki frowned, irritated. Chip was right, and Suzuki should have pressured Milos for more information. No mission Milos had ever sent them on was easy. It was stupid of Suzuki to assume the dwarf had changed. "So, what do we have to be aware of?"

"Plain and simple? Everything here is gonna try to kill you. Even the trees have a touch of the ol' murderous intent, so keep your peepers peeping. Otherwise, you might not survive to peep another day."

A rustling sound came from the jungle. The Mundanes and the Horsemen drew their weapons.

The elder Smuggle walked out of the jungle and bowed low before continuing toward the MERCs. "You wish to enter the sacred jungle?" the Smuggle asked.

Diana and Suzuki knelt to be closer to the Smuggle's level. Diana looked at Suzuki, giving him the go-ahead to speak with the elder. "Uh, we didn't know it was sacred," Suzuki explained. "We did not mean to offend."

The elder Smuggle shook his head and smiled sweetly. "No offense. Partaking in the ritual opened the jungle to you. It is your sacred jungle, as well. But warning, there is a creature in the jungle. Terrifying. Beware. It kills. It always kills."

The elder Smuggle motioned to the jungle, and a few Smuggles came out from behind a tree. They carried a large stick and placed it at Suzuki's feet. "This has killed many creatures," the elder said. "Use it wisely."

Suzuki picked up the stick. It didn't look any more useful than his axe, but he wasn't going to shit on tradition.

In fact, he was excited.

Diana wasn't the only person who was interested in other cultures, and this was the first time since joining MERC Suzuki had been able to spend time with anyone other than humans. The most he'd seen so far was an elvish city, and that was only for an afternoon. It didn't compare to this.

Suzuki bowed his head and uploaded the stick to his HUD inventory. "I will make sure to use it wisely. Should we bring it back when we're done?"

The elder shrugged his shoulders. "No worry. Jungle full of sticks. May the gods watch over you." The elder and the other Smuggles disappeared into the jungle.

Suzuki turned to the rest of the MERCs. "All right, you guys ready to find some fungus?"

3

The jungles of the island were thick with trees and plants, none of which Suzuki had seen before. The trees grew close together, covering the ground with their roots. Their branches stretched overhead and nearly blocked the sun. Shadows moved across the ground as creatures slithered in and out of the shadows cast by the trees, faster than any of the Mundanes could see.

Diana walked beside Chip, holding a notebook. Often, she would stop and make notes about a plant or tree she passed. Any time an animal darted in front of them, she noted it.

Her curiosity was infectious. Suzuki had never been much of a nature person back on Earth. His father had taken him camping a handful of times, but most of the outdoor activities Suzuki had taken part in had been in Middang3ard with the Mundanes.

And even then, most of the time, he was much more concerned with staying alive than taking in the natural beauty around him.

Not today.

Diana raised her hand and waved Sandy over to her.

They both knelt beside a bright red plant shaped like a tube with a protruding lip that hung over the rest of the plant like a veil. Diana took out her wand and prodded the plant's veil-like lip as bright blue liquid oozed out of it. Diana took out a vial, scooped up the blue liquid, and held it up to better see in the light. "Manna potions are made out of this liquid," Diana said as she tucked the vial away. "This vial alone is enough to make thousands of potions. The plants aren't hard to find, but the species that grows here is known for its exceptionally effective secretions."

They continued moving through the jungle, Diana occasionally stopping to comment on one of the plants they passed. Suzuki tried his best to memorize what Diana was saying. Most of them seemed like they had magical applications. Suzuki was interested in what kinds of things could be made from the more mundane plants. Most of the enchantments Suzuki had created were mostly based on runes or magical gems. He wondered if it were possible to use any of these plants for crafting and enchanting.

Suzuki realized Beth had been quiet for most of their walk.

Diana, Chip, and Sandy were talking excitedly about potion-making, a hobby all three had some experience with.

Stew was quiet and was giving off an air of sullenness. Whatever was bothering Stew wasn't Suzuki's concern, though. Stew tended to get morose when Sandy was giving anyone but him attention.

Beth, on the other hand, didn't seem to care much about what Suzuki was doing. It never affected her mood in any way. That was why it was so noticeable when something seemed to be on her mind.

Suzuki came up to Beth and squeezed her hand. She looked at him and smiled briefly before turning away. "Hey, Beth, everything okay?" Suzuki asked.

Beth nodded as she looked at the gray vines that hung over them. "Yeah, yeah, everything's okay," she murmured. "Just thinking, I guess. You understand."

If there was anything Suzuki did understand, it was thinking. In his case, though, it was more overthinking, obsessing, and backtracking than simply thinking.

Beth pointed to a section of vines that had burst into bloom, displaying bright yellow and orange flowers that looked like a collection of individual sunsets. "Those are beautiful, aren't they? I've never seen anything like this before. Back home, I lived in the city, a good three hours away from the closest forest. Never thought I'd care much about seeing a tree. Even when we got here, most of my time was spent going back and forth between villages and shit. This is a nice change of pace, seeing something I didn't care about seeing."

Suzuki stopped to touch where the vines met the trees. "Yeah, same here. Never thought trees were very interesting. Guess the trees back home are different."

"These are something else. They must be so old. Look at how thick their roots are. Can you imagine how long they must have been growing here, Smuggles evolving around them? Life starting to take off in this forest."

Suzuki laughed as he pushed his hair out of his eyes. "Here I thought you might be upset about something. I didn't know you were having an existential experience. Did you sneak any of Diana's shrooms?"

"Fuck off, Suzy."

"I'm just joking. Never pegged you for someone who meditated on the vastness of existence the first time they walked into a forest."

Beth pointed at Stew. "It's better than staring straight ahead like a zombie. Look at him."

Stew was slouching, practically dragging his feet as he walked. His eyes looked dull, and he was drooling slightly. His movements were drawn out and exaggerated. Suzuki thought he looked like one of those depictions of a caveman.

Suzuki ripped a piece of hanging leather from his gloves and wadded it up into a small ball. He tossed it at Stew, shouting, "Hey, Stew! Too much green for you?"

Stew turned to face Suzuki. He was foaming from the mouth, and his eyes had rolled back in his head. He took a step toward Suzuki, jerking violently as the veins in his chest started to turn black. Stew lunged forward faster than Suzuki had ever seen him move before, swords drawn.

Suzuki jumped out of the way as he drew his axe. He rolled across the jungle floor as Stew turned his attention toward Beth, slashing at her erratically with his swords. Beth pulled out her shield and blocked the attack. She unsheathed her sword and took a step back. "Sandy!" Beth shouted.

Sandy looked at Stew, and he glared at her from across the jungle. He ran toward her, dropping his swords and grasping the massive battle-axe that hung from his shoulders. He swung at her head.

Sandy ducked, pivoted the side, and drew her wand.

A concussive force burst from her wand and tore up the ground in front of her. She didn't pull any of her strength. It still wasn't enough to move Stew, who raised his axe, ready to cleave her in half.

"Oh, shit," Sandy muttered as she dodged Stew's axe, her body breaking up into a thousand small pieces of ash and reorganizing behind Stew, where she could see the source of Stew's sudden violence.

A slug-like creature had attached itself to the back of Stew's head. It was covered in slime and veins and was pulsing rhythmically. A tube from what could have been its mouth was plunged in the back of Stew's neck. "What the fuck is that thing?" Sandy yelled.

Diana came up behind Sandy and pointed to the slug. "That is a glarry leech," Diana noted. "They live in the vines Suzuki and Beth were admiring. They're relatively harmless when they're that size."

"What do you mean, that size?"

"Well, it's just using Stew for a host. Hold on. Let me take care of this."

Diana stepped forward and waved her wand in Stew's direction.

Stew's feet floated off the ground. He continued trying to walk, his eyes still dim and stupid. He didn't even realize his feet weren't touching the ground.

Diana motioned for Chip to go to him. "You've removed one of those before, right?" Diana asked.

As Chip reached out for the back of Stew's neck, her hand separated into thousands of small mechanical pieces—the advanced tech of the Dark One. Chip's hand contorted into a spindly, delicate operating device. "I've picked off a leech or two," Chip answered as her fingers lifted the leech, revealing the long tube filled with blood attached to the back of Stew's neck. "I'll make sure not to pull out his brain stem. Leave all the gray, juicy stuff where he needs it."

Chip's thumb shot a small laser bolt that severed the

leech from Stew's neck. She tossed the leech to Diana, who caught it and put it in a bag. "Can be used for a valuable neurotoxin," she commented as she walked over to Stew to observe his wound.

Sandy was doing her best not to look too worried, but Suzuki could see she was freaking out. Chip put her arm around Sandy's shoulder.

Diana leaned over Stew as he relaxed onto the ground and rolled him over. "Oh, there's nothing to worry about," Diana said. "The leeches don't have a lasting effect, and Chip expertly removed the creature. Stew should wake up in no more than half an hour with a very interesting story to tell. They say that once the leech has you under its control, your mind melds with its mind. That being said, though, Chip, would you be a dear and check the vines for any other leeches?"

Chip saluted Diana and pointed at Beth. "You fancy coming along?" she asked. "Noticed you guys are a little heavy on swords that swing all about, but none of you know anything about tracking or that type of shite. You could benefit from rogue-ing. Eyes look sharp enough on you. Come on, pick up your britches. Today you're learning how to tree-run."

Beth shook her head and lifted her sword and shield. "I'm a fighter, not a rogue."

"One of the things you newbies need to learn, especially military brats like you, is that you can always learn new skills. Don't mean you have to toss down your pointy and shieldy things."

Beth took a step toward Chip. "I'm not a fucking brat," Beth growled.

"Then come along for the ride. Unless you're feeling bratty..."

Beth looked ready to fight, then she smiled and laughed. "All right, I'll check it out," she finally said. "Beats sitting around waiting for that douchenozzle to wake up." Beth followed Chip as they walked toward where the vines connected with the ground.

The rest of the Mundanes sat beside Stew. Sandy anxiously bit her bottom lip as she held his hand. Diana sat down next to Sandy and smiled sweetly at her. "Really," Diana offered, "I'm not just saying this to make you feel better. He might as well have gotten bitten by a bee. It's just that in Middang3ard, the bees bite a little bit harder than back at home. Don't worry about him. You should put up a barrier around us, though, just in case any more leeches fall from above. It'll give you a chance to work on your rune and sigil work. I'll critique, all right? Now come on."

Sandy nodded and sniffed as she stood up. She walked the circumference of the area around the remaining Mundanes, then, with her index finger, she traced a circle around them all and walked into the center. When she was done, she drew a sigil in the air with her finger, which caught fire immediately, the shape burning bright for a few seconds before exploding and casting a magical barrier around the MERCs. The half-sphere shimmered light-blue and looked as if stars hung from its top.

Suzuki whistled as he admired Sandy's work. Even though he was something of a mage, he could not handle magic like Sandy did. Her work not only was powerful but beautiful. The last time they had been drinking at the Red Lion, one of the MERC mages had walked up and asked Sandy for tips. From the rumors Suzuki had heard, Sandy's prowess was starting to rival Diana's. Diana was one of the MERC's strongest mages, so that was saying a lot. Diana couldn't have been prouder of her protégé.

Diana inspected the barrier, clicking her tongue as she made her observations. Then she came to Sandy and explained how it could be improved. Sandy nodded as she took notes in her small notepad.

Suzuki felt a pang of heartache as he watched Diana and Sandy together. It hadn't been that long since Chip and José had mentored Suzuki. Now José was gone, and Chip was broken. She hadn't been the same since they had returned. Still, she was at least out with them on a mission, and she had taken Beth with her. Chip might not have been all there yet, but she was working on it. That much was certain.

That left Suzuki.

He didn't know how he was handling everything. His mentor had died. He'd fallen in love with Beth. The war with the Dark One. He was looking forward to having a breather soon and being able to figure out how he felt.

But life wasn't slowing down.

Chip and Beth stood in front of a very large tree covered in what could easily have been confused for Spanish moss.

Chip pointed to the top of the trees and along the branches. "That's where we're going."

Beth folded her arms as she looked up. "I can jump up there, but after I do, I'm up Shit Creek without a paddle." Beth sighed. "I'm not exactly what you would call graceful."

Chip nodded as she laughed. "Oh, you don't have to tell

me that. I've seen you in a fight. Fast as lightning but lacking in any subtlety. 'Pointy end goes in' type of thing, right?"

"You don't have to dodge if it's dead."

"Right you are. But lacking in grace? Far from the truth. Rarely have I seen a fighter who looks as natural as you. A lot more than pointy, stabby things, you know? Got a sense of rhythm. Flow."

"Okay, maybe, but I'm not going to be able to Naruto this shit."

"*Yet.* You Mundanes might have been raised on games, but you're forgetting the most important part. This is real life, which means you can learn. And the ol' HUDs will help out along the way."

Beth took off her HUD and looked at it. "How's this thing going to help?"

"Plain and simple? You saw how I'm all gears and whistles inside? After the battle, I had to be locked up for a bit. Quarantine, seeing as how I went all bang-bang on my fearless leader under the Dark One's influence. The powers that be found out the HUDs share a lot of similarities with the shiny stuff in me."

"How the hell did that happen?"

"MERC doesn't know. Our HUDs were based on mil-tech. Maybe the military bigwigs got their hands on Dark One tech and reverse-engineered. Either way, we noticed something about the adaptive processing unit's integration with the cerebral cortex and familiar human synergetic adaptation in relation to—"

Beth held her hands up to cut Chip off. "Dude, I don't speak cyborg or nerd. What the fuck did you just say?"

"Oh, laymen, laymen."

Chip cleared her throat. When she spoke, her voice

changed dramatically, an almost perfect replication of Diana's studious, bookwormish, lecturing tone. "In short, HUDs learn. The skills you access and the way familiars help with the wiggle room for connecting you to magic? All of that's learned behavior. We ain't gone far enough to see if the buggers are alive, but they're something. So, if—"

"If I try rogue-like shit, the HUD will learn and help me."

Chip's voice returned to normal. "Bingo. Feeling a little more comfortable?"

Beth cracked her knuckles and leapt onto the closest branch. "Fuck, yeah. Don't tell anyone, but I fucking love learning new shit. I never got to try anything new in the military. So, you gonna teach me how to be the next Hokage?"

Chip landed next to Beth. "Even show you why running all flail-armed makes sense. Now follow my heels."

Stew woke up giggling, holding his sides, his face bright red, gasping for breath. After he finished choking, he laid there quietly for a few seconds before getting to his feet, stretching and chuckling.

The first thing Stew did was give Sandy a huge hug. He lifted her off the ground and spun her around, kissing her on the cheeks and the lips. "I love you so much," Stew shouted.

Sandy, bewildered, looked at Diana and Suzuki. "Uh, I love you too, babe," she said. "Are you feeling all right?"

Stew put Sandy back on the ground and touched his toes. "Yeah, I feel great," he answered. "Feels like my head is on straight. Kinda want to go for a run. Don't know why, but I feel like I could run for a while. How are all of you feeling?"

Sandy threw her arms around Stew and kissed him,

knocking him over. They rolled over in the lush grass for a second before they became aware of those around them and sat up, blushing and giggling before standing and smoothing their clothes out. "Glad to see you're up and ready to go," Sandy joked.

Stew was all smiles. He looked like he had been given an injection of youth. "Yeah, I'm ready to fucking get going," he exclaimed. "What are we doing next?"

Suzuki stepped forward and broke into the conversation. "We're waiting for Beth and Chip to clear out the leeches," he explained. "Same leeches that were gnawing on your brain."

Stew gave Suzuki a confused look. "My brain? Are you telling me I had a leech sucking on my head?"

"Dude, more than sucking. That thing was using you like a puppet."

Stew grew solemn for a moment as he tried to recall what had happened. "Are you saying I got mind-controlled? I don't remember anything. The last thing I can remember was you guys talking about boring shit. And then I felt...I don't know, I thought it was Sandy giving me a kiss on the neck. I woke up here."

Diana sat down and scooted close to Stew. It was obvious she was interested in what Stew had to say about the experience. She looked like she was staring at a specimen to be dissected. Her eagerness was palpable to all the Mundanes. "Do you remember dreaming anything?" Diana asked. "In the time you...weren't yourself?"

Stew scrunched his face as he thought, stroking his chin. "Now that you mention it, I do remember dreaming," he finally admitted. "They were confusing. You know, I don't dream much. Never have. But I did have a dream. It was weird, and you were all in it. We were out in...space or something like that. Floating along. I was choking. I couldn't breathe, no matter how much I tried to. And there was a dragon. It was thrashing around against the stars. It looked sad. I tried to do something to make it feel better, but it was moving away from me. And Suzuki, you were there while it was happening. You reached out and grabbed the dragon, and it started breathing fire everywhere. The stars caught fire, and then we were in the sun. And the Dark One was there. He was watching everything, but it was hard to tell he was watching because, you know, he doesn't have a fucking face or anything. But it felt like he was watching. It was unbelievable. But, yeah, that was the dream."

Diana stood up, looking somewhat disappointed. "Hm. That wasn't what I was expecting. If you have any more dreams like that, please let me know."

As Diana spoke, leeches started to fall from the branches overhead. They hit the barrier Sandy had built with sickening thuds. Their dead bodies littered the jungle around them.

Chip and Beth jumped down from the branches, landing in a pile of dead leeches that exploded and sent blood and entrails flying. Chip reached down and grabbed one of the leeches. She tossed it in the air, smiling. "Your girl is a prime assassin-in-training," Chip said to Suzuki. "Picked most of it up in a jiffy. Wouldn't be surprised if she ditched the sword and shield and started doing something a little bit more sophisticated."

Beth was blushed brightly as she stepped away from everyone and picked up one of the leeches. She brought it to Chip and asked, "So, what can you use these for?"

Chip grabbed the leech from Beth and twisted it in her hands. The leech bled a blue substance that Chip caught. She tasted it on a fingertip. "Oh, there are all sorts of fun things you can get up to with this one's guts," she said. "But none of them are 'work appropriate' at the moment. If we start sucking on leeches, we might be in the jungle for a fortnight. Everyone might see a god or two. Much better to enjoy that tucked away under your blankets, I'd say. So, the big one is finally awake. Time to get moving instead of wasting time talking about slugs and leeches, eh?"

Suzuki nodded as he helped Stew to his feet. "Yeah, might as well get going. That ambrosia isn't going to find itself."

4

The Mundanes and the Horsemen wandered through the jungle. They had no clear-cut plan of action. The jungle was just too much, and despite them trying to point out landmarks they had seen before, the jungle continued to confuse and surprise them.

At first, they marked trees they had seen, behemoths of bark and leaf that were as distinctly individual as any of them. Yet after an hour of walking in one direction, they were in front of the tree again.

Diana cautioned that the jungles were known for causing madness. Many a traveler had spent days to months in the forest, ruminating over their life among the trees that dominated the landscape, their ancient weight hanging heavy over all who walked into their grasp.

It was sobering for all who walked through the black and green jungle that day. Nothing was said, yet it was evident to all who paced through the trees, ferns, and vines. Something weighed heavy on them. All the MERCs seemed to be trapped in pits of their thoughts and anxieties. Except for Stew.

Stew smiled and chatted throughout the entire walk. His optimism knew no bounds. He was a different man than he had been before. To everyone's surprise, when Beth mentioned she was tired of walking, that she felt like they had been meandering through the same circle of vines the entire day, it was Stew who suggested the MERCs sit down and rest. Once everyone had taken up a comfortable station, Stew asked Beth why she felt so depressed. When Beth was hesitant to answer, Stew pressed the subject delicately, which surprised the MERCs who sat huddled together in the dim jungle.

Beth stared wide-eyed at Stew, unable to explain why she was so uncomfortable with this sudden change of character. "What the hell, Stew? Are you saying you want to talk to me about my feelings?"

He laughed as he struggled to make his chain mail kilt more comfortable. "Yeah, I'm asking you how you feel," Stew exclaimed. "You seem like you're having a hard time out here. I was just wondering what was making this so difficult for you? I know we're all tired. It feels like we've been at this for a really long time. But you seem to be more bothered by it than anyone else. I just wanted to make sure you were feeling all right."

The rest of the MERCs looked on in confusion and awe. No one quite knew how to put into words how bizarre it was to see Stew showing the slightest modicum of human decency and understanding. Suzuki thought it was odder than Stew being controlled by a leech and attacking them. Somehow that made more sense.

Beth scooted away from Stew and eyed him with growing

suspicion. "I'm okay," she said. "Just tired of walking. It feels like we aren't getting anywhere."

Stew leaned forward, his eyes bright with intensity, focus, and empathy. "I was thinking the same thing," Stew exclaimed. "We've been walking for hours, and we haven't gotten anywhere. What do you think is the reason for that?"

Beth continued to eye Stew as if she were worried he was not who he said he was. "Uh, I don't know," she finally said. "I just know it's bugging the fuck out of me." At that moment, Chip beckoned to her, and they went aloft again.

Stew laughed and rocked back and forth, holding his kneecaps. "I know!" he shouted. "I'm very tired of walking around in circles. This jungle is obviously fucking with us." Stew turned to Suzuki. "What do you think we should do about it?"

Suzuki was caught off-guard by the question. Even though he had been wandering the jungle for the better part of four hours, he hadn't once thought about how he or the rest of the MERCs were going to find a way out. Now that he thought about it, it was kind of odd that he hadn't entertained the idea. He had just accepted they were going to wander for as long as necessary.

Listening to Stew talk and reflecting on his thoughts, it became very apparent there was some force in the jungle that was hindering his ability to think, and maybe his ability to feel. The assurance he felt that everything was going to be all right in the jungle seemed to come from outside his mind, almost as if it had been planted there.

Stew leaned close to Suzuki and placed his hands on Suzuki's knees. "What do you think is going on, Suz?" he asked. "I can see those gears grinding in your head."

Suzuki was uncomfortable with Stew's straightforwardness, and he leaned back and cleared his throat. "I don't know what's going on." Suzuki groaned. "Up until a few minutes ago, I didn't think there *was* anything going on. Now that we've stopped, and I've had a little bit of time to think, I can tell something's not right. Especially with you, dude. You are way too... I don't know, you seem a little bit off."

Stew leaned back and smiled brightly. "You know, I was thinking the same thing," he said. "I feel like...I don't know, in touch with everything around me. In touch with the trees, with the grass, with you guys. I just feel...so open."

Sandy poked Stew in the face. When he didn't react, she grabbed him by the cheeks and pulled. "Where is my boyfriend?"

Stew laughed, a sound full of mirth and joy. It was drastically different than his usual coarse, sarcastic laugh. "I'm right here, babe." He chuckled. "I'm more here than I've ever been in my entire life, and I want to tell you that you're beautiful. You're the most beautiful woman I've ever seen. And I love you."

Sandy smiled and blushed as she hid her face behind her hand. "Shut up, Stew," she cooed as she playfully slapped his hand away. "You're embarrassing me."

"I mean it, though. And not just you. I mean, you're beautiful, and I love you in an entirely different way. But all of you —you're all great, and I fucking love you guys. So much."

Suddenly, Beth and Chip fell from above in a crash of broken branches. Chip landed on her feet, while Beth fell on her ass, staring up at the branches overhead, laughing as the bodies of dead leeches fell from the canopy of trees overhead. Chip helped Beth to her feet, saying, "A wee bit of work on the landings, and you'll be right as rain."

Beth was elated and hugged Chip, then backed off awkwardly. "Thanks," she muttered. "You're a good teacher."

Chip nodded and turned to the other Mundanes, who were still crowded around Stew. "Looks like your boyo is in tip-top shape," she said.

Stew stood up and rushed over to Chip. He grabbed her hand and pumped it three times with the enthusiasm of a politician. "It's so good to see you, Chip," he gushed. "Thank you so much for getting that leech off me."

Chip backed away, caught off-guard by the overflow of sincerity coming from Stew. "Uh, no problem, mate. Just glad to see you up and about," she muttered before turning to Sandy and whispering under her breath, "Is Muscles all right?"

Sandy smiled and shrugged. "I don't know," she said. "But whatever the hell is going on, I think I might like it."

Suzuki looked at the sky. The sun was beginning to set. Waiting for Stew had taken longer than he had expected. Traveling through the jungle during nighttime seemed like a terrible idea. Even in the bright of day, they had been obstructed by creatures they weren't even aware they should have been looking out for. Suzuki cleared his throat to get the attention of the other MERCs. "Hey, so it's getting late," Suzuki started. "Maybe we should make camp for the night and head out tomorrow. There could be worse shit out there we don't even know about."

The rest of the MERCs agreed to varying degrees. Diana wanted to find out what was hiding in the night. Beth was restless and didn't want to set up camp just yet. Sandy was extremely worried about Stew's sudden personality change. Chip was the only MERC who was indifferent toward the plan. She said it didn't matter when they left, there was going to be something that desired to feast upon their flesh.

Suzuki didn't feel comfortable giving a straight-out order. He wasn't the leader of his party since the MERCs didn't have a strict hierarchy. It was mostly based on an unspoken rule.

He also knew Chip and Diana were a party completely separate from his, and they had their own way of figuring things out. However, it seemed like everyone was waiting for him to tell them what they were going to do. "We should make camp for the night," he stated.

There were no disagreements.

Everyone went about setting up their tents. It was not long before a fire was roaring and they were sitting around it, roasting meat rations Diana and Stew had brought along. Diana conjured bottles of mead and tankards and passed them around. Within the hour, Diana and Chip were singing old war songs that had been passed down through the MERCs for who knew how long.

Suzuki sat by the fire, watching the flames lick up the wood. Beth was across from him, her face highlighted by amber light and shadow. Stew and Sandy were trying to learn the words to the song Chip and Diana were singing. Stew's voice rang out the strongest of anyone's. Suzuki remembered that Stew had mentioned he liked to sing but was very shy about it. This was the first time he had ever heard Stew sing without fretting. Stew belted the lyrics he knew and hummed through the sections he didn't. His voice filled the campground as the Mundanes, and the Horsemen grew tired. Eventually, they put out the fire and retired to their tents.

Beth was already in the tent by the time Suzuki arrived. She was wearing a silk robe as she sharpened her sword by candlelight. She looked up at Suzuki as he entered. "Wild day, huh, Suzy?"

Suzuki sat down next to her and removed his shirt. "Really, you think so?"

"Uh, yeah. A long, meandering, and pointless walk through the jungle. Stew gets a brain leech and suddenly has an entirely different personality. I'd say it was pretty fucking interesting day."

"I don't know. I feel like that's just the norm now. What's a quest if one of your party members doesn't try to kill you?"

Beth put away her sword, laughing as she laid back on her sleeping bag. "Things definitely work differently in the MERCs than the military," she said. "I really like it. A lot more room to breathe."

"What was it like in the military? You don't talk about it much."

Beth stared into Suzuki's eyes. Her gaze was heavy, and she held his eyes for far too long. Suzuki had to look away. "It was, I don't know...the military," she explained. "You follow your orders. Do what you're told. Help your—I wouldn't call them friends—your squadmates when you can. No one tells you shit. I mean, not real shit. Like what Milos pulled on us, sending us out here without letting us know how dangerous it is. That's nothing compared to the military. Milos is just being an asshole. With the military, though, I mean, they treat you like pawns on a fucking chessboard. All of us were expendable. They never said it, but it was obvious. Made me wonder why the fuck I was fighting the Dark One for a while, to be honest."

Suzuki didn't know what to say. His experience with MERC had been the complete opposite. He wanted to be there for Beth, but he had no idea how to relate to what she was saying. Since he had come to Middang3ard, all he had felt was unrestricted freedom. He had felt like he had the ability to be whatever he wanted to be. It was nothing like what Beth had experienced. "Yeah," he finally managed. "That sounds really fucking rough."

"It was more than rough. I felt like I was losing myself, even though I was doing something I knew I was capable of. Every day, it just felt like I was a little bit less of myself, you know? It was weird. Serving for the common good. Trying to take down the Dark One, and the whole time feeling like I was losing myself. That's why I couldn't go back. I mean, of course, I wanted to be with you guys, but even if you had told me the MERCs weren't taking anyone else, I wouldn't have gone back to the military. I would have gone home. I'm not that person. I don't think I could ever be that person."

There was a time and place for words, and this was not one of them.

Suzuki wrapped Beth in his arms and they sat there in silence for some time, letting the weight of Beth's words sink into them both. They drifted to sleep, both of them thinking about what had been said and what was to come.

5

The MERCs awoke to their usual morning routines. Diana and Suzuki rose early and went about their business, the rest of them trickling in as they saw fit. After breakfast was finished, they packed up their camp and continued into the jungle, making sure to watch the canopy above for leeches.

Around noon, they stopped at Stew's request. He said he thought they should rest for a bit, seeing how the heat was accosting them no end.

Once they made camp, Stew began cooking. He coaxed Diana into sharing some of her coveted inventory and managed to whip up an amazing meal that was both reminiscent of home and paid tribute to the wilds of Middang3ard. All the MERCs were impressed. Stew had wowed them with his culinary skills before, but the meal he created that day was unprecedented. It was art, as Diana subtly put it.

After lunch, they broke camp and continued on, Suzuki watching Stew closely. For some reason, Suzuki thought "Steward" fit better than Stew. He pondered it for some time, knowing full well why he believed there should be a proper name change. The man at his side was not the same one who had been there before. There were only trace elements. The sophomoric humor had disappeared. Instead, there was what seemed to be a solemn, almost contemplative attitude, still drenched in good nature, yet at least twenty years older.

Suzuki was wary of the sudden change.

Sandy, on the other hand, seemed to be relishing Stew's sudden change of heart. While the rest of the MERCs trod through the jungle, slashing at the vines that fell in front of them, hacking away, trying to make their way through the jungle, Sandy fell into conversation with Stew in a way Suzuki had never seen them speak.

What he could catch was mostly in whispers, yet Suzuki could see how close Stew and Sandy walked next to each other. They were already very close, but this was unprecedented.

Stew asked questions about magic, but they were not the questions a novice would pose. His questions were insightful, the sort one asks when they have listened to a subject for some time yet are not as knowledgeable as those they converse with.

Sandy ate it up.

The conversation on the jungle walk pertained to magic and magic alone. Diana scooted closer at some point, and the three of them spoke of magical dealings, of curses and charms that had been forgotten for a millennium. The oddest part of the conversation was that Stew was completely keyed in to what was being said. He asked question after question, his earnestness almost tangible. In this way, they journeyed through the jungle.

Nearly two hours after lunch, Suzuki finally realized he

had forgotten why they were lost in the jungle. Ambrosia. That was the point of the mission. It didn't seem as if any of the Mundanes or Horsemen had any idea how to find the fungus. True, they had a photo of it, but they had hardly spoken about how to find the plant. Suzuki thought about it for a while. He assumed it was an effect of the jungle. Since they had initially arrived on the island, it seemed like the jungle had had some kind of effect on them. Being captured by Smuggles was something that wouldn't have happened on the mainland of Middang3ard. Suzuki thought it could be a form of ambient magic similar to what he had seen in the Dark One's defense rings, the sort of magic that disrupts without making itself obvious.

With that in mind, Suzuki stopped. He tried to gather his thoughts and focus on the purpose of their mission. They were here to find ambrosia, which was a fungus. "Diana," Suzuki said as he turned to her. "Are there animals that eat ambrosia?"

Diana scratched her chin as she thought. "Hm. Now that I think about it, yes, there are," she answered. "There is a type of beetle that exists purely on ambrosia. They search it out over anything else. Water. Sex. Anything. All they care about is the fungus. Needless to say, they do not have very long life spans."

"Perfect."

Suzuki pulled up his HUD. He opened the menu that pertained to his scent upgrade. It was the first SD upgrade Beth had sent him when she'd first introduced him to the MERCs. At the time, Suzuki had thought it was a completely useless addition to what was already shaping up to be an overwhelming experience. How wrong he had been. He scrolled through a multitude of scent settings, looking for something specific until he got annoyed. Then he remembered Fred.

His familiar had been extremely quiet since they had gotten to the Island. His pride was probably hurt from being tied up earlier.

Then again, it might have been more than that.

Seemed all the Mundanes' familiars had been silent since the Battle of the Viceroy. They still spoke to their owners if the occasion demanded, but they made no effort to start a conversation.

There had been something about that event—the chips and the monsters that spooked them—and the Mundanes had all agreed to give their familiars space.

So, instead of reaching out to Fred, the imp who dwelled in his body, Suzuki concentrated his thoughts on a specific scent, hoping Fred would pick up the slack and serve as a mediator between his desires, the magic, and the HUD.

Suzuki knew Fred had been paying attention when Suzuki become aware of the funky smell coming off his skin. *That must be the smell of ambrosia*, Suzuki thought. *Gross isn't the word.*

The rest of the MERCs looked at Suzuki, scrunching their faces with disgust. Stew was the only person who didn't seem to mind. He walked over to Suzuki and inhaled deeply. "That's a beautiful scent." Stew sighed. "Very floral. Almost like...lavender?"

Suzuki took a step back from Stew. "Uh, dude, you've been acting really fucking weird. Like, really weird."

Stew inhaled Suzuki's fungal scent again. He breathed it out slowly as if he were a perfumer. "Really?" Stew asked. "How weird have I been acting, my dude?"

"That! See, that right there. 'My dude?' Why the 'my?' Why the hell are you being so...nice?"

Stew smiled sweetly as he embraced Suzuki. "Because I fucking love you, my dude. You're my best friend. Why wouldn't I be nice to you?"

The rest of the MERCs surrounded Stew. Diana was staring at him as if he were a test subject. She looked like she was going to rub her hands with glee. She pinched Stew's cheeks, but Stew just kept smiling. Then she slapped Stew across the face. He took a step back, his eyes wide and worried. When Diana moved to strike Stew again, he grabbed her hand and held it steadily.

Diana slowly withdrew her hand as she began to pace around Stew. "Fascinating. He's had a complete temperament change, but it hasn't changed his cognitive function. Observe." Diana whipped out her wand and pointed it at Stew. She blasted a fireball toward him.

Stew yelped and jumped out of the way, then pulled out his axe and squared up.

Diana squealed with excitement as she put her wand away. "See! He still has his fighting techniques and his warrior disposition. He's become empathetic without losing his killer instinct, or at least his instinct for survival. We'll see if he still has a killer instinct when he's in a situation that requires killing despite having an emotional tie to the individual. We should test that as soon as possible."

Sandy came up to Stew's side and stared at him, her eyes scanning every part of his body. She grabbed his hand, and Stew pleasantly smiled as she looked at his palm. "Fuck you, Stew," Sandy shouted. "You're a fucking asshole!"

Stew's face instantly collapsed in contrition. "Babe, what

would make you say that?" he asked. "Did I do something to upset you?"

"You talked my ear off last night, even though I told you I needed to sleep. You just kept fucking talking."

"Babe, you told me you wanted to talk about things. That's why we were talking."

Sandy narrowed her eyes at Stew. "All right, he's definitely broken." Sandy sighed. "He's never this...reasonable, especially about something I just made up. I don't trust it, although I like it. A little. When is he going to go back to being, you know, Stew?"

Diana pulled down her HUD and scanned Stew. "There's no way to tell," she admitted. "I've never seen anything like this. There are no recordings of people being changed by a leech attaching to them. This is unprecedented. I think the most we can do is observe. Outside of that, this is all new territory."

Stew smiled brightly as he puffed out his chest. "So, I'm just Pleasant Stew for a little while?"

Sandy sighed as she shook her head. "You don't have to be so fucking cheerful all the time."

"Oh, I'm sorry, babe. I can tone it down."

"Or accommodating."

"I can work on that."

"Ugh, could you just go back to normal!"

Stew shrugged, smiling sweetly. "Don't know. Hope so!"

Sandy shook her head and leaned over to kiss Stew on the cheek. "You get into the weirdest shit. Even if you're suddenly a completely different person than the emotionally stagnant man-child I fell in love with, I'll still love you. Not even ironically."

"Uh, babe, that means a lot to me. I'm glad you can have a sense of humor about this."

Beth threw her hands up and walked away from the group of MERCs. "Jesus Christ, Stew, will you stop being so goddamn pleasant?" she shouted.

"I'm sorry!" Stew shouted back.

As Stew's voice rose, there was another rising sound. It was as if a thousand hands were clapping at once. All the Mundanes drew their weapons, Stew stepping to the forefront of their phalanx. He grabbed Beth's shield, pulling it off her back, and pounded on it, attempting to draw whatever was approaching's attention.

A swarm of insects flew out in.

Each was nearly the size of a baseball. Their compound eyes had multitudes of colors, and their thin, nearly translucent wings fluttered uncontrollably. Hundreds upon hundreds poured from the trees, each of them with a head like a mutated horse skull. Their jaws snapped, legs twitching as they flew and stumbled over each other, a plague from the confines of the jungle.

The swarm surrounded the MERCs. The gnashing of teeth and beating of wings was almost too much to deal with. The sound made the MERCs want to cover their ears. Fighting was almost out of the question; the sound of buzzing wings was so deafening.

Stew stepped forward and pulled out his axe. He swung blindly and ineffectively at the mass of insects as Sandy conjured her wand, her skin turning to ash and covering her body in a dark cloak, her face a death mask as her bones shone brightly in the fire ring she called up.

Suzuki called his hand axe and slid his fingers over the pommel, activating a charm he had placed weeks ago. The axe grew heavy and dense, its blade turning white with heat. Suzuki pulled down his HUD and scanned the insects.

His HUD read that he had a hundred percent chance of success.

His first instinct was to attack, but he stopped for a second. *They're just bugs, and they're what I need.* "Leave them alone," Suzuki shouted. "Don't hurt the bugs! They aren't trying to hurt us."

The MERCs slowly put away their weapons and, doing the only rational thing, ran away from the swarm. The insects did not follow through. They seemed content to stick around Suzuki, who remained where he stood.

Beth retrieved her shield from Stew as she shouted to Suzuki, "Suzy, get out of there! They're going to eat you alive!"

Suzuki shook his head as he smiled. "No, don't worry about it!" he shouted back. "They're here because I smell like ambrosia! It's all right." Suzuki felt something bite his shoulder, then his wrist. He looked down. The insects that had engulfed him were chomping down on him. "Fuck! I was wrong! Kill them! Kill all of them!"

The Mundanes stormed the insects, but they were too late. The flurry of wings had not stopped, and Suzuki felt his feet floating off the ground. The insects were taking him with them.

After the initial fear and pain wore off, Suzuki found the experience to be relaxing. He had been wrong twice within the span of a couple of seconds. The insects weren't chewing on him. They were only biting him so they had a way to lift him. Calling them bites seemed misleading. At most, they were nibbles. That being said, the rest of the Mundanes did not know this, and they anxiously followed Suzuki, despite him shouting multiple times that everything was okay.

The insects carried Suzuki and led the Mundanes out of the jungle into a green pasture. A river cut through the pasture, and the water was dark and brown—a river of mud. The Mundanes stopped short of the river and watched as the insects carried Suzuki and dropped him in the stinking, stagnant water.

Suzuki coughed and thrashed as he tried to keep from going under. He couldn't think of anything more disgusting than getting the water in his mouth. Then his feet touched the bottom, and he dragged himself out. Shit covered his armor—particularly aromatic shit. The rest of the Mundanes politely stepped aside as he walked toward where the insects were now swarming and then fell down. He wearily pointed at what the insects had crowded around. "Ambrosia," he muttered.

The MERCs walked up to where Suzuki lay and followed his finger. Sure enough, the insects were swarming around a massive growth of ambrosia. The insects hadn't landed on the fungus. They just floated above it, as if the scent was enough for them.

Stew leaned over and helped Suzuki to his feet. Suzuki exasperatedly tried to wipe the mud and gunk off himself but to no avail. He groaned, extremely irritated as Beth made a huge show of staying away from Suzuki due to his smell.

When the Mundanes and the Horsemen stood in front of the ambrosia, the smell was nearly overwhelming. It was almost nothing like what Suzuki's SD card had replicated. Somewhat. The smell was still there, but it was so intense that it was almost unrelatable. The air smelled so sweet, it was sickly, like rotten fruit. Yet the scent was strangely entrancing as well. Almost hypnotic.

Diana pulled a pickaxe out of her inventory and

approached the fungus. She sank the pickaxe into the fungus, chipping off a little bit of it. She looked over her shoulder and wiped off the sweat that was already starting to form on her brow. "Come on," she shouted. "This isn't going to pick itself. You should all have an axe in your inventory. MERCs get one pickaxe and shovel issued standard."

Suzuki scrolled through his inventory. There was the pickaxe. He wondered if he could get out of mining duty. *He* was the person who had been practically eaten alive on the search for the ambrosia. The thought was instantly discarded when Suzuki met Diana's eyes. She looked ready to crack the whip on all the MERCs. Even Chip had hastily grabbed a pickaxe and was mining the ambrosia.

For such a bookish person, Diana could swing an axe. All the MERCs, Chip included, had to stop multiple times to catch their breath. Not Diana. She continued picking the ambrosia as if she were incapable of tiring. It was good someone had that stamina because the ambrosia was thick and hard, tougher than iron or steel. For the hours of work the MERCs put in, there was hardly anything to show for it.

Frustrated, Sandy pulled out her wand, energy crackling from its tip, and pointed it at the veins of ambrosia. Diana jumped away from the fungus and pushed down Sandy's wand hand. "No, no, no, that's a terrible idea."

Sandy put her wand away and grasped her pickaxe again. "Why? It would go faster," she argued. "We're wasting time when we could be blasting this shit off. Chip could have gone all laser-hand and torn this shit apart by now."

"Did you stop to think about why Chip hasn't done just that? Ambrosia is very, very touchy. It takes on the molecular structure of whatever it comes into contact with very easily. If you use fire on it, it burns. A laser turns into refracting light.

You punch it? You have ambrosia that is the disturbing consistency of flesh. That's why we use pickaxes. Might take a while to chip it away, but the stuff is sturdy, and it lasts. Once you detach bits of ambrosia from the main fungus, its molecular structure stabilizes."

"This stuff better be good, for all the damn hoops we have to jump through."

Chip looked up from her work and scrolled her inventory for a bottle of water. "Oh, it is," Chip said. "'Twas José's favorite drink for a reason. The kind of stuff gods drink, you know?"

Suzuki sat down and tried to catch his breath. Stew sat next to him and handed him a handkerchief. "Where the hell did you get this, Stew?" Suzuki asked as he handed the handkerchief back.

Stew folded the hankie up and put it in his back pocket. "I always have a handkerchief," he said. "My mom always made me carry one when I was a kid. Never thought to offer it to anyone until today, though."

The Mundanes worked until they were all exhausted. All except Diana. The rest of the MERCs had gathered together, and Sandy had built a fire. Stew was roasting a rack of meat on the flames as Chip sang softly under her breath. Once the meat was cooked, Stew passed pieces to the MERCs.

Chip threw a rock at the pile of fungus Diana was working on. "Come on, Dee. Ain't that enough hacking today?" Chip asked. "Come sit for a spell."

Diana tossed down her pickaxe and walked over to the fire.

The last of the sun was dropping in the sky, painting the horizon different shades of orange and red, making it look as if the heavens had been wounded.

Suzuki took a bite out of the meat Stew had cooked.

It was fantastic.

Sweet and savory. The months of tutelage under Wendy, the owner of the Red Lion, had done wonders for Stew's cooking skills. He was obviously picking up tips from Diana as well. For the first time in a long time, Suzuki wanted to give Stew a compliment. He felt like Stew might be tolerable after being praised.

Before Suzuki could open his mouth, Stew faced Diana and asked, "Earlier, Chip said ambrosia was the stuff gods drank. It didn't sound like she was talking about the gods in the myths. Are there gods in Middang3ard?"

Diana poured a tankard of ale and passed it to the MERCs. "Of course, there are gods," Diana answered. "You lot killed one, remember?"

"So, that baby elder was actually a god? What the hell are gods, then, if you can kill them?"

Diana's eyes brightened as she sat up and leaned closer to speak with Stew. Sandy's ears perked up as well. "You see," Diana started, "the concept of deity and godhood is bizarre in Middang3ard. Not just here, but in general, I guess you could say. Earth and its realm have gods. All the old myths, religions, all of that stuff. Spiritual paths. Some gods have existed for as long as time, and others were dreamed up in caves, while still others introduced themselves along with technology or tales. What makes them gods is the intensity of the belief people have in them. Several world leaders, authors, and artists have been deified over time. Hemmingway, Frida Kalo...both of them are gods. Met them personally."

"What do you mean, you met them personally?"

By now, all the MERCs were hanging on every word Diana was saying. "You all know there are different realms.

They're stacked on top of each other, taking up the same space and none at the same time. Existing simultaneously. The seven realms of elves, men, dwarves, and so forth. Middang3ard is the neutral realm where all of the races mix. Beyond those realms are more, though—realms that are never seen. Even calling them realms isn't proper. Think of it like this."

Diana waved her hands and conjured the image of a piece of paper, then seven more pieces of paper. "Say each of these is one of the realms. This is what they look like and how close they are to each other."

Diana stacked the pieces of paper. "You see how the paper is so thin that you can't tell how many sheets there are?" She conjured a needle and pressed it through the stack. "That's why we can travel between realms so easily. We're right next to each other. But there are other places." Diana conjured a rock that floated a few feet away from the paper. "Other places that are nothing like our realms. Places people are terrified of going. Places that are so inhuman, we can hardly comprehend them. One of those places is the realm of the gods. Those gods are different than the ones each realm worships, though. They are the gods outside of the realms."

Sandy held her hands close to the flames, the shadows casting shapes on her face. "Have you been there?" she asked. "To the places outside the realms?"

Diana waved away the images floating above the fire. "A few times," she admitted. "It's different every time, but I have been there. Not for long, though. Only opened my eyes and saw what exists beyond reality. They say there's a realm we pull our magic from. A realm where you can gorge yourself on the source of magic. I was searching for it, and I found many things. It's how I became the mage I am today. But I did not find that place."

Suzuki cleared his throat as Beth grabbed him and pulled him under her arm. "That's where the Dark One came from, isn't it?" Suzuki asked. "He's not from any of the seven realms. He's from one of those...places outside the realms?"

Diana nodded as she spoke. "That's what I believe. At first, he just seemed to be a man with delusions of grandeur. He had tech, and that was the most we had observed. But at the defense ring, what came through those portals was not of the realms, and they were sent without hesitancy. As if they were of no consequence. We need to rethink our whole approach to everything concerning the Dark One. At least, that's what I've been trying to tell Myrddin."

Stew yawned and leaned back against a rock. "Why the hell are you trying to convince that old fart of anything?" Stew asked. "He's not the most forthcoming guy. Honestly, he's kind of an asshole."

Everyone turned to look at Stew before Diana burst out laughing. She grabbed her notebook and started taking notes, whispering under her breath, "Shows signs of increased emotional awareness while reverting back to former speech patterns." She put the notebook away and continued, "You aren't wrong, Stew. I've been trying to convince Myrddin we're fighting something bigger than an invader from another realm. Myrddin has never been to the place outside the realms. He hasn't seen what I've seen. He doesn't know what's capable of passing through. What they want..."

"What do you think they want?"

Diana stood and waved her hand so the sky became darker. "Magic is not merely for fighting," Diana said. "Magic runs through the core of all beings, of all existence. What we use in combat is the most banal application of magic. At its core, magic has the ability to distort and alter reality, depending on the strength and will of the individual, much like tech. In some realms, those distinctions aren't even made. I believe the Dark One is from a place such as that. I believe he, or it, is a creature beyond the distinctions of magic or tech."

The sky glowed green and took the shape of a turtle with a long white beard. The turtle stumbled a few steps forward, then opened up its mouth and vomited. Behind the turtle, a massive spider inched closer. It pounced on the turtle, and they intertwined into each other before breaking apart, their limbs scattered throughout the night.

Diana was floating, white light blazing from her eyelids. "I have seen how existence was created and met the first god. When he and his lover fought, they broke each other's bodies and cast them through the blackness of time and eternity. Each of those pieces became something we have never named."

Diana's voice changed. It grew dark and low as if something was speaking through her. "I know the being you speak around, for you do not speak of them. You use words to describe that which you do not understand. The Dark One, as you call it, is not a god. It is something beyond the very concept of 'god.' There is nothing which it is, and it is everything it wishes."

Diana stood and walked toward the river. In the water was a bright light.

The MERCs drew their weapons. Suzuki called his axe to him and it flew from his waist to his hand, catching fire instantly. Sandy pressed her hand to her amulet and turned

into a miasma of death and bone, while Chip's hand rearticu-
lated into a plasma cannon. Stew casually pulled his war axe
from his back.

There was a creature standing in the river. It looked like
an elk but was much larger. Almost as large as a full-grown
moose. It had spindly antlers that stretched toward the sky,
nearly five feet long. The fur covering its body was shaggy
and brown, the tuft of hair on its chest much longer than the
rest and white. The creature turned to look at the MERCs as
they approached.

Everyone stopped dead in their tracks.

The elk had the face of a human. It was covered in red
paint, six white lines drawn on the side of its face. It smiled at
the MERCs as it approached Diana, who rested her hand on
its side.

Suzuki felt the eyes of the creature pierce him straight to
his core. He was filled with fear, reverence, and awe. For some
reason, he felt extremely underdressed and self-conscious
about how he smelled.

Diana opened her mouth and the creature did the same,
and harmony rang out between them as Diana floated off the
ground. The fear and worry Suzuki had felt before disappeared. Whatever was standing before him was not a threat.
He knew that beyond a shadow of a doubt.

All the mud disappeared. As the elk stepped toward the
Mundanes, reeds and flowers sprouted from the water. The
mud disappeared, and the water turned crystal-clear. The elk
dipped its head and drank slowly before continuing to
approach the Mundanes. It came up the bank of the river and
sat down, folding its legs neatly beneath its body. Diana stood
next to it.

Diana spoke, her voice loud and completely unlike her

normal tones. "Do not be afraid, humans. My tongue is not made for your language, but I heard what you speak of. Diana seemed a worthy vessel for this conversation of importance."

Stew raised his axe and pointed it at the elk. "No, first off, you tell us what the fuck you are and what you're doing to our friend, or I will fucking end you."

The elk smiled sweetly as it tilted its head. Diana spoke for the elk, saying, "Your loyalty to your friend is beautiful. I am...I believe you humans call me *Yatsukamizuomitsuno*."

Stew looked at Sandy. "Do you know what that is?"

Sandy sighed and shook her head. "I think...I don't know what it means, but I know what he is. That's a fucking god. That's the god of the jungle. The *Shishigami*."

The *Shishigami* bowed slowly as it made some kind of guttural noise deep in its throat. Diana stepped away from the *Shishigami* and said, "You speak of what you call the Dark One. Your curiosity has led you in the proper direction. I have seen the places outside realms. I have walked its path. The Dark One is something beyond these places. He has existed outside of all known and unknown realms. He comes from a place beyond, and he must be named to be destroyed."

Suzuki didn't understand what was being said. "What do you mean, he has to be named?" he asked.

"The Dark One is not a name. It is a title that has been given. Yet, in his name, there is power, an old power many have forgotten about. The name is where one finds power in the old magic. If he remains unnamed, he will retain a power that cannot be defeated. Find his name."

Sandy stepped forward and knelt before the *Shishigami*. Suzuki didn't know why, but he felt he should do the same. After a few seconds, Stew and Chip also stepped forward and knelt. The grass beneath them grew nearly up to their waists as Sandy asked, "Where can we find his name?"

The *Shishigami's* smile disappeared. It looked at the sky. "In the place beyond realms. In the dark where there is nothing. In the place of magic."

"The place magic comes from?"

"Find his name."

Diana looked at the stars above. "Did you come here in shapes made of thoughts and intention as well?"

The MERCs didn't know how to answer. Suzuki finally stepped forward. "Is that the way the Dark One came here?"

Diana looked at Suzuki, her eyes beaming white light. "He is here. One of the Dark One's minions."

A blast of ice came flying from the jungle, and the icicle hit the *Shishigami* in the throat. The god went down, blue blood flowing from its neck and pooling in a halo around its head as it gasped, trying to suck in air.

Diana fell to her knees, also gasping for breath, her eyes returning to their regular color. She looked around in a daze, confused, trying to figure out what was happening. At her side, the *Shishigami* was bleeding out. She tore off a piece of her robe and pressed it to the god's throat, trying to staunch the blood. "What the hell is going on?" she shouted.

Another icicle came out of the jungle. An uneasy purring like that of a giant cat followed as a black figure slunk through the darkness. Suzuki couldn't see the creature well, but he knew it was huge. He also saw that the creature was fading back into the jungle, having done what it intended to. "We need to stop that thing," Suzuki said. "Whatever the hell it is."

Diana was frantically crying. She seemed as if she didn't even know why there were tears in her eyes. "I don't know what's going on, but I need to stay here with him," she said. "He was...in my head. We were... Please, I can't let him die. Go."

Suzuki stared into the darkness of the jungle. "All right, Mundanes. Time to hunt."

The Mundanes drew their weapons and stalked toward the trees. Whatever had attacked the god was going to pay. Suzuki was going to make sure of that.

6

N o sound came from the jungle. Whatever had attacked the *Shishigami* had either disappeared or was the quietest creature ever to stalk a jungle. Suzuki doubted it was the latter. That didn't change the fact that the Mundanes were hardly able to see anything past the thickest of the trees, and whatever had felled the forest god was capable of sniper-level accuracy. Suzuki knew the odds were stacked against him in the current situation. He checked his HUD to see what they were.

The HUD gave him a ten percent chance of success.

Being out in the open was going to get them killed. That much was obvious. Making a dash for the jungle seemed just as risky. Whatever was in there probably had a better layout of the land than any of the Mundanes. If Suzuki was honest, the whole jungle looked the same to him. He could hardly tell one tree from the other.

An icicle shot out of the forest. It was smaller than the last two that had been fired but twice as sharp.

The icicle was heading straight toward Sandy, who raised

her hand at the last minute and cast a defensive shield that shattered the icicle. The force of the attack was still enough to fling her back.

Stew helped Sandy to her feet as more icicles shot out of the forest. They were all small but extremely sharp, coming so rapidly that the Mundanes had to run for cover. Suzuki wondered if there was more than one assailant, or if whatever was attacking was just proficient with ice magic. He leaned more toward one enemy. The grouping of the attacks was too close. If he had that many bodies to work with, he would have spaced them throughout the jungle. And he did have that many bodies to work with. Now, what the hell was he going to do with them?

Beth pointed to a pile of large boulders as icicles crashed behind her. "Come on!" she shouted. "We can use it for cover."

The Mundanes bolted for the rock pile and cowered behind it. "Any bright ideas?" Sandy asked.

Suzuki peeked out from behind the rocks. The moment his face was free of its cover, icicles came flying at him, and he ducked back behind the rocks. "Whatever is sending those things at us is obviously proficient with ice magic," he mused aloud. "Using it exclusively. Which, I'm betting, means it has an elemental weakness. It's also making the most of being behind cover. It might not be a tough-ass bastard in the open."

Stew cracked his knuckles and rolled his shoulders. "That is a lot of words and a lot less killing," he grumbled.

"There's the Stew we've all come to love. If you were a little more patient, you'd find out I wasn't done yet."

"Dude, by the time you're finished talking, we could be dead."

"All right. We're going to flank it. Sandy, I want you upfront, giving us distraction and alchemy. Chip, take to the trees and work your way around back. The rest of us are going to try to draw it out while Sandy buffs and covers us."

Chip raised her hand as she stood up. "Excuse me, boss man. D'ya mind if I hijack Beth for a little scampering?" she asked. "Nothing like a little in-the-field training."

Suzuki turned to Beth and shrugged. "You down to try something new?" he asked. "Knowing full well this is the worst possible time to start trying out new strategies."

Beth smiled as she inched closer to Chip. "Let's do it!" she exclaimed.

Chip beamed at Beth and gave her a high five. It was an oddly uncharacteristic amount of enthusiasm from both of them. Suzuki figured it was just a battle high. He raised his axe to the sky and shouted, "For honor!"

Beth raised her sword as well. "For glory!"

Stew held his axe high as Sandy pointed her wand skyward. "For XP!"

Suzuki turned to Sandy and pointed toward the jungle. "All right, Sandy, take point. Move us forward slowly!" he commanded.

Sandy stepped out from behind the pile of rocks.

The moment she was out from behind cover, the icicles started to fly. Hundreds of small, razor-sharp icicles the size of bullets shot out from the jungle. Sandy held her hands in front of her, her ashen cloak changing from gray to green as flowers started to bloom across her bony hands. A clear barrier popped up in front of her. The icicles that passed through the barrier turned to lavender petals.

Once the barrage was over, Suzuki and Stew stepped out from behind Sandy, Suzuki holding his own small magical barrier, and Stew casting a Stoneskin spell over himself. Sandy hummed slightly, harmonizing her magic with Stew's to buff his spell.

As Stew, Suzuki, and Sandy slowly advanced across the river separating them from the jungle, Beth and Chip slipped into the shadows. They went around the riverbank, sticking as close to the stones and rocks as possible. They were low to the ground and moved quickly as they went around where they thought the creature might be.

Chip leapt into the trees and landed effortlessly on a tree branch. Beth jumped next and wavered as she tried to maintain her balance on the branch. Chip grabbed her wrist to keep her from falling and held a finger to her lips.

Chip's eyes glowed bright red for a second as she stared into the darkness of the jungle. She surveyed the area before pointing to a spot in the darkness. A moment or two passed, then the dark spot Chip was indicating lit up as something conjured a handful of icicles that flew toward the Mundanes who were still near the river.

Sandy stopped and transmuted the icicles again as Suzuki and Stew hid behind her. They all waited for a few moments until they were certain it was safe to move again.

Chip headed in the direction where she had seen the flash of magic. Beth followed her as they moved to a position behind where the flash had come from. Chip's hand converted to a cannon, and she took aim as Beth drew her sword. As Beth was preparing to leap down, Chip lightly touched her on the shoulder. When Beth turned around, Chip was holding a short bow and quiver. She handed it to Beth, who took it, looking down at the bow and arrows as if she didn't know what to do with them. After a brief hesitation, she slung the quiver over her shoulder, drew an arrow, and nocked it.

Chip leaned forward and whispered in Beth's ear, "It's got a nice little upgrade too if you wanna try being fancy. Just think...*fire*."

Beth smiled as she concentrated on fire, imagining flames in her mind's eye.

The end of her arrow caught flame. "Fucking sweet," she murmured.

Chip pointed down to where there was another flash of magic. "All right, let's see what we can rustle up," she whispered.

Chip fired a plasma shot directly behind where the magic had been conjured. Beth fired right afterward as well. Her arrow hit a tree and burst into flames, creating a wall of fire. There was a loud screech—not of pain, but of fear, followed by crashing. Chip and Beth continued to pepper the area, preventing the creature from retreating and pushing it toward the river. Every time the creature screeched, Chip would zero in on its position and give Beth a visual cue, and they would rain fire from the trees.

Below, the Mundanes advanced as quickly as possible, taking advantage of the respite from attacks. Suzuki readied his axe. He knew it was only going to be a few moments before the Mundanes and their enemy converged.

Suzuki saw a flash of magic on the outskirts of the jungle. He flipped his axe once in his hand, caught it, and tossed the axe at the point the magic was coming from. His attack was greeted with a screech of pain that harrowed him down to his bones.

A massive cat burst out of the jungle. It stood ten feet tall and was deep orange with murderous green eyes. The cat,

Azrael, was all lean muscle, its long body plunging into the cool river water as it rolled over, dousing the flames in its fur. As it rose, smoke coming off its singed fur, its eyes fell on Suzuki.

Suzuki had no time to react. The cat had surged forward in a torrent of speed and muscle. It connected with him a few seconds later, knocking the wind out of him as it sent him skipping over the water like a stone thrown by a child. Suzuki continued to skip across the water until he hit a tree, and his head swam as he tried to pick himself up. As he stood, a paw clawed him across the face, and he was tossed to the ground. Azrael towered over him, the jungle cat's mouth foaming, its green eyes glowing in the dim light.

Azrael lunged forward to bite Suzuki's throat, but stopped mid-attack and cast a look over its shoulder. Stew had it by the tail. He smirked as he pulled back, dragging the cat away from Suzuki, then threw the cat over his shoulder.

Azrael flew through the air, flailing. It landed on its feet and hissed at Stew as he unsheathed his broadswords, screaming, and ran at the cat. Sandy was right behind him, flinging fireballs in the jungle cat's direction.

Stew leapt and brought both swords down on Azrael, who simply stepped to the side in an elegant movement nearly too fast for any of the Mundanes to catch. Using that same speed, it tackled Sandy, pinning her under one of its paws.

Sandy wasted no time launching her own attack. She screamed as her ash cloak burst into flames, her entire body covered by fire, looking like a demon wraith from the very pits of hell.

Azrael cried out in pain and bolted away from Sandy. It looked down at its singed paw before leaning over to lick it in such a feline fashion that it looked like a domestic cat. Then its fur burst into flames, its eyes glowing with fire. The water it stood in instantly evaporated. The jungle was filled with heat, the cat feeling like the sun, radiating warmth.

Sandy stood to her feet as Stew circled the cat, slashing but unable to get any closer. "Are you fucking kidding me?" Stew shouted.

Suzuki had caught his breath and was racing back to the battlefield as he recalled his axe back to his hand. He flipped down his HUD to check their chances of survival. The HUD read five percent. He gritted his teeth, determined to make that count. "Sandy!" he shouted. "End those flames!"

Sandy nodded and levitated. She raised her wand toward the skies and dark clouds gathered. A crack of lightning was followed instantly by a godlike boom of thunder.

Azrael took no notice of Sandy. Instead, the feline turned its attention to Chip and Beth. Azrael turned to face them, effortlessly knocking Stew away with its hind leg. Chip fired at it, but the cat was too fast. It leapt to the side and pounced on her. Azrael bit into Chip's cannon hand and ripped it off with hardly any effort. Chip screamed in pain as her other hand contorted into a cannon, firing a sizable plasma blast, which sent Azrael flying.

Chip stood and held her arm to her side as blood poured from the wound. She knelt and searched the water for her hand as Beth pulled out her sword and shield, dashing toward the cat, which was rearing up on its hind legs like a lion, roaring loudly as it shot fire from its mouth toward Sandy, who swerved out of the way as she waved her wand around, pulling water from the sky and river, rolling it up into a watery sphere. She brought her wand down and the sphere came crashing down on Azrael, sending a tidal wave of water crashing into the river.

Beth tossed her shield down and jumped onto it like a surfboard. She rode the tidal wave to get closer to the jungle cat, then leapt, her sword in both hands, flying straight toward the cat's head. She brought her sword down in between the cat's eyes.

A second before Beth's blade connected with the cat, Azrael's skin changed to the consistency of water, and Beth passed straight through. She hit the river's surface hard as Azrael's new form swirled into a watery version of itself, still attached to the water of the river.

Azrael looked around at the Mundanes, who surrounded the cat. Its fur was bristling. Then it hissed and collapsed into the water.

Suzuki looked down at the water to see if there was any way to see where the cat was. All he could see was water. "Sandy, everyone in the air now!" he shouted.

Sandy's voice cracked as she answered, "I can't levitate everyone! It's too many people!"

"Sandy! Mundanes! Air! Now!"

"Goddamn it!" Sandy shouted as she catapulted into the water.

Sandy's wand transformed into a gnarled, wooden staff. She slammed the staff into the water like some sort of pagan Moses, causing the water to explode into the air around her.

Suzuki's feet started to levitate off the ground. He looked around, and the rest of the Mundanes were also floating up. Sandy was the only one still on the ground. "Uh, Sandy, that includes you," Suzuki ordered.

Sandy looked back over her shoulder at the floating Mundanes. "I can't do it and all of you too," she explained calmly. "It's too much mana."

"You're an open target down there!"

"Yeah, I know. You better be coming up with a fucking plan."

Suzuki wracked his brain. If Diana was here, this would have been an easy problem to solve. Diana could have frozen the river while Sandy kept everyone out of harm's way. But that was too much of a strain. All Suzuki knew was Azrael could counter any elemental magic Sandy threw its way. The elemental magic Suzuki could work was limited. Same with the rest of the Mundanes, if they were able to. There weren't a lot of options.

The water beneath the Mundanes swirled, coming together in a wave with the roaring mouth of Azrael. The tidal wave came crashing down on Sandy, who raised her staff, the water that would have hit her converting to steam as the Mundanes above her started to fall.

The tidal wave passed. Sandy remained standing. The falling Mundanes halted in mid-air. Suzuki turned to Chip. "How strong is that plasma cannon?" Suzuki asked.

Chip looked down at her damaged hand. "Could be a tad stronger," she muttered.

"If that cat comes at me, will it be strong enough to break apart the water?"

"Disrupt it, yeah. It'll blow a hole through a water wall."

"All right, get ready." Then Suzuki turned to Beth and Stew. "When that thing takes solid form, I want you two to put everything you got into putting it down. This one is gonna be heavy on you, Stew."

Stew nodded as he pulled out his hefty battle axe. "I can go berserk," he said. "It'll take a lot out of me, but I can take the cat. It's just a fucking cat."

"All right. Sandy, get ready. You'll know what to do."

Sandy stumbled forward a little bit but caught herself.

"Whatever you're planning on doing, just fucking do it!" she grumbled.

Suzuki pulled up his HUD and went to change his scent. He concentrated on what he felt was the dumbest idea he'd had to date. Catnip. After he focused on the idea of catnip, he closed his eyes and tried to see if he could smell any change. *Does catnip even have a smell,* he thought to himself.

Suzuki's answer came in the sound of an increasingly loud and feral roar. He looked down beneath him as the water of the river began to pull together, taking on the shape of the massive jungle cat. Before Suzuki had any time to react, Azrael had thrown itself through the air. The cat flew at Suzuki with an impressive measure of grace. If Suzuki was going to die today, at least he was going out with some style.

Before Azrael could connect with Suzuki, Chip aimed her cannon and fired off a shot of steaming, hot plasma. The blast went straight through Azrael, sending its body off into different places, its head separating from its chest, claws and arms flying back down the river. The cat screamed in pain as its eyes rolled around in its head, trying to find where its different appendages had gone. Already the water that formed its body was reaching out, trying to pull itself together.

As Azrael tried to recombine itself, Sandy let the Mundanes fall back to the ground, her staff changing back to the wand, herself floating through the air toward Azrael. As she waved her wand, the air around her became cold enough for icicles to form on the noses of the Mundanes. Bringing her wand down and taking aim, a blast of arctic cold shot forth, instantly freezing Azrael.

Azrael fell to the ground, its eyes wide at being converted to another solid. The cat was obviously confused by the change of events. Its body started to change, reverting back to flesh and blood, the form Suzuki thought was its default. He figured a big enough shock to the jungle cat's system would force it to have something like a hard reset. Turns out, he was right, though he wasn't ready for what stood before him.

The cat had indeed returned to flesh and blood, but its body had pulled itself together in the same shape it had been frozen in. Its legs were stretched to thin noodles while its arms were hulking, grotesque parodies of muscle, and its neck was long like a snake's as it hissed and swatted at the Mundanes in front of it.

Beth lunged forward, using her own spectacular speed to take aim at the creature's back paws. She sliced through both strings of flesh with one flourish while Stew stepped in front of the cat, his chest growing larger and larger, all the muscles in his body swelling as his eyes went red and foam poured from his mouth. Raising his axe high above his head and bringing it down in between Azrael's eyes, the creature's skull split in two, right down the middle.

The Mundanes gathered around the bizarre remains of Azrael.

Stew laughed as his body started to shrink down to its regular size. "Now, that was a fucking fight." He chuckled.

Sandy stood by the guts of Azrael, which had exploded all over the river. The body of partially digested Smuggles floated in the water. "I guess this thing preys on Smuggles," she explained. "Wonder if they've ever wanted to try apex predator before. I know I have."

Beth turned her face up at Sandy. "Are you serious, dude?" she asked. "You'd eat a cat?"

Sandy nodded without turning to face Beth. "This is

Middang3ard. It would have eaten us if it killed us. It's the least we can do to return the favor."

Suzuki raised his hands to put a stop to the discussion. "Let's table that," he interrupted. "First, we find Diana and the Forest Spirit. Then we'll talk about whatever disgusting ideas you guys have."

The Mundanes found Diana upriver. She had dragged the Forest Spirit to the riverbank and they sat together, the *Shishigami's* head resting on Diana's thigh. Diana gently stroked the Spirit's head as it breathed slow and shallow.

At the approach of the Mundanes, the *Shishigami* raised his head, eyes slowly opening as if waking from a dream. His lips turned up in a smile as he shakily got to his feet. Walking to the Mundanes, his head bowed slowly and he softly licked Suzuki's hand, then went to the next Mundane, showing his thankfulness in his own way.

Diana stood and came over to the Mundanes, her face worn. She looked like she hadn't slept for days, her eyes red from either tears or stress. She moved with the weight of one who has been running for some time and looked as if she had just been through a battle.

The *Shishigami's* antlers stretched out toward the branches of the trees as if they were growing slightly longer. "I almost left this world," the *Shishigami* said. "It was almost my time to see another adventure. But your friend insisted on me staying here with Middang3ard."

Diana laughed, and a little bit of color came back to her face. "You make it sound like I was pestering you," she said.

"You almost died. Not to be dramatic, but you were this close to slipping into wherever the hell you go."

"There are many places one can go. You know this better than anyone."

Chip stepped forward. She was troubled by something. "Where do you go?" she asked.

The *Shishigami* smiled again. Something about its smile put Suzuki at ease. It was familiar yet foreign, haunting yet comforting. "You wish to know where the dead dwell?" the *Shishigami* asked.

"Just one."

The *Shishigami* looked at the blood that covered the Mundanes. "You felled Azrael?" he asked.

Stew picked at his teeth and then looked at the *Shishigami*. "You mean the big cat?" he queried. "Yeah, we killed the shit out of that thing."

Diana took out her notebook and jotted a note, muttering to herself. "His speech pattern has nearly completely returned to normal. Personality still off, hasn't said anything insensitive in a while."

Stew reached out for the *Shishigami's* antlers. "Do you mind if I?" he asked.

The *Shishigami* bowed. "Please."

Stew ran his hand over them. Bits of bark broke off in his hand, and he stared down at his palms. "You know, these would fetch some decent cash if you were ever hunted."

Diana jotted another note. "I stand corrected."

Stew pulled out a knapsack and tossed the antler shavings in. "Not that I would do anything like that," he quickly added. "I just meant you must be in danger a lot. Your antlers are...beautiful."

The *Shishigami* laughed, a sound as beautiful as the river

flowing beside him. "True, true. Not here, though. I am the sacred guardian of the forests and jungle. My subjects revere me, and none but the most loyal of the Dark One's servants would dream of harming me. If I were to fall, the entire island would collapse into the sea. It has happened once, but that is a long story, and you and your friends must have many questions. I believe the Smuggles would appreciate the body of the cat you felled."

Suzuki gasped in awe as he tried to keep his words somewhat reverential. "You heard us saying that?" he asked, shocked.

"I hear all that comes and goes within my domain. Now let us go. The Smuggles will wish to provide an ample feast."

The *Shishigami* turned away from the Mundanes and walked into the jungle without saying another word. Stew leaned over to Suzuki and whispered, "Do you think that thing is really a god?"

Suzuki knew the Japanese legend of the *Shishigami*. He had seen it in animes growing up and had done a little more research as he had gotten older. It seemed right that anime was full of stories that were only seeding the human race with inclinations toward the truth. At least with the *Shishigami,* it went back even further than anime and mangas. So much Japanese media was rooted in folktale and legend. It was as if the Japanese had been told a long time ago that certain things were true, and they never allowed themselves to forget it. The same could be seen in English literature based on legends of fairies and brownies. Every culture probably had the same thing going on.

Suzuki nodded as he followed after the *Shishigami*. "Yeah, I think so," he replied to Stew. "Next time we meet a god, don't tell him his antlers would make a good trophy."

"Dude, it just slipped out. At least I didn't tell him I would have been the one hunting him."

"You do know he hears everything that happens in the forest."

"Goddamn it."

"Even when you're trying to be polite, you still manage to shove your foot in your mouth. At least some things never change."

The Mundanes were gathered around a large fire near where they had originally been captured by the Smuggles. They had brought the cat, which they had butchered and quartered, leaving only the head intact, to be dragged by Stew to the Smuggles, offering it as a gift. The Smuggles had been delighted, and thousands of them poured out of the jungle. Suzuki was surprised there were so many of them since they had only seen a small number during their battle and the Smuggle's ritual.

The many hands of the Smuggles made preparation of the cat, decorations for festivities, and general merrymaking quick work. It hardly took any time for the cat to be further butchered into smaller, more manageable pieces for the Smuggles. The meat for the Mundanes was kept separate, and Diana and Stew tended to the preparing of their allotted food.

The elder bearded Smuggle made a great show of bestowing the meat on the Mundanes. He attempted to drag it over to them, and eventually opting for a couple of carts to stack the meat on and dragged them toward Chip and Diana, who he had decided were the leaders.

Suzuki didn't mind the mistake. He was happy anytime someone assumed he was just a member of the party. The pressure he felt from his party members wasn't intense, but it was there. His knack for being able to strategize and rally his friends had situated him as the de facto leader. Furthermore, he actually enjoyed it. He had never been one to call the shots until he had started playing Middang3ard VR. When he was thrust into the real thing, with stakes larger than anything he had ever imagined, he had initially floundered under the pressure. It was starting to feel normal now. He had pulled off some pretty crazy shit. He felt comfortable with the title, the Most Mundane of Mundanes.

Once Diana and Stew seasoned the cat meat with spices Diana had "borrowed" from the Red Lion's kitchen (she was very adamant that the Mundanes not let Wendy know of the loan), they got to grilling. They talked quietly and with an air of excitement. There seemed to be only one thing Stew and Diana had in common, and that was a love of food.

The rest of the Mundanes broke off into their own clusters to take care of whatever they thought was important until dinner. Chip repaired her arm, sitting cross-legged, eyes closed. She held the severed hand close to the wrist, and her techno-organic skin started slowly reconnecting itself.

Beth sat on a rock with her HUD pulled down, listening to an old AM radio. She was wearing a large, military-grade headset. Suzuki took a seat over near her, and she looked up at him before he leaned over to kiss her. Beth absentmindedly kissed Suzuki back before turning to fiddle with the radio that was hooked up to her headset.

Suzuki leaned over to get a better look at it. It looked like something that had survived the Vietnam war, and was years and years behind the tech the local military or the MERCs had. "What's with the old tech?" Suzuki asked.

Beth continued twisting knobs, her eyes focused and her brow furrowed in concentration as she answered. "Best way to communicate now," she explained, drawling her words, absorbed in the task of finding the right station. "After the military found out about all our tech being reverse-engineered Dark One-tech, they went through everything. You remember when our HUDs got confiscated once we got back? That was to make sure they weren't susceptible to the Dark One's influence like Chip was. Can you imagine an entire platoon going haywire?"

"Yeah, that would be pretty fucked up. But if the Dark One could have hijacked all of the MERCs and military, he would have done it."

"That's what the bigwigs figured too. Still, the military wanted to make sure none of our communications had the slightest chance to fall into the Dark One's hands. So, we went straight old school. Most everyone got retrained."

"How about you? You had left the military by then. You've been with us pretty much all the time."

Beth looked up, smirking smugly. "Got friends in high places," she admitted. "Plus, I still have friends in the military. I want to make sure they're safe. Also, MERC intel sucks troll cock. You guys...I mean, *we* don't get anything until it's already passed through bullshit military brass. So, I figured, why not just keep checking the source?"

Suzuki stared at Beth. If he could have seen himself, he would have laughed. He looked like a high schooler who'd just met his crush for the first time. "How did you learn all this stuff?" he asked. "Like, the radio and dispatching and that military nerd shit?"

"My dad and I used to do military cosplay and games. He served a while ago. It fucked him up. A lot. He never really got over it, but it was a huge part of his life, you know? It was part of his identity. He couldn't go to the base or anything because of his PTSD, but cosplay was something he could do. It helped him work through a lot of shit. Just running through drills and teaching stuff he learned. I fucking loved it."

"Yeah, that sounds really sweet. Your dad seems like a cool guy."

Beth chuckled. "You'll find out for yourself. Once we kick the Dark One's alien ass, we're going home as heroes. And we're throwing a hero's barbeque in my backyard with the parents. You're meeting the whole family. You better start prepping. They don't take to nerds very much."

Suzuki laughed as he leaned against the rock Beth sat atop. "Not even a nerd who rode a dragon in the biggest battle Middang3ard has ever seen."

"They don't impress easily. And that dragon only let you ride her because she was sprung for you. Now, please, be hot in silence. I'm trying to listen."

Beth reached down and scratched the back of Suzuki's neck before returning to her communication device. While Beth worked, Suzuki looked across the small camp and saw the *Shishigami* speaking with Sandy. Sandy was holding the head of an orc necromancer she had taken as a trophy while they had been fighting their way through the Dark One's defense rings. When Sandy noticed Suzuki staring, she reached up and pulled down her hood to hide her face.

Suzuki sighed and pulled out his axe, flipped down his HUD, and started looking through his list of ingredients and tools. "She has gotten so weird since we got to Middang3ard," Suzuki muttered under his breath.

Beth laughed from above. "You're fucking telling me, Suzy."

Suzuki looked at his hand axe through his HUD. Some of the enchantments were wearing off. The stronger ones, namely the enchantment that gave his axe the ability to be recalled through thought, were still holding strong. Those were deeply rooted in the axe. There was a chance they would never grow dull. Other chants were mostly superficial —small homing or sharpness buffs. They got the job done, as did the enchantments on his armor, but tonight Suzuki wanted to try something more interesting.

Stew's voice broke Suzuki's train of thought. "Dinner's on!" he shouted.

The Mundanes surrounded the fire as Diana and Stew dished out plates of cat. The meal was completed by a collection of mushrooms and vegetables the Smuggles had acquired for the Mundanes. Once everyone was served, they sat around the fire as if they were family. For the first few minutes, they ate in silence, relishing the salty, sticky cat meat that had been roasted to perfect succulence. The vegetables balanced the meal, cleansing the palate almost like water so one could more fully taste the cat.

About halfway through the meal, Diana started pouring everyone drinks. Chip opted out, preferring to suck on one of Diana's beetles instead. The rest gladly took a tankard of ale as the remaining Smuggles brought their plates to the Mundanes' fire. The elder, gray-bearded Smuggle took a seat next to a blond smuggle, who also had a beard. The blond Smuggle pulled on Suzuki's pants and said, "We are honored to have you tonight."

Suzuki, not knowing what to do, humbly bowed his head and said, "Thank you. The honor is all ours."

"You saved the *Shishigami*. You saved our forest. We owe you much."

Suzuki waved away the Smuggles thanks before realizing how rude it might look. "We're glad to help," he said. "That's kind of what we're here to do."

Across the fire, Chip beamed at Suzuki. "Only part of the truth." Chip chuckled. "We also came for the flavor of the gods. Can't forget the finer points of adventuring, am I right?"

Diana snapped one of her beetles in half and tossed it in her ale. "Wish we had some of that ambrosia right now."

Chip leaned over and grabbed Diana by the shoulders. "Might want to hold off on guzzling that there bugger," she said. "Feast your eyes on my ingenuity." Chip pulled down her HUD and went through her inventory until she squealed with delight.

A machine conjured itself into Chip's lap. It looked almost like a food processor had been taped to a jet engine. There were elaborate pipes running through the whole thing. The machine was split into two sections with what appeared to be a processing or distilling section and then another one that looked to be good for holding liquid.

Diana clapped her hands together with excitement. "No, you didn't!" she shouted.

Chip, a smug smile on her face, stood up, hands on hips. "Yes, I most certainly did."

"Care to let any of us in on why you're both so excited," Suzuki asked.

Chip held her arms out at the odd machine like a game show host unveiling a prize. "This, my dear ladies and chums, is my patented, easy fixing and mixing, ambrosia distiller," she exclaimed. "Make a short task of the painful ass fucking which is distilling this shite. Care to wander down a wild road?"

"You said this stuff was pretty strong, right?"

"Strong ain't the right word. Strange fits best. Some folks feel it like a creamy ale, others go down a rabbit hole of bleakness and odd sights. Most just get royally fucked. Care to join?"

Stew fist pumped and leaned over the fire to give Chip props. "Hell, yeah, dude. Let's do this!" he shouted.

Chip bowed low to the Smuggles sitting at the fire. "Care to partake, perchance?"

The elder Smuggle looked at the blonde Smuggle who, in turn, looked at the other Smuggles. They all stared solemnly at each other, eventually passing their looks back to the elder Smuggle like some sort of ocular wave. The elder Smuggle pulled out a pipe and began to puff. "It would be our honor."

"Then let's get-a-cracking."

Diana stood to help Chip unpack the ambrosia and begin loading it into the machine. Stew also went to give a hand. He was obviously interested in the extraction process. That left the rest of the Mundanes to entertain themselves and the *Shishigami*.

Beth sipped her ale and stared into the flames. "The Dark One is ramping up his forces," she said softly. "There are reports he's taken over almost all of the Eastern Encampments of Middang3ard. The guys said it's getting real fucked up."

Suzuki looked at Beth. Her face was stony, hardly betraying any emotion, but Suzuki could hear it in her voice. She was scared. "That's not news," Suzuki offered. "He's been pretty aggressively expanding over the last few weeks."

"That's not the only thing. They said there's shit they've never seen before. Creatures...they don't know what they are. Everyone keeps saying it's, like, when they see them, they don't see them. And they're taking people away. Just dragging them into thin air. Everyone sounds pretty fucked up about it."

"You think they might be like the creatures we saw back at the defense rings?"

"Could be. Who knows? I'd have to see it, you know."

Suzuki reached out for Beth's hand, but she folded them together in her lap and continued staring at the flame. He wished there was something he could do or say to help her know it was going to be okay, but he knew that he couldn't. He hadn't seen what the Dark One was capable of like she had. Even then, he wasn't sure if he knew everything was going to be okay. They had managed to survive their encounter with the Dark One's Viceroy, but it had been a narrow victory. It also didn't seem like the Dark One had any lack of resources. There could already be a new Viceroy.

Sandy was still speaking with the Forest Spirit. Whatever they were talking about absorbed both of them. Diana had even gone over to join them. Suzuki couldn't tell, but it felt like their words weren't traveling, not in the way that happened when someone cast a sound dampening spell. That was more like muffling. Suzuki felt like their conversation was simply disappearing, as if their words were being sucked into the air once they had trickled off their lips.

Across the fire, Chip was staring at Diana and the rest of them. Her pupils were large, and she looked to be agitated. "You said..." she started, "You said that you would tell us what happens after death. Do you really know?"

The *Shishigami* turned to face Chip. Its face was soft and

understanding, as if the answers within its heart were truly encouraging.

Suzuki had wanted to ask the same thing Chip did. When the Mundanes had first arrived back from the Battle of the Rings, Suzuki had gone to mourn and celebrate with the rest of the MERCs. He hadn't felt like drinking. The rest of the MERCs were either getting shit-faced because they were surprised they were still alive or because they were attempting to stave off the pain of losing their friends.

Suzuki couldn't do either. Neither could the rest of the Mundanes. They had sat in shock, playing over how they could have done better, how they could have kept José from dying. It was at that moment that Suzuki looked up from his bed and saw something. He wasn't sure at first, but as the glimmer of light approached, he saw it was José.

José, or the vision of José, had said something to him he couldn't remember now. He still wasn't sure if he had a vision or if it was just shock manifesting itself in a different way from anyone else's. He had heard of soldiers having flash-backs or going off at the sound of fireworks. Only a few hours before, he had seen someone he looked up to obliterated right before his eyes. Maybe he was just having a shitty time with it.

Chip was still looking eagerly at the *Shishigami*. She looked ready to cry, her eyes tearing up yet still somehow hopeful. "What happens?" Chip asked.

The *Shishigami* stood up and approached the fire. It bent its head low and plunged its face into the flames. The flames flickered different colors as the *Shishigami* fell into the flames. The fire instantly extinguished itself.

Chip leaned back, her eyes wide enough a little bit of the mechanics behind her eyelids were visible. "Well, that's a bit fucked," she muttered as she took a small cup of ambrosia away from her machine and passed it around the fire as everyone stared mutely at the now-dead fire. In a few moments, everyone had a cup of ambrosia.

Diana pointed toward the sky. The sky had grown blacker, and the moon and stars had disappeared. It was like looking into a black veil. There was something moving behind it. Slowly, a few bright lights came into view. They swirled around each other, taking the shape of a familiar face—that of the *Shishigami*.

The fire roared back to life.

The *Shishigami* sat beside Chip, its legs neatly folded up the way a baby doe would. "There are many kinds of life," the *Shishigami* said. "And along with those lives, many deaths. There are deaths of gods, death of those who follow those gods, death of those who follow no gods, and death of those who know of no death. Each person creates their own after-life. They do it from the moment they are born. Their beliefs spark new realities. Some people share the same reality. Others, only vague similarities. Each person creates a perfect universe to themselves that awaits them when they close their eyes for the last time. Except for some. There are some who understand the truth of life and death, who will not be placated by a holding space for eternity."

The Mundanes and the Horsemen sipped their ambrosia. Suzuki instantly felt the effects. He felt more awake and hyper-focused yet, oddly for him, much less critical. He was aware he would have probably not cared much about this conversation, other than for its practical uses. As he listened, he thought that was something he might want to change. He also was aware it was the ambrosia talking. That didn't really bother him.

The rest of the MERCs were also leaning in to better hear the *Shishigami*, who was now looking at the stars and humming softly. The Smuggles echoed the melody with soft voices.

Chip reached up and petted the back of the *Shishigami's* neck. "And what is that truth?" Chip asked.

The *Shishigami's* antlers stretched toward the heavens. They looked to touch the stars, where his face still beamed down upon them. "There is no life or death. Everything continues, and there are those who have learned how to continue as they see fit. Nearly immortal. They pull themselves through any plane of reality, no matter how painful."

"How do you find them? If I need to find someone, how do I do it?"

"It is discouraged. Many lose themselves in the place between realms. It is chaos and madness. It is not a place to go to find things. If they want to find you, they will."

Suzuki shook his head. He was trying to piece everything together, but none of this made sense. Nothing really died, yet there were places you went once you died. Alternate dimensions for everyone who's ever existed? Except for people who found their way out of the cycle. Who brought themselves back. "That's what the Dark One is, isn't it? One of those...immortals?"

The *Shishigami's* antlers touched the antlers of the *Shishigami* in the sky. Everything went white, and suddenly it was dawn. The sun was rising between the *Shishigami's* eyes. "There have been many iterations of the Dark One. He has been known by many names and believed to have been vanquished many times as well, yet the realm between realms cannot hold him. It has become his birthplace and kingdom. And he wishes to spread it to everything."

"No, that can't be right. We saw the Dark One. We fought his army. All he seemed to care about was making organic life technological instead. It was just about control. It wasn't as big as all this. He's just some asshole who feels like he needs to control everything."

"Sometimes, even we are a mystery to ourselves. I have seen this cycle. Watched it run its course many times. Make no mistake, what the Dark One wants now is only a shadow of what he will become. He is an evil that presents itself with a new voice. But what is underneath is always the same."

Suzuki thought over what the *Shishigami* said. He'd heard of this trope before. It wasn't one that often made its way into literature but was more often seen in myths, in folktales of evil and malice. Few authors believed in absolute, unkillable evil. It went against all stories about the nature of good and evil, the everlasting battle. If evil was something that was unbeatable, what did it say about goodness? Maybe there was no good and evil. Maybe there were just ambivalent forces. But that was more of the elder god type of stuff. The Dark One did not seem ambivalent. From everything Suzuki had seen, the Dark One was intentional and methodical in his desires.

The tone of the fireplace had changed. The MERCs sat around and watched the flames in silence. What had fallen over them was not fear, yet it was different for each of them. They looked into each other's eyes and could see that a note had been struck. Each of those notes formed a chorus, a harmony that was unspoken. Whatever the Dark One was, they were going to be the ones to stop him.

Chip poured herself another cup of ambrosia. "Usually, I'm not one to turn down a nice pitter-patter on doom and gloom, but yeesh. What's the vote on lightening the mood the fuck up?"

There was a general murmur as the *Shishigami* smiled and rose. "On that note, I shall be going. I greatly appreciate all you have done for me. I wish you luck on your travels." The *Shishigami* turned to Suzuki, his eyes boring into the MERC's. "And for your sake, I hope that you are correct."

Chip passed everyone a new cup of ambrosia, and they all sipped while watching the stars above. Even though the stars had returned to normal, it still seemed like *Shishigami* was above them, watching over. Suzuki wondered if the creature really was a god. It was hard to tell what things were in Middang3ard. Suzuki was still surprised he hadn't met a Norse God.

Suzuki reflected on the name of Middang3ard for a little bit longer as the world around him grew pink and purple. "Hey, why the hell is this place called Middang3ard anyways?" Suzuki asked.

Diana laughed as she sipped her ambrosia. "The naming conventions that we've had to use are...complicated, to say the least. Some of the worst magic that Myrddin's used, in my opinion," she explained.

Sandy did a double-take, practically spitting her ambrosia out. "Wait, are you saying that the reason that we call this place something that ridiculous is because of magic?"

"It's hard to explain. Like I said, it's pretty sloppy work. So, think of it like this...name a book. Just pick one off the top of your head."

Stew threw back his ambrosia and shouted, "Jules Verne!"

Diana shook her head, pinching the bridge of her nose. "That's not a book, but sure, we'll use it. Happens to work perfectly, so I'll let you off the hook. Verne wrote *Journey to the Center of the Earth*. You remember the volcano, the one they use to get to the center?" Diana pointed at the volcano.

Stew whistled and murmured, "Fuck me."

Sandy leaned over and rested her hand on Stew's crotch. "Later, babe."

Stew completely ignored Sandy, leaning forward and almost knocking her over. "Are you saying that shit is real?"

Sandy collected herself, brushing the dirt off her thighs. "Didn't peg you for a Verne fan," Sandy teased. "Let alone a fan of, you know, books."

"I love Verne! Everything he ever wrote. Those books were like magic."

The childlike glee on Stew's face was contagious, and Sandy smiled at him as she took his hand. Suzuki thought back to the first Verne he had ever read. He couldn't have been older than twelve. He remembered it vividly, being trapped in those worlds that Verne had created. He had lost time there.

Diana was nodding in a far off way as if she were listening to music, her eyes closed, lost in memory as well. "That shit is real. Not everywhere. Not on Earth. But Middang3ard is hollow as hell. Anyways, the way the magic works is that Myrddin would find authors and use magic to bring out their latent talent. It basically helped them concentrate. Then what Myrddin did to seal the spell was tie it to the words that they used. They became words of power. Because of that, there are a lot of descriptions and so forth we can't use until the copyright date runs out."

Suzuki burst out laughing. He wasn't sure if it was the ambrosia or if that was the funniest thing he'd ever heard. "Are you fucking kidding me." He guffawed. "You're saying that using the names of copyrighted materials weakens the spell?"

"Exactly. Even after the author dies. It starts to affect the potency of their work, which is why we avoid calling certain places, like this realm, which bears a strong resemblance to a certain realm with halflings, by their true name. That Myrddin tied his spell to something as complicated as legalities is beyond me."

"So, why don't we just call this place Middang—"

"Shush. It was one of the first spells Myrddin tried, and he botched the whole thing. Also, if I remember correctly, a fantasy author named a spectacular book that, and has the copyright for another few years."

Beth rose and yawned loudly before finishing her drink. "I can't wait until that shit is over and I can stop stumbling over Middang3ard. All right, I'm off to sleep, douchenozzles. Later."

Suzuki got ready to stand up and go after Beth. "You want me to come too?" he asked.

Beth shook her head. Her eyes looked sleepy and distant. Suzuki wasn't sure if it was the ambrosia or something else that was bothering her. "No," Beth said almost curtly. "Just because I'm going to sleep doesn't mean you have to. Be your own person, Suzy." She turned and walked off to their tent.

Suzuki sat down, dejected. Something was wrong with Beth, and he wanted to do whatever he could to help. But the way she had spoken to him, the little bit of bite in her voice, had cut Suzuki in a way he hadn't thought Beth capable of. She probably didn't even realize she had, so it wasn't anything to lose sleep over. He turned his attention back to the conversation at hand.

Stew was still very excited about the prospect of his

favorite science fiction books being real. "Okay, what about Burroughs? What about Tarz—"

Chip shook her finger at him. "Ah, ah, ah," she cut in. "Don't be spewing names all willy-nilly. And that one's out, as well as that Percolator one or whatever it's called. Burroughs ain't gonna roll around to public domain for another twenty-one years. 'Til then, try to keep your fanboy hard-on away from the literature, will you?"

"All right, all right. Don't want to fuck up the magic, right?"

"Exactly."

The Mundanes and the remaining Horsemen continued to drink long into the night. They spoke in quick bursts, laughing for extended periods of time as if they had only just realized how funny their companions were. It was lamented that Beth had gone to sleep so early, but it was understandable. Why had they not gone to sleep? No decision was agreed on across the board, but they did slowly drift away to their tents. Tired yet rested somehow. As Suzuki opened his tent, he could understand why José loved ambrosia.

Suzuki returned to his tent, trying not to stumble over the little bit that was inside, namely, Beth's feet. He found the corner of the tent and plopped down. He looked around, trying to figure out what he was going to do with his time. Sleeping didn't seem like a good idea. Whatever the ambrosia did, it wasn't the same as alcohol, but it was similar. There was a general sense of relaxation, but it also provided an intense amount of energy. *That's not quite right,* Suzuki thought to himself. *It's more like...I'm interested?*

It seemed like a waste to just go to sleep, so Suzuki grabbed his axe and pulled down his HUD. He had been thinking about working on his enchantments earlier but had been distracted by dinner and the conversations that had come afterward. Now seemed like a pretty good time. Everyone had headed to sleep. Beth was snoring softly.

The enchantments Suzuki had on his armor were mostly passive, charms and enhancements that boosted his strength slightly while also helping him with his balance. Enhancements that were simple to work with and would expire after considerable use. But the ambrosia had Suzuki's mind going. He realized he was using enchantments in the most boring way possible. If he could cover his armor with charms and enhancements to distort and buff different properties, there was almost a limitless number of possibilities he had never even begun to play with.

Suzuki pulled out the book of runes Sandy had found for him a few months ago, dug from the catacombs of the MERC library. The book was still musty. The smell of thousands of years. Suzuki cracked the book open, along with the rune compendium Diana had gotten him after finding out the book of runes had sat on his desk unopened for nearly two weeks.

The premise of the book was simple. There were runes. Each represented a different thing. If one was to etch that rune into an object, that object would take the properties of the rune. It was a process similar to the SD card attachments his HUD had. The difference was that he didn't need Chip to fine-tune them. Even further, there was something he found extremely comforting about working on his own armor and weapons. Carving the runes himself made him feel as if he were creating something of permanence in Middang3ard, as if he were making something for himself and only himself.

It was a time consuming process. To begin with, there were thousands of runes. It was one of the reasons Suzuki had kept to basic ones. It was not a problem of carving the runes but rather finding the proper runes to carve.

Suzuki wasn't worried about that tonight, though. He flipped open the book to a random page and started reading, cross-referencing with his dictionary. He found two he thought would be fun to try out. There was a rune for levitation and one for carrying out tasks with haste. Suzuki didn't know why, but he decided to pull off his boots and get to carving. He worked for nearly an hour before he felt the pull of sleep. He yawned, went outside to stretch, and came back in, taking off his shirt and tossing it into a pile of Beth's clothes before getting back to carving.

The weight of his axe in his hand and the way the steel cut into the soft leather soles of his boots brought a smile to his face. In Middang3ard, there was always loot to find, just like in the VR. Sandy always found or searched out loot that called to her. Stew tossed away each old axe for a new one at a moment's notice. Suzuki had never had that kind of luck or relationship with his gear. What he had found through enchanting filled that void. For the most part, he had much of the same gear as when he'd first come to Middang3ard but every time he worked an enchantment on a piece of his gear, it felt like something just for him. He was never one for tinkering before. It always surprised him that enchanting was one of the most calming things he could do.

Suzuki hummed to himself as he worked, a slow song of sorts. He could not remember where he had heard it or why he felt it must be hummed, but everything felt right about this moment. He finished the last rune and held his boots up, looking at his work. As he turned around, he saw that Beth had woken up. She was rubbing the sleep out of her eyes, smiling slightly. "Shit, I'm sorry, I didn't mean to wake you up," Suzuki said.

Beth waved away Suzuki's concern as she stretched her arms. "You don't have to apologize, Suzy." She yawned. "I was hoping you'd wake me."

Suzuki held his boot up to the dim light thrown by the magical fireflies they had cast when they first pitched the tent. The fireflies cast a soft blue light that was easy on the eyes for sleeping but offered enough illumination for working or reading. "Oh yeah, you were?"

"Yeah, I just wanted...ugh...I fucking hate saying this, but I just wanted to say I was sorry. About earlier. About you being your own person. You know, I haven't ever done this whole dating thing. Like, the whole being in a relationship shit. It's weird. I feel like I could be smothered. Not that you're smothering me. Just, I don't know, kinda afraid that could happen. But that's not even what I'm trying to say. That's not why I said that...I just...I've been feeling weird. Not weird. I been feeling shitty. All that talking about death and shit. Gods and whatever. I don't know why, but it really set me off."

"I can see why talking about death had you—"

Beth sat up straighter and stared at Suzuki, her eyes full of an emotion Suzuki could not easily place. "That's not it. It's what I heard from my friends, from the military about what the Dark One is doing. The military is pulling back. They're retreating. I think... I think we should take the fight to the Dark One."

"We are taking—"

"No, I mean us. The Mundanes. Chip and Diana. We could bring the fight to them. We don't have to wait for the military or for MERCs. We could lead them."

"What are you trying to say, Beth?"

"Suzy, I saw you out there at that battle. I saw what you can fucking do. You could lead an army. We don't need a bunch of MERCs waiting around to fight the battles they want. And we don't need that bureaucratic military bullshit. We need people to take the fight to the Dark One. I think that's us. Time is being wasted. If no one else is going to step up and fucking end this, we have to."

"Myrddin is—"

"Myrddin has been taking over 5,000 years to deal with this. Now we're here."

Suzuki looked deep into Beth's eyes. She had that look he had fallen in love with, the one where she looked like she was capable of anything. He would follow her into any battle. He knew that better than he had ever known anything his entire life. "I love you," Suzuki said.

Beth laughed and whipped the little bit of hair she had out of her face. "Fuck off, nerd. I love you too, Suzy."

Beth leaned forward and kissed Suzuki. He could taste the love on her lips, could see it in her eyes as she pulled away and smiled at him. "Are you tired?" Beth asked.

"Not anymore."

"Good. You wanna try something new?"

"What kind of new?"

"Get your book?"

Suzuki looked down at the rune book in his lap. "You wanna try Nordic runes?" Suzuki asked.

"No, Suzy. The other book."

Suzuki suddenly remembered. Back when the Mundanes were still hunting down Beth, Suzuki had come across an elvish novelty book. The book itself was blank, but it had been enchanted so that if you opened the pages, it would tell you a story you wanted to hear. It didn't matter what it was. And the book had a habit of being able to pry the most sensitive and embarrassing information out of you. Suzuki had mostly been using it to dream up different battle tactics, to imagine situations in combat he had never thought of before.

But that was only how he had spent some of his time before he and Beth started dating. There were lots of other things the book was able to illustrate for Suzuki. He hardly missed the internet since he had gotten the book.

Suzuki scrolled through his inventory until he found it. He hoped he had made sure to close it since the last time he had used it. Or cleaned it. It was much more important that he had cleaned it.

The book materialized in Suzuki's lap. He breathed a sigh of relief when he saw the pages were closed and there weren't any unexpected fluids or stains. "You mean this one," he said, tossing it to Beth.

Beth caught the book and flipped it open. "Stop being cute. Of course, I meant this one," she said. "You think I want to read old world history with you?"

"Well, you could have wanted a runic tattoo."

Beth continued flipping through the pages, grinning to herself. "Suzy, this thing is fucking raunchy," she exclaimed. "I can't believe you been walking around with your own literary porn site in your bag."

"Honestly, it's been a lifesaver. I mean...uh..."

Beth scooted closer to Suzuki and placed the book in between them, resting on both of their laps. "What do you mean, it was a lifesaver?" Beth asked.

Suzuki blushed and looked away until Beth took his chin in between her fingers. "You wanna show me what you jerk off to?"

"Seriously?"

"Why the fuck not? I used to wank off to pictures of you all the time."

Suzuki couldn't believe what he had just heard. Pictures of him? Any anxiety he had had instantly left him. "Are you serious?" he asked.

"Oh yeah, all the time. I mean, not *all* the time. I had to do stuff like patrols or eating. But anytime the barracks were closed, you know, I had all those screenshots from VR."

"Wait, you used to jerk off to my VR avatar?"

Beth giggled and clasped her hand over her mouth before turning red. "I didn't have any real pictures of you," she admitted. "And we only ever met once in person. And all the videos you sent always had Stew or Sandy walking in and being obnoxious and shit. So, yeah. I used to cum imagining your super scrawny paladin with that god-awful color –that puke green sash you used to wear. Ugh. I can't believe I'm talking to you about this."

Suzuki kissed Beth, holding her as close as he could until the edges of the book started to dig into his skin. When he pulled away, he took a deep breath and prepared himself. "I used to jack off to you too," Suzuki breathed, feeling like a weight had lifted.

"Uh, yeah, I know. Sandy totally walked in on you once and told me."

"Oh. Well, that's...goddamn it."

"She said you were looking at this book, and I was in it, you know, getting weird. So, I wanted to check it out with you. Kinda like watching porn together? And we could get some ideas. Some weird ideas."

Suzuki grabbed the book and scooted closer to Beth so they were sitting side by side. "I've never looked at this with anyone before," Suzuki said. "I don't know how it works. But, I mean, I'm down to try it."

"Yeah, I think it'll be fun. You know, I feel like this is something we could really enjoy. Together."

Beth was grinning, running her fingers over the blanket. Suzuki thought she looked like she was swelling. Not growing larger but taking up more space, like the tent was filling up with her, whatever she was. "You want to?" Beth asked.

Suzuki closed the book, grabbed Beth's hand, and placed

it on top of the book. "Yeah," he exclaimed. "Let's open it together."

The two held hands and opened the book together, longingly staring into each other's eyes for a few moments before looking down at the blank pages.

At first, there was nothing. Then a swirl of color, black and tans mixing together into a medley of contrast and hues. Suzuki heard a voice in the back of his head and wondered what it was Beth heard as the colors on the page took on starker tones, the blacks becoming deep and the tans becoming more sand-like. A scene painted itself. First the blackness of space, followed by an explosion of stars, of planets that were foreign yet somehow familiar. Suzuki couldn't tell where he had seen these planets, but he knew them deep down in his core. Almost as if he had been there before.

The planets rushed up at the pages, and Beth tightened her grip around Suzuki's hand as they both stared down. Now the book was zooming through space, the stars blurring in a tunnel vision of whiteness until suddenly, it stopped. The pages were an inky black depiction of space, a moonlike structure floating in the void.

Suzuki gasped as he grasped his chest. "Are you fucking serious?" he murmured.

At his side, Beth was smiling widely, almost mischievously as she leaned over the book. She flipped the page.

The illustrated version of Beth was wearing a golden bikini with a tannish brown rim. It was the spitting image of the bikini worn by Princess Leia. She was gripping her throat. Standing across from her was Suzuki dressed as Darth Vader without a helmet. His skin was pasty and looked to have been severely burned as he stretched out his hand, force choking Beth.

Beth sighed heavily as she leaned back and looked at Suzuki. "That is so fucking hot...you wanna try it?"

Suzuki raised his eyebrow. "You mean roleplay Princess Leia and Darth Vader? You do realize Princess Leia is Darth Vader's daughter, right."

"Yes, of course, I know, Suzy. But that's in the story. You aren't my daddy. Or are you?" She gave him a wicked smile.

Suzuki shifted uncomfortably.

Beth rolled her eyes before scooting closer to Suzuki. "Come on, we can just put the whole incest theme on the backburner. I think it'd be fun."

"Where are we going to get the costumes?"

"Already on it."

Beth ducked out of the tent, leaving Suzuki alone. He looked down at the pages of the book. Beth did look really good in that bikini. A little odd that when she fantasized about him as Darth Vader, it was without the helmet. Suzuki thought the helmet was the coolest part.

It was only a couple of minutes before Beth poked her head back into the tent. "Come outside," she whispered.

Suzuki did as he was told and stepped outside. Sandy was there, wearing her pajamas and yawning loudly. She pointed her wand at Suzuki, waved it, and then rubbed her eyes. "All right," Sandy said to Beth. "You guys should be good. All the details tomorrow, okay."

Beth gave Sandy a high five and hug and said, "You got it," before rushing over to Suzuki and dragging him back into the tent. "All right, Sandy said all we have to do is close our eyes and concentrate on how we want to look. She called it glamour or something."

Suzuki nodded to show he understood the instructions. Then a question popped into his head. "Wait, do you want me to wear the helmet or not?" he asked.

Beth laughed as she squirmed with anticipation. "No helmet. And not old man Vader but fresh, juicy Anakin burns, okay?"

"Gotcha."

Suzuki closed his eyes and concentrated as hard as he could. It didn't take much. He had memorized Vader's armor since he was a child. Even though he wasn't sure about looking like he'd been in a makeup chair for six hours, he was glad he wasn't going to have to listen to a breathing apparatus all night.

Slowly, Suzuki opened his eyes. There Beth was in all her nerdy, hot glory. She smiled bashfully as she let the transparent silk robe she was wearing open, showing her bikini. Suzuki wasn't sure what he was more turned on by, seeing Beth dressed as Leia or how obviously into this she was.

Beth raised her hand and a chain materialized over her neck. She handed it to Suzuki before getting down on her hands and knees. "How are you going to stop the rebellion, Lord Vader? Are you going to force-choke me, Daddy?" she cooed.

Suzuki raised his hand in the iconic choking gesture. "I grow tired of your insolence, Princess! Where are the plans to the Death Star," he growled.

Beth ran her hands down her bikini bottom as she smiled and whispered, "Lord Vader, I've hidden them. You're going to have to search for them. Thoroughly."

Someone coughed in the room. "Well, this is extremely awkward."

Suzuki turned around, calling his axe to him without

even thinking. What he saw was enough to make him forget about his costume, which instantly vanished, leaving him naked, his axe raised in the air.

José stood before Suzuki. He was nearly transparent but still tangible. He looked younger than when Suzuki had first met him. His hand rested on a large, glowing, golden sword. He was smiling, shaking his head as if he were embarrassed for Suzuki.

Suzuki could not believe what he was looking at. He remembered seeing José blasted by Chip, his body completely obliterated by her plasma cannon. "José," Suzuki finally managed. "Is that you?"

"It only seems appropriate that I show up at this moment. I am kinda like your Yoda. Though I would have preferred not to have seen your lightsaber."

"Shit," Suzuki exclaimed as he turned around and grabbed his pants. He looked back at José and asked, "What the hell are you doing here? Aren't you dead?"

"Oh, I am dead. And that's why I'm here."

Beth cleared her throat. Suzuki turned to see Beth standing, wearing her robe, tapping her feet impatiently as she twirled the chain. "Uh, Suzy, who the hell are you talking to?"

Suzuki eyed her suspiciously. He knew the mood had been killed, but why would she be asking who he was talking to when José was right in front of her. "José," Suzuki explained. "How the hell did he get here, right?"

Beth stepped closer to Suzuki and looked over his shoulder. Then she looked Suzuki long and hard in the eye as if she were a doctor. She pressed her hand to Suzuki's forehead. "Suzy, if you weren't feeling it, you could just say something," she said.

"No, no, I was," Suzuki said as he grabbed Beth's hand and pressed it to his crotch. "See?"

"Okay, that is pretty convincing. But what's up with the José thing?"

"He's standing right over there."

Beth checked over Suzuki's shoulder again. Then she checked Suzuki's temperature again. "Holy shit, I think I broke you."

"You can't see him?"

"There's no one there, Suzy."

Suzuki walked over to José and ran his hand through José, who sighed, irritated. "José, do something, so Beth doesn't think I'm crazy."

José chuckled to himself as he walked over to the book Beth and Suzuki had been using. He picked it up and held it over his head.

Beth's jaw dropped as she watched the book levitate over to her and open, its pages spelling out, "It's me, José. I'm glad you got out of that orc prison all right. Glad to see you and Suzuki are together."

Beth took a step back and tripped over herself. "Ros'ten," she called to her familiar. "Can you see anything?" She waited for an answer before shaking her head, getting up, and hiding behind Suzuki. "Fuck this," Beth said. "I don't do ghost shit. I did not sign up to be haunted. What the fuck are we supposed to do? Is he pissed at us or something?"

José put the book back down and sat cross-legged. "No, I'm not pissed at either of you. Or anyone, for that matter," José said. "I'm just here because I need to talk to you, Suzuki. Your training isn't over."

Suzuki conveyed the message to Beth. She still looked freaked out, her face white as paper and her lip slightly trembling, but she agreed to trust Suzuki. The whole ghost situation was too much for Beth, and she decided she was going to crash in Sandy's and Stew's tent. She could catch them up on the fact that José was apparently now haunting their campgrounds. And in the meantime, Suzuki could have his chat with José.

After Beth left, José came over and placed his hand on Suzuki's shoulder. "We have a lot to talk about, kid."

8

S uzuki and José sat alone in the tent. It felt as if all the heat in the room had been sucked out. When he first saw José, he thought the man looked the same as he had in life. Now that he looked closer, he could see that was not the case. José's armor was busted and cracked as if he had laid down and had men hammer on him for no obvious reason. He also looked younger but more worn. His face was gaunt, and he looked thinner. The sword that hung on him was not the same one he had been buried with. In addition, his armor wasn't MERC armor. It bore no insignias.

José looked at Suzuki, large, black bags under his eyes as if he had never known the meaning of sleep. When he spoke, it was with a measured control Suzuki had never heard from him before. There had always been a seriousness, a solemnness when José chose to speak. This was something more. It seemed like every word José said was weighted with life and death. "He's out there," José said, his words sounding like they were dragged through gravel.

Suzuki knew exactly who José was speaking of—the Dark One. It was always the Dark One. "We know he's out there, José. That's why the MERCs are trying to take him out."

"Trying and doing aren't the same thing."

"We're working on it. We need a plan. We're still trying to figure out what to do. Every few weeks we find out something different about this guy. First, we think he's some techno freak. Then we find out he's some kind of alien. Now, some forest spirit is telling us he's a fucking god. How the hell are you supposed to find something you don't even understand."

José smiled sadly and nodded as he reached into his pocket and pulled out a pipe. He puffed on it as he spoke, the smoke looking more real than José.

"How do I even know you're real?" Suzuki asked.

José let out a cloud of smoke and his smile faded. "When you were five, you fell down a flight of stairs," José whispered. "You cracked your head open. All your family thought you were going to die. You have a steel plate in your head, and you never tell anyone about it because you're afraid they're going to assume that is the root of your oddities. You don't want to be a meme, the nerd who has social anxiety because he was dropped on his head. You've never told anyone this. Not even the Mundanes."

Suzuki's heart stopped and he felt his veins flood with ice. He wanted to run screaming from the tent. To say he was scared was an understatement. He felt like he might shit his pants. "How did you know all that?" Suzuki asked.

"The dead see many things. We are privy to all kinds of information. Your parents miss you, but they know what you're doing. They know how important your work is, and they're very proud of you."

Suzuki's heart dropped. He couldn't remember one time he had really thought about his parents since he had come to Middang3ard. There was always something going on. He had been so focused on finding Beth he had forgotten he had left his entire life behind. Now that life came rushing back to him at breakneck speed. He did miss his parents. He missed his friends. Surprisingly though, and he knew this in the core of his person, he didn't miss it. He didn't miss being a nobody. He didn't miss not knowing what he was doing with himself —living through a virtual reality video game.

Old insecurities came flooding back into Suzuki, and he felt like maybe all this was a dream. Maybe this was just something he saw when he went to sleep because he was so pathetic in real life he had to build a fictional world to live in.

José continued to smoke his pipe. He packed a new bowl before he spoke. "These are things you should never forget," José explained. "You aren't the person you used to be. You should remember that, so you can understand who you are now."

Suzuki wiped a tear from his eye. He hadn't even been aware that he was crying. "What are you doing here?" Suzuki asked. "Did you come here just to remind me that I used to be a dweeb, and that I need to kill the Dark One."

"It is much deeper than that. I heard you spoke with the Forest Spirit. Speaking to you as soon as possible afterward was important."

"How did you know I spoke—"

José raised his right hand. In the palm of his hand was a hexagram. Its corners were bright white lights. "I am connected to you all," he explained. "I do not see and hear everything, only what is important. You speaking to the Forest Spirit was important. He told you things you must understand and make sense of. Things the rest of the Mundanes may overlook, simply because they were not aware of them. These are the sort of things we must talk about."

Suzuki smiled and shook his head, thinking José was just trying to flatter him before sending him on a suicide mission. "And what do I need to be thinking about that no one else would notice?" Suzuki asked.

"What is the Dark One?"

"I have no fucking clue."

"You have multiple clues."

Suzuki sighed in frustration. He wasn't used to the kind of José who spoke in riddles. "Are you going to elaborate on what those clues are?" Suzuki asked.

"Suzuki, do you believe that everything is related? That everything happens for a reason?"

"Sure, I guess. I mean, there has to be a reason for anything to happen. That doesn't mean those reasons have meaning. They're just a cause and effect relationship. Like the distribution of energy. What does that have to do with anything?"

José had already packed another bowl. His face was shrouded in smoke as if he were exhaling himself. "Why don't you think the Dark One is an alien?" he asked.

"Why? Because aliens are fiction. Or, I mean, not like any of the stuff I've seen wasn't fiction before. But aliens in pop culture are...I don't know, they go against the basis of physics. Traveling from other planets and shit? The way we think of it is impossible. I can't believe Myrddin is thinking about sending a rocket to fight him in space. It can't be that simple... because...if...holy shit...everything the Forest Spirit said is true, isn't it? And so is what I thought. He is an alien, but not like from another planet. He's from another dimension. And he's godlike, just like what's in the earth. The hollow earth. In the center. But it's not on Earth. Diana said Middang3ard is hollow. Are you saying the Hollow Earth theories are real?"

"What do you think you would find if you were to search?"

Suzuki stood up, his fists balled up in frustration. "Could you cut the riddle bullshit?" Suzuki shouted. "Just give me a straight answer. You can't show up here like this and just..." Suzuki stopped midsentence. His face was hot, and it was hard to speak. He felt like he was choking on something and suddenly needed to sit down. There was a heavy weight on his chest, and he was gasping for breath. Before he knew it, the tears were coming. Through the sobbing, Suzuki managed to say, "I didn't even get to say goodbye, you know. And then you come here...it's all riddles, all..." Suzuki broke off, crying.

A warm presence touched Suzuki's shoulder. He looked up to see José, smiling down at him. "I know it hurt, Suzuki," he said. "But I'm not gone. Not from you all. I never will be."

"But you died. I watched you die for me, for all of us."

"No one lives forever, Suz."

"Except for the Dark One."

"I came for three reasons. To remind you that the Dark One is your responsibility, and yours alone. To speak to Chip. And I don't know why completely, but to speak to Sandy."

My responsibility? Suzuki thought. That made no sense. All the forces of the realms were trying to take down the Dark One. What made him Suzuki's responsibility? José must have been confused or meant something else. Maybe all that he was trying to say was Suzuki must share responsibility with the rest of everyone. *But he did say "yours alone,"* Suzuki thought.

José stood up and held out his hand for Suzuki, who tried to take it, completely lost balance, and tumbled through José. José's laughter filled the tent. "Honestly, I'm surprised you didn't try to make a Jesus joke." José chuckled. "I'm very glad you're over that phase."

Suzuki stood up and brushed himself off. "Why is it my responsibility?" Suzuki asked.

"There are things I don't understand about where I am. It is chaotic. Nothing seems to make sense. Ideas come into my head that I know are true, but I don't know why or how they got there. This place is a battlefield—the Dark One's battlefield. There are some of us fighting, but we are greatly outnumbered."

"How do I know these aren't ideas sent from the Dark One? How do I know you weren't sent by him?"

"Have I told you anything that would make you think so?"

Suzuki wracked his brain, going through everything José had said since he first appeared. There was nothing. He sighed as he accepted this was another thing he was just going to have to take on faith. "Come on, you said you wanted to talk to Chip and Sandy, right?" Suzuki asked.

Suzuki walked out of the tent, followed by the ghost of José. The rest of the Mundanes and Horsemen were sitting around the remains of the fire, Smuggles sleeping in the ashes as the sun began to rise in the east, peering through the tangled jungle of the island. Beth looked up at Suzuki as he looked around at the Mundanes. He could see the worry in their eyes. Obviously, Beth had told them all what she had seen. To be honest, he would have done the same thing.

Suzuki raised his hands in assurance. "All right, I know what it probably looks like, but hear me out."

Stew stepped forward first with a soft smile on his face as if he were about to deliver a hard truth to a confused child. "José's dead," Stew said. "I know it's hard to accept, and none of us have really been talking about it, but the guy is gone. It's fucked up, but he's gone. That's one of the reasons we're out here, one of the reasons we're fighting. So this doesn't happen to anyone else. As long as the Dark One is out there..."

Stew stopped talking as his eyes fell to the ground. He followed a stick floating in the air as it traced letters into the dirt. It simply said, "When did Stew become sensitive?"

Sandy laughed as she knelt by the floating stick. She ran her hand through the air where an arm would have been. She smiled wide and almost squealed with surprise and glee. "Holy shit, Suzy," she exclaimed. "You aren't crazy. We were so fucking worried. Can you actually see José?"

Suzuki cast a quick glance at José and nodded. "Yep, as clear as day," he said. "And he didn't come to speak with just me. He wants to talk to Chip and you."

Chip's face looked as if it were about to fall apart. There were tears in her eyes, and her lips trembled as she backed away from the rest of the MERCs. "Me?" she murmured.

"He says he's not angry, not with any of us. He just came back to talk."

"I want to see him. I need to. Can I try?"

Suzuki checked with José, casting him a quick glance. José nodded his assent, and Suzuki told Chip she could give it a shot. Chip stepped forward as Suzuki directed her to where José stood. Her eyes changed color and began to cycle through different light ray spectrums. As she cycled, the corners of her eyes opened up as if to allow more light in.

After a couple of minutes of trying, she sighed and said, "I can't see him. Could you...talk to him for me?"

Suzuki nodded and asked, "What do you want to say?"

"Tell him I'm sorry. I'm so fucking sorry."

Chip's voice quivered as the usual robustness disappeared. She fell to her knees, her whole body shaking as she wept and repeated over and over, "I'm so sorry."

Sandy turned and went to her tent. She returned after a few moments, holding the head of the orc necromancer. She crouched next to Chip and took Chip's hand. "Here. Let me help you. Hold this."

Chip took the head, its eyes wide and white, mouth hanging open as if it were in shock. Sandy ran her hand over the head's face and whispered something quietly. A cold wind rushed through where the MERCs stood.

The lips of the orc moved, as if an electric jolt had gone through the head. The mouth began gumming back and forth, the eyes rolling about as if they had been seized by a vision, whirling about, mad and searching. The skin took on life again, as much life as you could see within an orcs head to begin with. The mouth yammered back and forth as spittle trickled down its chin, from where nobody knew. A hoarse voice, somewhat similar to José's yet different, like a multitude of other voices were speaking in unison, some of them pained, others in what could have only been described as ecstasy, came through the mouth of the orc. "Chip?" the voice wheezed.

Chip held the head up so she could look into its eyes, which had taken on José's soft brown. "José?" she asked. "Is that you? Is it really you?"

"I have so much to say to you. I never stopped loving you. I'm sorry. I'm so goddamn sorry."

Chip cried as she held the dead head close to her cheek. "Don't be daft, you idiot," she managed. "If anyone should be apologizing, it's me. I'm the git who snapped you from this world. I—"

"It wasn't your fault. I know it wasn't your fault."

Chip was silent. The head muttered something and Chip held it to her ear, listening intently, her eyes growing wider and wider. "I love you too. I'll always love you. I'll never stop loving you," she whispered. "And I will. I promise. I'll take care of it when it's time." And with that, Chip stood and handed the head back to Sandy. She walked over to Diana and sat next to her. Diana took her hand and held it tight.

Sandy stared at the eyes of the dead orc. "What do you want to talk to me about?" Sandy asked.

A sigh like the rustling of leaves came up out of the orc. "I need you," José said through the orc. "I need you to come with me. There...there is a thing I need you for. A way-line... the planes... I need to take you with me."

Diana jumped up, her eyes flashing as she held back tears. "No!" she shouted. "Whatever you need her for, I can do it! You will not take her when you can have me."

A roar came from the orc's head, a thousand screams of pain and pleasure. "No!" José shouted. "They will need you and Chip. You cannot leave them for what is ahead."

"And you will risk her? Risk her fucking life? She can't go there. She's never been. It could destroy her."

"Did it destroy you?"

Diana shook her head as she looked at Sandy, who looked more than confused. "What is he talking about?" Sandy asked.

"He wants to take you to the realm between realms. The

realm of the dead, chaos, and life. The realm where the Dark One came from."

"Then I'm going."

"Do you have any idea of what you're talking about?"

Sandy nodded her head solemnly as she stood. Suzuki had never seen her look this serious. The corners of her mouth were tight, and her eyes were focused on something that could not be seen by the rest of the MERCs. "It's what the *Shishigami* told me," Sandy whispered. "Someone has to find the Dark One's name. There's power in a real name, a true name. And José is right. We can't lose you. I won't pretend I don't know how strong I am. But there's still so much I don't know. If I–if something happens to me, the Mundanes will keep going on. But if something happens to you, what are we going to do? This is beyond simple fetch quests. This is a war. We need to be realistic. You aren't expendable."

Stew grabbed Sandy and turned her to face him. "What the hell are you saying?" Stew asked. "What makes you think you're expendable?"

Sandy caressed Stew's cheek and smiled sadly. "Babe, we have to be honest with ourselves. We're at war. We can't keep pretending all of us are going to make it. We're going to have to make sacrifices."

"You can't just run off on some—"

But Suzuki didn't hear what Stew had to say because Fred chimed in, speaking for the first time since they had come to the island. *Suzuki*, the imp said while stirring in the Mundane leader's body. *Sandy is right. She must go. There are things in the nether realms only certain people can access. Certain people like your extremely violent and very pretty magic-user.*

You think Sandy is pretty, Suzuki mused, not because he

was teasing Fred, but because the imp never expressed any appreciation for beauty in any creature, human or otherwise.

Shut your foolishness, human, Fred retorted.

"Ah, sorry. I was just—"

I know what you were just. But Child of Dust, human... Suzuki...if José is right, this is exactly what we need to stop the Dark One. Send Sandy, but she cannot go alone. She needs someone to guide her. Someone more knowledgeable.

José is—

Fred hissed. *José, as great as he is, is only human. She will need a guide who understands death. I will need to go with her.*

You? But—

But you worry about your magic, whelp.

Suzuki pursed his lips before nodding. *That and I worry about you. And Sandy. We haven't agreed for her to go, and—*

This is what could end the war, foolish human. If there is only a small chance of that, we must try.

Suzuki knew Fred was right, but losing his familiar would mean he was out of the fight, too. Humans couldn't remain on Middang3ard without a tether to magic.

As if reading his thoughts, Fred answered, *I can leave behind an imprint of me. The imprint will lack my wit, but you will maintain your tether. And your magic.*

Suzuki shook his head. *It's not just that. What about you? Sandy? You'll need to die to go there and—*

You and I have both seen things worse than death, Suzuki, Fred hissed before pausing. Then in a soft voice uncharacteristic for Fred, he added, *Suzy...this is a chance. Perhaps our only one. I will need to join her if she is to have a chance of success and—*

Fred's thoughts were cut off by Sandy yelling, "I'm not

sacrificing myself in vain! But I'm going to do what I think has to be done to stop the Dark One. You should too."

"This is to stop the Dark One? Is that what you're saying this is about?"

Sandy looked away, unable to meet Stew's or any of the other MERC's eyes. "There are things I need to know," Sandy finally said. "There's a reason Diana went to the place between realms. I need to go there, too. Otherwise...oh, fuck it. It's why I'm here. It's the whole reason I'm here on Middang3ard. All of us have a role to play. I don't know mine completely, but I know I'm supposed to go there."

Stew was angry; it was evident from his face. But even Suzuki could see this anger was coming from fear. "Why do you have to?" he shouted. "Why do you have to risk your life? Is it because of something a fucking deer with a face told you? How the fuck do we know any of this is actually real? How the fuck do we know this isn't something the Dark One is orchestrating just to fuck with us, huh?"

Stew yanked the orc's head out of Sandy's hand and held it up so it was eye level. "All right, if you're José and all this is on the up and up and you're reaching out to us from beyond the grave, give us a sign. How's that sound? If we're supposed to trust you, how about you give us a reason to, other than just playing with everyone. Give me some proof we should be listening to you!"

In the distance, there was a powerful roar. The earth shook and trembled strongly enough that the MERCs almost lost their footing. An earthquake rolled through the jungle as smoke rose from its highest peak. The MERCs couldn't help but watch as molten lava began to pour from the tip of the island's mountain.

Stew shook his head in disbelief. "There's no way you orchestrated a fucking volcano."

The lava stopped flowing. It had been nothing more than a spurt of the hot red stuff, but the earth continued to shake. The Smuggles who had been sleeping around the fire jumped to their feet and went screaming into the jungle after they saw the humans, leaving the MERCs alone. One of them was holding an orc head, staring into it to gain some kind of understanding. The rest were quiet.

Suzuki knew it was José.

This wasn't some test from the Dark One.

If there ever was a sign, the exploding volcano was it.

He just didn't know what he was supposed to do about it.

Suzuki turned to ask José what was going on, but he was gone as if he had never been there. "Okay, can we all admit something really fucking weird just happened, right?" Suzuki asked.

The MERCs all nodded in agreement. "All right, so what are we going to do about it?" Suzuki asked.

They deliberated for nearly twenty minutes. Diana was adamant about Sandy not going to the place between realms, especially since José had vanished. She said it was a terrible idea to go there, try to find José and take care of whatever it was that she thought José wanted her to. Unsurprisingly, Sandy hadn't changed her opinion. She was going. Either Diana was going to tell her how to get there, or she was going to find out herself. Finally, Diana agreed that she would show Sandy how to slip between realms.

The next order of business was what do concerning the volcano. Stew thought they should either investigate or leave the island. It wasn't that far away but, as Stew put it, "What the hell are we doing here if we're just going to let a volcano go off after our friend's ghost responds to me asking for a sign?"

Stew had a point. The MERCs decided they would see what was going on with the volcano.

Now all that was left was saying goodbye to Sandy. No one had actively spoken about the dangers she was going to come across other than Diana, and even then, she had been uncharacteristically quiet. The only indication this might be more than a simple goodbye came when Diana threw her arms around Sandy and told her she loved her and she had to come back; there was nothing more important than coming back. "You're my daughter," Diana whispered through tears. "I didn't even know I wanted a daughter, and you're my daughter."

Sandy didn't bother trying to say anything in return. She hugged Diana, and her eyes were wet when she released the embrace. Then Sandy went down the line of friends, hugging them all and giving them a kiss on the cheek.

She saved Stew for last.

Stew kissed Sandy on the forehead before wrapping her in his arms. "I love you, babe. I'll be waiting for you."

Sandy rested her head on Stew's shoulder as she squeezed him as tightly as she could. "I'll be back. I promise." She gave him another kiss on the cheek and let him go.

Go to her, Fred said. *Embrace her. I will join her now.*

Suzuki did as he was told and hugging her, he felt Fred leave him and enter her. But he also still felt the imprint within him.

"What was that?" Sandy asked.

"A guide in the form of one imp," Suzuki answered.

Sandy nodded with understanding and walked over to Diana. They both went into Sandy's tent. They were gone for some time before Diana walked out alone. "It's done. Come on. We should get going."

"How long is she going to be gone?" Suzuki asked.

"Best not to start thinking about it."

And with that, the Mundanes tore down their camp. An unspoken tension filled the air. No one mentioned it, but all felt it.

Once the camp was broken down, the Mundanes headed toward the volcano, Smuggles scampering around them as the mountain spewed smoke in the distance.

9

The Mundanes stalked through the jungle for what seemed like hours, hacking at vines that grew thick as a forearm.

They hardly spoke, each of them wrapped up in their own thoughts. Suzuki wished there was something he could say to get everyone out of their heads. That was what a leader was supposed to do.

He had seen José pull that shit more than a handful of times. José would have just the right words to get everyone laughing, to remind everyone they were on an adventure, that they were doing something important, and they could have fun doing it.

Suzuki realized this was probably what everyone else was thinking. They were all in some way thinking about either José or Sandy, and that was what was weighing them down. Suzuki looked from one MERC to another. They looked to be stumbling their way through the forest, their eyes far off as they concentrated on something that wasn't in front of them.

This was more than just an awkward walk through the

jungle. If something happened, if they were attacked, no one was focused. They would fall apart like a house of cards. Suzuki had to get them paying attention to more than their feelings about José. *How the hell do I do that,* he thought.

Then it hit him. "What do you think is going to happen to us if we die?" Suzuki asked.

The MERCs looked up from their feet and at Suzuki. He had brought attention to the elephant in the room, the one thing no one wanted to talk about. Sure, José showing up as a ghost was definitely disturbing, but it hinted it something even larger. Every mission, they faced death. Yet they had never spoken about it, and they had never spent time trying to understand what they were facing.

Things seemed even odder since they had spoken to the Forest Spirit. The afterlife had been explained to them, at least somewhat. Then a spirit walked into their camp like the ghost of things yet to come? Why the hell not just talk about it.

Chip looked up at Suzuki with wet, bloodshot eyes. "Why would you go and ask that?" she asked.

Suzuki shrugged as he leaned against a tree. "We're all thinking it, aren't we?" he countered.

Diana crouched and sighed. She shook her head as if she were trying to get out of a bad dream. She opened her mouth a couple of times to speak, but it took a few moments before she was able to squeeze out the words. "You really want to have this talk right now?"

"We just talked to our dead friend. I think this is as good a time as any."

Diana laughed as she wiped the sweat from her brow. The jungle was sweltering. She looked happy to take a break from walking. "All right, I'll shoot. I didn't think anything happened after you died. Not really. You know, everyone has their own myths, stories about the afterlife. Humans tend to think there's either a good or bad place you go. Elves believe you become part of the trees. Dwarves don't think you go anywhere, which makes sense because they don't even dream. But me? I just thought you stopped existing. It was that easy. You die, and then there's nothing. No spirit. No soul. You just cease to be. José kinda proved that one wrong today. So, fuck if I know."

Beth knelt by Suzuki's side, leaning against the same tree. Going through her inventory, she pulled out a flask of something special.

She took a sip and passed it around, taking another sip when it returned to her. "I never believed in heaven or hell. My parents didn't teach me anything about it. Not religious people. But my Nana used to talk to us about...I don't know, where she thought she was going, just like stories her mom told her before and that kind of shit. She said she was going to the place of our ancestors, like it was a huge family reunion or something. That's why she would always be watching over us, because that's what family did. They watched over you to make sure you were safe."

Stew took the flask next and took a long drink before speaking. "My dad was terrified of dying. Not like he was sick or anything. He just was scared of the idea. I asked him once what happened, and he didn't want to talk about it at first. But then he finally did, and he said you just go on living another life. You know, reincarnation. But it wasn't something that made him feel more comfortable or anything. He was terrified of having to live all over again. He said he just wanted one go, and that was it. But I liked the idea a lot. You know, you get to try a couple of runs, get it down until you can live your life the right way or however you want to. Sandy helped me with that. It's kinda what she thinks."

Beth laughed as she motioned for the cigarette Diana had just rolled and lit. "I didn't peg you and Sandy to be having deep conversations about life and death," she joked.

Stew laughed as he waved away the smoke floating toward him. "You know, I'm more than just a cute face and muscles. I have feelings and shit."

Diana took out her notebook and began scribbling notes as she muttered under her breath. Next to her, Chip grabbed the flask and took a sip. "Not even sure if I get granted an afterlife," Chip said softly. "The whole not a person thing kinda puts a damper on a soul. Maybe I just deactivate. On and off switch. That whole shit."

No one was quick to speak.

Suzuki realized he had taken his soul for granted. He hadn't really thought about what a soul was, but he knew that if human beings had one, so did he. In that sense, he had taken it for granted. He and the rest of the Mundanes had only just recently found out Chip wasn't a human or an elf.

She was a machine.

And it was a fact it seemed Chip herself was still reconciling.

"Do you dream?" Suzuki asked.

Chip looked up from her cigarette, confused. "Why?"

"It's from a book. Philip K. Dick. *Do Androids Dream of Electric Sheep.* It's a question about what consciousness is and whether it exists across the board, or if it's just something humans have dreamed up."

"Yep, I dream with the best of them. Nightmares, too. That proof of my soul?" Chip asked.

Suzuki shrugged. "I don't know. I'm not sure if it matters, though."

"That's easy for someone walking around with a soul to say, boyo. Only recently come into this whole not-a-person situation, so excuse me if I'm a little wary of getting all excited about any kind of existential statement about me own existence."

Diana burst out laughing, choking on the little bit she'd sipped from the flask. "Are you fucking kidding me, Chip?" She cackled. "You bet your soul on a card game last month. Literally, last month. How are you going to act like you give a shit about having a soul?"

Chip smiled despite herself, and Suzuki could tell she was itching to play into this. That was one thing he respected about Chip. She handled her shit and never let it change the kind of person she was. Even being extremely vulnerable about her fears couldn't stop her from seeing a gag and wanting to roll with it. "I only bet me soul because I had a killer hand," Chip pointed out. "It ain't a bet if you know you're going to win."

"Chip, you were down three hands, drunk as shit, and you lost an entire month of pay. Even if you had a soul, you don't know."

Chip waved away Diana's concerns as she cackled madly and slapped her knees. "The moment, the moment is what I live for," Chip said. "Souls be damned! Can I get a toast to that?"

Beth raised her flask and took a swig. She passed it around, and each MERC did so as well. Once it returned to Beth, she put the cap on and stood up. "What about you, Suzy?" she asked.

Suzuki considered it. In all honesty, he had never thought

of it before. Death was something he had recently become more accustomed to, but he tried not to think about the afterlife. His job was killing minions of the Dark One, minions who didn't seem like they had any control of their own actions. It was a murky gray area that made him extremely uncomfortable when he thought about it.

Suzuki took a deep breath. "I try not to think about it. I try not to think about a lot of this shit. If I think about it too much, I will go crazy. I hope there is something after death. At least for orcs and goblins. At least for people who don't have control of their lives. I hope they have something after death."

Beth rested their hand on Suzuki's shoulder. "You know they're trying to kill us, right?"

"Yeah, I know. And they don't have a choice."

Chip stood up and walked over to Suzuki. She embraced him and squeezed him tight. Suzuki was caught off guard and didn't know what to do, so he hugged Chip back. And he felt something deep within him trying to get out, something he had been pushing back for longer than he could remember. He tried to continue to squash it, to bury it as far in his gut as he could, but it came screaming out of him as his body sagged, and he started to cry.

Chip held Suzuki tightly as he wept. "No, we didn't have a choice," Chip whispered in Suzuki's ear.

They both stood there, crying and holding each other.

Beth came and put her arms around both of them.

Diana came over next.

Finally, Stew folded them into his arms.

For a while, they stood there in silence, the only sounds Chip's and Suzuki's muffled sobs.

This was Middang3ard, the brutal reality of their childhood games and books. This was a realm where entire races were enslaved, brought in to enact horrors they had no control over. A place where friends were turned against each other regularly. A place where heroes died. A place of pain, suffering, beauty, and friendship.

It was a place for MERCs.

A place for family.

When the tears stopped, the MERCs silently broke apart, giving each other space to breathe. They did not hide their eyes from each other. Whatever had been felt, experienced, it was important for them all. There were no words for such things. They were not just a party. They were kin. It had not been spoken aloud, but the Horsemen no longer existed. They were all Mundanes now. It could be seen in Chip's and Diana's eyes. It was as if that were an unspoken part of José's visit. A closure of sorts.

The Mundanes walked farther into the jungle, each of them in their own heads, but in a different way than before. Suzuki watched his party as they stalked through the hot, humid jungle. He was proud of them. And he loved them. Both things he felt weren't necessary to be said often, but it was true. They had all come through the worst the Dark One had thrown at them. Nothing had broken them. Nothing would break them.

As they walked through the jungle, bending to avoid trees and vines, Chip came up to Suzuki's side. "Thanks for all that."

Suzuki pushed a vine out of the way with his axe as he ducked to avoid it slapping him in the face. "Don't worry about it," he replied.

"No, really. Not to shine you on too much, but that shite back there was intense. And necessary. You got a good handle on these types of things. Not much seen in the likes of MERCs. It's appreciated."

"Thanks. That's really good to hear."

"José would be damn proud of the kind of leader you're shaping up to be. Damn proud. Thank you."

Chip took Suzuki's hand and squeezed it before walking ahead and slapping Beth on the back of the neck. "Come on, padawan," she shouted. "Senpai says it's time to get in them trees."

The two of them went running off ahead of the rest of the Mundanes. Chip leapt into the trees first, landing effortlessly. Beth flew up next. She didn't land as gracefully, but she sprinted to catch up with Chip, springing from branch to branch almost as effortlessly.

On the ground, the Mundanes continued their pace, Stew, Diana, and Suzuki walking side by side. Stew coughed loudly as if he were warming himself up to say something but remained silent. They continued on in this way for some time.

The jungle thinned out over the course of their journey. It was as if the trees tucked themselves away to hide from what was ahead. The air had changed as well. It had grown hot and difficult to breathe. The air smelled like sulfur and felt thick in the lungs. Still, they pushed on until the jungle was left behind and they stood in a clearing, standing before the leviathan volcano as it spewed columns of black smoke.

Chip and Beth jumped from the trees and landed next to the rest of the Mundanes. "Oh, that there is a flaming one, ain't it?" Chip asked.

Suzuki stared at the volcano. The smoke coming from its top was disconcerting. The sky above was dark and ominous as if an omen of things to come. If Suzuki had ever seen a sign, this was it but he was not certain what it was a sign of. It didn't matter though. Whatever José had wrangled them into was going to be difficult. That was just the way things were.

Stew was pacing, looking at the volcano. "How do you tell if it's going to pop?" Stew asked. "I mean, have you seen footage of volcanos going off? That's like apocalyptic shit, dude. And if it's smoking, that means it'll pop soon. Right?"

"Actually, volcanos smoke all the time without blowing. Besides, we're already here. If it went off, it wouldn't matter where we were on the island. We'd be dead. But since we are here, let's check it out. There's got to be a reason José was trying to get us to come here."

The Mundanes went toward the volcano. There was a sudden rumbling. The ground trembled as the earth quaked. "Fuck, dudes, it's happening," Stew shouted as he turned to run.

Nothing came from the volcano. The ground shook again. Suzuki figured out it wasn't the volcano quickly enough. That didn't answer the question of what was shaking the ground, though. "Sandy, can you...oh, yeah." Suzuki sighed as he realized Sandy couldn't help them out. It would be nice to get a better view of what was going on around them. Instead, he turned to Diana, feeling extremely uncomfortable ordering her to do something. "Hey, uh, Diana, could you do me a favor?"

Diana was staring in the distance, no doubt trying to figure out what the source of the earthquake was. "Yeah, what do you need?" she asked.

"To see what's going on. Could you?"

Diana nodded as she levitated into the air. "Oh, shit," she gasped.

"What is it?"

"Get fucking ready, guys!"

Diana whipped out her wand as the rest of the Mundanes drew their weapons. The quaking of the earth grew stronger. It had gone from a slight rumble to shaking so much Suzuki was hardly able to stay on his feet. He was about to ask what Diana was talking about when he realized there was no need. He saw the source of the commotion coming over the hills in the East.

A herd of brontosauruses was coming over the crest of the green hills. They were majestic and terrifying. The Mundanes went silent in awe as the creatures stampeded over the hill. Suzuki was beside himself. He couldn't express how badly he was freaking out. Dinosaurs. The child in him could not help but shriek as the massive lizards ran past the Mundanes—which begged the question, what were they running from?

The answer came swiftly.

Once the brontosauruses had run into the jungle, destroying the trees in their path, the predators came.

Seven tyrannosauruses came up over the hill, roaring loudly, towering at least fourteen feet in the air. Their massive jaws were lined with razor-sharp teeth, and their heavy bodies were moving at a speed that seemed unnatural.

They were a mile behind the brontosauruses, but their beady eyes had keyed on other prey.

Stew pulled the axe from his back and stepped to the front of the Mundanes' formation. "I know we were being all emotional and sensitive earlier, but there's T-rexes. Everyone ready for this?"

Suzuki didn't need to be asked.

This was still Middang3ard and shit was going to keep getting real. And the Mundanes were going to rise to every occasion. Orc, troll, whatever—it didn't matter. They were coming for the Dark One, and they were going to cut down whatever stood in their way.

Beth pulled out her short bow and stood next to Stew. She nocked an arrow and aimed at one of the T-rexes. "What's the game plan, Suzy?" she asked.

Suzuki laughed to himself. *Game plan? Against dinosaurs?* It wasn't something he had ever run scenarios of. "They're fucking dinosaurs," Suzuki finally said. "I don't think we're going to need a master plan to be able to figure this out. Hit them fast and hit them hard. For honor!"

"For glory!"

"For XP!"

The Mundanes charged at the stampeding T-rexes. Suzuki was certain this was something they would easily be able to handle. They had fought of trolls, orcs, and dragons before. What were a couple of flightless reptiles compared to that?

Stew leapt, his axe raised high above his head, toward the closest T-rex. He screamed, his eyes wide with the bloodlust as his body bulked up, entering into his berserker mode.

As Stew brought down his axe, the T-rex stepped to the side and a rex behind the first stepped forward and head-butted Stew hard enough to break every bone in his body. When Stew fell, the other rex brought its foot down on Stew's entire body. Instead of taking a bite, it kicked Stew to the side and turned to the other T-rexes. It chuckled, a sound Suzuki wasn't aware dinosaurs were capable of making. That didn't prepare him for what happened next.

The largest T-rex cleared its throat and spoke in a deep voice. "Ah, we've come across humans. I believe we should expedite this, so we do not lose track of our current prey."

The T-rex's scales broke apart, showing a level of techno-organic symbiosis Suzuki had never seen before. It was as if the tech and the skin, the organs, the entire creature were gone. The scales of the T-rex gleamed like liquid steel as its fangs grew larger and sharper, the whole creature bulking up yet slimming down as tech rippled across its body, opening its jaw and firing a stream of plasma as it roared.

"Goddamn it," Suzuki muttered. "Why isn't anything ever easy here?"

10

S treams of plasma tore across the open clearing, cutting up the earth and leaving huge scars across the ground.

It was all the Mundanes could do to avoid the onslaught of energy cutting through the air, leaving a steely sizzle as if it were not meant for this plane. Suzuki found himself scuttling across the ground, trying to get to his feet as fast as possible as the T-rexes rampaged toward him. The rest of the Mundanes were in similar situations.

The rexes were fast.

Faster than Suzuki would have imagined creatures that large could move.

Suzuki managed to get to his feet just as a T-rex brought its foot down on where he had just been. Hardly taking a moment to aim, Suzuki tossed his axe at the T-rex's right eye. It landed with a sickening thud, and the T-rex screeched in pain as it thrashed.

Before Suzuki had a chance to celebrate, the T-rex reached up with its stubby paws and rubbed the axe out of its eye. Then the wound began to heal; Suzuki could see thousands of nanofibers stitching the T-rex's eye closed. *What the hell?* Suzuki thought. He had seen that kind of healing before; it was the same way Chip reattached parts of her body that had been lopped off. He'd never seen Chip heal this fast, though. Within a matter of moments, the T-rex's eye was fine. If the T-rexes healed that fast, the Mundanes were in for a difficult fight.

Across the battlefield, the rest of the Mundanes were struggling as much as Suzuki. Stew had only just gotten to his feet before he was smacked in the chest by a stout, scaly tail. The impact of the attack sent him soaring over the rest of the Mundanes until he skidded across the ground and slammed against a tree.

Two of the T-rexes looked at each other. The larger turned to the smaller and said, "The big chap—we should address him first." The other T-rex nodded and they both took off after Stew, who was getting to his feet and trying to shake his head clear.

A plasma bolt whizzed past Stew as Chip and Diana came chasing after the T-rexes, Chip firing her plasma cannon, trying to catch the dinosaur's attention but failing.

The rexes were zeroed in on Stew. For some reason, they had identified him as the primary threat and were working in tandem to separate him from the rest of the Mundanes.

Suzuki could see this from afar. He also noticed the T-rex he had squared off against was doing its best to keep Suzuki from getting closer to the rest of his party. Within a couple of seconds, the T-rexes had figured out Suzuki was the one issuing commands, while Stew's main position on the field was to absorb and dish out damage.

They're smart, Suzuki thought to himself. *I'll give them that.*

Suzuki recalled his axe back to his hand and sent it flying

at the T-rex. The Rex dodged the axe, but that wasn't important to Suzuki. He just needed room to breathe. The most important thing was that he get back to the Mundanes. He wasn't worried they couldn't take care of themselves, but he knew the closer he was to the rest of the Mundanes, the easier it would be to coordinate attacks. If the T-rexes were working in unison, that meant the Mundanes were going to have to as well.

Ahead of Suzuki, the T-rexes were launching streams of plasma at the Mundanes, who had gathered around Stew.

Diana was busy trying to heal Stew, who had been knocked unconscious and was bleeding from the head.

Beth had whipped out her shield and was using it to deflect the plasma bolts. Whatever the shield was made out of was strong.

Chip had converted both of her hands to a large shield that unnervingly looked like flesh.

Even though it seemed to be different tech than whatever the T-rexes were made of, her shield still held up. Stew finally came too, and Diana turned her back to him and started casting defensive spells.

Suzuki was closing on the Mundanes when he felt the heat on his back. He didn't need to look over his shoulder to know what was coming; he just hoped he could avoid it as he flung himself to the right. Plasma seared the ground to his left and he hit the ground, rolling, then quickly getting to his feet and sprinting ahead without breaking his stride. He focused on his axe, raised his hand, and caught it as it came flying toward him. Behind him, the T-rex roared, and Suzuki hoped he had managed to at least wing the giant dinosaur. Then he leapt toward one of the T-rexes accosting the Mundanes.

The T-rex turned to face Suzuki at the last minute before contact. Suzuki brought down his axe on the T-rex's head between its eyes. He didn't wait to see if the attack made any difference before leaping off the T-rex and landing next to the rest of his party. "These guys are moving like a fucking wolf pack!" Suzuki shouted. "We need to regroup and put them on the defensive."

Diana whipped her wand and sent a firebolt flying at one of the T-rexes as Suzuki called his axe back. "They're healing too fast to do any damage!" she cried.

Suzuki looked around to assess the situation. There wasn't enough time to think, though. He pointed to the jungle and shouted, "Haul ass back to the trees!"

The Mundanes didn't waste any time heading back to the trees. They booked it, plasma bolts screeching behind them as the T-rexes roared and quipped to each other. Suzuki was glad he was out of ear's reach and didn't have to hear them gloating. He pointed up to the trees and ordered, "Chip, Beth, you two get up there with Diana. Me and Stew will draw their attention, and you take care of the rest. You feeling up to it, Stew? You got your ass handed to you pretty hard."

Stew smiled as he ran. "Just got caught off-guard, that's all. I'll make them regret not putting me in the fucking ground."

The Mundanes exited the clearing and reentered the thicket of the jungle. Beth and Chip soared into the air and landed easily in the trees while Diana levitated up into the canopy leaves. Suzuki ran until he found an area where the trees didn't crowd as much.

The ground shook from the heavy trampling of the T-rexes as Suzuki and Stew turned to face them. The T-rexes looked at each other greedily as they licked their lips. Just as

Suzuki had expected, part of their natural instincts had been displaced by their intelligence. They were doing something natural T-rexes would never do: toy with their food. That was just the edge Suzuki needed.

As the T-rexes closed in, the largest one grinned—a toothy, frightening image—and chuckled. "It looks as if we have scared off the other two. Three? No matter. Two humans are not much against us and our sophistication."

Suzuki was going to act. He hoped the Mundanes above got the drift of his plan. "Yes, we are!" Suzuki shouted, causing the T-rexes to stop in their tracks. "I've never come across such a well-led group before. Your tactics are unbelievable. How? You have to tell me before I die!"

"The gifts of the Dark One are numerous. If only you would allow yourself to embrace his grand designs, you too could be elevated to our level."

Suzuki was still sizing up their weak points. The techno-organic flesh made them more resilient, but it didn't make them immortal. Anything could be severed if you hit it hard enough. He remembered how easily his axe had sunk into the soft spot between the T-rex's eyes. That was probably their safest bet—go for the kill spot and keep hacking at it until it's over.

"You can hulk out now," Suzuki said to Stew. "Try not to get killed, all right?"

Stew cracked his knuckles and his body began to swell, his muscles growing larger, his legs and torso stretching to give him nearly an extra foot of height. He turned toward the T-rexes as he tossed his axe in the air and caught it. Then he threw his axe at one of the T-rexes before sprinting toward the creature, his two swords in hand. The axe he threw went straight through the T-rex's leg, completely severing it, and Stew slid under its leg, slashing the other one.

Suzuki ran his finger over his axe, enchanting it with the fire and lightning runes he had etched into the hilt. A flame spread over the blade, and lightning crackled. "Aim between the eyes, and don't stop until its dead!" Suzuki shouted as he leapt.

The T-rex Suzuki was aiming for opened its mouth and shot a plasma bolt at him. The blast hit Suzuki square in the chest and sent him flying. His skin burned and he felt like he had been hit with a truck, but he knew he could keep going. He climbed to his feet, and his axe came flying back to him.

From above, Chip fell from the trees, slapping her hands together, fusing them to create a larger cannon than usual. She fell onto one of the T-rex's heads and fired a massive blast between the dinosaur's eyes. The plasma tore through it and exploded out of its neck. As the dinosaur toppled, Chip leapt into the air, splitting her hands apart and firing shot after shot with deadly accuracy. Each blast tore farther into the T-rex's head until there was nothing more than a bloody pulp.

Beth leapt from the tree along with Diana, who was freefalling, firing arrow after arrow as fast as she could at the T-rex's eyes. Her arrows landed true, blinding the dinosaur as Diana raised her wand. A bolt of lightning cracked through the air, hitting the soft spot between the dinosaur's eyes. The dinosaur went down, but Diana did not relent. She aimed her wand and another lightning bolt hit the dinosaur, jolting its body as its legs convulsed.

At their side, Stew had thrown his weapons away and was ripping into the T-rex's head with his bare hands, punching until the skin was nothing but pulp. He didn't stop there. He kept going until he hit the skull, and then he felt the bone shatter and the soft, squishiness of the T-rex's brain explode. By the time he stood, covered in blood, all the T-rexes lay dead.

Suzuki walked up to Stew as he shrank back to normal. The barbarian warrior was covered in blood and sweat. The rest of the Mundanes converged and took stock of what they had just killed.

The T-rexes looked to be a perfect amalgamation of flesh and machine. It was difficult to tell where organic life began and inorganic life ended. The difference between the T-rexes and Chip was noticeable immediately. When Chip's body contorted and took the shape of her alien tech, the machinery was noticeable. It looked as if corruption had set into her body, which was not the case with these hulking creatures of the past. There was no distinction. The transition in their bodies was seamless.

Stew knelt and looked at the busted head of one of the T-rexes. "This would probably be terrible to eat, huh?" he asked.

Diana pulled out her notebook, jotting notes as she paced around the dead dinosaurs. "Bad would be an understatement," she explained. "It would be like eating a microchip."

"Shame. I've always wanted to eat something that's extinct."

"Looks like whatever that leech did, the old Stew is back. I think I'm glad."

Suzuki looked in the direction they had run from. "We should go and see if we can figure out where they stampeded from," he suggested. "I know the Dark One's forces have to be on the island, but, as far as we've seen, they're pretty sparse. But these guys got me a little interested. The cat that attacked us earlier seemed like something that was sent to get us.

Maybe a patrol or something. These guys, though? It seemed like they were concerned with something before us. We just happened to be here, so they attacked. And, not to sound cocky, but they didn't know who we were. From what I've been able to gather, we're on the Dark One's shit list, so why didn't they recognize us?"

Diana nodded her head. "That's a good point," she assented. "They could be out of the loop. Maybe this island is something like a dark spot for communication. We have them as MERCs as well. People stationed out in places that are too remote to get in contact with. That would be surprising for the Dark One, though, seeing how he has the tech to be able to communicate between realms."

Chip raised her hand, her skin breaking apart into sections of organic tech. "Not too unreasonable," Chip said. "Looks like there's leaps and bounds in the shiny things the Dark One dabbles in. These fuckers make me look like a bucket of gears out the Jurassic period."

Suzuki nodded his head as he took a closer look at the T-rex Stew had pummeled to death. The hole in its head was sizable. When Suzuki looked closely, he could see that the nanotech that made up to T-rex's skin had already been trying to close itself. The stuff worked fast. Luckily, Stew had managed to reach the T-rex's brain, killing it and any hope of healing. Still, it was impressive to see how resilient the creature was. "Hey, Chip, do you think you could interact with the Dark One's tech?" Suzuki asked.

Chip's hand returned back to normal as she shrugged. "Ain't been raring to try, to be honest," she confessed. "Last time I interacted with dark tech, I blew my ol' flame to pieces, only to have him come back and haunt us later. Not sure it's such a good idea for me to go around touching things."

Suzuki could see the pain in Chip's eyes despite the unaffected persona she was trying to put on. Chip's language had generally fascinated Suzuki. It didn't belong to any specific region or fantasy trope he could understand. Instead, it seemed like a hodgepodge of different idiosyncratic dialects and linguistic ticks. Suzuki had figured out they were directly related to what Chip was feeling at the moment. Sometimes she was hiding behind words. Other times she was using them to bolster her own confidence. And there were times her syntaxial tricks fell apart and Suzuki could see how fragile she really was.

Diana was the complete opposite.

No matter how hard Suzuki tried to get a read on her, he drew a blank. She was always professional, always held the air of one who was knowledgeable of what was going on, and it didn't matter what situation.

Even hallucinating from magic beetles did nothing to her demeanor. Suzuki still felt uncomfortable with what seemed like her stepping back and letting him take charge of the mission—if you could even call it a mission. All they had to go on was a volcano had started smoking and they had been attacked by a group of ultra-intelligent dinosaurs. He had no idea what José was getting them into.

Stew was observing the dinosaurs as well—another wildcard Suzuki needed to keep an eye on. Even with Stew seeming to have returned to normal after the leech bite, Suzuki felt like something was still off. It wasn't something he thought was cause for immediate concern, but he had been caught off-guard by how quickly Stew had been taken out earlier. Not too surprising, though. Stew had been known to rush into skirmishes unprepared. What had surprised him more was how quickly Stew had taken care of that T-rex.

Suzuki knew Stew was capable of enormous amounts of strength, but he had never seen Stew fight methodically before. Suzuki was surprised he hadn't thought to take the legs out from under the T-rexes. But not only had Stew figured that out with his gut, but he had also torn into the dinosaur's skull with nothing other than his fists.

That was the part that troubled Suzuki.

It was no secret that Stew was strong, probably stronger than any of the other Mundanes. And there was a level of savageness he threw himself into battle with. But what Suzuki had seen earlier was different. He had only caught a bit of it out of the corner of his eye, but there had been frenzy on Stew's face. He wasn't all that surprised Stew had torn that T-rex apart with his bare hands.

Then there was Sandy.

Suzuki still hadn't had a moment to try to grasp what Sandy had signed up to do with José. He hadn't asked any questions, but he wished he had. Now she was gone, off to whatever plane the Dark One inhabited with the ghost of a dead man. What the hell else could go wrong?

The only stable thing Suzuki knew he could count on was Beth. She had meshed instantaneously into the flow and rhythm of the Mundanes.

And she was picking up new skills.

It wasn't that Suzuki felt he couldn't depend on the rest of the Mundanes. It was more that he realized there were multiple variables at play in a mission he didn't even comprehend. He hadn't even started to take his own role into account. Probably better not to. He was already spending too much time up in his head.

Suzuki held up his hand, and his axe returned to him. "The dinosaurs had to have come from somewhere," Suzuki started, thinking out loud. "And I think it's a safe bet they weren't sharing space with the herd we saw stampeding. The herd looked freaked the fuck out. So, I'm gonna say the T-rexes had come as a surprise. The next step is finding out where they came from."

Diana clicked her tongue as she paced around the fallen dinosaurs. "You think they might have a different natural habitat?" she asked. "That's why the other dinosaurs would have reacted that violently?"

"Something like that. I don't know what it was José was trying to point us in the direction of, but that volcano and these rexes are the closest things we have to a clue. We might as well start by checking it out. That sound good to everyone?"

There were no disagreements, so the Mundanes prepared to leave. Before they disembarked, Diana decided it would be a good idea to retrieve some samples from the T-rexes. The only bit of the Dark One's tech MERC had any access to was Chip, who refused to be a test subject. MERCs had tried to send a few parties into the Dark One's broken defense rings, but after the fall of the Viceroy, the Dark One's forces had scrubbed the place clean. This would probably be the only chance the MERCs were going to get to study whatever it was the Dark One was creating.

As Diana and Chip dissected pieces of the T-rexes off, Beth came up and crouched beside them. "You should send some of that to Hyatt," Beth said, referring to her former platoon captain. "He could make some good of this."

Diana narrowed her eyes at Beth. Her eyes darted to Chip, the T-rex, and then back to Beth. "We're not really in the habit of sharing intel with the military," she said. "They have a less-than-stellar track record of giving us useful intel. In fact, we're often given the opposite. If we're given anything, I'd think they'd have already found a sample worth working with."

Beth made a sound as if she were trying to hold back a laugh. "Are you seriously pulling that bullshit right now?" she asked. "We're in this together. All of us—elf, human, gnome, military, and MERC. It shouldn't matter who finds what. We still need to be sharing information. What if they find something we aren't aware of?"

"I think as a show of good faith, the military should start providing information first. They have a host of technology we've only received secondhand, valuable military recon, not to mention the sheer amount of research on healing spells, the libraries—"

Beth's face was beginning to turn red as she shouted, "We're at fucking war! Is this really the time to—"

There was the slightest change in Diana's face. Her skin showed the beginnings of decay from constant magic use, and the area around her hairline and on her neck looked to be cracking around the edges as if powerful energy sat right beneath the surface of her epidermis. In an instant, it was as if that energy ceased to be contained. A rush of blue light pulsed through the air, knocking Beth over.

Diana floated in the air, her eyes white, flashes of energy coming off her as if she were an atom waiting to split. "Do not lecture me on war," Diana's voice boomed, sounding as if it were composed of hundreds of voices speaking at once. "I have known war beyond your understanding. A millennium of war. Do *not* fucking question me."

Another blast of energy tossed Beth across the ground, flooring the rest of the Mundanes. Suzuki didn't know what to do. Whatever'd happened to Diana happened so fast he wasn't quite sure what was going on. He slipped down his HUD, thinking for a second he might have to defend himself against Diana. His HUD said he had a -67% chance of success. Was she really that powerful?

Whatever was happening to the former Horseman was difficult to understand. It was as if her entire body had ceased to exist in the physical sense. She still had the shape of a human, but pure energy radiated off her, distorting the air around her like she was reshaping reality. The sky was darkening, and yet there seemed to be two suns in the sky. When Suzuki looked down at his hand, he saw multiple versions of it stretched over each other. As he looked at Diana, he had a sudden feeling of falling. What he saw looking was even more confusing. There seemed to be dozens of Dianas, each in a different position—some of them running, others screaming, and yet others calm and distinct, each of them a glowing being of pure energy.

Chip reached out to Diana and she grabbed her hand. "Dee, it's going to be okay," she whispered, and just like that, it was over.

Diana fell next to the dinosaur corpses, dressed in her robes, made of flesh and bone again. "Oh, my God," Diana murmured, her eyes wide and frightened. "I am so sorry. I am so sorry." Her eyes widened further, growing frantic as they searched around, deerlike, as if she were afraid not of what she had unleashed but of what her teammates might have thought of her.

Beth was already back on her feet, drawing her sword. "What the fuck was that?" Beth shouted.

Diana raised her hand, wand between her fingers. "Hold on," she said before placing her wand on the ground. "I can explain."

Suzuki stepped between Beth and Diana. "Everyone needs to chill the fuck out right now," he said. "Beth put your sword away. Diana—"

Beth pushed Suzuki away and stalked toward Diana. "The fuck I am," she shouted. "Did you see what just happened?"

Diana was backing up, her hands still in the air. "I can explain," she pleaded.

"The fuck you will."

Suzuki didn't think. He reached out and grabbed the back of Beth's armor and yanked with everything he had, pulling Beth behind him. He whipped around, his voice loud and commanding, and shouted, "Stand the fuck down, Beth!"

Beth glared at Suzuki. She looked like she was prepared to fight him, then she spat on the ground and sheathed her sword.

Suzuki turned to Diana, his gaze and voice just as firm. "Explain."

Diana spoke, her voice trembling for the first time Suzuki had heard, stumbling over words, and stuttering. "It...it wasn't me. Not really me. You see, I lost control a little bit. Not enough to be worried about. I would never hurt any of you. Never. It's just, sometimes when I'm too... But, you see, it rarely happens, and—"

Chip walked up behind Diana and rested her hand on the woman's shoulder. "Dee, darling, allow me," Chip said. "She's afraid. Afraid for me. There have been comms that the military's thinking of getting all mad scientist like on my body. Thinking about it enough to send someone after me to nab me and all my goods. She's just righteously spooked, that's all. 'Tis the reason she don't want to be sending any recon to the uniforms."

Beth had calmed down some but was still noticeably

angry. "And that's what fucking happens when she gets a little upset?" Beth shouted. "So, we have two fucking berserkers in a party, and one of them is capable of whatever the fuck that was! What the fuck?"

Diana pushed her glasses up and took a deep breath. "Please allow me to explain," she said, her normal calm returning to her voice. "Years ago, I spent an extended time in the realm between realms. There were some ramifications. I came into contact with beings of higher planes of existence than I was prepared to handle. I was young, naïve, and arrogant. Through a series of poorly thought out decisions, I was forced to embody one of the spirits within my own body to return home. For the most part, our personalities have assimilated due to my...restraint. But...there are times when I struggle with control. It is impossible for the being to act outside of my own desires, but it does make it difficult for me to communicate in a fashion that is...less confrontational."

"What kind of being is in your fucking body?"

"The easiest way to say it is that a trans-dimensional god is held somewhat captive in my body."

Suzuki shook his head, trying to understand what Diana was saying. "Wait, you mean like what the forest spirit was saying the Dark One is?" he asked.

"Yes, very similar. I assume you saw the reality manipulation radiating from me. That was the effect of multiple dimensions and alternate realities conflating upon themselves. They show themselves as echoes on our plane of reality."

Suzuki sat down as he rubbed the back of his head. "Holy fucking shit..."

"How do you think I became the most powerful mage in the realm?"

"Why don't we just sic you on the Dark One if you're so powerful?"

"Because I'm not nearly as powerful as him. By keeping this being in me, I substantially decrease its power."

Stew was the next one to speak, although his voice was shaky and frightened. "That's where you sent Sandy?" he asked. "You sent her to a place like that?"

Diana looked ashamed but did not back down. "I told her what to expect, what was possible, and how to avoid it. We are remaining in contact, and I will not let anything happen to her," Diana explained. "I promise."

Stew didn't look like he trusted or believed Diana. Suzuki could understand. The brief lapse in Diana's control had frightened everyone. Suzuki was surprised that he had been so ready to attack Diana. He was even more surprised that he had broken up the potential fight between Beth and Diana. How was Beth going to take that?

While Suzuki was lost in his thoughts, Stew stepped up to Diana. He was staring at her, and she returned the gaze with just as much intensity. Out of nowhere, he extended his hand to Diana. "Do you promise Sandy will be okay?" he asked.

Diana took a deep breath and let it out slowly. "I can promise I will do everything in my power to make sure she's safe," Diana finally said. "Everything in my power."

"That's good enough for me."

Diana clasped Stew's hand, and they shook. When the two broke apart, Diana walked over to Beth and extended her hand. "I'm sorry," she said again. "I really don't bear you any ill will. And I want you to know you can trust me."

Beth was still glaring at Diana. She looked like she would hit Diana at any moment. Instead, she laughed caustically and took Diana's hand. "Jesus Christ, this is the most touchy-feely group of douchenozzles I've ever quested with," she said flippantly. "Are we going to have to have a group therapy session every time we disagree with each other?"

Suzuki let it out a sigh of relief. It seemed like everything had blown over just as quickly as it had erupted. "All right, if we're all done being emotional, how about we go find where those dinosaurs came from."

There were no disagreements, so the Mundanes made their way back to the clearing they had been chased from. Suzuki made sure to get as close to Beth as possible. He couldn't gauge how she was feeling, and he figured it was better to ask now than wait for it to worsen. As they walked, Suzuki brushed his hand against Beth's to get her attention. She jumped in surprise, flinching from his touch. "You okay?" Suzuki asked.

Beth looked at Suzuki and her face was tired. She smiled nonetheless and nodded. "You mean, because of the way you manhandled me back there?" she asked.

"I wasn't trying to man—"

Beth gave him a loving punch on the shoulder. "Just fucking with you, Suzy. I know what that was. Didn't like it at the time, but I know what it was."

"What was it?"

"You diffused a dangerous situation like a good leader is supposed to. What, did you think I was going to give you crap about not taking my side or something?"

Suzuki sighed in relief. "I don't know. I thought you might be pissed off at me."

"I'm not gonna say I'm in a really great mood and want to cover you in kisses or anything at the moment. But I'm not pissed. It's what any of my captains would have done. I don't like being told whether or not I'm right or wrong, especially when I know I'm right. But I'm also not stupid. We can't be wasting time fighting each other. Especially when everyone's got such specific reasons for fighting each other. Someone gets their brain hacked. Someone else is the containment vessel of a god. And I heard through the grapevine that you almost killed each other because you were being poisoned by a witch?"

Suzuki nodded, remembering one of the Mundanes' first real quests and how close they had been to ripping each other's throats out. Apparently, MERCs trying to kill each other due to outside forces was such a common thing the MERCs even had a name for it: aggressive friendship. Diana had once said if MERCs held grudges about every MERC who had tried to kill them, they wouldn't have anyone left in their party.

Beth wiped the sweat off her forehead and spat. "Yeah, so don't make a habit of throwing me around," Beth said. "Though it was *a little* hot. Just a little. Now come on, Fearless Leader. Get your head back in the game."

Chip went to the front of the party's formation. She motioned for Beth to come up and join her, which Beth did. Once they were standing together, Chip knelt and pointed to the ground. She showed Beth the indentations that had been left by the T-rexes and the other dinosaurs that had gone stampeding through the jungle. The indentations were faint, and Chip explained how one could find them; how one allows their eyes to find the natural pattern. Suzuki was glad Chip was still planning on mentoring Beth. Even with the brief bit of tension, it didn't seem as if anything had truly changed.

After a few minutes, Chip and Beth stood. They spoke

with each other for a bit, figuring out which direction was best to travel.

Chip encouraged Beth to lead the Mundanes along the trail, and they set out in the direction of the mountain. The trail went cold a few times and Beth walked back and forth, growing more and more frustrated. She finally kicked up a clump of dirt and slashed it apart with her sword.

Chip took a second and took Beth away from the rest of the Mundanes. She spoke to her quietly, speaking with great care, and Suzuki wished he could have heard what they were saying. In the last twenty minutes, he had seen sides of Beth he had never known.

As far as he had known, Beth was a cool and collected person.

That was not what he had seen today.

Maybe there were things that set her off he had just never experienced. This was the longest time they had ever spent with each other.

Once Beth was calmer, Chip and Beth returned to the path. It did not take long before Beth picked the trail up again. This time, instead of relying on the markings in the grass, they tracked based on the stools that had been dropped during the stampede. It took them about twenty minutes, but the Mundanes eventually circled around the volcano until they found what looked like a camp.

Beth looked it over and then began to pace, scratching the back of her head. "I don't understand," she said to Chip. "We followed the trail. There's nothing here. Just some abandoned shit."

Chip checked around the camp while the rest of the Mundanes watched. As Suzuki watched Chip and Beth work,

Stew cornered Diana and was asking her about Sandy. There didn't seem to be any reasoning behind his questions; they were open-ended, grasping at concepts he didn't understand. His fear came through in each of the questions. Even if he didn't understand, he was terrified of what could happen to Sandy.

Over in the camp, Chip pointed to an overturned bowl, then to a series of footsteps that looked very different from anything else they had seen. These footprints seemed to accompany those that were obviously from the T-rexes. "Beautiful," Chip murmured. "One of these toes ain't like the others. You see that, right? Sometimes you just have to take a moment and look around, see what you can glass with your peepers. You're a keen bit more observant than you give your-self credit for."

Beth nodded as she led the Mundanes along the trail. For another twenty minutes, they walked. It was beginning to get dark, the sun slipping from the sky. In the last bits of the sunlight, Beth pointed to what looked to be an entrance carved into the side of the volcano.

Chip opened up her HUD and pulled up a map. She scrolled through looking for the volcano on the island. Once she located it, she rendered a 3D image of the map, walking around it, rubbing her cheeks obsessively. "All right, darlings, looks like this ain't on any of our maps," Chip finally said. "Got us a brand, spanking new entrance to spelunk with. What's the game plan?"

Suzuki looked at the 3D map. "This is the volcano, right?" Suzuki asked. "The one like Verne talked about. The one that goes straight into the middle of the world?"

Diana pointed at the map and it changed, showing a pathway straight through the volcano down into Middang-g3ard. "It was closed a long time ago," she said. "It was briefly explored before it was determined to be too big a risk. There were...magical artifacts. Well, not quite artifacts. It was discovered there was something in the cavern that provided the natives with a large amount of magical power. That was why the Smuggles were able to easily defeat you earlier. They draw their power from within the world. If the Dark One has decided to start messing with whatever is within the hollows of Middang3ard, it could be catastrophic."

"So, you don't know what is down there?"

"Not exactly. There were theories before the observation spaces were shot down. We believed it might be something. A ley line."

Beth threw her hands up in exasperation before crouching down on the soles of her feet. "Okay, can you just assume you aren't talking to people with a degree in nerd," she groaned.

Diana couldn't help but smile, and Beth returned the gesture, albeit more of a grin. "Certainly," Diana continued. "A ley line is a point in a geographical plane that aligns with other points in a straight line across the world that are used for magical purposes. From this volcano, if you were to draw a straight line on the map..."

The 3D map Chip had produced now changed so it showed all of Middang3ard. The volcano was a sole point. A line cut through the volcano and circled the globe. There were other points on the map that fell on the vector. One continuous line.

"Each of these points are on what we call ley lines, places in Middang3ard that produce intense amounts of magic. In all honesty, we still aren't sure what magic is. What is conjuring a fireball or casting a sound-dampening spell? My theory is that magic is nothing more than reality manipulation. All forms of magic boil down to that, and each individual is able to manipulate reality to different degrees, depending on their innate ability or learned skill."

Some of the ideas were starting to click for Suzuki. "Like what we've been talking about with the Dark One?" Suzuki asked. "He's in some way trying to control or distort reality, right?"

"Exactly. We don't know how. We're not even sure we know how we are capable of doing it. Familiars, innate racial magic, all of it is a dark forest, and we can hardly take in the whole thing for being focused on the trees. But what we know beyond a shadow of a doubt is that these areas called ley lines produce magic on such a level you wouldn't be able to find it across the whole realm. They are places that are in flux with other dimensions. With time. You can no doubt see why the research areas were closed down. To say these areas are dangerous is an understatement."

Suzuki nodded as he walked out of the shade of the trees to take a better look at the opening Chip and Beth had led them to. The sun was descending over the horn of the mountain. Darkness was coming soon. "We should make camp for the night," Suzuki suggested. "Do you have any idea how long it's going to take to get to the center?"

Diana shook her head and shrugged. "Most of the technical records we have, the very specific ones, were lost," she admitted. "The military has the bulk of the research, and... well, we already talked about all that."

Neither Beth nor Diana looked as if they were capable of meeting each other's eyes. An awkward silence descended over the party until Suzuki spoke up. "If that's the case, let's make camp. I want everyone to be rested before we get to this," he ordered. "Who knows what the fuck we're going to come across down there."

Chip was already pitching her tent with an ale in hand. She looked over her shoulder and grinned at Suzuki. "Glad you can read minds," she joked. "Anyone care for a tankard of good 'ol grog?"

The Mundanes did not need to speak. There was nothing words could say. They went about their own tasks, although broken in some ways. Beth and Suzuki built their own tents, and Stew erected his. Chip and Diana set their own up, as was their fashion. There was little said between the members of the party.

They ate in silence, then went to their tents and slipped into their sleeping bags or cots. Sleep came fast and without warning for each of them, heavy and deep. No one awoke until morning. The sun rose, and they traveled to the volcano.

11

The Mundanes approached the volcano with little thought or words.

The morning had been sunny enough. If Suzuki had believed in omens, he would have assumed this was a good one. But as he had already come to understand, there were no good omens in Middang3ard. Nothing was certain.

The side of the volcano had been carved out by what could have only been a large machine. It was the only option. The hole in the volcano was at least twenty feet high. Somehow, it looked as if the rock of the volcano had been changed. Suzuki thought it was the techno-organic corruption he had seen touch the various aspects of the Dark One's army.

That was not the case, though.

As the Mundanes got closer to the volcano's entrance, Suzuki could see it was an entirely different construction.

It was a distinction that almost would have been unobservable to the layman's eye. The Mundanes stopped to look at the volcano's entrance. Before they passed through its threshold, each of them stopped and looked up at the ceiling or at the walls as they walked through.

The porous rock of the volcano had given way to something else, something which looked to be growing out of the rock itself. It was almost as if the rock had become pregnant on a cellular level. Life was bursting out of the rock, but it was a type of life none of the Mundanes recognized. Even Diana was confused by what they saw.

Something like black bean sprouts were forcing themselves out of the rock. They moved in unison with each other, almost like the way sea anemones wave in accordance with the waves around them, although the black sprouts did not actually move. Suzuki couldn't quite understand what it was he was looking at; it felt like an optical illusion. The sprouts were definitely moving and also absolutely still. That, coupled with the bizarreness of them growing out of the solid rock, left an impression that was more akin to horror than anything else.

Stew reached out to touch one of the sprouts, and Diana grabbed his hand. "Don't touch anything," she whispered. "I have no idea what any of this is. It could be deadly. Poisonous at the least."

Stew eyed the black sprouts, obviously not impressed by them. "And we're supposed to go in there?" he asked. "If this shit is growing outside, you know there's gonna be a lot more once we get in there."

"That's a good point. It doesn't seem like there's anything to be done for it, though. As I said before, I have no idea what is down there. We need to be careful. And not go around touching anything that catches our attention."

Stew withdrew his hand and shrugged as the Mundanes continued to look at the volcano's threshold. There was something deeply unnerving about the black sprouts. No one seemed to be able to put their finger on it, so they did the only thing they could, which was to stare at the threshold until someone coughed or made a joke. It took a long time for someone to cough. Finally, Suzuki suggested they cross the threshold and delve into the volcano.

The Mundanes began their descent.

It was unsurprisingly hot, and the tunnel they traveled down sloped at an extremely vertical degree. Suzuki felt as if he did not have a choice to walk but was compelled to keep moving forward, or he would have fallen flat on his face. It seemed to be the same way with the rest of the Mundanes. They moved at a slow jog for some time before the tunnel evened itself out.

The tunnel itself was also extremely claustrophobic.

The tunnel was tight, and the Mundanes had to walk in single file as the walls grabbed their shoulders. It was almost the feeling of being hugged.

Suzuki tried to stay on the lookout for any more of the black sprouts they had seen at the onset of their journey. He had seen none but was also aware that even if he had, it wouldn't have made a difference. There was only one way to go now, and it happened to include rubbing the internals of the volcano.

Farther and farther, they descended. Suzuki wasn't certain how long he had been walking. Time had ceased to exist the moment the Mundanes had begun walking through the dark, hot tunnel. Diana had cast multiple illumination spells, but the lights were of no use. It was not as if they fizzled out; it was something else. Suzuki could see the light, see the brightness, but it was as if the light could not cast its rays anywhere. The space immediately around the lights was bright, but it was like the tunnel sucked the light away.

Suzuki wished they had torches. Not because he thought it would be any different. He was just curious to know how much light this place could gobble up.

They continued through the tunnel. Suzuki wasn't sure why, but he felt like he was having a hard time breathing. It confused him because he could feel the air in his lungs despite the feeling. He wanted to ask the rest of the Mundanes if they were experiencing anything similar, but he thought it was a stupid question. No one else seemed as if they were having an issue. That was, until Beth stopped walking and knelt against the tunnel walls. She raised her hand and coughed loudly and said, "Gimme a minute. Just a minute."

Suzuki took a seat next to her. He was worried about her, but more than that, he needed to take a breather. "Are you okay?" Suzuki asked.

"I can't fucking breathe. I can't fucking breathe."

The rest of the Mundanes took a seat as well. The tunnel filled with the sound of wheezing, stressed lungs.

Suzuki filled his lungs with whatever air he could. He wasn't certain it was air, but he knew he needed it. There were words he wanted to share, but he knew he could not spare the air. He hoped the rest of the Mundanes were aware of this as well.

They sat there. The only sound was the sound of coughing. After some time, Stew stood up, tried to walk away, and fell against the increasingly suffocating tunnel. "What the fuck?" Stew whispered as his eyes swam toward the back of his head.

Suzuki looked around, trying to figure out what was

causing this reaction. And that was when he saw the black sprouts. The walls of the tunnel were covered. He hadn't even realized the entire time he had been journeying into the depths of the volcano, he had been brushing against these sprouts. His mind flashed back to a point when he was younger, when his parents had been looking for a place to live. The first apartment they had checked out was filled with black mold. At the time, Suzuki hadn't known what black mold was. He had been a child, hardly capable of under-standing the concept itself. As they had toured the apart-ment, he had clenched his chest and tried to express to his parents that something was not right. Something was off.

Suzuki stood and stumbled farther down the tunnel. "We need to keep moving," he wheezed. "We can't stop here. We need to keep going."

The rest of the Mundanes looked up at Suzuki with clouded eyes. He wasn't sure if they had anything to say but realized this was not the time to try to understand that. The most important thing was they kept moving. That was the only thing that mattered.

Slumped against the wall, Suzuki took Beth's hand and pulled her up. He shoved her forward. Next, he took Stew's hand and dragged him up. He grabbed Stew and said, "You need to make sure she's still going forward. Do you understand?"

Stew looked up at Suzuki, his eyes misty and red. "Wait, what?"

"Fucking listen to me. You don't stop walking, you under-stand? You keep moving, you keep her moving. You look behind you and make sure they keep moving. Do you under-stand me?"

Stew nodded solemnly. He opened his mouth as if he

thought there was something to be said and then closed it again, then he turned and followed Beth, who was already slumped against the tunnel's wall. Stew leaned against the wall next to her. After a couple of seconds, he straightened up, placed his hand on her shoulders, and guided her farther down the tunnel. He cast a look over his shoulder as if inviting the other Mundanes to follow him.

That was all Suzuki needed. He pulled Diana and Chip up and shoved them after Stew. They didn't bother asking questions. Once they had been given a direction, they continued walking.

Suzuki did not know how long it took for him to be alone in the darkness. Faintly, he realized he was alone. The black sprouts looked beautiful. Even more than beautiful, they looked delicious. He wanted to eat them. He felt if he were to take a bite, everything would work itself out. If he were to sit down and enjoy their saltiness, the world would expand around him, and he would be able to get the answers he wanted. But his arms were so heavy. He couldn't lift them even if he wanted to. All he could do was sit and smell. The perfume of the black sprouts wafted up, filling him with craving. If he could have, he would have cried.

The tunnels fell in on themselves.

Suzuki saw the blackness folding, distorting itself. He knew he was alone, and this was the way he was going to die.

Blackness and the soft petal sprouts against his neck.

In the darkness, there was a voice he had never heard before. It called out to him, singing softly. If he could have, he would have reached out and held the voice in his hand. There had never been anything more important to him than the voice at that moment. It was almost as if he could run his hands across it, to have held it in his hand, to have felt it creeping into the crevices of his fingertips, to have felt it pouring into each and every part of his cells.

If death had been a thought in Suzuki's mind before, it had never been as present and tangible. He felt it wrapping around his throat, creeping into his bones, hollowing out the marrow. This feeling, these emotions, they were the same things he had caused so many orcs and trolls to feel. They had watched their lives flash before their eyes, remembered their friends, their lovers, and their families. They had seen those moments play across the back of their eyelids as Suzuki's axe had come crashing down on their skulls.

It was a fear Suzuki did not want to think about. The last few months came rushing back to him, slamming into his head, cracking him open. He was screaming. He did not know when he had started. His voice was hoarse. *If he could, he would have stopped.* But the terror was within. It was deep and he had not been aware how far down it went.

Suzuki felt someone grab his arm.

They lifted him, and it seemed as if he were floating despite how heavy his body felt. The black sprouts grazed his face. Suzuki wanted to lean his face against the wall, to feel the gentle caress of the sprouts.

But he kept moving.

Not of his own accord.

When I close my eyes, only when I close my eyes... I don't understand it, it's almost like... I don't know, Suzuki thought.

A strong slap brought Suzuki's attention back to the present. He looked around, his eyesight still blurred, until he could make out the Mundanes surrounding him. "What the hell happened?" Suzuki finally managed to ask.

Beth helped Suzuki sit up as he started hacking. He spat black mucus into the palm of his hand and stared down at the mess. It looked like there was blood in the black gunk. "Did this happen to any of you?" Suzuki asked.

Diana leaned forward and took Suzuki's hand in her own. She turned it over a couple of times and held her wand over the gunk. The little bit of light that came off the wand was enough to see that the mucus had a bizarre texture, almost like sandpaper.

Diana took a vial out of her robes and handed it to Suzuki. "Wipe that off in here," she suggested. "Whatever caused this to happen to you is something I haven't seen before. And it no doubt was caused by those black petals we walked through. Everyone was affected in some way, although you seemed to be more deeply bothered by the sprouts."

"What happened to the rest of you?"

Stew coughed loudly and spat into his hand. His mucus was the regular color. "It was like allergies or something. I used to live in a place that had tons of black mold. It wasn't any worse than that. Just a tight chest, and that's about it."

Suzuki tried to stand, but his legs felt weak. He thought he could hear singing in the tunnels. "How far down are we going?" Suzuki asked.

Chip pulled up her map and projected it for everyone to look at. The map cast enough light so everyone could see the diagram of Middang3ard. "Can't say for sure how long," Chip admitted. "Don't know if anyone has ever tried to walk the path before, but it's doable. Straight shot all the way to the guts."

"Do you think those sprouts go all the way down?"

Chip shrugged as the map she was projecting changed to a visual dictionary of all the flora and fauna in the volcano. "Years old," she muttered as she scrolled through the information. "Don't see nothing 'bout sprouts. Might be something new. Might have been overlooked before. Only thing I'd say for certain is not to put your mitts on them. Especially you, Suzuki. You already got a little too carnal for my approval."

Suzuki finally made it to his feet.

He coughed again but didn't bother looking to see what was in his lungs. He didn't feel as tired as he had a few moments before. The feeling of fatigue had disappeared so quickly that Suzuki wasn't sure if he had felt it. He nearly reached out and leaned against the wall until he remembered he probably shouldn't touch anything.

Another fit of coughing racked Suzuki's body, but it wasn't as violent as the first few had been. "All right, I guess we should get going. No need to slow down because of me."

The Mundanes continued on through the narrow tunnels of the volcano. The tunnels themselves were widening, with nearly enough room for three of the Mundanes to walk side by side, something they all unconsciously started to do. Suzuki thought it made the walk feel less lonely. There was something about the darkness that was oppressive. Suzuki couldn't put his finger on it, but the feeling couldn't be shaken. In the darkness, Suzuki felt Beth's hand reach out and grab his own. "You feeling okay?" Beth asked.

Suzuki nodded and took a deep breath. "Yeah, I feel a lot better." Suzuki coughed. "Lungs still feel like shit."

Beth continued to hold Suzuki's hand, forcing him to walk more slowly. The other Mundanes walked far enough ahead that Beth was able to comfortably lean closer to Suzuki and whisper in his ear, "They were being very careful with their words. Careful enough that I don't think you got the whole truth."

"What are you talking about?"

Beth pursed her lips. "We were all lost longer than any of us understands. Stew's the only one who doesn't seem to have any lost time, but we had no idea where you were for what seemed like hours. Me, I felt like I was gone for weeks."

"You're joking, right?"

She shook her head. "Diana didn't want to say anything because she doesn't understand what's going on, but I don't think we should be keeping it a secret from you just because you can't remember what was happening. There's something else. This one I thought we probably shouldn't tell you, but secrets can be deadly, you know? You were singing. That's how we found you—leaning against the wall, practically rubbing your face in the black plants. You were just standing there singing."

"That sounds extremely freaky."

Beth laughed, but there was no humor in her face. Suzuki could tell she was worried. "It *was* freaky," Beth admitted. "Whatever the hell is going on here, things are very different than on the surface. I wouldn't be surprised if Chip and Diana have no idea how fucking far we've gone down so far. I don't blame them. This doesn't sound like whatever their last experience was. And that makes a lot of sense if the Dark One is behind this."

"Sounds a little mutinous."

"Not. I just understand what they're doing. They're worried, and they were supposed to be the adults on this trip. I've seen this look before. Things are going bad way faster than they were prepared for, and I don't think either of them is used to being caught off-guard like this. I think they both thought they had some kind of handle on the situation. Just thought you should know, since, you know, you're the one who does all the last minute planning. Now come on, I don't want them to think we're up to anything weird."

Beth pulled Suzuki's hand, and they finally caught up to Chip, Stew, and Diana. The three other Mundanes were talking. Suzuki tried to make out their words, but they sounded far off. This was another one of those odd occurrences Suzuki was going to have to make sense of.

Whatever was going on, it seemed like there was some kind of distortion of time and space. Suzuki had read about this sort of thing happening with alien abduction.

But whatever he had read about was nowhere near as severe as this.

In addition, when people related their abductions, they rarely remembered or understood what was going on when it happened. It was something that only came back to them later.

Suzuki knew a trace amount of quantum physics and mechanics. Just the sort of knowledge you pick up from being interested enough to try to understand.

That was about all Suzuki knew, and it was apparent that whatever was going on was happening on a quantum level. It was more than met the eye. Suzuki thought through some of what the Forest Spirit had told him. Gods, alternate realities, stacked dimensions. It had all seemed to be way too weird, but here he was, descending a volcano and trying to find the center of Middang3ard.

This was a new realm for Suzuki to explore. The dark catacombs were outside of Suzuki's comfort zone, but to be honest, so was coming to Middang3ard. It was just something that Suzuki was going to have to figure out before it ended up being the cause of his death.

What else was new?

The Mundanes lunched at some point in the dim cavern.

Whatever petals had been growing along the side of the cavern walls were gone now, replaced by slick rock that felt as if it were covered in slime. The tunnels had grown much larger, and in the dim light, Chip mentioned there were dinosaur footprints.

How the dinosaurs had gotten through the narrower sections of the tunnels was not clear to the Mundanes.

They talked it over as Stew and Diana crafted a fire and fumbled for their cooking supplies in the dark.

Chip was doing everything in her power to figure out why they didn't seem to be able to use their lights. She had opened her operations panel, something she only did because there was hardly any light, to tinker with some of her settings.

Suzuki tried not to watch too closely because he felt like it might be on par with watching someone get dressed. But he was interested, and there was no way to hide that. While Chip worked, she muttered to herself under her breath, her voice occasionally punctured by the crackling of her soldering iron.

The Mundanes huddled in the dark, the light of their fire hardly casting itself against the slick rock walls. The mood was drastically different than any of their meals before. It was like a black cloud was hanging over them as if a darkness that could not be dispelled with light had sunk deep into their brains and wormed behind their eyes.

The inside of the volcano felt unbelievably cold. A stiff breeze blew through and chilled Suzuki to the bone. He could hear the other Mundanes shivering. It made no sense. They huddled as close as they could to the fire, so there should have been some kind of heat to warm themselves with. And they were also in the middle of a volcano. Shouldn't the magma beneath them have been enough to keep them warm?

With the cold came dread. It was unspoken, but it could be seen on everyone's face. Once more, it had become difficult to remember how long they had been walking through these tunnels. Suzuki thought this was his first meal of the day, but if he pondered long enough, he could remember multiple meal-related incidents in the tunnel. He remembered having lunch in another section, not too far away. He even remembered the conversation he had with Stew. Did that actually happen? Or was there something else going on?

Suzuki turned to Chip and grabbed her arm. "How long have you been working on your arm?" Suzuki asked.

Chip looked down at their arm and the soldering iron. "Honestly, couldn't tell you the slightest," Chip admitted. "Thought it was a couple of hours a few minutes ago. Now it feels like this is the same thing I've been doing for the last week."

Suzuki leaned over the fire and grabbed Stew by the shoulders. Even standing directly above the fire wasn't enough to bring him any warmth. "Stew, how many stacks of provisions did you bring with you?" Suzuki asked.

Stew pulled up his HUD and yawned, bored with the conversation. "Why do you need to know?" he counted.

"Because if we know how many meals we've eaten, then we can tell how long we've been here."

Stew looked through his HUD's inventory. "So, it looks like we...uh, that's fucking weird. We haven't eaten anything."

"What do you mean we haven't eaten anything?"

"I mean, none of the provisions have been touched."

Suzuki shook the plate of food in his hands. "We're eating right now," Suzuki practically shouted, fear creeping down his throat. "That's impossible."

"Maybe it's a mistake. You know, an error or something. We can't have been down here that long."

"Yeah, but do you—"

"Better than you. I don't know what's going on with you guys, but it isn't hitting me as hard as you. I can still remember things, sort of, and I'm the only one not freezing my ass off. So trust me, we haven't been down here for any longer than a few hours. This is our first meal. It's just the darkness, dude. It's freaking everyone out."

Diana blew on the flames in front of her. Then she inhaled deeply, trying to take in as much air as she could before leaning back against the walls. "No, that's not right," Diana said. "Not completely. This is not our first meal. Nor is it our last. There is something distorting time, maybe the ley line. These places are frail and easily broken. Reality itself is on edge here. We just have to push through it."

Suzuki didn't quite understand what Diana was saying. It was like she was talking in another language, yet he remembered having learned the language she spoke. As Suzuki tried to wrap his head around what Diana had explained, he turned and saw that Beth's nose was bleeding. "Oh, shit, Beth, your nose," Suzuki said as he mimed touching where she was bleeding.

Beth lightly touched the small stream of blood coming from her nose. She looked down at the blood. "So, you're saying we just need to push through this?" Beth asked.

Diana nodded and wiped the blood beginning to pool in her own nostril away. "Exactly," Diana said. "We just need to keep pushing, like pushing a needle through skin. There's resistance the entire way, but you can pass all the way through."

"And what if you're wrong?"

"Wrong?"

"I know you aren't used to the idea of being wrong but it could happen. Maybe that's why all of this was abandoned and the researchers left. What if places like this are too unstable to even come in contact with?"

"Oh, I am not wrong. And neither are you. We are not meant to be in places like this. It is too unstable. But I have an ace up my sleeve. It was supposed to be a surprise but the situation has gotten more confusing than I thought. But we have some help."

Diana leaned over the flames and blew them again, harder than the first time. The flames flashed up and tickled the top of the tunnel. There was a flash of heat that faded quickly. Something could be seen in the flames. A figure. As they watched, the figure reached a hand through the flames, which split into dozens of other hands that faded with the rising smoke. It was difficult to make out through the flames, but there was no doubt it was Sandy, and on her shoulder sat Fred.

Stew jumped up, looking as if he were ready to throw himself into the flames. Diana reached out as soon as he started moving and held him back. "It's Sandy!" Stew shouted. "What's she doing in there?"

Sandy faded as Diana fanned the flames with her hand. "Guidance," Diana said. "José sent her to the realm between realms to find the Dark One's name, and I told her I would help her navigate through the realm. Somehow, Sandy came across a further distortion in the different realities and came looking for us here. She's been providing a link to keep us from being torn apart by the ley line."

Beth laughed loudly as she slapped her knee. "So, you were going to get us killed." Beth chuckled.

"No, I planned for this before we decided to enter the volcano, although I did realize it would be uncomfortable. But we might as well keep moving if you are all finished with your meal."

"You seem to be handling this pretty well for someone who could have gotten us killed."

"I've been through ley lines before. It's no more dangerous than mountain-climbing, albeit more confusing and disturbing, and potentially more spiritually enlightening."

They continued sitting there for some time after Diana finished speaking. No one was trying to make sense of anything, let alone what Diana had said. Suzuki looked at his hands in the light of the flames. Now it seemed as if the entire tunnel was nothing more than a beam of light. Suzuki was no longer cold. He was quite comfortable. But in the light, he could see the walls were not as bare and slick as he had thought. There were black petal sprouts here as well, just not as many as they had first come across.

Suzuki yawned and stood up. He was starting to get sleepy again. The sort of tired that comes after a filling meal. Now that he thought of it, he had no idea what he had eaten. He only knew he enjoyed it. "Thanks for the food," Suzuki said as he stared down the direction of the tunnel they were heading to. "You guys ready to do this?"

Stew stood and stumbled to the side. Beth reached out and kept him from falling on his ass. "Okay. I take back what I said about not being affected like you guys. I feel like fucking shit. It feels like someone's stretched me out. Like, really stretched me out. I feel...thin. Like, paper-thin."

"Same here, dude. And there's too much on my mind. Like, way too much. I feel like I've thought everything that's ever existed in the world before. Beth, how are you holding up?"

Beth was staring the dying fire. Her eyes were filled with tears, and she was rocking back and forth. Suzuki came as fast as he could to her side. He wrapped his hand around hers and squeezed it tightly. "Babe, babe, are you okay?" Suzuki asked.

When Beth looked up, her eyes were red and her bottom lip was trembling. "I think I saw how I'm going to die," Beth whispered.

"What? What are you talking about?"

"Or maybe it was when I was born. I can't tell the difference. Either way, I'd like to unsee whatever it was."

Diana offered Beth her hand. "Come on. We just need to pass the threshold. We're all getting fatigued from too many realities converging. If we stay here and don't get through the threshold, we'll be too inundated with other realities. Come on."

Beth took Diana's hand and stood.

The Mundanes didn't waste time breaking down the small campfire and getting back to making their way through the tunnels. Suzuki still didn't feel great, but the sense of dread that had been hanging over him was gone.

In its place was an almost warm feeling of positivity.

The journey continued on, fluctuating between moments of intense darkness, moments when it seemed like death was at their heels, like the darkness they walked through was much more than a physical occurrence, and other times, when there was intense light and it felt as if they were walking on clouds. Then suddenly, the Mundanes stood before what could have only been called a portal. It was a hole in existence.

Suzuki had seen portals before.

Myrddin had brought them through one to get into Middang3ard, and the Red Lion had their own fast-travel portal specifically for MERCs needing to get someplace. This one was different, though. All the portals Suzuki had seen before felt as if they belonged where they were. You could tell they were leading you someplace.

This portal was nothing like that.

It seemed as if it had been plucked from somewhere else and dropped into the volcano. There was an odd singing coming from it, and Suzuki realized it was the singing he had been hearing all along. It was coming from the portal.

Diana walked up to the portal and circled it quickly. Then she turned to the Mundanes and motioned for them to join her. "This is the threshold," Diana explained. "Once we walk through it, we should be free from all of the reality disruptions."

Beth eyed the portal and Diana suspiciously. "And what's going to be on the other side?" she asked.

"Ideally, it'll just send us farther into the volcano. It's most likely a portal that was being used by someone who traveled this before us. I doubt the ley line created its own portal. It's highly unlikely, and in the event it did, we would only be transported to another ley line. At worse, it would be mildly inconvenient."

Stew put his face up to the portal, and a strong wind blew his hair back. "So, we're not going to get our atoms smashed or anything like that?"

"Not with Sandy watching over us. You've all heard the singing, no doubt."

The Mundanes nodded their heads silently as they looked from one to the other. "Sandy's song has been anchoring us to this ley line, this plane in reality. From what she's explained to me, she's come across a couple of variations of herself in the realm between places. One of those Sandys happens to be well versed in oral song magic. She's also much older, and very aware of how the realm works. Apparently, in some realities, Sandy is something of a big deal."

Stew looked away from the portal and to Diana, his face brightening with curiosity. "An old Sandy?" he asked. "I have to see this."

"I'm afraid we don't have time to satiate your curiosity. The different versions of Sandy are on a mission, and they've been using valuable time to protect us. After this, they're going to return to the task at hand, and we will return to ours. But I'll continue to stay in touch with her, although it seems like she's playing the role of protector more than me. Are you all ready?"

Suzuki couldn't wait to get out of the tunnels. They had gone from feeling claustrophobic to a funhouse mirror to a hall of horrors. He looked down at his hands, confused by the different after echoes of his own movements. It looked like he was generating new alternate realities as he moved. This was something he wanted to talk with Diana about. If there were alternate versions of Sandy, couldn't there be alternate versions of the rest of the Mundanes? Maybe that was something they could use to their advantage at some point.

Diana reached her left hand into the portal. "When you pass through, things are going to get very weird," she explained. "I can't tell you specifically because it's going to be different for everyone but be prepared for whatever comes at you. Stay focused on moving forward." Then Diana stepped through the portal and was gone in a flash of light. Chip followed closely after.

The younger Mundanes' eyes jumped from one to the other. "So, who wants to go first?" Stew asked.

Beth stepped forward and walked into the portal without taking a moment to slow down. She vanished in the same white, bright flash. Stew nervously shifted his weight from foot to foot before running into the portal, screaming as if he were running onto the battlefield.

Suzuki paced for a moment. He didn't know why he was so scared, but the prospect of crossing through the portal terrified him. Perhaps it was the fear of the unknown. Or it could have been the fear of the slightly known. The little bit Diana had told him had done nothing to soothe his fear. It didn't matter now, though. Everyone else had gone through, and this looked like the only way they were going to get farther into the volcano. He took a deep breath and walked through the portal.

All at once, Suzuki's atoms began to sing. Not that they began to vibrate or Suzuki perceived feeling in a different way. The atoms themselves started to sing a melody. The world around Suzuki was bright, and he struggled to continue walking forward as his eyes adjusted. As the whiteness faded, Suzuki started to be able to make out some of the shapes around him. In the distance, directly in front of him, was a door. Planets and stars and nebulas whizzed past him faster than he could see as he continued to walk a direct path to the black door. It was like walking through mud, though. Each of his steps was heavy and leaden.

Suzuki lost his footing and fell down, banging his knee up pretty badly. As he looked up, preparing to stand, he saw another version of himself continuing to walk forward. Then he looked over his shoulder and saw another version of himself, just a few steps away. When he leaned to his right to get a better look, he could see dozens of versions of himself walking in a queue. Although they were all walking, it did not seem as if they were moving. Suzuki stood and turned around to see a version of himself, still on the ground, holding their knee, which was bleeding profusely. This version of him was covered in the black petal sprouts he had accidentally inhaled before.

Suzuki reached down to help the other version of himself and was surprised when he grabbed onto someone's flesh and blood.

Deep down, he had thought this was some kind of visual illusion.

But he was holding onto his own hand.

Or something like his own hand.

The other Suzuki smiled and muttered his thanks as he got to his feet.

Both of them made their way to the door.

Suddenly, the space around them stopped moving. It stood deadly still, and Suzuki realized he was in a vacuum. There was no air, only the coldness of space. As he looked around and tried to regain his perspective, he saw that he was upside-down, not quite floating, but also not quite standing. He turned and turned, looking for the door. Finally, after a few moments of feeling sick to his stomach, he found the door and headed toward it. The rest of the Suzuki's weren't faring as well. The only Suzuki who seemed aware of what was going on was the one Suzuki pulled along his side.

In the space above the threshold, or perhaps around the threshold, the space grew darker and darker. The lights of the planets and stars faded until the darkness of the threshold looked to be bright. Out of that darkness came a voice. It was deep and calm like that of the sea, and it filled Suzuki with a terrifying dread.

Suzuki didn't know where the voice was coming from, but he knew he wanted to be as far away from it as possible. A primal fear surged up through Suzuki, and he found himself running to the threshold as fast as he could. The space broke apart. It was as if someone had reached out and cut a thin slit in the space before him.

The slit opened and a man stepped out.

The man was nearly seven feet tall.

His body had evenly toned muscles, and his skin was so transparent that the blood vessels and technological additions could be easily seen. The same veins covered his face. Long, curling blond hair cascaded down his face, if you could even call it that.

He wore no shirt but had a long black robe that melded with the darkness around him.

"Ah, Suzuki," the Dark One purred.

Suzuki turned to run.

Before he could get his feet off the ground, he felt something wrap around his legs and hold him in place.

He was turned to face the Dark One.

The Dark One did not walk. His body vibrated, and then he was in front of Suzuki. The first thing Suzuki noticed was the smell.

The Dark One did not smell like anything he had a concept for. It was not that the Dark One stank or smelled beautiful. It was beyond those distinctions. He smelled like something ancient and foreign to existence.

Suzuki struggled to get out of his bindings, as did the other Suzuki.

The Dark one towered over both Suzukis, his body still vibrating. "What has brought you to the realm between places?" the Dark One asked, his voice burrowing deep into Suzuki's skull. The feeling was unbearable. Suzuki wanted to scream, to do anything to keep the Dark One from speaking again.

"Answer me, boy!"

The command nearly sent Suzuki spiraling into madness. It was as if someone had taken a sledgehammer to his brain. He felt sick to his stomach. "You know," Suzuki muttered, "I had the day off. Thought it might be fun to check it out."

There was no indication on the Dark One's face, but Suzuki knew he was smiling.

He also knew it was not a mocking smile.

There was genuine goodwill and humor in it.

Yet that goodwill did nothing to undercut the atmosphere of violence that radiated from the Dark One.

The Dark One's body contorted briefly.

It was as if there was another person behind him who had been shoved into his body and forced to move.

The disturbing part was that it looked extremely natural. "You have hardly been of notice to me," the Dark One said. "Yet it was you who destroyed my elder god. And it was you who realized my experiments. You who killed my Viceroy. Which makes me wonder, exactly who are you, Suzuki?"

The Dark One pressed his finger to Suzuki's forehead.

Suzuki felt as if someone had run a thousand knives down his body, splitting him into thousands and thousands of versions of himself. He could feel them stretching back in an infinite line. As Suzuki's body trembled from the strain, the Dark One practically waltzed around him. "Ah...a boy from Earth," the Dark One said. "One of the Dragon-blooded now. Exceptionally normal. Is it you who has been destroying my best-crafted plans?"

Suzuki did the only thing he could think of—he leaned forward and thought of his axe. He didn't know the last time he had held it, nor did he know if his enchantments were strong enough to hold through multiple realms of reality, but he knew he was not going to stand there and be taunted by the Dark One.

Even though Suzuki had not said anything aloud, the other Suzuki must have been thinking the same thing because they both surged forward at the same time, their axes flying to their hands, and brought the axes cleaving down on the Dark One's head.

The axes passed through as easily as butter, and the Dark One was gone. In his place was a large black petal sprout, reaching to the dark skies.

Suzuki looked at his doppelganger. "Uh, that was pretty intense," Suzuki said.

The other Suzuki nodded as he rubbed his sore leg. "Always wondered what it would be like to meet another version of myself," he muttered. "Would have thought we would have more to say to each other."

"When I thought of meeting alternate reality versions of myself, they never had to deal with anything like this."

"True. I guess I was thinking time travel or something like that."

Suzuki could see the other Suzukis walking around him, all of them approaching the threshold, their after images faint and hardly noticeable. "Do you think any of them can see us?" Suzuki asked. "I don't think anyone's acknowledged each other except for when I helped you up."

"That was you?" the other Suzuki asked. "I didn't see you, just felt your hands around my arm. Honestly, I didn't even know you were there until we were attacking the Dark One."

"Huh...maybe our alternate timelines aren't that different from each other's."

"You'd think that would hold for the rest of them too. Doesn't look like any other version of us was stopped by the Dark One."

"I mean, if there are infinite timelines, then it would make sense that the odds of any of them being too similar would be pretty infinite too."

"You know what? I was wrong. We obviously have a lot to talk about."

The two Suzukis started to make their way to the threshold again, Prime Suzuki helping his wounded alternate along.

After a couple of seconds, the other Suzuki assured Prime Suzuki that he was able to walk. As they proceeded, the world around them turned even blacker than before.

The threshold was not visible.

Deep in the darkness behind them, there was a rumbling, the sound of something awakening. Suzuki wasn't sure how he knew that, but he knew it beyond a shadow of a doubt. He also knew the only thing he could do was run. He set off, straight ahead, unsure if the threshold was still in front of him, but very aware he needed to get away from whatever was behind him.

A roar shattered through Suzuki's mind, and he wanted

nothing more than to drop to the ground. He had to see what was behind him.

He looked over his shoulder.

In the darkness, there looked to be lightning.

But it was not lightning.

More like fire.

Suzuki did not know how to describe what he saw.

There were only images of things which he had seen, images that did not make sense with each other. What he believed he saw was a giant mountain. The ridges of the mountain were deep and formed what looked like a furious bearded face. In each of the ridges of the face marched thousands of people holding torches. Then, without warning, the thing opened its eyes, and within those eyes Suzuki could see a thousand of his deaths in painful detail. The face surged forward, its mouth opening, the deep maw taking up all the space in the realm between realms.

The two Suzukis ran as fast as they could. Suddenly, there was a light. Suzuki wasn't sure where the light was coming from, but it was enough to let him see where the threshold was. On his back, he could feel the heat coming from what he now knew was the Dark One. Suzuki threw himself through the threshold. As he slid across the ground, he turned back to the threshold, and his jaw dropped in horror. The other Suzuki's hand reached out, and Suzuki saw black jaws clamp down on that Suzuki's arm. The threshold closed, and the other Suzuki's hand lay on the ground, bleeding.

An intense feeling welled up in his chest as if he were having an asthma attack. His head suddenly grew hot, and he felt like he was swimming. The feeling passed quickly, though, and he sat there staring at the hand.

Beth knelt beside Suzuki and tried to get his attention. "Suzy, are you okay?" she asked, her voice thick with fear.

Suzuki nodded as he stared at the bleeding hand. "Yeah, yeah. How is everyone else?" he asked.

"Fine. We've been waiting here for you for like an hour or something. It didn't take anyone else that long to get through. What the hell was going on in there?"

"I saw the Dark One. Really saw him. He's not like what we saw before. That's not him. He's so much... How was he just in there?"

Diana stepped forward and knelt across from Suzuki. She held out her wand. "Watch my wand, all right?" she commanded as she moved it back and forth in front of Suzuki's eyes. "Doesn't look like you have a concussion or anything. And you are right, he is something much larger than the military or MERC want to acknowledge. We can all play our war games, but whatever the Dark One is trying to do is going to be as vast and terrible as he truly is.

"If you saw what you say you saw, it explains a lot of what's been going on here. The Dark One is obviously using this spot for something, and he knows you're here. You've piqued his attention. But he isn't omnipresent. He can't be everywhere at once. The ley line was his chance to get to you. It was an echo of him. But that was it, and that lets us know he's not really here."

Suzuki pushed away his fears and the questions in his mind. This was simple enough. "All right," Suzuki said as he stood up. "So, we find out what the Dark One was up to here. If anything else is still happening, we shut it down. No matter how weird things start to get. You guys in?"

The decision was unanimous.

The Mundanes were going to get to the bottom of this.

P ast the threshold, the nature of the volcano had changed.

The psychedelic visions and feelings that had been plaguing the Mundanes before were gone, as was the suffocating nature of the tunnels. This new section looked as if it had been hollowed out by giant machines. There was a lot of open space that looked unnatural. There were no rock formations to be seen. Instead, there were stretches of empty cavern.

The Mundanes were not certain what time it was but, judging by Stew's embarrassingly loud stomach, they figured it was about time to eat. Chip and Beth went farther into the caverns to scout to see if there was anything else to be worried about. They returned after fifteen minutes, certain there was nothing remotely alive in this section of the cave. Suzuki was slightly unnerved by the fact there was *nothing* living in the cavern. Though with how things had been going since they started going deeper into the volcano, this was a little bit of luck. Also, it would give him a bit of time to recoup from his harrowing experience.

Suzuki wasn't one to sit and think about his situation. Most of his thoughts revolved around handling different battle or relational scenarios. In his head, he was somewhat of a background character. Trying to rescue Beth? That was about Beth. Watching the temperaments of his party members? That was about trying to make sure they were all in a space where they could work easily together. Now? It had been brought to his attention that the Dark One knew him by name, had noticed him, and picked him out. That was something big, and he was going to need to understand it.

Stew and Beth worked together, building a small fire from the stores they had brought along. Just as Stew had said, none of the food they brought had been touched. Even though Suzuki had a few questions, Stew assured him it wasn't anything they should be wasting time thinking about. Even if they did know where the food had gone, it hadn't negatively impacted them. They'd been eating just fine. If the curse of the cavern was that their food inventory was never depleted, Stew let Suzuki know he would be completely fine with it.

Suzuki walked away from Stew to speak with Diana. Stew's personality change was still obvious, even if it wasn't in your face. His generally immature attitude had almost completely vanished. Oddly enough, it made Stew seem much less like Stew. Or maybe it was just that Sandy was gone and Stew was worried. That would be another thing on the list of things to talk with Diana about: Sandy. She was part of the Mundanes. Suzuki wanted to know how she was faring.

Diana sat away from the fire but still close enough to benefit from its warmth. She was working on her wand, balancing it on her fingertips, occasionally levitating it before splitting it into thousands of pieces and pulling it back together. Once Diana had reassembled her wand, Suzuki took a seat next to her and cleared his throat. "That's really fucking impressive," Suzuki commented. "Must take a shit ton of control."

Diana continued to levitate her wand as she nodded to Suzuki. "Yes, it does. Control is one of the highest principles of magic. It doesn't matter how much raw force you have. Means nothing if you don't have any control."

"Makes sense. Diana, I wanted to talk to you about some shit. If it's not completely obvious, I am utterly out of my element. I know you and Chip are kinda expecting me to put on my big boy pants and everything, but I don't even know where to start with this shit."

"What's bothering you the most?"

"In the threshold. I saw the Dark One."

Diana's wand drifted down into the palm of her hand, where it stood up by itself. "Yes, you did. Is that confusing to you?" she asked.

"Obviously, but I think that one might be beneath you. I don't need to understand all the alternate dimension shit to figure out what I'm worried about. He knows who I am," Suzuki answered. "He picked me out of all the chaos in that realm and came to speak with me. There are thousands of other people trying to take out the Dark One who are doing much more important shit than me, and he came out of the middle of fucking nowhere just to intimidate me. Why?"

"What did you see in the realm between places?" Diana asked.

Suzuki knew Diana was either trying to figure this out or she was intentionally making Suzuki answer his own questions. Either way, it was frustrating as hell. "I saw different versions of myself," Suzuki finally said. "None of them could see me, though, except for one, and that was the one the Dark One could see, too. That was the one who got killed."

"I can see why you would be confused. That's not an easy thing to explain."

"You wanna give it a fucking shot?"

Diana's wand floated up and stopped in front of Suzuki's eyes. The tip glowed brightly, and a little bead of light floated up from it. "When I was born, this little light came into existence. From that moment on, every decision I ever made created another version of me."

Five smaller lights split away from the larger light. They were tied together by a string of light and floated a couple of inches apart. "Each miniscule decision," Diana reiterated. "Down to how large of a step I would take getting out of bed. Whether or not I choked on my spit. Within a couple of hours, there were so many different variations of these versions of me that it didn't matter. They got lost in infinity and have literally nothing in common with each other."

Now there were more lights stretching all the way up to the ceiling of the cavern. More than Suzuki could ever dream of counting, but each was tied back to the light that came before itself, going all the way back for the first light near the tip of the wand.

"Now some people are not like that. It happens every couple of thousands of years. They don't make unconscious decisions that differ much from the other versions of themselves. As a result, they don't have limitless, infinite possibilities. The versions of themselves that exist in alternate timelines are very, very close to each other."

All the lights disappeared but the first. From that light

came five more lights close to each other. Then more lights came from that one. Rather than stretching out like the bright lights Diana had conjured before, these lights remained close to each other and were more jumbled together. "An energy ties all of these alternate lives together, but when that energy is only split between a few thousand individuals, it doesn't dilute itself. That's what the Dark One is. An individual who could have had endless possibilities, and, for some reason, after some freak occurrence, unconsciously chose not to. Each version of the Dark One is going to be the Dark One. And he's learned how to harness that energy to become whatever the hell he is."

"Okay, fucking great."

"And you, Suzy. You're like that as well."

Suzuki's jaw dropped open. The idea that he could be anything like the Dark One was hilarious. If it was not for how seriously Diana was watching him, he would have assumed she was playing a joke on him.

Diana grabbed her wand and the lights disappeared.

"If you could even see one alternate version of yourself, that means you have significantly less than anyone else," Diana said. "All of us walked through the same unconscious chaos as you did, and none of us even picked up on the fact that we were walking in a sea of infinite versions of ourselves."

Suzuki heard Diana's words, but he didn't know what it all meant. "Are you saying I'm a chosen one?" Suzuki asked.

Diana laughed out loud before noticing how confused Suzuki was. "Kid, it might feel like we're in an epic fantasy novel, but no one out here is chosen. José had the same number of limited possibilities. I did for a while, until the whole god thing. Sandy does too. It makes you different than a few other people, but no one is destined for greatness. All it means is that you're one of the few people the Dark One is going to take notice of. How great you decide to be is up to you."

"Okay, one last thing. The dragon blood. From Ashegoreth. She never explained to me what it did, and I haven't had a chance to talk to anyone about it. I figured you would know as much as anyone else."

Diana scratched her chin with her wand as she thought. "Honestly, that might be harder to explain. Dragon's don't often share their blood. There aren't a whole lot of examples I can think of, and in most cases, the person who had the transfusion died way too early on to be able to gather long term information."

"Died? Why did they die young?"

Diana laughed again as she stood and ruffled Suzuki's hair. "It's because dragons always choose warriors. Anyone swinging a sword is liable to get killed by one. And MERCs don't usually have a long life if you haven't noticed. Now come on. Let's get some food before something jumps out and tries to kill us."

The two MERCs returned to the rest of the Mundanes. Stew had finished cooking up a small meal of spiced meats and a vegetable that tasted like a cross between cabbage and broccoli. After they were done eating, Chip poured everyone a shot of ambrosia, and they toasted their fallen comrades and themselves. Then they packed up their camp and continued farther into the cavern.

Chip was the first one to notice the massive shape looming in the distance. It looked like a giant man sitting on a throne of some sort, hunched over as if he were in a state of duress. The Mundanes watched the figure for some time just to be certain it was not going to move. Stew burped loudly and asked, "How strong is that ambrosia, dude? We only had one shot."

Chip shook her head as she pulled out a pair of binoculars. She scoffed when she held them to her eyes before passing them to Beth. "Fucking bonkers some days, as if my peepers need these," she muttered as Beth took the binoculars and Chip fiddled with what could only be knobs on the side of her face. Beth took a look, then passed the binoculars down the line until they came back to her.

Suzuki took the most time with the binoculars. His initial impression of the monolithic creature in the distance was correct. It was a man, but it looked like something was wrong with his body. The seat he sat in was far too bizarre-looking to be a chair. He knew they were going to have to get closer to figure it out. It was the closest thing they had gotten to what amounted to a clue as to what this cavern was being used for.

The Mundanes continued on through the cavern, slowly approaching the behemoth of a creature. Finally, they stood before the thing. A rusting ruin of a creature, it was covered in mold and lichen and more of the black petal sprouts that had been peppered throughout the caverns. The creature sitting atop the throne was at least sixteen feet tall. Its body was covered with an exoskeleton of some sort, not that different from a carapace of an insect. The throne itself was more of a small rocket or console of some kind. It was impossible to see if there were dials or if it had a computer screen from where they stood. Suzuki could tell the dead creature had been interacting with whatever it had slumped against when it died.

The throne itself could not be a throne proper. It looked to be more a floating seat. As Suzuki looked at everything, he was reminded of the grocery carts you can sit in if you have trouble walking. That was what first popped into his mind. Whatever this creature had been, it had used this throne to move around.

Suzuki walked closer to the creature. If the creature was dead, it had been dead for some time. The only smell in the cavern was of rock and the black petal sprouts and their acrid discharge. There was no smell of decay.

The closer Suzuki looked at the creature hunched over its device, the odder it seemed to him. There were tubes sticking from the creature and black stains ran down its mouth and sides, pooled in a frozen puddle on its thigh. The back of the creature appeared to have split from its exoskeleton, and what could only be described as organs and bones were spread almost like wings.

The rest of the Mundanes came up beside Suzuki, walking the breadth of the creature, trying to make sense of what they were looking at. Finally, Stew asked, "Hey, is Myrddin's whole thing just for book nerds?"

Suzuki was wondering the same thing. "Yeah, do you know if he ever worked with Cameron or any of those guys? This looks eerie similar to the Space—"

"Dude, shut up. Remember what Diana said about the magic?"

"Oh yeah, sorry," Suzuki said, surprised Stew remembered specific instructions, instructions about magic Suzuki had forgotten.

Beth walked behind the ruined creature. She seemed really interested in the creature's back. "It looks a little bit like an angel," she called before returning to the group.

Suzuki agreed before turning to Diana and Chip. "Do you think you guys could find out if Cameron or those guys ever worked on something with our 'Angel' here? Could give us a tip of what we might be up against. Though reading Verne didn't really prepare me for having an existential, physic experience."

Stew scoffed as he stretched. "Dude, you obviously were not reading Verne the right way," he said. "Every one of those books put me in a crisis."

"You? Having an existential crisis?"

"Yeah, I think about my own existence sometimes. It's called introspection, ass-hat. Maybe try it some time." *That was a little bit more like the old Stew.*

Chip pulled up her HUD and started writing a message. After a couple of minutes, she sent off the message and then gazed at the Angel. "The HUD don't register our beauty as threatening." She whistled. "I say we keep on moving if we're all done with our little detour."

Diana walked away from the rest of the Mundanes, back toward the Angel. "I wanna take a couple of samples before we leave," Diana yelled back. "It could be useful. There's a lot of flora in here I've never seen before. It could have a link to the Angel."

While the Mundanes waited for Diana, they crouched and talked amongst themselves. "That was a pretty good name," Suzuki said to Beth. "Didn't even realize how freaky that thing's back was."

Beth spat on the ground and absentmindedly rubbed it in with the bottom of her boot. "Yeah, the whole back thing is freaky. Funny, I would have thought anything here named an angel would have been all EVA style. Glad that's not the case, though. Could you imagine having to run after giant mechs with your mother's juices inside? God, that sounds horrifying."

Stew cast a glance at the dead Angel. "Really?" he asked. "I don't know. I think that thing is freakier than anything I've seen in an anime."

Suzuki laughed as he ran his finger over his axe, checking to see how well his enchantments were holding up. "Apparently, you aren't watching the right kind of anime," Suzuki said.

"True. Sandy's shown me a couple of *hentai* that made me want to pull my dick up into my stomach. I was regretting my balls ever dropping."

Beth laughed so hard she had to grab her side. "Goddamn, Stew, I forgot how much I like questing with you," she exclaimed. "I've hardly heard anyone crack a joke since we started this damn thing. Everyone's been so in their fucking heads. Don't blame you, though. Walking through that ley line seemed like it was fucking everyone up. Suzy didn't even make everyone uncomfortable by talking about nerd shit for too long."

Suzuki's eyes narrowed as he turned bright red. "Wait, I make people feel uncomfortable?"

"And we were way overdue for some of that classic 'Suzy Insecurity.' God, how I know you all must have missed that shit."

Suzuki was right.

It was the first time he had heard anyone laugh in a long time.

It had been a while since he had felt like laughing as well. Hopefully, it had just been the ley line hanging over them earlier.

The only thing Suzuki could still notice was off was his chest. It felt like there was an intense pressure on it ever since they had gotten out of the ley line.

Suzuki chalked it up to the number of odd sprouts that seemed to be everywhere.

Ever since he was a kid, he had a hard time with pollen.

There wasn't much more time to sit around and think, though. Diana had finished her sample gathering and was waiting impatiently for the rest of the Mundanes to stop sitting around and enjoying themselves. Suzuki was slightly annoyed at how quickly Diana wanted to get moving. Maybe they could all have benefited from sitting around and relaxing a little bit more. That shot of ambrosia had calmed Suzuki down a lot. He definitely wouldn't have minded more.

The temperature of the cavern was changing dramatically. It was not nearly as hot or cold as earlier, but the air had taken on a definite chill. Suzuki thought he could hear running water up ahead, which he knew made no sense. They were too far down in the mountain for there to be any rivers or whatever. But that could also have been said about giant relics of creatures from days gone past. And the whole reason why they were down in a volcano was to try to make it to the center of Middang3ard to see where the super-intelligent dinosaurs had come from. Running water was hardly a stretch.

The cavern looked as if it dropped off in a few feet. There was a cliff in the immediate distance, and the Mundanes made their way over it. Just as Suzuki had thought, there was water. Underneath the cliff's edge, there was a waterfall and what sounded like a coursing river. A massive chasm stood between the cliff's edge the Mundanes were on and the one across from them. On the other side of the chasm was something like a military facility.

Beth took out her binoculars and glanced across the chasm. "What the fuck? That looks like one of ours," she muttered. "I mean, one of theirs. Sorry, I keep forgetting I'm a Mundane, not whatever nickname those douchenozzles have for themselves."

Suzuki checked around his immediate vicinity for something that could give some clue how to get to the other side. After a little bit of searching, he found what looked like a switch built into the side of the mountain. It didn't look like any tech he had seen before, and he wasn't sure how to operate it. "Hey, Chip, can you come check this out?" Suzuki asked.

Chip came up to Suzuki's side and leaned over to look at the switch he was pointing at. "Now, that's an interesting piece of tech," Chip admitted. "Any idea how to turn the bugger on?"

"I was wondering if you could help me out with that?"

"Flattering, but just because I'm mostly wires, it doesn't mean I'm an idiot savant at tech."

"Actually...I was wondering if you were capable of interfacing with it?"

Chip looked warily at Suzuki as she bit her bottom lip. "What you going on and asking? We all saw how that ended up last time anything interfaced with me," she said quietly.

"That was different. That was someone overriding you. What if you could actually connect with tech on your terms?"

Chip shook her head as she backed away from Suzuki. "Ain't happening, boyo. Too big a risk. I know you're supposed to be a big leader and such now, but that is a lot of trouble you could be bringing down on yourself and everyone around."

"Hold on, hold on. Our HUDs can read threats, right? How about you see how much of a threat that switch poses. Anything over ten percent we don't bother with?"

Chip crossed her arms and looked at Suzuki as if he were joking. "The HUDs pick up on enemies. Do you think—"

"Enemies and traps. And if you think a switch can be a trap to you, doesn't that mean the HUD should as well?"

Chip sighed and turned back to the switch. "I'll humor you because you're cute when you're all hopeful and naïve. But don't get your... All right, you little bugger, you win this one. Less than a two percent chance it'll be a danger to me. You happy?"

"So, you'll try?"

Chip flipped Suzuki off.

Then the tip of her middle finger broke off, showing a series of small wires that stretched out as if they were autonomous tendrils.

She turned to the switch and touched it, letting the tendrils snake around and worm their way into the switch. "Oh, gods, that feels a touch odd," Chip murmured. "Ain't ever done this before. And definitely never felt anything like this before. And...oh, there goes another computer system."

Chip's eyes went white and her body went rigid. Suzuki tried to see if everything was okay, but Chip didn't respond to him. He called her name and waved his hands in front of her eyes, but to no avail. He was getting ready to wave the other Mundanes over when Chip's eyes snapped back on and she let out a nervous giggle. "Do you mind?" Chip said as she straightened her clothes. "We're in the system, and we got a nice little trolley coming across to meet us."

Up above, Suzuki could hear gears and machinery whirring. Something like a large warehouse elevator lowered itself from the ceiling. Now that Suzuki knew what he was looking for, he could see the cables overhead and the rail that ran beneath the trolley. When the trolley came to a standstill, the gates opened.

Suzuki cast an over-the-shoulder glance at Chip. "And this is how we're getting across?" he asked.

Chip walked past Suzuki toward the trolley. "Of course," Chip said. "Nothing to worry about, either. No tech in there. AI, things of that sort, yes—just good old-fashioned folders and instructions. Like popping open a HUD."

Stew ran his hand over the rusted trolley. "This thing looks ancient. What if it falls apart on us?"

"Falls apart?" Chip exclaimed. "Is there no trust in my skills at procuring comfortable travels for us? Why, I would trust this thing with my life!"

Chip knocked twice on the iron frame. There was screeching and a labored groan, then the cables the trolley were attached to snapped and the trolley fell into the chasm. Chip went red and sucked her lips back so her teeth were bared. "Okay, so I was certain about the trolley," Chip said. "Not a lick of diagnostics on the cables, though, loves. But I got a backup. Got some directions for how to get to the other side through the little computer box, although it's not what I would label as easy. If anything—"

Beth interrupted Chip. "Did you happen to at least find out what this place is before we start risking our necks trying to get to it?"

"Always pragmatic, my darling. You are going to make a great ranger. And, uh, no. That information was unavailable."

"So, the place isn't military then. There's no way a military base wouldn't even have the bare minimum of information. It would have been classified, but you would have been able to find something that would let you know there was classified information on there."

Suzuki looked at the base across the chasm. "If it's not military, I got a pretty good bet who's behind this."

Stew shook his head as he held up his hand. "The Dark One? This tech is way behind what we've seen him working with before."

"Yeah, that was until we pulled that tech off the dinosaurs. And Diana said so herself, no one ever comes to this island. This could have been abandoned a long time ago. It would make sense that the tech is so outdated. I say we check it out. We're already here anyway, and it doesn't seem like there's a whole lot of options we have for exploring further."

"I don't know, dude. I'm really not into getting killed underground."

Beth gave Stew a look as if he had just said he was an elephant. "Wait, are you into getting killed in other situations?" she asked.

"Of course. There're definitely ways I'd be down dying. Doesn't everyone have a preference?"

Chip raised her hand, but none of the other Mundanes did. Even though Diana looked annoyed with the conversation, she seemed unable to keep from asking Stew, "How do you *want* to get killed? And we are talking about being killed, not just dying?"

Stew's eyes lit up brighter than a Christmas tree. "Oh, yeah, of course, those are two entirely different questions." He beamed. "I could talk about that all night. If I was going to die, I would want it...and guys, this is totally hypothetical, all right? Don't laugh. But if I were going to die, I would want it to be in a three-way fight with a dark dragon and a chimera. I think that would be fucking sick."

"Are you saying you want to die in a free-for-all with two

creatures that greatly outmatch you in power? That you would hardly have a chance against one on one?"

"Yeah, can you imagine if I got a couple of solid hits in there? I'd be so fucking stoked."

Diana rested her face in her palm as she shook her head and laughed. "There are many things I haven't been able to understand about yours and Sandy's relationship, and the more you talk without her around, the less I understand. Gods bless you, Stew. Gods bless you."

Stew's eyes jumped from the rest of the Mundanes as if he were trying to gauge their reactions to what he had said. "That's a compliment, right?" Stew finally asked.

"Yes, Stew. It is a compliment and a blessing."

"Sweet."

Chip cleared her throat as she bashfully kept her eyes lowered to the ground. "It'd be pretty sweet to be torn apart by an eldritch sea monster," she muttered.

Diana's eyes widened the way a schoolteacher's did when she caught a student misbehaving. "Chip, are you serious? You would throw your—"

"No, nothing about throwing my life away. This is a hypothetical ideal final epic battle, nothing more."

Chip's HUD went off, indicating she had just received a message. She opened it up, skimmed through, and smirked. "All right, young'uns, just got word back, your pop culture knowledge is spot on," Chip said. "Cameron was working with Myrddin. Did a couple of projects 'till he claimed to be abducted by aliens…Myrddin wasn't sure about working with him much after that."

Suzuki couldn't believe what he had just heard. A guy who was supposed to lace humanity's consciousness with the idea of aliens got fired from his job because he thought he was abducted by aliens. "So, what Myrddin doesn't even believe in the stuff he's trying to get humans to believe in?" Suzuki asked.

"Could have thought it was bunk. You know, folks tapping into the collective unconscious is hit or miss sometimes."

Suzuki shuddered, thinking back to the first time he had seen Cameron's aliens with his parents. "For our sake, I hope we don't have to deal with any of that shit," he said. "You guys remember those movies? They were horrifying."

"Obviously not hitting the point home in the right. Either way, I don't think anyone is going to be too excited about how we're crossing this here chasm."

Diana pulled out her wand and pointed it at the chasm. A bright light stretched out, and in a flash, returned back to her. "From my estimate, we have to cross more than a hundred feet. So, however we do it is probably not going to be easy or enjoyable."

Chip smiled before leaning over the side of the cliff. "You guys ever done this before?" she asked as hocked up a loogie and spat over the cliff. "You should give it a try. 'Cause that's where we're on the way to. Hopefully much less quickly."

13

Suzuki had never done anything like this before in his life.

The closest he could think of was when he was a kid and used to jump down from trees he had climbed. As he peered over the cliff, he thanked God he didn't get vertigo and wasn't afraid of heights. Or at least, he wasn't sure if he was afraid of heights. The longer he stared over the edge, the more certain he was it was a terrible idea.

Chip was manning the descent.

She said it was the least she could do since the lift hadn't worked out. It took her nearly fifteen minutes to scope out the potential depth. During that time, the Mundanes paced, each of them airing whatever misgivings they had about leaping off a cliff to descend into a volcano. Chip was undeterred by their complaints and reassured them it was the fastest and safest way down to a bridge below that they could use to cross.

Beth crossed her arms and clicked her tongue as she looked over the side of the cliff again. "I know you're saying it's the safest way, but I don't see anything remotely safe about this," Beth said.

Chip was assembling what looked like a giant harpoon gun. The tech looked newer, and Suzuki wasn't sure if Chip had built it out of her own body. The gun was nearly the same size as Chip and a thick rope ran from the harpoon's edge to the shoulder stock. Chip aimed the gun over the side of the cliff. "Well, I mean safer by comparison," Chip said. "Compared to flinging yourself over this cliff."

"Goddamn it, Chip, those are both fucking dangerous options."

"All jokes aside, I don't see us picking and choosing from a shite-ton of options."

Beth didn't have anything to say, so she sat down next to Stew and pouted. Stew occasionally looked over the side of the ledge. It was impossible to discern what he was thinking. His eyebrows were knit tightly together, and every so often, he would purse his lips before sitting back and then leaning over the edge of the cliff again.

Suzuki couldn't stop thinking about how far down they were going to have to climb, and Chip was being coy about the numbers. He figured he would have to find out for himself. He recalled his axe to his hand and threw it over the side of the cliff. The rest of the Mundanes listened as Chip whistled. They were listening for quite some time before Suzuki realized throwing his axe had proved it was an awfully long way down. Suzuki called his axe back to him. It took a long time for it to return. "Okay, Chip, could you give us some more details?" he asked. "It would make putting my trust in you a lot easier."

Chip smiled as she looked over her shoulder, and Suzuki could see the mischievous child behind her eyes. "Aye, you need more of a reason to trust me than my knack at staying one step ahead of that gray-eyed death?" Chip sang. "Well, then here's the plan, all placed out nice and easy to digestion. I'm gonna fire this here line-gun down the side, and it's gonna hit the bridge at the bottom. After that, me and your lady lover are gonna—"

Beth jumped to her feet, raising her arms and bringing them down in the universal sign for "no fucking way." "Hold on just a fucking minute," Beth exclaimed. "You didn't say anything about me going down there with you."

"Why would I have? You're my lucky protégé. Thought it went without saying that we'd be defying death with each other."

The color had drained out of Beth's face. "Okay, I wasn't sure I could do the whole action hero thing you're talking about, but I am one hundred percent certain I am not up for this."

Chip patted Beth on the back and pushed her away from the rest of the Mundanes, who were still looking dubiously over the side of the cliff. "Ain't nothing to it," Chip explained. "You just follow my lead. Easy enough?"

Beth sighed as Chip sat down and dangled her feet off the cliff. Chip held her harpoon gun and took a deep breath as she lined up her shot. The gun went off, and the harpoon went flying into the darkness. Chip leaned a little farther over the cliff to get a better line of sight. After a couple of minutes of waiting, there was a faint *clink* and Chip smiled, much more delighted than any of the other Mundanes—Beth in particular.

Chip stood, still holding the gun. She popped off the heavy shoulder stock, showing another harpoon underneath. She drove that harpoon in the ground, covered it with a couple of large rocks, and then used her plasma gun to fuse the rocks together. "See?" Chip exclaimed. "We're gonna be extremely secure as well. Nothing's pulling out. All we gots to do is slide on down. Granted, at a reasonable speed. No adrenaline-junkie shit. Straight-and-narrow prudish. Now, let's get sliding."

Beth groaned loudly as Chip pushed her to the rope that hung over the cliff. Chip went first, holding onto the rope tightly and slinging herself over the side of the cliff as if she had done this thousands of times. Beth went afterward, nervously looking over the side a few times before finally sitting down, dragging her legs over the side and lowering herself down.

Suzuki was surprised at how not worried he was watching Beth climb down the cliff. If there was anyone he thought was capable of anything, it was Beth. He had been pleasantly surprised by how quickly she seemed to be adapting to the entirely new role she was playing in the party. But not just the party. Beth had never played anything other than a fighter in any of the VR sessions they had been in together. Granted, for the most part, everyone stuck to their own classes, but the rest of the Mundanes had back up characters they had worked on in case they had to change roles for an unforeseen reason. Not Beth. She had one fighter, and that was it.

That summed Beth up pretty accurately. One fighter. One save file. One life. Even if she didn't like to say it, she loved living on the edge, especially if that edge was defined by her abilities.

Chip's voice came from below. "All right, next one get started. We got enough space for at least twenty of you!" Chip shouted.

Stew, Diana, and Suzuki exchanged glances. No one was

going to jump at the chance to go first. After an uncomfortable pause, Stew sighed loudly and theatrically in case his attitude about the situation wasn't clear and walked over to the rope. He held it in his hand for a moment before leaping off the side of the cliff. If he was afraid, he didn't show it that last second.

Diana and Suzuki stood around awkwardly, waiting for the announcement that the next one should descend. Suzuki cleared his throat and tried to think of something to say to fill the silence. He realized this was the longest he'd ever been alone with Diana before. "So...does Chip do stuff like this often?" Suzuki asked.

Diana jumped at the sound of Suzuki's voice. "Huh? Oh... like this?" Diana asked. "Not usually, but close enough. She is somewhat impetuous. It pays to have someone like her around. Helps to bring attention to some of the less obvious options."

Stew's voice came from the cliff. "Next one is up!"

For some reason, Suzuki didn't want to be the last one on the rope. He walked over to the side of the cliff and took the rope in his hand. It was rough and thick and felt like something that could hold up to a lot of stress. Using that to reassure himself, he turned around and lowered himself over the cliff.

Suzuki knew he wasn't supposed to look down. He'd seen it in every movie. It was a meme in every video game—don't look down. Despite knowing that, Suzuki looked down. The first thing he noticed was his friends directly beneath him. There was some space between them, but they were all close enough that they could communicate. The next thing he noticed was the waterfall against one of the walls of the chasm. Gray mist came off the waterfall, catching the ambient light. It was hauntingly beautiful.

From below, Suzuki heard Chip shout, "Send Diana down!"

Suzuki looked up and shouted, "Your turn, Diana!"

Below, Suzuki could feel the slack on the rope go taut. He figured that meant they were moving down. Even though Suzuki had never done this before, it felt natural. Moving was straightforward. He planted his feet against the mountain and held tight to the rope as he lowered himself down.

"Use the hook and loop on your belt," someone shouted from below.

Suzuki looked down at his belt. He had been issued one when he first became a MERC and had never thought anything about it. MERCs weren't necessarily known for providing their mercenaries with too many useful items. All of the gear Suzuki had learned to rely on (as with the other Mundanes) had been found out in the field. But Suzuki had never come across a belt. Now, as he looked down at his belt, he could see there was a strap that was perfect for attaching to the rope in front of him. He breathed a sigh of relief. He knew he was physically capable of making the climb down, but it was comforting to know that if he lost his grip, he wouldn't go plummeting to his death.

It was kind of funny Chip had managed to leave out that important piece of information. She was probably enjoying freaking the rest of the party out.

Suzuki felt Diana pull on the rope, and he looked up in time to see her fly over the side of the cliff, her boots hitting the wall with a heavy thud. Diana took out her wand and aimed it into the dark, and there was a bright flash. A ball of white light floated away from the wand and to the middle section of the MERCs climbing down the cavern. "Always brightening up my day," Chip called.

Diana's face was too white and grim to look anything other than terrified.

The MERCs made their way down the cliff in this fashion. The gray mist seemed to float up and kiss their faces, cooling them as the heat from deep within the earth wafted up. Suzuki could smell whatever was down there. It was something deep and ancient, and he hoped they weren't really planning on descending that low into the hollows of Middang3ard. Whatever was down there was best left for another adventure. Checking out the abandoned buildings across the chasm would have to suffice. Suzuki couldn't help but wonder if one day he would find out what was in the deepest depths of Middang3ard.

As Suzuki continued down the rope, he noticed the walls had the same black sprouts he had been seeing throughout the caverns. These sprouts opened up wider anytime Suzuki got a good look at them. Once the petals widened, there was an intricate swirl pattern, like that of a conch, which glowed bright blue. A sweet scent also came off the petals once the womb of the sprouts was exposed. "Hey yo, these sprouts things are everywhere!" Suzuki shouted.

Stew lost his grip and slid down a little faster than he expected. The hook on his belt stopped him midfall, and he took hold of the rope again with his hand. "Yeah, I've noticed," Stew called back. "What the hell are these things?"

The Mundanes waited for Diana to answer, but she was too busy gritting her teeth. "How much farther are we going?" Diana asked.

From below, Chip laughed. "What's wrong, Dee? You scared?" Chip quipped.

"I don't like being suspended mid-air over a chasm and would like to end this as soon as possible."

Stew leaned back to look up and see Suzuki. "Hey, Diana, you know Suzuki can see up your robes?" he shouted.

The rope slipped out of Diana's hand and she fell toward Suzuki as he raised one of his hands over his head and shouted, "I wouldn't fucking do that!" His protests meant nothing. Diana's foot collided with Suzuki's head, and they both went sliding down the rope until their belts stopped them abruptly. Diana looked at Suzuki, and her face bloomed bright red. She and Suzuki were face to face, almost close enough to kiss. "Please do not look up my robes," Diana muttered before climbing higher up the rope.

Suzuki grabbed his axe and chipped off a piece of stone from the cavern wall. It was small, about the size of a quarter. Perfect. He wound up and threw the rock at Stew's head.

Stew grabbed the top of his head and screamed, "God-damn it, it's raining fucking rocks now!"

Neither Beth nor Chip needed to have seen what had happened to know.

Suzuki could hear them snickering. "Oh, it must have fallen from above. Don't worry about it. I think I knocked it loose."

"Well, be more careful."

Beth stopped laughing and shook the rope. "All right, douchenozzles, stop fucking around," she suggested. "We need to get going."

Suzuki felt a rock hit him on the head. He didn't think Diana was the kind to join in on the joke. Humor never seemed like an interest to her. Maybe she was pissed off at him because she thought he had tried to peek up her robes.

"Hey, Diana," Suzuki started. "I really wasn't looking up

your skirt. I wouldn't do something like that. The regular Stew is back, that's all."

Suzuki waited for a response. What he got in return was a surprise. Diana's voice was hoarse, gripped with fear, tight in her throat. "Go. Now," she whispered.

The walls of the cavern shook violently, tossing the Mundanes away from their hold on the rope. The only thing that saved them from plummeting to their deaths was their belts. "What in the ass-crack of the gods was that?" Chip shouted.

Suzuki looked up and could see Diana staring up as well. There was another tremor, and what Suzuki saw sent a shiver of fear up his spine.

A head was poking out of the stone wall. It was vaguely serpentine but also reminiscent of a human, its skin covered in wet-looking scales, its neck long and slender. The creature's mouth, the mouth of a human, hung open, and its jaw dislocated so it could have easily fit any of the Mundanes in its throat in one try. A stench like rotten eggs came off the monster. Its torso was like that of a cobra. It had no legs but instead had two longs arms that bent the way a spider's would. Yellow snake eyes peered from behind human eyelids.

Without warning, the creature surged, moving nearly too fast to see, toward Diana, its mouth hinged open as it flung itself into the air, its arms stretching out and puncturing the rock. It used its momentum to close the gap between it and the Mundanes.

Diana let go of the rope and pushed off the rock with her boots, swinging into the air as she pulled out her wand. A fireball went flying toward the creature, who opened its massive mouth wider and swallowed the fireball whole. "Move!" Diana shouted.

Chip let go of the rope and slackened her hold on her belt to slide down the rope at breakneck speed. The rest of the Mundanes did the same, except for Suzuki.

Diana was trying to maneuver around the creature, who was taking advantage of her lack of solid footing. She spread her arms and levitated before casting a barrier around herself.

Suzuki pulled down his HUD and scanned the creature.

Eighty-five percent chance of survival.

He pulled out his axe and sent it toward the creature as it turned. The creature swerved its neck out of the way, and the axe went flying into the darkness. That was all Suzuki needed, though, and he unloosened his belt. Diana did the same, and they both went screeching into the darkness after the rest of the Mundanes.

The creature screamed, a sound akin to the mewing of a cat if it had its intestines ripped out, and went after the MERCs.

The MERCs were sliding down the rope as fast as they could, the creature screeching after them, its tongue lolling from its mouth, slobbering. The drool burned away whatever rock it fell on, the smoke sizzling up, the creature still screeching.

At the bottom of the queue, Chip kicked off the wall and slammed her hands together, converting them to a plasma cannon, and fired two shots. The creature easily dodged them, acid still dripping from its mouth as it bounded after the MERCs.

Suzuki recalled his axe to his hand and threw it at the creature, but it dodged again, and then, without warning, the creature turned and slammed its head into the cavern wall. It continued on, blood forming in a halo around its crown until the wall gave way, and the creature slipped into the cracks of the rock.

Suzuki unclipped his belt and stopped. Diana nearly slammed into him, but she managed to stop at the last minute. Suzuki shouted for the Mundanes to stop. "We need a fucking plan!" Suzuki shouted.

As Suzuki tried to formulate something in his head, he could hear the rock wall shaking around him, cracking, beginning to give way. He wanted to stop and catch his breath, but that wasn't an option. "How far down does this go?" he asked Chip.

Even though Suzuki couldn't see Chip, he could imagine her scanning the potential drop and shrugging. There wasn't time for her to give an answer. The rocky wall of the cliff broke apart and the creature burst out, its jaws open, its acidic spit trickling down its face as it reached out and grabbed the rope the Mundanes were hanging by in its mouth.

The sensation of freefalling was almost beautiful. Suzuki felt his body hanging in the air as if there was no such thing as gravity. He looked around as Diana floated next to him, her hair hanging above her head as if she were underwater. They stared at each other, and Suzuki realized he was falling to his death, to be consumed by whatever was living in the middle of Middang3ard. *Guess my curiosity is going to be satisfied after all,* he thought.

As Suzuki twisted in the air, calling his axe back to him, a harpoon went flying through the air, grazing his cheek. He looked down and saw Beth holding Chip's harpoon as she fell. She shifted in the air, grabbed Chip's body, and used it to fling herself closer to the cavern's wall. She hit the rock, accompanied by the sickening sound of bones cracking, but this did not deter her. Her hand was wrapped tightly around the harpoon's point, and she jammed it into the wall's surface.

The rest of the Mundanes continued to fall, cinching their belts. Within seconds, the slack of the rope had caught, and they slammed against the wall, safe from crashing into whatever lay at the bottom of the cavern.

Chip coughed up blood as she held her chest. "Fuck me and all the gods." She laughed as she converted her arm to a cannon. The rest of the Mundanes also drew their weapons, Stew pulling out one of his axes, Suzuki brandishing his own, and Beth nocking an arrow to her short bow.

The creature was nowhere to be seen. The rocks were still. There was no sound.

Suzuki looked around to see if he could gather any information. It was too dark. The light Diana had cast was gone. There were only darkness and the rushing of water.

Beth shouted, "Suzy, we need a fucking plan!"

Suzuki had nothing.

He knew this was so far beyond the realm of things he had experienced or even gauged the likelihood of happening. "I almost got something," he lied. "Don't worry."

The cavern's rocky walls burst open as the creature flung itself out of the rocks, its jaws hanging open. Its acidic spittle dribbled down its mouth, and a bit of the spit hit Stew in the chest. Stew screamed in pain as he clasped his chest, losing his grip on the rope.

Diana wasted no time. She disengaged her belt and levitated to where Stew was. She cast a healing spell and Stew's chest stitched itself back up, the burned skin and muscle coming together again. Once his body was intact, he turned around to try to find the culprit. The creature was already gone. "How the fuck am I supposed to kill something I can't see?" Stew lamented.

There were rocks, and they were on a rope.

Cornered.

That was all Suzuki knew for sure. Something was missing from the equation. If he could just figure it out.

Chip fired two more shots into the darkness.

The plasma lit the cavern for a brief second before everything was plunged back into darkness. She looked around, trying to find the creature, but much like the rest of the Mundanes, she couldn't make sense of what was around her. The creature must have burrowed back into the stone. As Suzuki watched Chip, Beth, and the rest of the Mundanes flail, something clicked.

Suzuki turned to Stew and shouted, "Go berserker now!"

Stew gave Suzuki an incredulous look. "Why the fuck would I do that?" he asked.

"Go berserk now and pound on the rock."

"But they're covered in those—"

"Pound on the fucking walls, Stew! That's a fucking order!"

Stew stopped hesitating and listened. His body swelled, the muscles bulging out as his torso and his legs stretched. His eyes went red, and he turned to the rock walls. When he slammed his fists into them, the walls quaked. Suzuki had been expecting something of the sort, but he was not prepared for how strong Stew was. It felt like an earthquake had just ripped through all of Middang3ard.

Almost as soon as Stew's knuckles pulled away from the rock, the creature came screeching out. Suzuki didn't have time to think or explain. He undid his belt and threw his axe at the creature, who dodged it effortlessly.

Suzuki fell, his body weightless.

His axe was coming back. He knew that, but he wasn't sure if it was going to be fast enough. In the meantime, the creature had thrown its body toward Suzuki, the only obvious prey.

Suzuki pulled down his HUD with one hand as he waited for the inevitable impact, either from whatever was below or the snake thing quickly gaining on him from above.

Even in the dark, Suzuki could see the creature coming for him. Its serpentine eyes glowed in the little bit of light shimmering across the slick sprout-covered walls. The creature's jaws opened wider still, preparing to slip around Suzuki. A droplet of its spit fell on Suzuki's throat and it erupted in pain. It felt as if someone had laid him out on the ground and taken a knife to him, deciding to slowly dig the blade around as if they had no care in the world for how long it would take for him to bleed out.

Suzuki screamed in the emptiness of the cavern, and it echoed across the cold, dead walls.

In the distance, Suzuki could hear the Mundanes screaming. He could hear the snapping of rope and belt, the gnashing of teeth, and screeching of the abominable creature. All he could concentrate on was the pain. He felt as if his heart was going to slip out of his chest. Cool air brushed against his face as he gasped for breath.

Suzuki's rope hit a snag, and his body went limp as his belt clung to the rope. His eyes forced themselves open as he coughed up blood, a thick, black substance that stung his mouth.

Beth swung from the rope, throwing herself with all her strength until she landed next to Suzuki, her bow drawn, waiting for the creature to make itself evident again. She did not have to wait long. The cavern walls shook.

The creature burst from the rock near Suzuki. Beth saw the rock moving as if it were experiencing a seismic upheaval, kicked off the stone, and cinched her belt so the rope was taut. She swung past the creature, nocked two arrows, and let them fly. The arrows hit the creature in the back of the head. Its blood spewed and hit Suzuki in the face, burning off his flesh instantly.

Suzuki grabbed his face out of reflex, unaware of the pain that would come afterward. He vaguely thought about how he had never wondered what his skull and his bones felt like. There would be no reason to wonder ever again. His fingertips grazed the cold bone of his skull, and he screamed in horror as he fell into the darkness.

The feeling of weightlessness disappeared. His body went slack, and whatever held him up, he accepted as his savior. He felt the side of his face melting. If he had wanted to say anything, it would have been pointless. His jaw worked idiotically in his skull, the skin melting off it.

In the dark, the creature flew forth from who knows where. None of the Mundanes were prepared for another attack. The creature slammed into Suzuki, its body crushing him against the rock as its jaw retracted and slammed shut, grasping at Suzuki, dripping its acid spit over him. Suzuki screamed and his body seized as he tried to call his axe toward him. He was not capable of forming the thought. He held his hand out in the dark of the caverns as his axe lay someplace he could not reach.

Chip jumped from the rope, disengaging it from her belt, her hands forming into two plasma cannons. Sweat beaded her forehead as she exhaled, taking aim. Beth came to her side, leaping through the air, her bow drawn. Diana came as well, her wand inches from her hand as she conjured an immense fireball. Stew's hulking body climbed down the cliff wall, detached from his belt, eyes wide and full of red hatred. They all converged on the creature.

To call it an explosion would do a disservice to what happened. It was as if a comet had punctured the earth. The rock gave way, and the creature shrieked its last cry as it fell into the darkness of the chasm. Diana scooped Suzuki into her arms and cinched her belt against the rope.

Suzuki tried to keep his eyes open.

It was difficult.

He wanted to know what was going on around him, but he couldn't seem to focus. Each time he blinked his eyes, he felt like he could close them forever. There was nothing he was going to miss. There was only the song beating in the back of his head and the black sprouts.

He would be okay.

That was all he needed.

The world around Suzuki faded.

It grew gray and cold.

The pain in his neck ceased to exist.

He looked around and saw only blackness, then the faint trace of a star went past him, too fast to catch. He was sorry he didn't make a wish, but deep down, he knew there were no wishes to make. Wherever he was, it was a place without wishes, without possibilities, perhaps only built on intention, hope, and will.

Suzuki looked around, trying to get his bearings. Even with the bleak nothingness, he was experiencing, he felt deep down that there should be some order, some kind of understanding. At that moment, Suzuki understood he was dying.

This was the end of his life. It had never been clearer to him before.

In the distance of the darkness, there was a song. Suzuki did not know how to sing along with it, but he was certain he knew the words. He felt them deep in his chest. He looked down. His skin was burned away. There was a hole in his chest. His heart peeked through, and he watched it beat through the ivory of his sternum.

Still, there was a song. It was strong. It continued on. Suzuki remembered what he had heard Diana say about Sandy singing their safety into existence. Suzuki didn't know how to put it into words, but he tried to compose his own song. Not thinking of notes or measures, he let his heart and soul call out in the only way it could in this place of blackness and chaos.

And there was an answer.

The song changed its tune.

All around, the universe began to change. As Suzuki floated through the darkness, he split into thousands of versions of himself flailing for their lives in the black. He reached out for them, but none took notice of him.

A face came to him in the dark.

It was ridged as if had been carved from the most ancient of stones. Fire burned in its crevices. Suzuki knew he had seen this face before, and he knew it was important that he did not look at it again.

He turned away, and in the distance, he saw a light bright enough to obliterate the darkness threatening to consume him.

It was Sandy.

A bright white glowing light in the black. She hardly had a form. Suzuki didn't know why he knew it was her.

Until she spoke.

"Get the fuck away from Suzy!" Sandy shouted as she pointed her hand at the vestige of the Dark One. A beam of light shot from her fingertip.

The world collapsed on itself. Everything turned to white and then to black. The universe collapsed.

Suzuki woke up in a place he had no remembrance of. It was similar to places he had been before. Places he had been to recently. Still, his mind did not seem able to grasp onto those concepts. There was chaos around. No doubt. Yet, somehow, there was more sense here, more conciseness. In the deep void, Suzuki called out.

In that calling out, there was an answer. It did not come with a boom or a shout, nor a whisper or a whimper. It came as a voice Suzuki understood. "What are you doing here, Suzuki?" Sandy asked.

Suzuki was a child.

He did not know how, but he was a child.

He looked at his hands, and they were those of a babe. When he cleared his throat, he was surprised it was his voice he heard. He assumed it would have been a child's. "What's happening, Sandy?" he asked.

"You are in a place where you should not be," she replied.

Suzuki tried to look around. It didn't matter. What he saw made no sense. Universes falling into collapse. His body, the many iterations of it, lambasted by the cosmos, morphing into forms he had never imagined, their limbs growing long and confusing. "Why shouldn't I be here?" he asked.

"This is not a place for you."

Suzuki looked around, trying to make sense of where he was. "What is this place?"

"You are not ready. This is a place where you can understand yourself and…"

The fabric of the fragile reality began breaking apart. The universe sped up. Stars came into existence and died with hardly a notice.

And Suzuki woke up.

The Mundanes were sitting on the bridge above the chasm. Diana was crouched above Suzuki, trying to stem the blood oozing from his face. These were the worst burns she had seen in her life.

Suzuki tried to breathe. Each breath felt like his lungs were ripping open. He tried to sit up to get a better idea of the state he was in, but his body wouldn't respond. His eyes fluctuated between open and closed as he choked down whatever it was he was coughing up.

The rest of the Mundanes were quiet as they watched Diana working. Diana moved with the efficiency of a surgeon. She held her wand above Suzuki, reciting through incantation after incantation to find something that would stitch up his chest. It was as if the wound was beyond magic. Sweat beaded her forehead as she became more frantic, and Suzuki's breathing slowed.

Black mucus oozed out of Suzuki's wound. It was the same color as the black sprout petals they had been seeing throughout their journey.

Stew was standing guard, waiting for the creature to return. They had lost track of it in the commotion, but they knew it was not dead. There had not been time to talk about what they thought it was or where it came from. The only thing that was important right now was making sure Suzuki didn't die.

Diana cast her wand aside. She leaned over Suzuki and pressed her head to his chest, to the wound, and screamed. Her robes exploded in light as the magical cracks across her skin spread. The god shone through her, and the entirety of the cavern vibrated with her power. The light leaked into Suzuki, pouring from her eyes as if it were tears, Diana weeping, her body shaking as the god within her lent its power.

Suzuki's wounds healed within seconds, and the light vanished. He sat up, grasping at where the wound had been, and he gasped as he sucked in air as if he had never breathed before. "Oh, my fucking God," he whispered.

At his side, Diana slumped over, struggling to breathe. She grabbed the side of her head as her body returned to normal, and the light faded. She was still for a moment before Beth rushed to her side and shook her awake. "Diana! We need to move!" Beth shouted.

Diana's eyes fluttered open, and she looked Beth in the eye and smiled. "I know," she replied. "Help me up."

Beth pulled Diana up. Then Beth called Stew over and motioned to Suzuki, who still lay on the ground as if he were a child waiting to be picked up by his parents. Stew was still in berserker mode and easily picked Suzuki up and slung him over his shoulders.

Chip led the way as they crossed the bridge. She watched the water pouring from overhead and the dark rocks covered in shadow as closely as she could. There was no light. They couldn't risk it. They moved within the darkness toward the destination Chip reminded them was true. It did not take long to cross, even with two of the Mundanes carrying their wounded comrades. After a while, they stood before the cliff on the other side of the chasm.

Beth looked up at the heights they were going to have to scale. "They're not going to be able to get up there. Not Suzy, at least."

Chip nodded as she paced back and forth, trying to come to a solution. "All right, someone has to get up there and place the harpoon. I'll do it."

Beth grabbed Chip and shook her head. "No," she said quietly. "You have more firepower than me. You need to stay with them. If anything happens, you and Stew in a fight will be a better match than anything else."

Chip shook her head as if she disagreed but didn't say anything. Instead, she opened her HUD and went through the inventory until she found a second harpoon gun. She pulled it out, and when the gun materialized in her hand, she handed it over to Beth. "You need to plant one down here and then one up top. Just make sure it's secure," Chip advised.

"Got it."

Beth aimed the harpoon gun and fired it, the harpoon driving into the ground. Then she slung it over her shoulder.

Chip reached out and grabbed Beth's shoulder. "Wait," Chip said. "Take these. It'll make it easier." Chip handed Beth two daggers. They were worn with age and covered in rust. Their hilts were engraved with words in a language long dead, without meaning.

Beth took the daggers. They were heavy in her hand, much heavier than such small daggers should have been. And still, they felt as if they were an extension of her body. She looked at Suzuki as she stood before the great rock wall she had to scale. Then she plunged her dagger into the rock before her, the second dagger after that, kicked her boot into the rock, and began her ascent up the chasm walls.

As Beth ascended the wall, Stew placed Suzuki onto the ground next to where Diana was leaned up against the rock. Suzuki's eyes closed and opened rapidly, time and time again, but he focused on nothing. Stew took a seat across from Suzuki, crouching low and looking Suzuki in the eyes. "Dude, you need to get out of this," Stew said. "We need to get the fuck out of here."

For a moment, Suzuki's eyes connected with Stew's. Then they went foggy and gray. Stew shook his head and took a seat next to him. Suzuki's head tilted over and fell against Stew's shoulder. "You know you're my best friend," Stew said. "As long as I've known you. Nothing's ever going to change that, but you're not pulling your weight right now. You're sitting on your ass like a fucking baby, and you can't be sitting here like that. Not now, not ever."

Stew took Suzuki's hand in his massive one. It was like a giant holding the hands of a child. "You need to get up, Suzuki," Stew whispered through his tears. "We need you to get up."

Suzuki looked at Stew. His stare should have implied he understood what was going on, but that was not true. There was nothing behind his stare. The wound in his chest had healed physically, but his body was still trying to make sense of how close he had been to death. He wished he could explain that to Stew, but his mouth wouldn't work. No matter how hard he tried to speak. All he could really focus on was the song he heard playing in the back of his head. The sweet voice. The voice he now knew was Sandy's.

If death was so simple to slip into, why weren't other dimensions? Wasn't that what death was? José had died and gone onto an entirely different plane of existence, one that could still interact with the living world. Sandy had disappeared within seconds. Diana had brought back a god to reside within her body. Only minutes ago, he had almost died and slipped into that same realm. What was to keep him from doing it while living?

Suzuki smiled at Stew and closed his eyes. He concentrated on the singing, on the voice he knew and understood.

He felt his body grow weak and frail and break away.

Suzuki opened his eyes, and he was no longer in the cavern.

The room he was in was familiar, but at first he did not know why. As he settled into the new situation, he realized it was familiar simply because it was normal. It was someone's bedroom. Someone from Earth. He hadn't realized how long it had been since he'd seen the room of someone who was like him, back before he had been drafted into Middang3ard.

The song was still present, but it was clearer than before. Suzuki felt like he should get up and follow the song. The voice was pleasant. And he didn't want to be sitting in someone's bedroom. There were clothes strewn about. Underwear that made him feel uncomfortable. It was like he had just walked into someone else's life. So, he stood and went after the voice.

Suzuki walked out of the room and down the hallway. The walls were covered in pictures. Suzuki felt like he knew the people in the pictures, but he couldn't place any of their faces. He stopped and looked at one. It was a photograph of a child. She stared back at him, and he thought he saw her blink, but he wasn't sure. Either way, the song was clearer out in the hallway. It sounded as if it were coming from downstairs. He went toward it.

From the stairs, Suzuki crossed the living room and went into the kitchen. A young girl was sitting at a table, singing softly. Suzuki took a seat across from the child. The child was playing chess against herself. The pieces were black and white, but a kind of black and white Suzuki had never seen before. It was almost like the pieces were radiating black and white energy. The child did not pay any attention to Suzuki.

"Glad to see you finally made it," a voice said.

Suzuki turned around to see Sandy.

She wasn't wearing her MERC attire, but a baggy sweat suit instead. Her hair was pulled up in a messy bun, and she looked tired. She crossed the room, poured herself a cup of coffee, and sat down next to Suzuki. "Do you want any?" she asked.

A cup of coffee appeared in front of him. "Uh, yeah, I guess so," he said.

"I've been waiting for you to get here for so long."

Suzuki sipped his coffee and stared at Sandy.

He was confused. He still didn't know where he was, or what exactly was happening.

All he could remember was closing his eyes and trying to find the source of the song that had been playing in his head. He remembered a sharp pain in his chest and the feeling of coldness spreading across his body. But that coldness had disappeared and had been filled with something warm. And the feeling he should not have gone after the voice. Now, it didn't seem like that big of a deal. "Sandy, where are we?" Suzuki finally asked.

Sandy ran her hair through the young girl's hair. At that moment, Suzuki understood the young child was Sandy, albeit, a different version than the Sandy Suzuki knew. The child had a long scar running from the crown of her head down to her chin. "We're in me," Sandy said. "I think. I'm still trying to figure this place out, but I think this is my mind. Or something like that. Maybe the mind of all of me."

"Why am I here?"

"Because I was calling you."

The child version of Sandy moved her black chess piece. She stared at the board with an eerie amount of focus. Then a white piece moved, the rook. It took her pawn, and the child pouted as she crossed her hands.

Suzuki stared at the board. He didn't know why, but he was obsessed with the game. There were patterns he could see, moves the child version of Sandy didn't seem to make out. Even though she had just lost a pawn and the white rook was on the prowl, she was still winning the game. She did not seem like she knew. "Why were you calling me?" Suzuki asked.

Sandy stirred her coffee with her finger. "I've been hiding in here," she explained. "José didn't quite tell me all I was supposed to expect. Diana told me, but it was hard to understand. Very hard to understand until I got here."

"And here is the place between realms. The chaos the Dark One lives in?"

"Yeah. So, I built this place. To hide from him."

Sandy looked up at Suzuki and her face changed. It was subtle but all-encompassing. Her hair was now white, and her face was lined with wrinkles. She sighed and sipped her coffee. "I feel like I've been here for my entire life," she whispered, her voice sounding frail and broken.

Suzuki reached across the table and took Sandy's hand. He didn't know why, but it felt like the right thing to do.

Sandy looked up at Suzuki and smiled the way a grand-mother does at a child. "What are you doing here?" Suzuki asked. He felt like he already knew the answer but had forgotten along the way.

Sandy leaned over and moved one of the chess pieces. Instantly, the black rook moved forward and took another pawn. "Looking for the Dark One's name." Sandy sighed. "It's been exhausting. This entire place is him. That's why I built myself someplace to rest. Me and my others. But we can't find it. His name, I mean. No matter how many of us are looking. But it's because this is all him. How the fuck do you name an entire reality?"

"What do you mean, an entire reality?"

"The Dark One doesn't reside in the place between realms. I don't know when he did it or how it happened, but he *is* the place between realms. He's this entire universe. At first, I thought the place was built on all the unspoken things, all the places that reside in us that we don't know about. And maybe it was at first. That's what it felt like, at least. But the longer I've been here, the more it feels like that's a lie. It's all him, and maybe he's seeping into all of us..."

Sandy's face returned to normal. She sighed again, sounding as if her soul were escaping through her gritted teeth. "I just wanted to see you, Suz," Sandy said. "All of you. But I couldn't get Diana to come back here, and Beth would have been torn apart. She doesn't have a very good handle on magic, if you haven't noticed."

Suzuki laughed, and his laughter broke into a thousand pieces that floated up and contorted into different versions of himself that hung on the wall and scurried away. "Yeah, I've noticed," Suzuki said after he gathered himself again.

"And Stew, God, I want to see Stew so bad. I've seen a

million of him live and die, fight and breathe. I've talked to some of them. But none of them are my Stew. And I miss him so much. I'm afraid I'm never going to see him again. Not the way I want to. It's this fucking place, this fucking name. I can't figure out how I'm going to find it."

Suddenly, everything clicked. Suzuki could see all the Sandys standing in the room, pacing and talking to each other. They all looked to be going out of their minds with frustration. Old versions of Sandy and young versions. Sandys who were missing limbs, Sandys who glowed with an upsetting bright light. Some of them were taking notes. Others were writing on the walls.

It was madness, every Sandy trapped in a small routine of insanity.

Suzuki reached over and moved the chessboard to face him. The child Sandy's eyes went wide, and she looked as if she were going to cry. Suzuki did the only thing he could think of; he scooped the child into his lap and kissed her on the forehead. He pointed to the chessboard and he felt he should say something, but he knew his words would carry no meaning in this place, not the kind of meaning he wished for.

Instead, Suzuki moved a pawn forward and pressed his finger to his lips so no one would speak.

The black rook moved again, taking Sandy's pawn. Suzuki moved another pawn. The rook pounced once more. Suzuki gave away three more of his pawns as both Sandys watched, their eyes wide with horror and their lips trembling.

One more of Sandy's pawns disappeared. It was the last one Suzuki needed. He grabbed his queen and moved her across the table in a classic move he had seen Bobby Fisher perform. His queen waltzed over the board and took the black king.

Suzuki stood up and drank a little more of his coffee. He felt his back and stomach expanding and looked over his shoulder, only to see thousands of Suzukis laughing and congratulating each other. He turned back to the Sandy in front of him. "You got this, Sandy," he said. "You fucking got this."

Sandy was crying, her head buried in her palm. "Thank you so much, Suz," she said. "I'll be back soon. Be safe."

"You too."

And then Suzuki opened his eyes.

Suzuki was strapped to Stew's back when he woke up. At first, he tried to move, but the bindings were too tight. Then the flood of memories came back, and he understood what had happened. "Hey, Stew, I'm awake," he said.

Stew was holding onto a rope, scaling the side of the cavern wall. He kicked off the wall and pulled his sword from its sheath. "Not now, dude!" Stew shouted.

It didn't take long for Suzuki to see the reason. The creature they had seen earlier was running up the side of the cavern wall after Stew. Suzuki looked up and could see Stew was close to the summit of the wall. He wished he could call his axe to him, but his hands were bound too tightly.

Stew scrambled up the rope as the creature clawed up the wall of rock, its mouth slack and open as it screeched, its arms stretching so it could grasp the rock. It was a thing of nightmares and Suzuki almost screamed, seeing the creature approaching so fast and not having a way to defend himself. Stew was very aware of the threat, though, and threw his sword at the creature, nailing it in the chest. Then he turned back to his rope and leapt up the side of the wall, landing on the edge of the cliff.

Beth reached out and grabbed Stew and pulled him to safety. Then she leaned over, disconnected the rope from the harpoon gun, and took off running. Stew was right behind her, unhooking Suzuki from his back and stopping for a moment to undo his bindings.

Suzuki hit the ground and got to his feet, taking off after Stew. There was more light on this side of the cavern, but Suzuki did not stop to think why. He was trying to figure out the best way to take care of the monster at their heels. The creature was too fast for a full-on fight. It might have had the advantage while the Mundanes were tied to a rope, but that seemed like too strong a gamble to make at the moment. If the creature was still pursuing, it meant it felt comfortable enough with its own strength to keep the fight going. It could still have the upper hand.

The rest of the Mundanes had gathered up ahead and were preparing to make their stand. It didn't take long for Stew, Beth, and Suzuki to meet them.

Diana was standing, wand in hand, and at her side, Chip's plasma cannons were ready.

Suzuki skidded next to them as he turned and called his axe. "It's too fast," Suzuki shouted. "Even with all five of us!"

Beth drew her short bow and aimed in the darkness. "Yeah, and what do you propose we do?" she asked.

"Diana, bless Stew with a protection spell."

Diana waved her wand, and a blue aura appeared over Stew's body.

Suzuki grabbed Stew's shoulder. "Look out there with your HUD and tell me where you're at!"

Stew flipped down his HUD and stared into the dimly light cavern. "Sixty percent chance of success," he replied.

"Perfect. Leroy this shit right now!"

Stew smiled as he grabbed another of his swords. "Are you serious?" he asked.

"Hell-fucking-yeah."

"*LEROY JENKINS!*"

Stew went running into the darkness toward the creature just as it pounced into the light. The creature hit Stew in the chest and they fell to the ground, Stew struggling to get the monster under him. The creature's tail slashed and flicked about as its arms and jaw stretched out. Acid dripped onto Stew, but the protection barrier held.

Suzuki pointed his axe at the creature. "Stew's tanking! Everyone on Stew, and we kill this fucking thing! Find its weak points, and we take care of this!"

The Mundanes wasted no time. They ran toward the creature Stew had managed to put into a headlock. Diana cast a lightning bolt from her wand as Beth leapt, firing arrow after arrow while Chip darted forward, taking her time lining up a shot and firing, hot plasma flying through the air.

The creature couldn't escape Stew's grasp, and it got hit with everything, Stew along with the beast. He screamed in pain as the creature screeched. When the smoke cleared, Stew held the dead creature's body, cradling it as if it were a child.

Suzuki reached down and helped Stew to his feet. "You okay?" Suzuki asked.

Stew looked down at his chest. He was covered in scratches, but most of them were from the friendly fire of the Mundanes. "Yeah, I'm good," Stew replied.

"I figured we got fucked up so badly before because we were out of our element. Whatever that thing is, it works on surprise. And it stuck to climbing through the walls as well. It's not a fighter. It was an opportunist. The only thing we had to worry about was that acid. Which is why it's lucky we have such a good fucking tank, something you need to remember. We need you to tank because no one does it like you. You got it?"

Stew smiled as he wiped the blood off his chest. "Hell-fucking-yeah."

"Good job, Mundanes. And thanks for keeping me alive. Now, let's figure out what the fuck is going on here."

14

The Mundanes were filled with a renewed sense of purpose as they approached the facility ahead. Suzuki thought it was good he had managed to pull off a pep talk to bolster the party's morale because what he saw as the Mundanes closed on the facility would have broken anyone's spirit.

There was nothing particularly off about the facility, but it was much different from what Suzuki had expected, seeing it across the chasm. For one, the facility was much larger. Now that he was closer, Suzuki could see it was the size of a few city blocks. Its height and width had been diminished by the gray mists that hovered over the chasm.

The style of the facility was obviously military, just as Beth had said, but there weren't any noticeable sigils or flags or anything of that sort. It looked as if it had been purchased from the military and then scrubbed clean of anything that remotely reminded one of the military's authority.

The closer the Mundanes got, the easier it was to pick out distinct aspects of the facility that stood in the face of reason.

The first one that stood out to Suzuki was that this facility was deep underground. If the dinosaurs they had fought had come from here, how would they have gotten up to the surface? The path the Mundanes had taken was difficult despite how small they were. There was no way a T-rex was going to fit through those spaces.

The second thing that stood out was the lights. Stadium lights were placed all over, and they shone with an intense brilliance that reminded Suzuki of the first time he and his dad had gone to a baseball game. There were also lights on inside the facility, which made no sense because the place was obviously abandoned.

Who the hell was paying the light bill?

Suzuki sighed as they walked up to the main mechanical door. He felt like he was in a bad science fiction movie, one that wasn't plotted well and probably had spent the entire budget on monsters.

Stew reached out to open the front door when Beth grabbed his hand. "Hold on," Beth said. "We should check the perimeter."

Suzuki thought it was a good idea. They still weren't certain about how large the place was, and they had no idea what was around them. This would at least give them an idea of whether or not there was a chance of an ambush or something. "Good idea," Suzuki admitted.

"It's army shit. Old habits die pretty hard."

"All right, we're going to split into teams. Me and Chip will take the left, and Stew, Diana, and Beth are going to take the right. We will scope out the entire building from the outside, meet up in the middle, and go from there."

Diana cleared her throat, her glasses catching the light and giving the illusion that her eyes were glowing. "Actually, I think it would be better to go with you, Suzuki," Diana suggested. "More firepower, you know?"

Suzuki didn't really care and shrugged his shoulders as he nodded. "Sure, works for me," he said. "Ready?"

The party broke apart, the MERCs banding together as Suzuki and Diana had suggested. Diana and Suzuki went down the left, stepping over industrial size piping that plugged into the side of the cavern. As Suzuki and Diana tried to find the easiest way to approach exploring the area, Diana cleared her throat and stepped closer to Suzuki. "I need to talk to you," Diana whispered. "You went to the place between realms, didn't you? While your chest was healing."

Suzuki watched Diana. For some reason he couldn't put his finger on, he didn't trust her. He had no reason to mistrust her before and, even now, he still didn't have one. But there was something off that made Suzuki wonder what it was Diana was thinking. "Yeah, I did," Suzuki finally admitted. "What about it?"

"It's interesting. Very interesting. Usually, the only way between the realms is through magic. Mostly very powerful magic users. Myself. Sandy, you know what I mean. But you? You don't use magic much. You don't seem to have a knack for it. So I'm interested to know how you got there."

"Don't know. I just closed my eyes and kinda slipped into it. Sandy said something about calling me, but I couldn't make much sense of anything I saw in there. I've been thinking about it since I got back, but nothing clicks."

"That's how things are in there. All you have is the knowledge of the immediate. It is very difficult to bring anything back."

"So, you don't want to know what I saw?"

"No, I don't care. I assume you got in contact with Sandy. Until Sandy comes back, none of it matters, though."

Suzuki stepped over another pipe. There were more and more of them feeding into the side of the building. The longer Suzuki and Diana walked, the more apparent it was that the place was huge. Suzuki wondered where the pipes were coming from, where they went, and what purpose they had. There were far too many for it to be an aesthetic. What could the facility need pumped in?

Diana was right behind him, taking a bit more time jumping over the pipes. "How did Sandy seem?" she asked.

Suzuki looked over his shoulder. He understood why he hadn't trusted Diana earlier. Diana was worried about Sandy but didn't know how to express it. That's why she had been acting so weird. There were probably feelings Diana hadn't tried to explain for some time. The one that was apparent now was her love of Sandy. Diana's face looked hollowed out in the darkness as if something had sucked out all of her life. Her skin was sallow and her face gaunt as she chewed her bottom lip.

Suzuki took Diana's hand for a moment. "She looked tired," he answered. "She looked very tired. But she also looked like she knew what she was getting herself into, and like she could handle herself."

Diana relaxed a little bit, the wrinkles going out of her face, the blue cracks in her skin shining less brightly as if a volatile reaction with her had disappeared. "That's good to know. I'm glad you got in touch with her. It's been difficult with everything going on, but I'm glad you got in touch with her."

Suzuki's HUD crackled, and Beth's voice came through. "Hey, are you guys done fucking around?" she asked. "We got something important over here. You're going to want to see it. Fast."

Diana and Suzuki exchanged glances, uncertain of what to expect.

The rest of the Mundanes were on the other side of the facility. They weren't even close to the halfway point. Suzuki and Diana had to backtrack to the front and then work their way through that way. It was apparent the facility was much larger than any of them could comprehend, although it looked regular-sized. There was no doubt magic at play. It took a little under twenty minutes to find where the rest of the Mundanes were. No one bothered to take notice of Diana and Suzuki. They were staring straight ahead, slightly downward. As Suzuki got closer, he could see what had grasped their attention.

What Suzuki saw was something akin to a garden. It was an empty space quite different from the rest of the pipe-covered area around the building. It looked as if someone had intentionally cut away a bit of space away from the rest of the facility for this project. In the area were hundreds of the black sprouts. They were not the small things Suzuki had seen before. These pods were the size of a small dog and stretched toward the sky like a row of fingers. Other than the size, the other major distinction between these sprouts and the others was that a clear, thick liquid was oozing out of the tops of the flowers.

All the sprouts were closed, not unlike the first batch Suzuki had seen when he first got into the cave. Still, the area was filled with that syrupy sweet smell. It was so strong it made Suzuki's head swim, as if he had been baptized in the scent. He was feeling dizzy. He wanted to sit down, to try to gather his thoughts. Suzuki wondered if the rest of the Mundanes were being affected so strongly. "Hey, guys, do you...do you feel that?" he asked.

Beth nodded as she stared at the sprouts. "That's why we called you guys over here," she said. "This didn't seem like something to ignore. There is definitely something going on."

Diana crouched in front of one of the smaller sprouts near her. "Very true. Coming across these in the tunnels earlier seemed like a minor inconvenience and seeing them as we've gotten farther into the cave led me to believe they are naturally occurring plants, albeit annoying ones. But this? These make it unlikely. Even if they are naturally occurring, this right here is intentional."

"What do you think they're for?"

Diana scratched her chin and pushed her glasses up. "What do we know so far?" she asked. "Suzuki inhaled a substantial amount of the pollen and coughed up a black substance. It doesn't seem to have had any long term effects on him that we can see. But since Suzuki inhaled that dust, he's experienced the most distortions of reality since we've been here. He was also able to slip into the place between realms easily. The sprouts also seem to react to him. None of us inhaled any dust, and none of those things have happened to us."

Stew watched the sprouts as if he were expecting them to jump out and attack him. "That's not true," Stew countered. "I inhaled a bunch of that dust shit too, remember? I was coughing up a lot of shit, but none of it was black like Suzy's. So, what the fuck does that mean?"

Diana shrugged as she left the sprouts. "I don't know. I

need more information. We should check inside and see if we can find anything that explains this," she said.

The Mundanes left the black sprouts and their odd, purple hue and walked back to the front of the facility in silence. Each of them trying to piece together a puzzle without knowing what the final picture was going to look like. All Suzuki knew was whatever was going on was deadly. He wouldn't have been surprised if the sprouts had something to do with why the facility was abandoned. Checking inside the facility was the best idea. They'd already figured out they didn't know shit about what was going on. Might as well start trying to make sense of something.

As Suzuki walked, his chest clenched. It was an odd pain that started in his torso and then moved on to his back, around his spine, between his shoulder blades. He had to stop walking as he grabbed his chest and hacked up a black loogie. The rest of the Mundanes stopped to see if he was okay, but Suzuki kept coughing. There was something large in his throat, and he needed to get it out, or he was not going to be able to breathe. He fell to his knees and finally coughed out a hardened black thing. It fell into his hand, and before he could get a good look at it, Diana had levitated it toward her.

Diana looked at the thing. It reminded Suzuki of an insect's carapace. Diana didn't say anything, though. She just placed it in a vial that she tucked into her robe. "We should see what we can find inside," Diana said as she walked away. The rest of the Mundanes followed her until they arrived at the front door.

The door was locked, and no one was able to pry it open, not even Stew. Finally, Suzuki turned to Chip and asked if she was willing to interface with door. It didn't take long to convince her to give it a try. Suzuki could tell she was excited about using her technological gifts without them backfiring on her.

It took a few seconds for Chip to find the proper bypass protocols, but the door slid open. The Mundanes gasped at what they saw.

The door opened to a dark corridor with a flickering light. The ground was covered in rust-colored stains. There were guns strewn about the floor. Six corpses were pressed against the wall, wearing some kind of uniform Suzuki had never seen before. Their bodies had been ripped open, and entrails lay scattered across the floor. The dead had been there for some time, but the smell of rot still filled Suzuki's nose. "What the hell happened here?" Suzuki asked.

Stew knelt next to one of the bodies. "Looks like someone got knocked the fuck out." Stew laughed. "These guys got the shit tore out of them."

Kinda miss the polite Stew, Suzuki thought.

Beth took a knee next to Stew. She grabbed one of the corpses and looked at its uniform. Then she picked up one of the guns and turned it over, looking for some kind of identifying mark. There was none. "These guys aren't military," Beth finally said. "Or at least not our branch of the military. If there's another shadow military out there trying to fight the Dark One, right now would be the time to let me know about it, vets."

Diana and Chip both shook their heads. "No, there isn't," Diana said. "Years ago, there were multiple armies fighting against the Dark One, but as our losses became too great, we banded together. MERCs are built up of nearly seventeen different armies that had been wiped out. The military is predominately the remnants of a large human military. As far as I know, we are the only people who are fighting the Dark One."

Suzuki had an idea, but he wasn't sure if it was bat-shit crazy. He was already trying to make sense of everything that had been dumped into his head over the last couple of days. "We're the only ones we know about in this plane," Suzuki ventured. "What if there are other realities fighting the Dark One as well?"

The rest of the Mundanes looked at Suzuki as if he was crazy, all but Diana. "All right, dude, it's time you lay off the magic beetles," Stew joked as he clapped Suzuki on the back. "Or stop having so many near-death experiences. I'm not sure that shit is good for your head."

Suzuki laughed to cover up how embarrassed he was. "Yeah, yeah, that's too fucking out there," Suzuki admitted. "We gotta focus on what we can actually see, what's in front of us. And what we have are a handful of people who were butchered. So, let's start there."

The Mundanes walked farther into the facility. The main hallway split up into two separate paths. "Looks like we're splitting up again," Suzuki said. "Beth, Stew, you're with me. How's that sound?"

Stew pumped his fist in the air. "Hell yeah, just like back in the glory days when we didn't know shit and were always almost getting killed," he exclaimed.

Beth rubbed her temples and sighed. "I'm so glad I wasn't around for that clusterfuck."

Suzuki ignored both of them and spoke to Diana and Chip. "We'll stay in contact with our familiars and meet up if we find anything," he said.

Chip and Diana exchanged glances that made Suzuki slightly uncomfortable. He had forgotten the two had known each other so long that they hardly ever needed to speak when it came to planning missions. He could see why it had initially been hard to trust them. "Yeah, we'll make sure to stay talky-talky on the proper channels." Chip chuckled. "Holler if you find anything or feel the need to get extra stabby. Also, try to get Beth to keep using that bow. Maybe take a minute to run through some of her abilities or something. Not like I'm telling you how to do your job, but..." Chip smiled as innocently as she could. "See you guys on the dark side."

The Mundanes split into two groups. Suzuki, Beth, and Stew took the left path, the lights overhead flickering fast enough to look like a strobe light. *Yeah, just like a fucking B-horror movie,* Suzuki thought to himself. He moved to the front of the group and recalled his axe. It didn't come at first, and Suzuki was left awkwardly holding his hand until he could hear the axe ripping through the steel of the wall.

Beth whistled as Suzuki put his axe away. "No matter how many times I see you do that, it never stops being hot," Beth said. "But speaking of axes, I have been wondering. Stew, where do you get all of your weapons? I've never seen you pick one up before, yet you are constantly chucking shit at people."

Stew smiled shrewdly, the way one smiles when they've been sitting on information for a long time. It's unclear whether the person is happy to finally have an audience or if they just want validation for having kept a secret for so long. "Well, it's something I figured out a little while ago," Stew started. "Our weapons only load back into our HUDs if we're holding them or sheath them. If we leave them on the field, they never come back. Well, I found out if you have a default number of weapons and leave them out, your HUD sends an automatic requisition order back to MERC 's main inventory, and they just load a new version of the weapon onto your HUD. You never know how good a weapon it's going to be. Like, I got these throwing daggers once that were enchanted, but you know, you kinda throw throwing daggers."

"So, you're getting free loot boxes?"

"Basically."

"Damn, Stew. That's genius."

The Mundanes turned a corner. This one was better lit but still felt wrong. It was obvious, the farther the Mundanes walked through the facility, that something terrible had happened here. There were no bodies yet, other than the first ones they had seen when they first came into the facility.

Suzuki held his axe up to the light, looking at the enchantments etched into its hilt. "Yeah, Stew, that is pretty smart. Do they know you're doing that?"

Stew's booming voice broke the dread with laughter. "Oh, yeah, of course, dude," he explained. "And it drives everyone fucking crazy, but there's nothing they can do about it. It's not even an inconvenience for them to smith something and pop it out. Honestly, the dwarves said they'd been going nuts because they were so bored until I started giving them work every day. You should have them take a look at some of your shit. Both of you. I mean, they aren't the best with enchantments and shit like that, but they can improve the overall quality within seconds."

Beth drew her daggers and tried to balance one of them on the tips of her fingers. "Maybe I'll stop by and give it a try. At first, I wasn't sure about this whole class switch, but it's actually a lot sicker than I thought. I mean, I hardly use my shield anyways. Feels like I'm casting off dead weight. Also, fuck, it's just nice to have a change. You know, put that whole military thing behind me. Start fresh."

Beth tossed her dagger into the air and caught it. "Also, it's pretty sick learning how to be a sneaky assassin," she continued. "Really fucking sick."

The Mundanes walked past an open door. It was dark inside. Suzuki tilted his head toward the door and asked, "You guys wanna check it out?"

Stew emphatically said yes and Beth agreed as well. As they walked into the room, Suzuki flipped a light switch next to the door frame. The lights flickered to life and illuminated a cafeteria. The cafeteria could have easily held over two hundred people. There were tables and seats everywhere, thrown about as if the people eating had left in a panic. There were plates still on the table, covered with rotten food. Roaches had scattered at the fresh light.

Suzuki stepped farther into the room. He picked up a plate of food. It looked like it had been there for a long time. Long enough to rot but not long enough to turn to ash. Whatever happened had just recently taken place. "What the fuck happened here?" Suzuki wondered aloud.

Beth was walking the length of the room, trying to pick up clues. She pointed to the ventilation system. The vents had been broken, and the sides of the vent had been clawed. "Looks like whatever got through was pretty vicious," Beth said. "Must have been a lot of them for people to have left so fast. Plus, those guards we saw earlier. Whatever they are."

Stew stood underneath the vent, his hand resting on his short sword. "Either a lot of them or something really fucked up," Stew posited.

Suzuki was looking through at the kitchen of the cafeteria. The food had been left, and it smelled disgusting inside. He jumped over the counter to see what else he could find. In the corner of the kitchen, propped up next to the oven, was a body. It was slumped forward, its back to Suzuki. The corpse's back had exploded outward, its intestines trailing down the open wound, its shoulder blades bent outward, much like the angel the Mundanes had come across earlier. Suzuki pulled the corpse away from the stove.

The corpse fell forward. Its face had been chewed off. All that was left was a broken skull and traces of brain matter. "Hey, guys, get over here," Suzuki called.

The other Mundanes came to Suzuki's side. Beth grimaced when she saw the body, but she still knelt beside Suzuki and pulled the body back to lean it against the side of the stove so she could see the damage that had been done. "It's the same as the angel," Beth murmured.

"Yeah, it is. Whatever happened to that guy happened to this dude as well."

"But the other corpse was so much older. What happened to the angel happened a long time ago. This is a week at most. All the corpses. This just happened."

Stew kicked the corpse and groaned with boredom. "Guess it pays to know how long it takes for something to turn to maggots," he said.

"You come across enough slaughtered villages, you start to get an idea of how long ago someone died. And stop being an asshole. Just because they're dead doesn't mean you can treat them like that. This was a person. A fucking living, breathing person. Show some goddamn respect."

Beth turned and stormed off. Stew gave Suzuki a look that said, "Well, someone is overreacting," but Suzuki shook his head. "What did I do?" Stew asked, exasperated.

"Maybe try not treating the dead like they're a stuffed animal your sister left in your room."

"Dude, you know I don't have a little sister."

"Goddamn it, Stew."

As Stew and Suzuki left the kitchen, Suzuki's HUD binged. He hit the side of it and opened his walkie talkie. It was a specific kind of magic the MERCs had worked on years ago for individual MERCs to use their familiars to communicate with each other over short distances. "Heyo, boyo," Chip sang. "Just heard back from the bigwigs about your boy Cameron. Turns out he was onto something. Him getting the boot wasn't quite a unilateral decision. Didn't sit well with most, but he did get axed."

Suzuki thanked Chip and hung up his HUD. *Great,* he thought. *Interplanetary aliens and a big bad who might be a whole fucking dimension. Fucking wonderful.*

The Mundanes continued to explore the facility. It was even larger inside than it looked from outside. Obviously magical. Suzuki hoped it would still be easy to navigate. He had heard rumors from other MERCs about places that were cursed so they would stretch on forever in hopes of confounding whoever had broken in. Hopefully, this wasn't the case. It could have been a spell that was meant to benefit the people who lived and worked there. More space for work without having to continue to build sections.

As the Mundanes continued to walk through the abandoned areas, they stopped to look through most of the rooms they passed. There were barracks that still had fresh linens, and a few smaller kitchens. A mess hall had three dead bodies, each of them with their backs popped open like the angels they had seen before. They spent the most time in what looked like a computer room for the folk who lived there to be able to communicate back home. There were three corpses in there, their bodies ripped open, a pair of feet hanging from the ceiling in a purple mucous membrane.

Stew walked under the membrane, took out his axe, and cut away at it until the feet fell. He held up his axe for Suzuki and Beth to see. "What the fuck is this shit?" he asked, his face turned up in the universal scowl of disgust.

Suzuki didn't want to take a good look at the mucous. He thought it was beyond revolting, almost like a giant piece of snot, but he knew they had to start trying to piece together the pieces of what happened. When he looked closely at the mucous, he saw it was the same hue of purple as the black sprouts they had seen in the garden outside. It was also the same color as what he had been coughing up.

Probably better not to worry too much about that, Suzuki thought. *But this does not bode well...*

For another hour, they stumbled through the facility, unaware of where they were. Occasionally they texted or called Chip and Diana. It was the same situation. None of them had been able to find something like a directory. But there were bits and information they were slowly uncovering. The facility was definitely some kind of research facility that also doubled as a type of school. Even though the Mundanes had come across guards at the entrance, there were hardly any other armed individuals. Whoever was working here hadn't been prepared for an attack. The odds were they were just scientists. And that narrowed down what the Mundanes were going to be on the lookout for.

Tech was the focus now. Whatever the Mundanes could get their hands on could let them know what they were up against, could help them piece together what happened. Suzuki already had his own ideas. The theory he thought was most likely was that the scientists here were experimenting with the different animals they found on and beneath the island. Whatever they were experimenting on must have gotten out and massacred the workers. Realistically, it might have been the creature they had fought before making it to the facility. That creature had the speed and viciousness to have easily disbanded a facility of unaware scientists. And the creature also had moved far from the facility. All Suzuki needed was proof of what was going on.

It did not take long for the Mundanes to find just that.

After another twenty minutes of wandering around, they took a right turn and found themselves in a long hall. This hall was different than the rest they had come across. The walls were lined with lights and glass windows. As the Mundanes walked past, Suzuki peered inside and could see the rooms were filled with the black and purple sprouts that had been outside. These were even larger, and many of them had opened in the same way Suzuki had seen while he was climbing into the chasm. All around the sprouts was purple grass, growing up even taller than the sprouts. A thick haze floated over all of the plants, almost a purple cloud.

Suzuki stared through the glass as the Beth and Stew looked on with him. "Hm, guess they weren't happy just working outside. Must have thought bringing it in was a good idea."

Beth's face was tight with worry as she tongued her gums. "Suzy, how've you been feeling?" she asked.

Suzuki did a double-take.

He had forgotten he had come into direct contact with the sprouts, but so had Stew, and there didn't seem to be any effect on him. It didn't make sense to start worrying about something he didn't understand. The only real option was to keep moving forward and hope they found something that would help clear up the mystery of what had happened. "I'm fine. We need to keep moving. Come on."

They followed the hall until they arrived at a large steel door. It whooshed open once the Mundanes stood in front of it. They crossed the threshold into a room that made the tech they had seen throughout the facility pale in comparison. The entire room looked to have been made from surgical steel. The surfaces were all stainless and gleamed in a way Suzuki had only ever seen once, in the research facilities of the Dark One's defense rings.

There were multiple desks with computers that were light-years ahead of anything that Suzuki had ever seen on earth. It was impossible to see where the computers began and the desks ended. Next to each computer was a small, cylindrical vat that held a black and purple sprout, but many of the vats had something more than just the sprouts. Looking closely, Suzuki could see what looked like a small squid swimming in the liquid. They were oblong creatures with a row of eyes running down their backs and a mouth that was all tentacles, the water occasionally causing the tentacles to stretch out violently and snag the glass that held the small thing.

Stew knelt in front of one of the vats and tapped the glass. "What the fuck is that thing?" Stew asked. "Looks like calamari."

Suzuki crouched beside Stew and exhaled his irritation. "Calamari is what it's called when squid is prepared, dude," Suzuki lectured. "What you mean is that it looks like a squid."

"Okay, but you understood exactly what I meant."

The swimming creature in the vat spread its tentacles out toward Suzuki. In the middle of the tentacles was something like a mouth, a large open circle rimmed with razor-sharp teeth. At the top of the hole was a hard beak the creature tapped against the glass vat.

Suzuki felt the tapping deep in his chest, and it suddenly became hard to breathe. He tried to catch his breath, but his heart was beating at the same tempo the creature was tapping.

Suzuki clutched his chest and said, "I need to go sit down." He walked away from the vats surrounding the computers, looking for a place to sit down that was not near any of the creatures. As he went farther into the room, his heart stopped racing, and it became easier to breathe. He finally found a seat in front of one of the larger computers, one that looked like something out of a time capsule-a hulking beast of machinery that was operated by punch cards and knobs.

Beside the antiquated piece of technology was a small datapad. Suzuki took a seat and grabbed the datapad.

The datapad had no password, and Suzuki started scrolling through the different options. Apparently, it was a collection of research materials tied to the facility. "Hey, dudes, get over here," Suzuki shouted. "I found something."

Stew and Beth came over to where Suzuki was sitting, and he showed them the pad. Beth scrolled through a few of the folders and options, then passed the pad to Stew, who was less than interested. Stew gave it back to Suzuki. "Looks like it's just a bunch of nerd shit," Stew said.

Suzuki snatched the pad from Stew. "If you haven't noticed, this whole place is a bunch of nerd shit," Suzuki snapped. "If we don't figure this out, we're not going to figure out what happened. Did you guys find anything interesting?"

Beth pointed toward the other side of the room. "Okay,

before any of that, let Chip and Diana know they need to come check this shit out," Beth suggested. "Maybe Chip could interface with some of the shit here and we could find out more answers. I'm not going to lie, everything in that pad looked like bullshit to me. Didn't make any sense."

"All right. Now show me what you guys found."

Beth and Stew led Suzuki across the room to a series of large tables akin to the metallic operating tables Suzuki had seen in the Dark One's defense rings. The difference being instead of the bodies of elves, dwarves, and humans, there was a large collection of tech. None of it looked like anything Suzuki had seen before. The tech on the tables was leagues more advanced than anything Suzuki had seen in the facility so far.

Suzuki picked up one of the pieces of tech. It looked like it was a plasma cannon, not that different from the ones Chip used. There was a connecting piece that looked as if it were meant for shoulder mounting. The cannon itself was not much larger than Suzuki's fist. It looked to be built from the most mercurial metal Suzuki had ever seen. He turned it over in his hand, trying to see how to activate the weapon. There was whirring, and the cannon heated up, firing a hot bolt of plasma at the ground, narrowly missing Suzuki's foot.

Suzuki placed the cannon back on the table as gently as he could.

Stew's eyes nearly popped out of his head as he reached for the cannon. "Okay, I call dibs on this shit!" Stew shouted. "That is so fucking sick. Can you imagine me chopping through an orc while that shit is firing off?"

Beth grabbed the cannon from Stew and put it back on the table. "First off, what makes you think you get first dibs on any of the gear?" Beth asked. "Secondly, we shouldn't be touching any of this shit until Chip and Diana get here. We don't know anything about this tech. We don't know how it works, what it does, or what it could do to us. So, how 'bout you put your fucking boner away and we just see what else we can find."

Stew's face contorted as he pouted strongly enough to give a baby a run for its money. "Whatever, dude," Stew muttered.

It took nearly two hours for Chip and Diana to find the Mundanes.

Suzuki had broadcast a distress signal with his HUD and had been certain there wasn't a strong enough signal for anyone other than Chip and Diana to have seen it. While the Mundanes waited for Chip and Diana, they shared stories from old games they had played back in VR and tales of what they had experienced both in the military and the MERC program.

Many of the tales Beth told were horrifying. The military didn't have any say over the kind of missions they were given.

Unlike MERCs, the military did what they were told.

Most of Beth's missions were some form of search and rescue. Her platoon very rarely found survivors.

Neither Suzuki nor Stew had experienced anything like Beth had. The few times they had come in contact with the ramifications of the Dark One's tyrannical madness, it had shaken them to their core. The most either of them had interacted with the bloody mess of the Dark One's campaign was their attempt at rescuing Beth.

Beth picked at the skin on her arm as she spoke. "I don't want to keep thinking about it," she murmured. "I mean, I'm here with you guys for the first time in forever. And it feels just like back when we were kids. Sounds stupid to say,

'When we were kids,' since that was less than a year ago, but everything feels like so long ago. Some days, I feel so fucking old."

Stew sat in one of the wheeled chairs in front of a computer, bobbing back and forth before spinning around. "Makes sense," Stew said. "I wouldn't want to talk about it either. There's a lot of easier things to talk about. But if you got shit you want to get off your chest, you know we're here for you. All of us are."

There was a loud crackle and a pop, and it felt as if the air had been sucked out of the room for a brief second. When everything returned to normal, Sandy was standing behind Stew, her hand resting on the back of his neck.

Stew whipped around and jumped out of his seat, picking Sandy up in his arms and hugging her so hard she started to cough through her giggling. "Babe!" Stew shouted. "You're back! And you're all in one piece, too!"

Sandy kissed Stew's forehead and pried herself out of his vicelike grip. "Of course, I'm in one piece. Did you think an alternate dimension was going to be enough to stop me?"

"How the hell did you know we were here?"

"I could bore you with all the information about scanning dimensions and signature auras and shit, or I could just let you know I could find you guys. I mean, I'm here, aren't I? Unfortunately, not for very long, though. I felt you three and thought this would be a cool time to check in and let you know I'm not dead. Not even close to it."

Suzuki and Beth stood, and each of them gave Sandy a hug. "I get you back for a minute, and you already bounce out." Beth laughed. "What about all that 'never split the party' bullshit?"

Sandy pushed her hair out of her face. "It still stands. I

didn't split the party. I'm still here with you guys, just in a different sense."

Suzuki was glad to see Sandy, but he knew her mission was draining her. Even if she was putting on a brave front for everyone else, Suzuki had seen what the place between realms was doing to her. "How much longer do you think you're going to be out?" Suzuki asked.

Sandy turned her attention to Suzuki and her face became serious, nearly as worn and tired as it had seemed in the place between realms. "Hopefully not too much longer. Things made more sense when I was in the place, but now everything is a little bit fuzzy," Sandy admitted. "Diana told me that would happen. She said it would take a little bit of time to figure out everything I had experienced. But hopefully, once I figure out what I'm looking for, it won't take too long to decipher it back home. But that's all I came here to say. Just wanted to say hi to you guys while I got a chance."

Sandy leaned over and kissed Stew's forehead. "Okay, I love you, Babe, be safe, all right?"

Stew nodded and hugged Sandy again before the air crackled and sizzled and Sandy disappeared before their eyes.

Suzuki hadn't seen Fred and wished he'd had a chance to ask about the imp... but it all happened too fast.

Beth sat down in one of the chairs and pushed herself back so she glided across the room and smashed into Suzuki. "Convenient little meetup, right?" Beth asked.

Suzuki pushed Beth away, but she just pushed her chair back into Suzuki. "Yeah," Suzuki said. "Nice of her to check in. I was pretty fucking worried about her."

"Yeah, I think all of us are."

There was a crash outside of the room and the Mundanes

jumped up, weapons drawn, ready to fight whatever was causing the commotion.

Chip stumbled into the room, practically tripping over her own feet as Diana followed behind her, moving with her signature grace and poise. "Sorry," Chip muttered as she walked farther into the room toward the tech that was laying on the table.

Suzuki stood up and walked over to the table as well. "Did you guys find anything?" he asked.

"Other than a bunch of dead bodies? Nope. Nothing. Found some corpses reminiscent of the big ol' angel we found hanging round out in the wilds."

"Yeah, we found some of those as well. Looks like something ripped its way out of their back."

"That would be Diana's theory as well, but we can talk science and junk after we take a look at the nice new shiny things. Any of it fun?"

Suzuki picked up what looked like an SD upgrade. "Don't know yet," Suzuki said. "We were waiting for you. Figured you could give a better idea of what any of this is before we start grabbing on stuff. Never know what might blow up in our faces."

Chip leaned over the table. "Aye aye," she murmured. "Well, might as well get cracking." She grabbed the shoulder mount Stew had been trying to claim earlier. "This one looks pretty much on the nose, but let's find out a little bit more."

Chip's fingers broke apart, and the tips converted to cables and wires that snaked across the shoulder cannon, finding a port to dock with. Chip's eyes rolled back and turned white as binary code flashed across them. Then her eyes popped back to normal, and she handed it to Stew. "Okay, so here's some good news and some utterly trash news," she started. "This is beyond a shadow of a doubt Dark One tech. His little grubby prints are all over it, which means this facility was his. Buuuuuuut, looks like the tech is coded differently than what we've seen before. It's just simple shit—plug and wear. Doesn't have any of the odd techno crap like what's going on in me body."

Stew grabbed the shoulder cannon. "Wait, which one of those is good news and which is bad news?"

Stew struggled to wrap the shoulder cannon on, and Beth walked behind him to help. She grabbed the strap and adjusted it so the cannon didn't wiggle back and forth. "God, I miss when Sandy was here to shut you up." She groaned. "Maybe we should take you back to the lake and get more leeches."

As Beth walked away, Stew stuck his tongue out at her. Then he yelped. The cannon had grown what looked like six legs. They stretched out and clamped hard into Stew's skin. "What the fuck is this?" Stew shouted as the cannon adjusted its height and then scanned the room.

Chip tapped the cannon with one of Beth's arrows and then pretended to hide behind Beth. "Neural uplink," she replied. "You know, so you can think and shoot."

Beth was looking at the different items on the table. "Yeah, that's a great idea. Let Stew shoot at things he's thinking about. If he's even thinking."

Chip pushed past Beth and grabbed one of the simple SD cards. She tossed it in the air and pulled down her HUD. "All right, looks like we got something pretty simple here," she said as she tossed it to Diana. "Light spectrum upgrade. I believe you could get creative with this."

Diana turned the card over in her hand. "Huh. I could probably find a use for it. Thanks."

"Figured the kids could have the fun stuff. Like you need any more upgrades. Fucking overpowered god. If this was a book, both you and Sandy would be getting nerfed real soon."

"I'd prefer to take upgrades you perceive as being useless over having my powers reduced."

Chip picked up what looked like two box cutters and an SD card lying next to them. She tossed them to Beth. "I'm pretty sure you'll like the card, but I don't know about the little metal things."

Beth held the box-cutter-shaped objects. Two small cable tendrils stretched out and pierced her wrists. "Fuck, that shit *hurts*," Beth gasped. Beth held out the box cutters and two energy beams shot out, vibrating loudly as they took the shape of daggers. The energy beam pulsed bright red and looked unstable from extending, but regardless, they maintained their shape. "Oh, fuck yeah, lightsaber daggers. That's so fucking sick. What about the SD?"

Chip motioned for Beth to pull down her HUD, which Beth did. Chip pulled out her soldering iron, her hands breaking apart into a variety of other tools, grabbed the SD card, and got to work. After a few seconds, she closed Beth's HUD and said, "All right, give it a go."

"What does it do?"

"Just access your 'new upgrade' menu. Don't want to wank on the surprise."

Beth did as she was told and found the menu. She hit new upgrade and shimmered out of existence. Where she stood emitted an odd light spectrum distortion. If Suzuki stared closely enough, he could see what looked like ripples in the air. "Holy fucking shit, am I invisible?" Beth shouted.

"Works top-notch with the new class, don't it?"

"You're damn fucking right, it does."

Beth shimmered back into sight. "I am going to be such a sick assassin," she exclaimed.

Suzuki looked on the table. "Too many choices, too many choices," he said. "What are you gonna pick, Chip?"

Chip waved away Suzuki's question as she hopped up on the table. "Oh, I'm done with upgrades like this," Chip said. "Been rolling what you said around in my skull for a bit. Figure you're right about interacting with Dark Tech, so I got a proposition for ya. We hook me up to one of these computers, we figure out what happened here, and I give myself a booming upgrade?"

Suzuki liked that Chip was ready to take a risk. More than that, he was happy to see Chip excited to take the risk, and looking forward to pushing herself a little further and seeing what she was capable of. "I think it's a good idea. We'll be on call to shut you down if anything happens," Suzuki said. "Do you have a kill switch or something?"

"From what I've been told, there's a few. Only one I'm comfortable with you fuckers knowing about is in the middle of my throat. Gotta chop my head off, but you hit that, and I go dead."

"Chopping your head off won't kill you."

"Convenient, ain't it? Now show me them computers."

"All right, let's get you hooked up."

The Mundanes went back to where Suzuki found the datapad and the supercomputer. Suzuki handed the datapad to Chip and said, "All right, this is all we've been able to find. None of the computers seem to work, and I have no idea how to do a punch card system or what they would even have on there that was relevant. But there's some info on the datapad. I figured that would be a good place to start, right?"

Chip took the datapad and looked at it for a moment before turning her attention to the supercomputer. "You know, they used these back in the day, at the military bases. The old tech makes it easier to store secrets. You don't have people trying to hack them as much because, you know, they're not fun. There's probably some really choice shit in there. All right, stand back fleshy mortals, I'm going to get deep in there."

Chip raised her arms, and her skin started to separate as if she were built of multiple sheets. From underneath, dozens of tendril-like cables came shooting out, some of them connecting with the datapad Chip held in her hands and then others connecting with the supercomputer, pulling panels away, inserting themselves into punch cards as Chip leaned back, forming a seat out of the cables coming from her back. "And now we get all that sweet knowledge juice," Chip murmured as her eyes rolled back and displayed binary code.

The entire room hummed with the sound of electricity. Whatever Chip was doing was sucking up all the power. Suddenly, Chip's cables withdrew, and she fell on her ass. She handed Suzuki the datapad and said, "You're not going to like this. Not one fucking bit."

Chip waved her hand as her eyes went white and the room went dark.

Suzuki grabbed Chip, fearing she had been taken over by the Dark One's system. "Chip, what the hell are you doing?" Suzuki shouted.

"Don't worry, it's still me, but there's a lot of bases we got to cover. Way too much for words. Just tune into Chip-o-vision, boys and girls."

Chip turned away from Suzuki and projected a blank

screen. After a couple of seconds, images started to crop up on the screen. Soon, it was obvious they were watching security footage. The footage was from all over the facility and wasn't in any particular order. The whole thing was chaotic, but Suzuki could see what Chip was doing. Slowly, the images started to make more sense. Chip was working backward, trying to organize all the videos into a cohesive story.

"Got it."

There were men climbing up and down the caverns of the volcano. They scraped the black sprouts the Mundanes had grown tired of seeing into small buckets or bags. Once they had gathered enough, they would leave.

Next, Chip showed the inside of the lab. Scientists were crouched over the sprouts. There was something different about these. They weren't like the ones Suzuki had inhaled too much of.

But they were close.

Next to the sprouts was a vial of a black liquid. The liquid swirled violently, as if someone had stirred it a few seconds earlier. Then the liquid ceased being a liquid. It sucked up into itself and grew hard but still somewhat sticky. It attacked its glass prison repeatedly until one of the doctors picked up the vial. They poured the contents of the vial onto the sprout. Instantly, the sprout changed colors to deep black and purple.

The footage jumped again. Scientists were back in the caverns, but this time, instead of taking sprouts, they were replanting their own in the rocky walls.

Again, the footage jumped ahead. Now the scientists were tending the garden of massive sprouts. They were cutting them down and moving them into the laboratory. The scientists brought the sprouts to what looked like a containment area. T-rexes were chained to what looked like feeding troughs in this area. It suddenly dawned on Suzuki why it seemed like the facility had continued to grow as they were walking toward it. A magically accommodating facility would have been necessary when working with dinosaurs of any size.

A scientist placed a large sprout in front of a dinosaur's face. The sprout began to blossom, its petals moving outward as a tube with a large spike on the end danced toward the dinosaur's mouth. The petals latched onto the sides of the T-rex's face and forced the creature's mouth open. The tube slipped into the dinosaur's mouth as it roared with pain.

Next, the Mundanes were watching a T-rex leaned against the wall, moaning in pain. Its body was contorted, and there were black spots of decay growing all over it. The bones in its back were beginning to protrude, looking as if they were ready to break out.

A scientist opened the door to the containment room and stepped inside. He approached the T-rex and started to install an implant into the dinosaur's head. The video became a time-lapse of the decay on the dinosaur disappearing as the tech installed in the dinosaur's head started to spread.

Suzuki was starting to pick up the pieces. "So, they were using some of the components in the sprouts as a catalyst for the tech they were using to modify the dinosaurs?" Suzuki asked aloud.

Diana nodded as she watched the images on the screen. "That is what it seems like," Diana responded. "Whatever experiments the Dark One was up to, he obviously needed more of a biological component. The dinosaurs probably just escaped and ate the scientists here."

Chip raised her hand and pointed at the screen. "There's more," she said.

The scientist were celebrating.

They were in the kitchen, opening bottles of wine, singing with each other. They were ecstatic about what they had accomplished. Two of the scientists near the door were doubled over laughing. One of them pointed to something off-screen, and the other one smiled and laughed. They left together. They walked down the halls of the facility, finally stopping at a door.

One of them pulled out their ID card, and the door slid open.

The scientists stumbled into the room, falling into each other's arms, kissing each other passionately. They sort of waltzed around the room, wrapped in up in each other, until they bumped into one of the feeding troughs in front of the dinosaurs.

Both the feeding trough and the scientist went down on the floor.

As the scientist tried to get to her feet, the sprouts of the petal stretched out and clasped her face. She screamed as the tube forced itself into her mouth. The other scientist tried to pull his friend away from the tube, but he couldn't until the sprout released her.

Finally, the other scientist stood and tried to laugh the situation off.

Weeks later, the scientist who had been attacked was sitting at her computer working. A peer came over and stood by the desk, talking. The scientist looked up. Even from the vantage point of the security camera, the scientist looked sick. Suddenly, the sick scientist leaned forward and grasped the sides of the desk. She started coughing as her back bulged outward. The scientist convulsed and bit through her tongue as the bones in her back burst out of her skin, and her back splitting down the middle, her spine flying onto the ground as her body spasmed.

A creature that looked vaguely human but with elongated arms and legs and liquid black skin rose out of the scientist's back. The creature had no face, only a mouth that appeared like a slit that ran from its forehead to its chin. It stretched open and showed row upon row of teeth, and a tube that rolled out of its mouth like some kind of pollinating agent. Its chest was concave, and the bones of its back were pronounced. Immediately upon exiting the scientist's body, it crouched over the corpse and pulled out intestines, biting into them with a savage hunger.

The other scientist screamed and ran out of the room.

Beth scoffed loudly as the images disappeared. "Okay, so, Mr. Theory of the Day," Beth said to Suzuki, "what the fuck is that?"

Suzuki looked closely at the creature as it stood and hunched over the scientist's face, biting into it with a disgusting crunch. "I have no fucking clue," Suzuki murmured.

The video cut off, and the lights flickered back on. Chip passed Suzuki the datapad. "There's tons of information in there," Chip said. "And an explanation. So, this is the Dark One's jam. We already know that, but it gets freakier. Those sprout things we keep seeing are plants made out of the Dark One's genetic material. He seeded the planet with them years ago. No one knows how long, not even the scientists. But these guys were working on culturing the plants so they could infect creatures with the Dark One's genetic material. Only problem was the shit was too out of control. That's why they were using implants on the dinosaurs, and you just saw what happens when you don't do anything to stop the Dark One's genetic code from rewriting your own."

Stew whistled as he sat down in one of the chairs. "Shit! That's much more extreme than using tech to make everyone listen to you. This guy wants to rewrite all of life with his genetic material?"

Suzuki tapped his knee as he thought about everything Chip had just said. "It makes sense, though," Suzuki finally mused. "You know, this place looking so much like all those Cameron movies. This is all that ancient aliens shit, aliens creating or doctoring creation with their genetic material. Just so happens in our case, the person doing the genetic manipulation is from another dimension. It's really not that far off. I feel like I'm living in a fucking conspiracy theory. So, what's the next step?"

Diana and Chip looked at each other awkwardly. Diana was the one to speak up. "Neither of us knew how to tell you about this earlier," Diana started. "They were mostly just theories, and we wanted to be certain before we said anything, but we're pretty sure you're infected with the Dark One's genetic material from the sprouts."

Stew burst out laughing, slapping his knees. "Uh, dude, you totally would be the one to get the Dark One's jizz down your throat," he screeched.

Diana looked at Stew, and her face was more serious than Suzuki had seen before. "This is not a joke, Stew," Diana chastised. "Did you see what happened in the video? I highly doubt that scientist was the only person to get infected. You have seen what's happened to this facility, so please behave as if you have a shred of decency because Suzuki's life is at risk."

Suzuki felt like the world had just been turned upside-down. There was something growing in him, some kind of monster, and it wanted to rip him open from the inside. If he hadn't already been sitting down, he would have needed to. "Okay, okay," he murmured half to himself, half to the rest of the Mundanes. "One of those...things is in me. We gotta get it out, but how are we going to do that? I don't want to end up like one of those angels."

Chip stepped forward and grabbed the datapad out of Suzuki's hand. "Real easy," Chip said. "The nerds had all sorts of protocols for this type of shit. Even pulled it off a couple of times. We just gotta find the operating and containment room, and I'll cut open your back and pull your little Dark One baby out."

"Are you fucking serious? When the hell did you learn how to do surgery?"

"One of the perks of being powered by a computer. I've already downloaded all their manuals on the surgeries. Also, I doubt cutting you up is going to be any more complicated than a HUD."

"Please stop referring to it as 'cutting me up?'"

"How'd you prefer it?"

"Let's just not talk about it. Where's the containment area?"

Chip pulled up a map and pointed to a blinking light. "Shouldn't take too long before we get there," Chip said. "And the incubation period for these fuckers is nigh eternal, so you'll be good. It's only been a handful of hours. Your back shouldn't pop open for another ten to twelve hours."

Suzuki stood and headed toward the door. He didn't want to waste any more time talking about what was inside him. The faster they got to the operating table, the better he was going to feel. He knew it was in his head, but he could already feel his back itching, could feel something crawling around in him. Thank god it wasn't going to be popping out of his chest. He couldn't imagine the pain of his chest exploding out around him, although it couldn't be that much worse than his back bursting outward. Yeah, the most important thing at the moment was to keep moving and not worry about what was growing within him. "All right, so are you guys ready to get going?" Suzuki asked. "Like, now instead of later?"

Chip ran over to the table where the SD cards were laying and scooped them all up. "Yeah, we should probably get going. But we don't want to forget any of these little guys. They could be a lot of fun later."

The Mundanes exited the room and headed down the hallway. They were silent. It had become a theme of this quest. It seemed like everything they had gotten themselves into was much bigger than they thought it would have been. And it wasn't even what they had gotten themselves into. This was José's big mission. It had become very obvious why José had called their attention to this place.

Even though the facility had been abandoned, it still posed a huge threat. The entire facility, no, the entire volcano, was filled with parasitic plants that were just waiting to inject a host with the Dark One's genetic material. Suzuki didn't even know what that would mean in the long term. Did the new creature have to follow the Dark One's will? Were they an extension of that will? Suzuki didn't want to find out first-hand. He thought this would be something better to observe from afar.

As the Mundanes were walking, Beth came up to Suzuki's side and took his hand in hers. She didn't say anything. Didn't look at him, just squeezed his hand softly and walked closer to him.

That was all Suzuki needed. He knew whatever was coming, he was going to get through it. Beth was here for him. The Mundanes were here for him. This was going to work out. They were going to cut that bit of the Dark One out of him and send it back to hell where it belonged.

15

The Mundanes arrived in the operating room. Much like the rest of the facility, the lights were flickering, and the room had been left in a state of disarray. Scalpels were flung to the ground, there were scrubs resting on overturned chairs, and a computer screen had been left on, its screen staticky and emitting a haunting buzz.

Chip crossed the length of the room and pointed to the operating table. Suzuki did not need to be told twice. He hopped on top of the table and pulled off his shirt. "Let's get this over with," Suzuki said as Chip looked around the room for the tools she needed.

Suzuki hadn't felt anything slightly troubling for most of the time he had been in the facility. That had changed about ten minutes ago while he was on the way to the operating table. His breathing had become constricted. He gasped for breath, trying his best to keep it from being noticed by the rest of the Mundanes. As far as they were concerned, he was in great health and just wanted to get the whole situation over with. That was not the case. His back felt like it was on fire, and he had an intense desire to scratch his shoulders. Every time he reached to scratch, his mind flashed back to the corpses of the scientist, their backs cracked open, their spines laying on the floor next to their slumped bodies.

Beth walked over and pulled a chair up to the operating table. She sat down and took Suzuki's hand in hers. "You keep finding your way into these things," she joked.

Suzuki laughed as he watched Chip busy herself around the operating room. "Yeah, it is becoming a theme," he agreed. "I'm just glad it hasn't been for any actual surgeries, except for this one. But Chip said it's hardly going to be anything."

Beth smiled at Suzuki. Her eyes looked tired and heavy, and the wrinkles in the side of her face were more pronounced. Suzuki suddenly realized just how old Beth looked. Whatever had happened in the prisons of the defense rings had taken a couple of years off Beth's life. Usually, it wasn't noticeable, but when Beth was worried, the stress was evident. The pain in her eyes could not easily be ignored.

Chip returned to the operating table as Stew paced, only stopping when Diana gave him a harsh glare and cleared her throat. Chip pulled up a seat next to Suzuki. She was holding a laser scalpel and wore hospital scrubs and a face mask. "All right, Suz, I'm going to need to you flip over," Chip explained. "I'm going to make a couple of small incisions along your spine, and then we're going to drain the genetic material out. You understand?"

"You know, I had a suspicion you could talk normally."

Chip laughed and pointed the scalpel at Suzuki. "It's called having a bedside manner, ya daft ass. Would you prefer me to have told you I'm gonna slice up your backside all proper and pull out all the nasty Dark One gunk?"

"Actually, you were right. The first one was much better."

"Exactly. Now turn your smart ass over. I got some vivisecting to do."

Suzuki did as he was told and tried to relax as he felt Chip's cold hands on his back, feeling down his spine to his ass crack. It didn't help that the burning sensation in the back of his shoulders was growing more intense. "All right," he heard Chip say, "gonna numb your back and then we're going to get started. You ready?"

Suzuki sucked in his breath and tried not to let his mind wander to the worst possible scenario. Everything was going to be okay. All he had to do was trust Chip was going to do what needed to be done. And that was that. Chip was right. He had only been infected with the Dark One's genetic materials a few hours ago. He had time. "Go for it," Suzuki said.

Then there was the sound of the laser scalpel turning on. It was a mix between a whistle and an electronic hum. Suzuki felt his body instantly tensing up. He hoped he would be able to relax.

All hopes of relaxing disappeared. There was a loud crashing sound outside of the operating room. Then the lights went black. Suzuki jumped up from the table and grabbed his shirt. "What the hell is going on?" he asked.

In the darkness, Stew stumbled over a couple of metal containers, sending them scattering into the dark, making nearly as much noise as whatever had caused the commotion outside. "Sorry," Stew muttered. "I have pretty bad night vision."

Diana flipped down her HUD and accessed her recently received SD upgrade. "Luckily, I don't," she said as she scanned the room. "Looks like everyone here is all accounted for. Let me see what I can find." She went out to the door, forced it open, and poked her head out. "Goddamn it." She sighed. "You know how you've all been wondering quietly where those angels are?"

"Angels? You mean the things that broke out of those guys' backs?"

"Yeah. If we're calling the hosts angels, why not the actual creatures?"

Stew's voice grew a little frantic as he started to pace again. "Wait, are you saying there are actual creatures?"

Beth scoffed as she fingered the switch to her lightsaber daggers. "Are you serious, Stew? Did you really think this was going to be as easy? We found the abandoned station, and Suzuki's DNA is being rewritten by the Dark One's genetic code. Of course, there are going to be monsters we must kill. Isn't that usually your thing?"

Stew's voice was trembling. "I don't know. I think I'm... Fuck, what the hell is this feeling? I feel like I'm going to throw up or something every time I think about what those angels did to those scientists. It...holy shit. I think I'm scared. Is this what being scared feels like?"

Diana walked over to Stew and put her hand on his forehead. "Guess the leeches are still having an effect on you," she suggested. "Interesting. Capable of blocking the Dark One's genetic material, and also causes the subject to experience new emotions they haven't experienced before."

Beth clapped her hands loudly to get Diana's attention. "Okay, we can do the science fair later," she interrupted. "You said those angels are out there? How many are we looking at?"

Diana shrugged as she peeked out of the door. "No fucking clue," Diana admitted. "It looks like a pack of them from the heat signatures, but other than that, I can't get any more information. But I can say there's a good number; that much I'm sure of. If we take into account the number of bodies we've already seen, there are at least six of them."

Beth came over to join Diana at the door. "That's not too bad. Totally doable. We just need to make sure we don't get overrun or taken by surprise. Any bright ideas, Suzy?"

Beth turned to face Suzuki, who was slumped on the operating table, trying to breathe. His temperature had shot up, and he was sweating through the fever. He coughed and blood trickled down his chin. Beth rushed over to Suzuki and tried to hold him up. "Jesus Christ, Suzy, are you okay?" Beth asked.

Suzuki was only able to mutter something softly under his breath. Beth brought her ear close to Suzuki's mouth, but she was not able to make out what he was saying. She turned to Chip, looking for some kind of answer or hope. "You need to operate on him right now," Beth shouted. "Something's happening to him."

Chip pointed at the lights as she knelt next to Suzuki and put her ear to his back. "Can't. The power was cut," she explained. "And all the tech I have is meant for exploding, not for delicacy. Could kill him."

Suzuki coughed again, this time with more blood than the last.

Beth stood up and started walking back and forth, frustrated and shaking her head. "We need to do something," she finally said. "And we need to figure it out fast. Come on, ideas, people. We gotta come up with some fucking ideas; otherwise, we're going to lose Suzy!"

Chip stood next to Diana, both of them looking out into the darkness, trying to gauge what their next move was going to be. Chip's forehead was tight with wrinkles, her tongue sticking out of the side of her mouth as she thought. Diana was the exact opposite, her face calm and emotionless. "You know, we could try that thing you were gabbing about," Chip finally said to Diana. "I left a quick transport at the Smuggle village and dumped one when we first got here. Try for a few leeches?"

Beth inserted herself between Chip and Diana. "Okay, this needs to stop right now," she said. "If we're all going to be Mundanes, you both need to stop with all the secret shit. We all need to know what the fuck is going on or whatever the fuck you two are discussing if it pertains to anyone in this fucking party. Now spill it."

Diana took off her glasses and wiped them. "We are not keeping secrets," Diana explained. "Both of us have advanced knowledge of plant life and tech. We were only exchanging notes and theories, but they are extremely applicable for this specific moment. One of the SD cards Chip found is encoded to be able to summon "aliens.' We think the 'alien' referred to is anything infected with the Dark One's genetic code. We thought it would be interesting to experiment with the nullifying agents of the leech while connecting the SD card to a host HUD. It was meant to be an experiment for when we returned, but at the moment, it seems like it might be the most viable option for keeping Suzuki from becoming an angel."

Chip nodded and held up crossed fingers, barely visible in the dark. "Scouts' honor," Chip chirped. "Just an unpleasant coincidence. Don't know how its gonna turn out, but at this rate, Suzy's guts might be on the outside soon enough. Can't really make the decision for him. Feel like girlfriend duty gives you the right?"

Beth pointed to Stew. "Fuck right, it does," she grumbled.

"Stew, strap Suzy to your back. We gotta start moving." Turning back to Chip, her face fierce with determination, she asked, "All right, you can get us back fast enough?"

Chip's eyes began glowing in the dark as binary started to flash across them. "I'm all plugged into the facility's map. Know this place better than any of the backs of my hands."

"Good. Let's get the fuck out of here and save Suzuki."

The Mundanes gathered around the doorway. Beth gritted her teeth as she mentally prepared herself for the task ahead. Chip tried to look as casual and confident as she could muster, and Diana was serious as always as if the obstacle ahead were nothing to her. Stew was the only person who seemed legitimately disaffected by the situation, Suzuki strapped to his back, his swords drawn. Even with the fear the rest of the Mundanes knew was flowing through his heart, Stew still managed to put on an air of confidence. "All right," Stew said. "You guys ready?"

It had not been said aloud, but the Mundanes knew exactly what it was they were facing and what they had to do. The only way to the portal was straight through the pack of angels who had decimated the facility. There was no telling how strong these creatures were, but they knew the angels had killed every person in the research facility. But those were scientists. They were the Mundanes. They had killed their way through orcs, goblins, trolls, and giants. Each of them had fought through the defense rings and watched dragons die in their wake. A pack of angels who had only ever killed scientists hardly presented a problem. At least, that was what they were telling themselves.

Beth exhaled deeply and said, "All right...for Honor!"

Stew ran the blades of his swords against each other. "For Glory!"

Chip and Diana looked at each other and then at the other Mundanes. "It's for experience, right?" Chip asked. "That's the phrase you dolts keep shouting?"

Beth laughed before she answered. "No, it's XP. We do it for XP."

"Oh, all right. Bollocks. For XP!"

The Mundanes ran out into the dark hallway, guided by Diana, who was using her light spectrum SD to see if anything was in front of them. From what she could see, the pack had diminished. She couldn't tell where the rest of them had gone, but there were fewer ahead than there had been before. But the angels were closer. A fight was brewing. And it would be happening in the dark.

Diana pulled out her wand and pointed it straight ahead. "We're coming up on them!" she shouted as she cast a series of illuminating balls to light the hallway.

In the dim white light cast by the magic balls, the Mundanes laid their eyes upon the angels who stood between them and their freedom. The creatures were just as they had seen in the videos, long lanky beasts with arms that practically dragged on the ground, their heads faceless, just one long slit that opened horizontally, lined with row after row of teeth as if their head was nothing more than a garbage disposal. Their sleek black bodies slid in and out of the shadows, casting a hair-raising screech as they squared up against the Mundanes.

There were only three of them. The Mundanes breathed sighs of relief before realizing Diana had said the pack had dispersed. If there were three standing before them now, how many more might there be, and where were they?

Beth did not have time for these thoughts. The only time she was aware of was the amount of time Suzuki had before one of these things ripped from his back. She slid her new daggers from their sheaths and clicked them on, the light from the blades illuminating the space directly in front of her. The hallway filled with the hum of energy coming off her daggers. "Let's fuck them up," Beth growled as her body slipped into invisibility.

Chip's hands converted to her plasma cannons, and she charged forward alongside the invisible Beth as Stew prepared to charge as well. Diana rested her hand on Stew's shoulder. "Not yet," she said. "Something isn't as it should be. I feel like we're walking into a trap. Stay behind with me."

Stew nodded his agreement and watched as Chip and Beth sprang forward, attacking the group of angels. Beth leapt, taking the first angel by surprise. She slammed her daggers into the creature's head as its body lashed around, trying to fight off its antagonist but only managing to succumb to death. As Beth stood, one of the other angels whipped around and struck her with its tail, sending her flying into the wall before pouncing on her, its tendril tongue snaking out from the deep maw of its cavernous mouth. The mouth moved like it had a mind of its own and that mind only had one goal: to force itself through Beth's skull.

Beth managed to raise her daggers in time and the tube connected with them, sizzling and drawing itself back into the creature's mouth. The angel stood to its full height, towering over Beth, reaching down and lifting her off the ground as if she weighed nothing. The angel slammed Beth into the wall, and Beth screamed as her body went limp with shock.

Chip fired shot after shot at the angel, who managed to easily dodge each of the blasts, sticking close to the shadows, fading from sight for a second, only to pop out to slash at

Chip, who jumped back, continuing to fire, until she bumped into the angel who was behind her, accosting Beth. Chip grabbed the angel by its throat with one hand, and with the other, pressed her cannon hand against its temple. Before she could fire, the angel's tail lashed out at her and slashed her across the face.

The angel dropped Beth and turned to Chip. It bounded on all fours toward her as she backed away toward the wall, firing and firing. The angel dodging each blast just as easily as the other ones. "Goddamn it," Chip roared as she slammed her hands together to form a larger cannon. The hallway grew hot with the plasma heating in her hand as she fired the blast. The angel jumped into the darkness.

The plasma blast ripped through the wall next to Beth. "Be careful where you fucking aim that thing!" Beth shouted.

Chip grabbed Beth and helped her to her feet. "More light, Diana!" Chip shouted.

Diana waved her wand again, and more balls of light went flying toward Chip and Beth. These balls of light were brighter than the first but smaller. The light reflected off the steel of the walls. Diana looked around, noticing the walls were indeed reflecting, but they were black nearest to her and Stew, quite different than the walls near Beth and Chip. "Fucking shit," Diana shouted as she jumped forward. "Stew, they flanked us!"

Stew whipped around just in time to raise his swords as six angels leapt off the walls and onto him. He screamed in pain as one of their tongues pierced his stomach, nearly driving straight into his intestines. Stew grabbed the angel's head, his muscles bulking up instantly, his eyes wide with rage as he ripped it off.

Farther up the hall, Beth dashed toward one of the angels.

She leapt toward it, her daggers raised. The angel slunk back against the wall, turning its back and slashing Beth with its pointed tail. Beth was flung back, her daggers knocked from her hand. She couldn't find them in the hallway, even with the light Diana had provided. Instinctively, she reached for her sword with her right hand. That was when she saw her dagger moving in the dark as if it were tethered to her wrists. "Oh, hell-fucking-yeah!" Beth shouted as she moved both of her hands, confirming her daggers were connected by some unseen chain. She backed against the wall and jerked her hands back so the daggers returned to her. Then she tossed one ahead, and as the angel dodged the attack, she pulled it back as she lunged forward with her other dagger, closing the gap between her and the angel, driving her dagger into its concave chest, whipping the other dagger around so it severed the angel's tail. Dagger still embedded in the angel, she circled it, dragging the dagger through the angel's body until the creature fell, convulsing in its own blood.

Chip was still firing at the angel, who was ducking in and out of the shadows, sidestepping its flailing tail.

Beth launched one of her daggers at the angel and shouted, "You got to get in close, Chip! They can't deal with close-range combat!"

Chip nodded and pulled her hands apart. Her fingertips stretched out and sharpened as she darted forward, slamming into the angel with all of her weight and throwing the creature off-balance. Its tail lashed around, trying to find a target. Chip slammed one of her clawed hands into the creature's throat, and her other hand converted to a cannon. She pressed it to the creature's mouth as its tongue snaked up and tried to impale Chip's head. She fired, and the angel's brains splattered across the wall.

Beth came over and helped Chip back to her feet. They turned around and saw the carnage behind them. Stew was covered in angels, screaming as he backed up against the wall, trying to keep Suzuki safe, Diana casting a smaller ball of fire, unable to cast anything large due to the confines of the hall. Chip grabbed Beth and pointed at the madness in the hall. "Precise shots!" Chip shouted. "We clean it up, you hear?"

Beth drew her short bow and reached for one of her arrows. Her quiver was gone, but she hadn't noticed. She still nocked, and as she drew back her bow, a bolt of pure energy not unlike that which her blades were made out of materialized. "Oh, fuck YEAH!" Beth shouted as she let an arrow fly. The arrow connected with the angel between her and Diana.

Chip fired four shots back to back. They tore down the hallway and scorched two of the angels on top of Stew to ashes. That was all the space Stew needed. He grabbed the angel closest to him, ripped it in two, and then slammed its torso into the other one. "Come on!" Beth shouted.

Stew and Diana ran to catch up with Chip and Beth, who had already turned the opposite direction and were running down the hall. Chip was in front, pulling up the map as she ran through the maze of halls that only seemed to get darker. All the while, the screeching of the angels followed them. It was impossible to tell how many of them there were, but it sounded like dozens.

Beth cast a glance over her shoulder. She could see hundreds of bodies moving in the dark, climbing the walls and ceiling. "Ideas, anyone?" Beth asked.

Stew turned for a second, just enough time to throw one of his swords at an angel who was getting too close. "We could try for the vents," he suggested.

"Are you fucking stupid? Have you never seen a horror movie?"

"No! I don't like being scared!"

Chip fired a shot over her shoulder without looking, taking out two of the angels. It meant nothing, though. There were too many for it to have made a difference. "All right, now is not the time for one of your pitiful nerd-offs! Any ideas? Any *real* ideas!"

Suzuki murmured something in his sleep. "What the hell did he say?" Beth asked.

Stew shook his shoulders around, trying to jostle Suzuki out of sleep. Suzuki murmured again, this time loud enough for Stew to hear. "He said *Backdraft*," Stew said. "What the hell is *Backdraft*?"

Diana laughed, a riotous sound that did not have a place in their dire situation. "Are you all really that young?" she asked as she slowed down and fell to the back of the party. "How far away from your portal are we, Chip?"

"Couple of minutes if we keep sprinting."

"You better run your asses off after this."

Diana stopped in her tracks, then turned around, her wand raised high. Her body started to emanate blue magical energy as she drew a sigil in the air. Then she blew lightly on the sigil, which ignited into a fiery sign. Diana pulled back her wand, then thrust it into the sigil. Flames burst from the sigil, covering the walls, the ceiling, the floor, spreading out like a wildfire, shooting down the hallway in the vacuum created from constraint.

The sound of screeching angels filled the hallway. But the fire was not contained. Most of it went shooting back toward the angels, but like many things in life, the fire could not be contained. Diana turned to run as the flames chased after her and the rest of the Mundanes.

Suzuki muttered, "Such a sick movie..." before drifting back to sleep.

The Mundanes moved as fast as they could, trying to outrun the inferno at their backs. Even with the fire roaring, they could hear the angels screeching. How many of the angels had perished, and how many of them would remain even after the fire? It was hard to say.

Beth pointed ahead, her forehead covered with sweat she had to wipe off just to be able to see. "The portal! I see it," she shouted.

Down the corridor was a shimmering green light. "All right," Chip shouted. "When you get through, hold your breath unless you want to be coughing up your lungs in a second."

The Mundanes pulled out everything they had as the flames licked their asses. They burst through the portal at the last minute, right before they were overtaken by the flames Diana had unleashed. Then there was darkness.

16

Suzuki opened his eyes. There was blinding light, and then he saw he was back in the kitchen with Sandy. She was sipping a cup of tea, and there was one in front of Suzuki. He watched the steam float up to the ceiling where it got caught in the corners, unable to move on.

Sandy blew on her tea.

She smiled pleasantly at Suzuki but didn't say anything. All around them, a thousand Sandy's bustled. Some were cooking. Others were pacing back and forth. Then there were those eating or snacking. One was smoking. And yet there were others who only stood. Staring into space as if they were waiting for an answer to a question long forgotten. "Getting in the habit of stopping by?" Sandy asked.

Suzuki took a sip of tea and winced at the heat. He hadn't realized he could feel pain here. "Uh, this time, I wasn't trying to show up here unannounced."

"Guess you're in the habit of almost dying."

"You know, I feel like out of all of us, I'm the one who ends up nearly dead the most."

"You're accident-prone. Or maybe just unlucky. Or it could be you keep putting yourself out there like you're some kind of goddamn hero."

Suzuki looked down at the tea leaves settling at the bottom of his cup. They looked like they formed a skull. "You're sounding kinda grouchy. Everything okay?"

Sandy sighed and slammed her hands on the table. The table shattered into dozens of pieces, as did the room they were sitting in. Now they were floating through space, both of them sitting in their chairs, planets and stars flashing past them. "I'm just sick of being here." She groaned. "José hasn't been back in, fuck, I don't know, a hundred-something years. I'm so fucking thin, I feel like you could just push your hand through me."

Suzuki reached out over what felt like lightyears and rested his hand on Sandy's shoulder. "Hey, Sandy, it's going to be okay, you're going to get through this."

Sandy threw her arms up like an angry teenager. "I know I'm going to get through it. I already know how it ends. All of this. I just want to go home so I can try to remember."

"Well, how do you get home?"

"I have to wait for everything to die. Every fucking star. Ugh, do you know how fucking tedious it's been? But at least I know, you know?"

"Know what?"

"Know how it all ends. Oh, and I guess you're gonna make it this time. See you in a little bit, dude."

Suzuki felt the stars melt away and a strong tug on his stomach, and then he spilled out into the real world.

Suzuki woke up surrounded by Mundanes. He was in a thatch-roofed hut on a bed of straw. His back hurt, and it felt as if someone had covered him with hot coals. His throat was sore, and when he tried to talk, all that came out was a raspy cough.

Beth leaned over and clapped Suzuki on the back. It looked like it was supposed to be a sign of comfort, but Beth's no-nonsense attitude made Suzuki feel as if she were just trying to help him keep from choking on his own spit. He knew there was something he had missed. There was a block of time he couldn't remember, replaced by what felt like an age with Sandy that he remembered almost crystal clear this time.

Suzuki rubbed his eyes, trying to wipe away the remnants of what he had experienced with Sandy and get the feeling of stardust off his eyelids. "So, who's going to fill me in on what's going on? I'm pretty sure I missed something important."

Stew knelt next to Suzuki, smiling. No matter how annoyed Suzuki was with Stew, he could never stay mad at the guy when he was smiling. No one could. It was like Stew's secret weapon—a disarming smile that also managed to make you feel stronger, make you feel like you were capable of anything. "Dude, you got to stop coming so close to dying," Stew joked. "You're starting to make me feel like a shitty friend for not rescuing you sooner."

"All right, all right. I get it, I get it. Sandy was saying the same fucking thing."

The Mundanes looked at each other. "Did you just see Sandy?" Diana asked.

Suzuki nodded as he tried to stand. Beth gave him her hand, and he pulled himself up with her help. "Yeah, just before I woke up. Why?"

"Sandy's outside. The Smuggles said she's been here for a while, but she won't talk to anyone. She only smiled at us when she saw us. But if you just spoke to her... Anyway, she's here. And we have things to talk about other than Sandy. We have a massive problem on our hands."

"What's new?"

"Chip has been going over—"

"Wait, could you guys please tell me what happened to *me* first? I know you're all getting pretty used to saving my life, but I still want to know some of the details."

Diana started speaking, and Beth held out her hand and cut Diana off. "You got infected with Dark One genes. Almost became an angel. Chip and Diana made some weird leech thing and shoved an SD card in you, and your body absorbed all the material instead of creating an angel. Now you have some of the Dark One's genes fused to yours. Then you didn't die. Got it?"

"Are you fucking kidding me? His genes fused with mine?"

"Something like that, but bonus, apparently you should be able to control anything with his genetic material. Kind of like an angel-caller or something. Sick, right?"

Suzuki pulled off his HUD and opened up the SD slot. He could see the new SD card. It wasn't hard to notice. The card looked like it had been shoved into the slot and had exploded. Black gunk was coming off the card and smoking from the HUD's heat. "This looks super gross," Suzuki muttered.

Beth crossed her arms and sucked on her teeth while she waited for Suzuki's attention. "Are you done having an existential crisis now? We need to brief you."

Suzuki was surprised he wasn't as disgusted as he thought

he was going to be. Over the last couple of weeks, he had gotten used to the idea of his body not being quite what it used to be. The dragon Ashegoreth had blessed him with the boon of dragon's blood back at the Battle of the Defense Rings. Suzuki still didn't know what it meant, but that had been hard enough to wrap his head around. At least he knew the Dark One's genetic material wasn't going to hurt him anymore. And, oddly enough, it also made him feel somewhat connected to his enemy. He had no idea why that was anything but a disturbing idea.

Suzuki placed his HUD back on his head. "All right," he said. "What's the juice?"

Diana stepped forward, pushing up her glasses and giving Beth an annoyed look. "As I was saying, Chip brought along the datapad we found in the facility. While you were recuperating, she went through and discovered more information. Unfortunate information. Apparently, this is not the only facility that is experimenting with the Dark One's genetic material. It is the only facility that went under. There is at least one more, to the east of here, on the adjacent island. It is fully operational and has nearly three times the subjects. The only recorded test subjects are humans. The Dark One must have made them his priority since he was having such issues with controlling humans before. It would be wise to assume there are members of other races there as well."

Suzuki nodded, remembering the different races he had seen under the Dark One's indoctrination at the defense rings. It had sickened him. The orcs weren't even aware they were under mind control. No one did. That was when it had dawned on Suzuki that he was killing people who didn't realize they weren't living anymore. Either way, the Dark One was still robbing people of their lives.

Diana continued speaking. "In accordance with a request from Beth, we've forwarded the information to the military as well as Myrddin. We have yet to hear back from either of them."

Stew was walking back and forth in the small hut, his head nearly touching the top of its ceiling. It was evident he was frustrated. "Honestly, we've been on hold for nearly three fucking hours!" he exploded. "For people trying to figure out how to defeat the Dark One, they sure as hell like to take their time making people wait around for them when we have important information."

"It's not much of a problem coming from Myrddin. This is the way MERC works. We don't have to wait until an official lets us know what we're allowed to do. We see a problem, and we go for it."

Suzuki headed for the door of the hut before turning to face the rest of the Mundanes. "So, we're going after the base, right? Let's get going. First, though, I need to speak to Sandy."

Diana raised her hand to halt Suzuki from leaving. "Just a heads up," Diana started. "She's...a little bit different than when she left."

"How different can she be?"

Suzuki stepped outside the hut. He was instantly answered.

Sandy was sitting in front of a fire, directly across from him. Her skin showed the signs of intense magic use. There were cracks all over her, similar to wrinkles. It gave the look of thinness, of frailty, as if she could be knocked over by a strong wind. Her hair had gone white, and her eyes were glassy, opaque, and white. She smiled when she saw Suzuki. "Oh, Suz," she whispered. "I'm glad you're finally awake."

The rest of the Mundanes came out after Suzuki. Stew

rushed over to Sandy and wrapped her up in his arms. "I'm glad you're finally talking," he said through tears. "How come you didn't say anything to me when you first got here?"

When Stew let Sandy go, she slowly floated back to the ground, her feet lightly touching it as if she could go flying off at any second. "A safety precaution," Sandy explained. "This isn't the first time I've been here, or at least it isn't the same time. It's difficult to explain, but I have stood here many times. This is the first time Suzuki didn't fucking keel over on me."

Diana motioned for the Mundanes to take a seat around the fire. "It's storytime, Sandy," Diana said. "You have a lot to let us know about, no doubt."

Sandy nodded as she crouched in front of the fire. "Too much to explain." She sighed. "I'll start with the easiest one. I'm ninety-nine percent sure I'm your Sandy, the Sandy from this reality. I remember all of you, and it felt right when I got here. But the Dark One came for me, and he obliterated so many different versions of me. Most of the versions of me are dead. For now. Secondly, I can't use magic anymore. I haven't been able to since I got back. I don't know what happened, if I burned myself out or something, but my magic is gone. My connection with my familiar is still here, but it's like I'm running on a dried-out fuse."

At that, Sandy looked down at the wand in her hand. She rolled it over in her palm. Her face looked crushed.

It was difficult to understand Sandy not being able to use magic. Since she had come to Middang3ard, learning magic was almost the only thing Sandy had cared about. And Suzuki had seen she had an amazing knack for it. Everyone had. Diana had even taken Sandy as her protégé. Now Sandy was saying she couldn't even cast a spell. Suzuki was surprised she wasn't doubled over crying.

Diana, who was sitting next to Sandy, took the woman's hand. "I know this must be hard."

Sandy wiped a tear away. It turned to salt in her hand, and she flicked it into the fire. "There is still magic in me. At least, that's what Fred said." At the imp's name, she looked at Suzuki and shook her head.

Suzuki knew what she meant, and nodding solemnly, asked, "Did he die well?"

Sandy nodded. "Heroically, but that's a story for another time. Right now, I need to think. To try to figure this out. I don't understand what's going on at the moment, but I will. More importantly, I found information about the Dark One. A lot of it is difficult to put into words. Everything I saw is still a little confusing, but I know where he came from. You guys remember your Norse mythology, right?"

There was silence amongst the Mundanes. The answer seemed pretty obvious.

"Are you guys fucking kidding me? We're in a realm called Middang3ard, and you didn't even think to give yourselves a refresher course? Some fucking nerds you are. Well, tell me if the name Odin jogs your memory."

The Mundanes collectively mumbled to cover their ignorance. Sandy sighed in irritation. "All right, I'm not going to give you all a fucking lesson in Norse mythology, but I'll explain what I can. Odin is the big god of Norse mythology. But there are like a thousand different versions. And that's just in our reality. Try to imagine how many different versions there are throughout the different realities. One of those Odins came from a reality with three others. The main one, Bolverkr, went insane and consumed the other two, which only fucked his mind up more. He hung himself on the World Tree to gain more knowledge. You know, typical Odin shit. But this time, the World Tree broke reality, and he ended up in the place between realms. That was when he got an idea. He started traveling through the other realms and kidnapping the different Odins. For the last who fucking knows how long, Odin has been crucifying different versions of himself on the World Tree and devouring them. Who knows how many he's eaten, but it's making him stronger, and, obviously, bat-shit crazy. Anyway, now we know his name."

Stew spoke up before anyone else. "What are we supposed to do with his name?" he asked.

Sandy laughed almost maniacally, the laughter of someone who is very aware they are closing in on their edge. "No fucking clue. That was all José told me. Find his name, and that was it. Now that I know his name, I can't use magic, and I'm intimately aware of what it feels like to see yourself die. Remember how into necromancy I used to be? Fuck that shit. I'm never fucking with the dead ever again. Shit is just too confusing."

Suzuki looked at the rest of the Mundanes. He knew he should say something. Everyone already looked beat. It wasn't that they had gone through so much, other than Sandy. It was that they didn't know where they were going. There was usually more structure to their quests, an end goal. Right now, it just felt like they were caught in the wind, following the lead of a dead man who only spoke in riddles.

Truth be told, Suzuki didn't think there was anything to say.

He trusted José.

Even if he didn't understand him.

And he assumed the rest of the Mundanes did as well. "All right, well, let's figure out how we're going to get to this facility. You got the coordinates, Chip?"

Chip nodded that she did.

"Cool. So, what are our options?"

Diana stood and stretched before pointing to the dense jungle. "We should speak to the Smuggles," she suggested. "They tend to be helpful in a pinch. Come on."

Diana led the Mundanes into the jungle. It did not take long to find the Smuggle village, despite its size. It was something akin to their lunchtime, and they had gathered around a small fire and were talking excitedly. When they saw the Mundanes, they grew even more excited. The elder Smuggle ran forward, nearly skipping with joy, exclaiming, "Mundanes, Mundanes! It is good to see you return!"

Suzuki knelt in front of the Smuggle leader and bowed slightly. "We've come to ask a favor of you. We know your magic runs deep through these jungles. We need to get somewhere fast, and we don't know how. Do you have any way to?"

The elder nodded gravely as he scratched his long white beard. Then he snapped his fingers, turned to the blonde female Smuggle, and whispered into her ear. When he returned, he pointed at Sandy. "This one has been outside the village for some time. We could feel her very strongly. She can work with us for your purpose," the elder said. "Bring the skull!"

The other Smuggles ran deeper into the jungle and returned in a couple of minutes. They carried the polished skull of Azrael on their shoulders. "Fearsome creatures," the elder said. "Fast and fearsome."

Sandy stepped forward and picked up the skull. "Yeah, and pretty dead. So what?"

"Not dead for long."

"Ugh, I literally just said I was done with necromancy. Besides, I can't even use magic. What am I supposed to do?"

The elder shook his head as he motioned for Sandy to return the skull to the ground. "The dead do not know magic. The dead know only the dead. You know the dead. Now I will speak the dead tongue to you. Then you will speak the dead. You will speak all the dead. Come. Come."

The elder stood on his tiptoes until Sandy got on her knees and bent over so he could speak into her ear. Her eyes grew wide as the elder spoke. As the elder whispered to Sandy, the cracks in her skin began to fade. Her hair darkened, even darker than it had been before, as did her eyes. Then the elder stepped away and said, "You now have the tongue of the dead. Speak now the dead tongue. Speak now the dead tongue."

Sandy stood straight.

She cleared her throat as if she were going to give a speech.

What came from her mouth was a song.

It was soft and gentle like a breeze, full of warmth and life. And as she sang, muscle and nerve wrapped around the battle cat's skull as bones pulled themselves from the ground all around in the clearing. Bones and skulls rose from the ground, tendon and sinew attached, and skin sprouted as if it were grass, then the fur grew in.

Before the Mundanes stood Azrael and five more battle cats. They were all about the same size as Azrael and just as fierce-looking.

Sandy stepped back and looked at her hands. She shook her head in disbelief. "Guess I'm not out of the game yet. This is going to take some getting used to," she murmured.

Beth approached one of the cats cautiously. As she stepped forward, the cat lowered its head and pounced. Before Beth could attack, the cat had knocked her over. The rest of the Mundanes drew their weapons, ready to attack.

Then they heard Beth laughing.

The battle cat was licking her face with its tongue and purring loudly.

Suzuki couldn't help but laugh as he put away his axe and approached the cat. "Thank fucking God." He petted one of the battle cats. "Such a relief that something doesn't want to kill me."

Stew was already wrestling with one of the cats on the ground. "These are so much better than axe-beaks. So much better!"

Suzuki turned to Diana and Chip. "So, what happened to the facility?" he asked.

Chip laughed as she pointed toward the volcano they had come from. Bright hot red magma was pouring from the tip of the volcano. "We accidentally popped the lid off the fucker." Chip cackled. "Don't worry, we checked with the Smuggles, and they're going to be okay. Apparently, most of the life on the island is immune to lava, even the daft plants. All right, guys, I'm loading all your HUDs with the coordinates. Let's see just how fast these things can go!"

Suzuki grabbed the fur of the battle cat. He wished it had reins or something to make riding easier, but the cat didn't seem to mind the scruff of its neck being pulled. In fact, it was the exact opposite. The cat turned around and slurped Suzuki across the face. "Well, let's fucking hit it!" Suzuki shouted as he pulled the cat in the direction they wanted to go.

The battle cat bounded forward much faster than Suzuki

had expected. He had to grip the cat's fur tightly to keep from flying off the damn thing. The cat was sprinting at a break-neck speed into the jungle, leaping between trees before flinging into the branches for a few minutes, then leaping back to the ground, hardly losing any speed, purring loudly as it ran. Suzuki cast a glance over his shoulder to see how the rest of the Mundanes were doing.

Sandy was atop Azrael, which only made sense. She was close to Suzuki, as were the rest of the Mundanes. Stew was hugging his battle cat tight, a smile as wide as the ocean on his face. The rest of the Mundanes looked to be having just as good of a time. The only Mundane who looked even remotely unaffected was Beth. Her face was sharp and serious. Suzuki wondered what she was thinking about. Then he remembered a trick he had learned while fighting through the defense ring. He could speak with Beth telepathically through the use of their familiars. He concentrated on sending Beth his thoughts. *Hey, Beth*, Suzuki thought. *Are you okay? Is something wrong?*

Beth looked at Suzuki, her concentration broken for a few seconds. "Just worried, is all," Beth said.

"Worried about what?"

"It seems like I keep getting closer to losing you. It kinda freaks me out a little. You know, how easily it could happen."

"That's exactly how I felt. It's fucking terrifying."

"It was different with you. You just heard about what happened. I've watched you just slip away for a few moments twice. Don't do it again, okay?"

Suzuki laughed at the idea he could control whether he was going to die. When he met Beth's face again, he could see she didn't think it was funny. "I promise," Suzuki said. "I'll try not to end up dead."

Beth smiled as she leaned forward and gripped the fur of her cat. "Good. That's all I wanted to hear," she replied.

Stew had caught up to Suzuki. He playfully ran his cat up, and the two cats nipped at each other while Stew and Suzuki laughed. "So, you know what we're up against, right?" Stew asked.

Suzuki reached over and tried to shove Stew off his battle cat. "A research facility filled with angels who want to rip us to shreds? Angels grown from the genetic material of a god? Maybe the end of all reality as we know it? Yeah, I think I have a pretty good idea."

Stew laughed again as he kicked the sides of his cat to speed it up. "Who would have thought we would be trying to save the world from a fucking god, right?"

"Me, obviously. Why do you think I spent so long in VR? That wasn't a fucking hobby."

"Fuck off, dude. Glad you pulled through. Seriously. We were all worried for a minute."

"Dude, what's there to worry about? I got dragon blood and god genes now. I'm set for life."

Stew nodded pensively before leaning forward and shouting, "By the power of Gray Skull!"

A little behind the rest of the Mundanes, Suzuki could hear Sandy shouting, "For the love of fuck, Stew, don't start with that shit!"

The Mundanes rode their battle cats through the jungle, joking and laughing the entire time. It was a good way to take a break from the last few hours. They knew once they got to the facility, they would have to be prepared for whatever came to them. All of them were going to have to be prepared. Really anything could happen.

17

The Mundanes rode east, their battle cats racing as fast as they could through the jungle. As they rode, the jungle petered away until they were in a field. The island was much larger than Suzuki had thought. He hadn't seen many maps of Middang3ard since he had arrived, but when Chip had spoken of an island, he assumed it was a small piece of land. He was surprised to hear it was roughly the size of Hawaii, which made sense. Hawaii was in fact an island.

As the Mundanes crossed the large field of vibrant green grass, Suzuki noticed there was something in the distance to his left. He pointed it out to Beth, who pulled out her spyglass. She said there was a row of people running down the hill. Chip noted it was in their general direction, and it was worth taking a look. There were many different people living on the island, and anywhere there were people, there was a chance the Dark One would accost them.

The Mundanes turned their battle cats in the direction Beth had glassed, and it was not long before the cats were bounding up the hill.

Suzuki jumped off his steed and approached the running folks, who turned out to be redcap goblins. On the surface, they were not much different from their gray cousins. The only discerning factor was they were completely bald and wore red caps, hence the name.

One of the goblins ran up to Suzuki and threw itself at his feet. This was the first time Suzuki had come across a goblin not actively trying to kill him. He wasn't quite certain what to make of the gesture but thought it best for him to say something. "Uh, nice to meet you," he managed.

The goblin threw its arms in the air as it wailed loudly. The rest of the redcaps took notice of the wailing goblin's prostration and crowded around the Mundanes. "Help us!" the goblins screamed.

The goblin who'd first prostrated itself stood up and wiped its face. It was crying profusely. "They are going to kill us," the goblin sobbed. "They've killed so many. The children! They killed the children!"

Beth knelt in front of the crying goblin and looked at it sternly. "Who killed them?" she asked, her voice soft and comforting despite her demeanor.

"The trolls. The Dark One's trolls," the goblin said, pointing toward the horizon.

Beth nodded as she stood. "Guess genetic manipulation isn't the Dark One's only plan," she spat. "He's still out to terrorize everyone in Middang3ard." Beth turned back to the redcap and told it, "We'll take care of them. You all get to safety."

Beth jumped back on her battle cat and pointed toward where the redcap goblin had indicated. "There have to be a lot of them," she said. "If they have this many goblins running. Let's make sure we send the Dark One another message."

She didn't wait for anyone to answer. Beth took off toward where the trolls were said to be. The rest of the Mundanes went after her. They crested the hill, and before them were the trolls—a pack of them, at least twenty.

The troll heading the horde, a large beast of a creature with flowing dreadlocked hair and war paint covering his chest, raised his axe high. His other hand gripped the head of a redcap goblin, and he roared at the sight of the Mundanes. He pointed his axe in their direction, and the charge was on.

The Mundanes ran toward the trolls, Beth leading them, her short bow raised, waiting to get close enough to fire. She stood up, balancing herself on the battle cat and, as the trolls closed in, fired ten quick shots that hit the leader of the horde.

The arrows sank into the troll's body, knocking him off his horse. It was not enough to keep him down, though, and as he stood, he let out another mighty roar. The other trolls rode past him.

Suzuki's battle cat leapt over the first handful of attackers and landed on one of the stragglers. The cat tore into the troll's horse, ripping its head from its neck as Suzuki jumped off the cat, bringing his axe down on the troll's chest. Then he whipped around and sent his axe flying at the nearest troll, hitting it in the back of the head, before calling his axe back to his hand and looking for the next fight.

Beth had also jumped off her cat, which was tearing into whatever it could get its claws on. She pulled out her daggers, and the hum of her lightsaber blades filled the air. She dashed forward, slicing through one of the trolls and ripping his stomach open for his intestines to tumble from. As she turned to look for her next kill, a troll grabbed her by her leather armor and lifted her into the air.

Stew came sailing through the air and tackled the troll. He hadn't even bothered to draw any of his weapons. He had already entered berserker mode, and his muscles were swollen as he increased in size. He grabbed the troll by the neck and tossed him to the ground before pounding his face in.

The trolls started to regroup, their leader rallying them around him. Even with the Mundanes' first kills, the trolls still greatly outnumbered them, and they seemed to know this. They pulled out their shields and rushed the Mundanes.

Diana floated into the air above the attackers, her wand drawn, and cast a shielding spell over the rest of the Mundanes. Once the spell was cast, she whipped her wand around again and a bolt of lightning came hot off its tip, hitting two of the trolls and scorching them.

A troll next to the ones who had just been set aflame ducked and launched his axe at Diana. It hit her in the shoulder, knocking her from the air, and she hit the ground with a heavy thud as Beth leapt toward her, pulling her away from a nearby troll. The troll continued to advance and Beth slung her daggers at him, taking his legs out from under him before pulling the blades clear through his chest.

Sandy was still atop her battle cat. She looked around the field of battle, trying to figure out how she could contribute. Suzuki saw her from the corner of his eye and absentmindedly thought about how difficult it must be to have to figure out how to use a new set of powers in the middle of battle. He couldn't give it too much thought, though, because two trolls were squaring up against him.

One of the trolls launched himself forward, his rusty axe

in the air. Suzuki stepped to the side and punched him before turning to the next, which was already rushing him. Suzuki caught the blade of the troll's axe but was off-balance. He stumbled back as the other troll regrouped from his prior attack, bringing down his axe on Suzuki, who barely managed to raise his own, losing more of his footing still until he stumbled back and fell. The two trolls came for him, but Suzuki rolled to his side, swiping one of the troll's legs out from under it. As Suzuki brought his axe up through the troll's crotch, a bolt of hot plasma came screeching through the other troll.

Suzuki looked up and saw Chip, still atop her battle cat, moving through the chaos of the battlefield, firing when she saw an opening, clearing up the stragglers who weren't engaged in heavy combat.

Suzuki quickly scanned the area, looking for his next kill. A greenish mist was settling over the battlefield. Suzuki looked around, trying to find its source.

Sandy had finally dismounted her battle cat. Her skin was paler than usual, and her hair darker. The green mist was emanating from her. The trolls near her, fighting Stew, started to slow. It was as if something had gotten into their joints, seizing them up. The trolls didn't seem to notice the change. Stew did, though, and he grabbed one of the trolls closest to him and hoisted the creature up, a feat that left the trolls near him stunned and frightened that a human could move such a massive creature with such ease. Stew slammed the troll into one of the others as Sandy walked past them all, touching one of the dead trolls, singing softly.

The dead troll's body exploded in a hailstorm of bones, impaling three nearby trolls as the green mist continued to pour out of Sandy's skin. She laughed as she levitated off the ground, the tips of her toes dragging as she launched herself at a troll. She grabbed his head and dug her nails into his skin as it began to rot. Then she plunged her thumbs into his head and ripped out his skull. She tossed the skull at another troll, the green mist compounded in the skull like some kind of grenade. There was an explosion of green mist and intestine and bone.

The leader of the trolls had singled Beth out, and they were circling each other. Beth swung her daggers and pulled them back into her hands. "Why'd you attack the redcaps?" Beth shouted.

The troll laughed and beat his chest. "Why do you care?" he countered before racing forward. The troll leapt at her, bringing his club down. Beth stepped to the side, narrowly avoiding being smashed. She leapt onto the troll and slammed her daggers into his chest. The leader was unaffected, and he grabbed Beth and tossed her away before hitting her in the chest with his axe.

Beth went flying and then skidded across the ground. She rolled once and was back on her feet, pulling her bow out and firing as she ran at the troll. Each arrow connected with the troll's chest, but he did not seem to notice. Finally, Beth fired again, and one of her arrows hit the troll in the eye.

The troll screeched in pain and tried to pull the arrow out. That was all the time Beth needed to slide under the troll, carving through his crotch with her daggers. Then she sliced his ankles. As he fell, she circled him and slashed his throat.

The troll fell dead at her feet.

Beth spat on him as the rest of the Mundanes finished off the others. Suzuki shot her a glance from across the battlefield and saw Beth pulling out her long sword and decapitating the troll she'd killed. When she was done, she went to another troll and removed his head as well. Suzuki came up to her, worried. He hoped she wasn't caught up in a battle frenzy. "Hey, Beth, are you okay?" Suzuki asked.

Beth looked over her shoulder, smiling. It was an odd combination, her face stained with blood and smiling so cheerfully. "Oh, yeah, so much better now," she replied.

"Why are you cutting their heads off?"

"Oh, this? It's a sign of disrespect. It shows any other trolls who come through that these trolls were killed by true warriors, and the rest of them should be more than a little afraid of what would happen to them. Serves these assholes right, too, fucking killing redcaps like that."

Diana joined Suzuki and Beth as she walked around, lopping off heads. "True," Diana agreed. "It was a senseless thing to do. Redcaps are some of the most peaceful creatures in Middang3ard."

Suzuki gave Diana a bewildered look. "I didn't know there was such a thing as a peaceful goblin," he admitted.

"Actually, the goblins in Middang3ard are generally very peaceful. That was the first tip-off that something might be wrong with the races following the Dark One. Everyone was quite surprised when goblins started forming raiding parties and attacking elves and dwarves. True, they war with themselves often enough, but it's honestly not much different than humans."

Sandy and Stew approached from across the field. Stew was holding a troll arm in his hand. He hadn't exited his berserker mode, and he was chewing on it.

Suzuki noticed Sandy's robes didn't change during battle. She also hadn't summoned her magical mask. He wondered if this was another ramification of her magic having changed. Maybe she didn't even need to use manna anymore.

Beth pointed at Stew and shook her head. "Are you fucking serious, Stew? That's disgusting," she shouted.

Stew looked from Beth to the troll arm and shrugged. "I'm hungry, dude, and everything tastes so good when I'm like this," he explained. "And this coming from you? Disrespecting the dead like that. Poor taste, dude. Poor taste."

Suzuki ignored Beth's and Stew's bickering. He had forgotten how much they argued when they played VR. It only made sense it would keep up outside of the game. Suzuki was more concerned with Sandy at the moment. "Hey, Sandy, how was all that?" he asked.

Sandy knelt beside one of the dead trolls. "Interesting," Sandy said. "I'm not nearly as powerful as I used to be. It's...a little unnerving. I was kind of expecting to come out of the place between the realms with more power. More knowledge, I guess. But I got nothing. I got worse than nothing. I got my powers drained."

"You still seem like you're a force to be reckoned with, though. That miasma-of-death shit you pulled was pretty fucking amazing."

Sandy sighed and rested her hand on the decapitated head of the troll at her feet. "It's not the same. I was a fucking powerhouse. Now...I dunno."

Sandy picked up the troll's head and looked into his eyes. "Or maybe I'm looking at this the wrong way," she murmured. Then she closed her eyes. Across the battlefield, all of the trolls opened their eyes. Sandy sang softly, and the trolls shut their eyes again. Then she placed the head back on the ground. "Yeah, I've been thinking about this the wrong way."

Chip pointed to the sun. "Fireside chat time should be about done," she shouted to the Mundanes. "We got precious hours of sun, so we'd best be hoofing it."

The Mundanes took off toward the east again. They doubled back for a moment to catch up to the redcaps to let them know the threat was taken care of. They did not stay for congratulations or thanks, although the redcaps did warn the Mundanes that the open space between jungles was especially dangerous at night. There were vicious creatures that moved through the darkness. The Mundanes thanked the redcaps for their advice, and then they were on their way.

In the evening, the Mundanes made their camp in the fields. They had left the jungles far behind. Now they sat beneath the stars, watching the fire crackling as Stew and Diana busied themselves with cooking. The battle cats had gone off someplace, hunting perhaps. Stew had floated the idea they could use the cats to get fresh meat, but the Mundanes soon found the cats only listened in regard to riding. Once they dismounted from the giant felines, the true nature of the battle cats could be seen. They were, in fact, nothing more than large cats. Needless to say, the Mundanes hardly noticed when the cats slunk off into the darkness.

Suzuki was calmer than he had been in a while. He stared up at the stars and tried to think through his feelings since the journey to the island had started. All and all, he didn't have much. Too much had happened but, more importantly, he had gotten used to just how frantic the life of a MERC was. Something always wanted to kill them. There was a constant stream of new information. People disappeared and returned. Sometimes your friends died. It was easy to see why the rest of the MERCs were the battle-hardened folks they were.

Across the flames, Suzuki caught Sandy's eye. She had

been staring into the fire as if there was some truth she could divine from its dance. When the flames cast more light on her, Suzuki could see she had been crying. Stew hadn't noticed since he was too busy cooking. Otherwise, he would have been by her side. Beth and Chip were fiddling with Beth's lightsaber daggers. Suzuki walked around the fire and sat next to Sandy. "You okay?" he asked.

Sandy nodded as she wiped away her tears. "Yeah, I'm cool. What's up?" Sandy asked.

"That wasn't really a question. I mean, not one you can answer without actually telling me something."

Sandy sighed as she arrived at the conclusion that she wasn't going to be able to get out of this. "All right, fine. I feel like shit," she admitted. "I was trying to cast a simple fire spell, you know, something to make the flames change color. A fucking parlor trick. I couldn't even do that. It's still...I don't know, it's frustrating more than anything else. I knew what I was doing. I know how to be a mage. I knew how to get more powerful. And I knew my place in the party. Now? All I know is that I kinda have a thing with dead shit."

"Didn't the Smuggles leave you with any kind of...instructions?"

Sandy shook her head. "Diana said they don't use magic like the rest of Middang3ard. It's more like ancestral magic. So, I just gotta feel it out."

"Basically, you're upset you can't just read about it to figure this shit out, huh?"

Sandy smirked and shrugged as the flames lit her face. "Fuck off, it's a lot more than that," she said. "But, yeah, all right. You got me. Reading shit is a lot easier than having to be all touchy feeling and weird about performing magic. Like when I picked up that troll head, dude, I fucking saw shit.

And, I mean, I've seen a lot of weird stuff over the last however long but that was something fucking new and fucking intense."

"What was it?"

"Hard to put into words. But it was like I saw all of the troll's life. Like every moment. In a flash. And then it was gone."

"What exactly did you do? We saw the troll heads reacting to you."

"Honestly, I have no idea what I did. No idea what happened. Or even why I felt so positive about everything earlier. It was weird."

Suzuki shoved Sandy playfully, almost knocking her over. "You'll figure it out. Plus, you were going on and on for so long about how you wanted to learn necromancy. It's kinda like a monkey's paw. Isn't that a magic thing?"

"Shut up, Suz, you're not cute," Sandy said as she laughed. "And thanks for cheering me up."

"No prob."

Stew came over to Sandy and Suzuki and shoved his head in between their shoulders. He eyes Suzuki suspiciously. "Whatcha guys talking about?" Stew asked.

Sandy kissed Stew on the cheek and said, "Suzuki was just telling me how it's perfectly normal to want to bring in a little corpse play into the tent. Just a little bit."

Stew's narrowed on Suzuki's as he stood up. "Not cool, dude. Not cool," he muttered as he backed away into the shadows. "Foods up!"

The Mundanes rose, Suzuki laughing to himself as Sandy giggled, noticeably pleased with herself. They all grabbed the small clay bowls Stew had provided and spooned chili in. The chili was hot, even by Beth's standards. It was filled with vegetables Suzuki had never seen before, things that grew only in Middang3ard, and the meat was soft and flavorful, reminiscent of goat. The Mundanes ate in silence, thoroughly enjoying their meal.

Beth's belch broke the silence. "What?" she asked. "I'm pretty sure in some places, that's considered a compliment."

As Beth and the rest of the Mundanes were finishing their food, the battle cats returned. All but one went to the Mundane who rode them, curled up, and quickly went to sleep. Azrael, Sandy's battle cat, slowly crept toward her. It held a massive bird in its jaws and laid it at Sandy's feet.

Sandy was elated. She grabbed the bird, which was almost her size, and held it close. "Oh, my God, thank you so much," Sandy exclaimed as she snuggled Azrael's face. "This is so sweet."

Stew leaned away from Sandy, not taking his eyes off the dead bird. "You know that when cats bring you shit, it's because they don't think you can take care of yourself, right?"

Sandy glared at Stew before rubbing her face against Azrael's nose again. "That is anti-cat propaganda, Stew," she said. "Cats give you presents when they respect you, and who doesn't like dead things?" Sandy cast her eyes against the flames, smiled, and laughed to herself. "Dead things...huh..."

The Mundanes continued to talk long into the night, the battle cats snoring through their conversation. Chip dipped into their store of ale and passed around tankards for everyone to enjoy. The night was filled with their conversation and laughter. The moon hung in the middle of the sky by the time they all retired to their tents.

Suzuki lay in his sleeping bag as Beth got herself ready for bed. He watched her cast away her armor in a fluid, effortless movement. Beth crouched and looked at it, then looked over her shoulder at Suzuki. "You're pretty good at enchanting, right?" she asked.

Suzuki sat up and grabbed his axe. He tossed it to Beth. "Yeah, I think I'm all right," he explained. "Still learning, though."

Beth looked over Suzuki's work, running her hands across the runes Suzuki had etched into the hilt. "I've seen it in action—really good work. I was wondering if you would take a look at my gear. The older shit, mostly the armor. Really, all of the armor. The military doesn't get as many loot perks as you MERCs seem to. All the shit I have is just fucking terrible. But, you know, I saw the basic-ass shit you started with and how you kind of made it your own thing, and, honestly, I'm a little jealous."

"I could teach you how to—"

"No, I mean I want you to work on my gear. Just you."

Beth grabbed her leather chest piece and brought it over to the sleeping bag. She handed it to Suzuki. "How do you, you know... Actually, just show me."

Suzuki took the armor from Beth as she politely looked away. He pulled up his inventory and selected the chisel he had used on his armor, which had multiple buffs, and on his axe. It felt comfortable in his hand as it materialized. "So, the first thing you need to do," he started, "is figure out what you want to enchant an item with. What are you looking to do?"

Beth smiled coyly.

Suzuki saw now that she was flirting. Most of the time when Beth was being flirtatious, it went over his head. It was only in hindsight he figured it out.

Tonight, that was not the case.

Suzuki could see her watching each of his movements, and she had scooted closer when he had started talking about the methodology of enchanting. Usually, he would feel extremely uncomfortable in situations like this, even though he was in love with Beth. But tonight, something clicked. He wasn't sure if it was the ale or if it was the way Beth's hair caught the sparse light in the tent. Whatever it was, it was making a difference.

Suzuki scooted closer to Beth and laid her armor on her lap. "What do you want?" he asked.

Beth bit her lip and screwed her face up as if she were deep in thought. "Well, I guess if I'm going to roll with the whole class change, I should probably get something that helps with being a rogue or assassin. So, I have that SD card that makes me invisible, but I still have to deal with being heard. How about we do an enchantment that makes me quieter? You know I'm a little loud sometimes."

"All right. I can work with that."

Suzuki pulled out his notebook. It was one of the few things he didn't store in his inventory. He liked to keep it on him, all the time. He had been journaling since he got to Middang3ard. Once he had started enchanting and doing research into magic, he had written it down in his notebook. He had collected hundreds of runes, most of them from books Sandy had given him. "All right, so let's get started," Suzuki said.

The leather would be easy to work with. The chisel could easily engrave the material. All he had to do was find the right rune. He knew there was something in the book that would be able to give Beth what she wanted. He had a faint memory of jotting down a rune that had to do with silence. He wasn't sure if it was a rune about the general concept of silence or if it was more practical. It took him nearly ten minutes to find it. He wasn't complaining, though. In the time it took him to find the reference, Beth had moved even closer, practically sitting in his lap while he was flipping through his notebook, her skin warm against his.

"Got it."

Suzuki worked the armor, chiseling in the rune slowly, cutting into the leather, occasionally stopping to check on the progress of his work. He and Beth sat in silence as he worked. Finally, after he was satisfied with his enchantment, he handed the armor back to Beth. "That was really hot," Beth said before she flung herself onto Suzuki, covering his lips with her own.

18

The Mundanes rose early and breakfasted, then broke down their camp and continued East. Chip let them know they weren't too far away from the coordinates of the enemy camp. It would be less than a day's ride, especially since the battle cats were so fast. The Mundanes arrived at the camp before they even realized it.

Beth glassed the coordinates with her spyglass. She saw there was a deep groove in the ground, the earth sloping forward into something like a massive ditch. It looked as if a lot of earth had been cleared away for construction. "Guess that's the place," Beth said. "You guys ready to take care of this?"

Stew pointed up toward the sky at something that was approaching the facility. It looked like one of those old science-fiction flying saucers. The saucer was remarkably flat and had a dome at the top. It moved quickly and seemed to have an erratic flight path. "So, now we got UFOs to deal with as well?" Stew sighed.

Suzuki motioned for Beth to hand him the spyglass. He

peered through it to get a better look at the UFO flying toward the ditch. He saw it stop in midair and suddenly descend into where the Mundanes assumed the facility was. "It looks like its dropping something off," Suzuki thought aloud as the UFO suddenly rose back into the sky and sped off. "We should probably take our time with this one. There's a lot of shit I don't quite get yet. Don't want any surprises."

Beth nodded in agreement. "Yeah, you're right. It would be better not to be caught off guard."

Chip nudged her battle cat forward, and they started toward the facility. "Oh, come on, where's your sense of adventure?" she chided.

Suzuki and the rest of the Mundanes followed her, each of them trying to rein in their battle cats' innate desire to run as fast as possible. "I'd rather not die again," Suzuki said. "It's kind of losing its novelty."

"Fair enough, fair enough."

The Mundanes closed in on the facility site and peered over the side of the wall erected in front of the cleared away earth. The facility was partially underground, explaining why the dirt had been cleared, but it could still be seen. Suzuki was reminded of going to the library near his home and seeing construction workers clearing out dirt and laying the foundations of a new building. It looked very similar to the state this facility was in.

There was a sound like a whirring buzz saw from above. Suzuki looked up and saw another UFO approaching at a ludicrous speed. The UFO flew straight above the facility and then stopped. After a few seconds, it lowered itself down into something that looked like a docking bay. It remained there for a few moments before rising up and jetting out of sight. "Looks like they're transporting something," Suzuki mused aloud. "They aren't staying for very long, but they're making routine drops. Maybe those are just transportation rigs or delivery drivers. What the hell would they need delivery drivers for?"

Chip pointed up at the sky as another UFO flew by. Her finger morphed into what looked to be a satellite dish. The dish spun as Chip tracked the saucer. As it rose and flew again, Chip continued to follow it. "This might shed a little light on our dark plight," Chip offered. "Quick scan shows that the UFO is empty of life, except for one of our little friends."

"So, it's automated? Like a remote-controlled delivery driver?"

"Not even the best part. Remote-controlled single angel delivery driver is the best part."

"Only one?"

"Yeah, but you saw how quickly the second craft came by. Maybe it's nonstop."

Suzuki crouched and passed the spyglass back to Beth. He really wasn't looking forward to stepping into another facility like the one he'd lost his life in. All the Zen thoughts he had earlier about coming to grips with death and danger were gone. They were replaced with something very akin to tiredness. This was going to be an experience, but this time, they had a better idea of what they were up against. Still, they could have an even better idea.

Diana knelt beside Suzuki. "What are you thinking?"

"Last time we walked into a shitty situation because we didn't know what we were up against. That wasn't our fault. José didn't or couldn't give us any information. Now we have a little bit more. We should keep from making the same mistake. I say we make camp for the day. Do some recon. Then we'll move in on the facility. How's that sound?"

Sandy was the only person who had a problem with the plan. "How exactly are we going to do recon?" she asked. "Send someone in there? I know we've used the whole magical cloaking spell thing before, but that was never someone just by themselves. And that place looks too small to have a couple of us sleuthing around."

Suzuki pointed up to the sky. "First, we need to figure out how many of these things are being shipped. We won't be able to get an exact number, but I'd like to know if we're up against something that gets delivered every fifteen minutes like a bus schedule. Secondly, call it a hunch, but I'm thinking if these angels are so dangerous they can't be transported in groups, there's a good chance they're too dangerous for anyone to be working around. I mean, they killed everyone at the last facility. Maybe the Dark One's learned from his mistake, and the facility is automated as well. Or it could just be a holding pen. Either way, I'll be the one to go check it out. I don't want to put anyone at risk. Besides, I have that alien upgrade."

Beth shook her head and chuckled. "You literally just promised me you weren't going to do something stupid and get yourself killed, and now you're talking about this? Suzy, you're supposed to be a good tactician, remember? And here you are forgetting the obvious choice. I'm the one with the new invisibility SD card. And you just enchanted my armor last night to make me more silent. If anyone is going, it should be me."

"Beth, it's really fucking dangerous. You saw how those things are."

"Yeah, I know it's really fucking dangerous, I'm not an

idiot. That's why it makes more sense to have someone go who has a chance of actually making it out alive. I know you love me and are probably just looking out for me and all, but you need to remember we're here on a job. We are all going to be taking risks. Don't jeopardize the fate of the party because of me. You're better than that."

An awkward silence settled over the Mundanes as Suzuki mulled over what Beth said. She was right. He hadn't really thought about it, but she was right. If he tried, he could probably remember a couple of situations where he had put Beth's safety over everyone else's, and here he was getting called out in front of everyone. It was fucking humiliating, but it needed to happen. There was no need for it to be a secret conversation. If Suzuki was going to be making calls that could end up with someone dead, every conversation needed to be in an open forum. He wasn't going to make the same mistakes Chip and Diana had by trying to protect everyone by withholding information for a more appropriate time. Beth's method was harsh, brutal, and quick. Just like her. And it worked.

Finally, Suzuki cleared his throat and conceded, "You're right, I didn't think that through. You're the one going in. We'll maintain contact through our familiars, and I want you to do a quick, thorough sweep. Use your HUD to take pictures, and we'll meet back up here. No longer than two hours, okay? If you get in a compromised situation, you radio us immediately. Understood?"

Beth saluted Suzuki and gave him her mischievous, playful smirk. "Yes, sir! When am I shipping out?"

"Immediately. Good luck."

"Thanks, Suzy. Love you."

Beth went over to where the earth sloped forward and

pulled out her daggers. She jumped off the cliff, throwing her daggers upward so that they connected with the rock and tethered her to the side of the cliff as she lowered herself down, shimmering out of sight. *Goddamn, she is beautiful,* Suzuki thought.

Stew shoved Suzuki, almost knocking him over. "Earth to Suzuki," Stew teased. "What are the rest of us supposed to do?"

Suzuki managed to regain his balance. "You are on UFO duty."

"Are you fucking serious? Beth gets to go be all badass, and I have to pull some X-files shit?"

"Stew, being quiet isn't your strong suit. But counting is."

Stew crossed his arms, pouting like a child as he accepted the role he was going to play. "Guess that's number one right there." He sat down in the grass and pointed at one of the crafts that flew overhead.

"That's what I'm talking about Stew. You count those UFOs."

"I fucking hate you."

"The truth is out there."

"I hate you so much."

The rest of the Mundanes got to making their stakeout more comfortable. Chip, Sandy, and Suzuki built a fire while Stew continued to keep track of the number of crafts coming and going. While the fire was being built, Diana went about the task of cooking. She built a meal off the dried jerky they had and disappeared to search for herbs. After some time, she returned, her hands full of tons of native vegetation from the island. She used these to garnish and flavor the jerky and they all sat around the fire afterward next to Stew, counting the ships that passed, snacking on the flavorful and sour strips of meat.

Beth continued to stay in contact with Suzuki. She reported in every ten minutes or so. It dawned on Suzuki one of the other reasons Beth was obviously the right choice for scouting was she obviously had experience from her time in the military. He really appreciated the routine and systematic way she held herself during quests. It was something he wished Stew would pick up on. It was doubtful, though. The most it seemed Stew had grown was when he was infected by a mood-altering leech.

Beth's reports were straightforward, and she didn't waste any time going into details that weren't important. The facility didn't seem to have anyone in it other than angels, which were kept behind glass windows. The angels didn't seem to take any notice of her. That might mean there was a chance their only mode of hunting was eyesight. From what Beth could tell, the craft was dropping the angels off directly into the glass rooms. She still couldn't find a reason for why they were being stored, but there were hundreds of them—a small army.

"When are you coming back?" Suzuki asked.

"Soon. I'm going to see if I can find any tech for Chip. See if she can hack it like she did that last datapad, so we can find out more information. I still feel like we're just shooting in the dark. All we've figured out is the Dark One is doing some kind of weird experiment with his genes, but we don't know the end goal. We don't know what he's planning or how he's planning it. I fucking hate being in this kind of situation. I want to know what I'm up against."

"All right, well, try to get back here before sunset."

"Gotcha."

It was nearing dusk when Beth arrived back at the Mundane camp. By this time, the tents had been set up and the Mundanes were talking softly as they finished their meals. Beth grabbed a bowl of chili and, without saying anything, took a seat next to Suzuki. She leaned her head against his shoulder and blew on her food to cool it.

Suzuki wrapped his arm around Beth and kissed her on the forehead. The two of them listened to the conversation around them, eating quietly, Suzuki thanking whoever had watched over Beth.

After Beth finished her meal, she started to speak. "The place is huge," she said. "Same deal as the last one we checked out. There weren't any of the sprouts, though. This one was even creepier. You know, the whole dead bodies thing is pretty terrifying, but this was worse. Nothing. Just those fucking angels behind the glass. I'm so glad they didn't know I was in there. It would have been fucking terrifying. But I did bring back some fun reading material."

Beth reached into her bag and pulled out a datapad. She tossed it to Chip, who caught it and exclaimed, "Right on! Let's crack into this bad boy and see just what secrets its holding."

Chip's fingers split and cables snaked out of her fingertips, locking themselves into the datapad. Her eyes went white and displayed binary code. Then they returned back to normal, and Chip started to scroll through the data. "Looks like the reason they don't have any sprouts is because the angels are grown somewhere else." Chip pointed to the sky as another UFO flew over the facility. "Little angels came from space, it seems." Chip turned the datapad around and passed it to Suzuki.

The datapad had a diagram of the UFO route. There was a large, moonlike object thousands of miles above the facility. From the diagram, it looked like the sphere was in space, outside the planet's atmosphere. Suzuki hadn't really thought about what space was like in Middang3ard. He had vaguely noticed the constellations he was familiar with on Earth weren't here. That hadn't unsettled him much before. He had never been a big space kid. Now it was starting to get a little bit under his skin. This realm was similar to Earth but also so different. Suzuki was surprised at how this place could still make him feel out of place and far from home.

Home. Middang3ard felt more like home now if he was honest with himself. His family was here. Still, he couldn't wait to take care of the Dark One, but then would he just be going back to his old life? How the hell was he going to be able to do that?

Diana stood and stretched. "Are we planning on checking out the facility?" she asked.

Suzuki shook his head as he answered, "No, I don't think it's necessary. I'm going to go over Beth's photos, but I don't think it makes sense for all of us to go down there. We gotta figure out what we're going to do about it, though. We can't let something like that just sit there. But at the moment, if we do attack, I'm pretty sure someone will be notified. Those ships are hitting the spot every fifteen minutes on the dot. How long did it look like the Dark One's been sending angels to the facility?"

Beth rubbed her cheeks as if she were trying to keep herself from falling asleep. "It looked like for years. You'll see in the pictures. There was literally nothing else in there except for angels. The whole place must have been built just for them."

Stew spoke up for the first time in a while. "We could blow it up?" he suggested.

"Anyone here have demolition experience?"

Chip raised her hand, grinning as if she were already anticipating what the explosion was going to look like. "If the occasion calls for it, I am capable of making many big booms with minimum assistance needed."

Diana yawned loudly. "Well, if we're done with a theoretical demolition discussion, I believe I am going to retire. I am exhausted."

Suzuki caught Diana's yawn and suddenly realized he was tired as well. The daylong ride had really taken it out of him. "You know, that's not a bad idea. I think I'm going to head to sleep as well."

He kissed Beth again and said goodnight to the rest of the Mundanes before retiring to his tent.

In his sleeping bag, Suzuki thought about whether he wanted to go home. It had only been a passing thought earlier. Now it came back, louder and stronger than before. There had been nothing going on back at home. Just work and playing video games.

True, he had friends and family, people close to him who loved him and probably missed the hell out of him. But that wasn't enough. Suzuki wasn't sure if he could ever experience a normal life again. Waking up to go to work? Clocking in at some bullshit pizza place?

It just didn't make any sense.

Suzuki drifted off to sleep without realizing it. His head was full of thoughts all night, and his dreams were a mix of those anxieties. He couldn't tell which was which. In his dream, he was in a tent, but he didn't know why. Beth was gone. She had been gone for a while. Then he heard her screaming. It horrified him, and he tried to find her, but she was nowhere to be seen.

When Suzuki woke up, he was drenched in sweat. He felt Beth's side of the tent. She wasn't there. Suzuki grabbed his axe as he tried to remain calm and stepped out of the tent.

Sandy, Stew, and Beth were all around the fire. They had fallen asleep next to the warmth. Sandy and Stew were in their sleeping bags. They had probably already decided they wanted to sleep outside. If sleeping was all they had planned. Beth was just lying on the grass. She must have fallen asleep without realizing it.

Suzuki came over and knelt beside Beth. He thought about waking her, but she looked like she was sleeping peacefully. One night sleeping by himself wasn't going to kill him. Maybe he'd even sleep outside too. It was a warm night, and it had been a long time since he had slept under the stars, watching them watch him.

There was a sound in the darkness. Past the light of the fire, something large moved. Suzuki thought it could have been one of the battle cats. But then he remembered how quiet the creatures were. And he had seen them all gathered in a pile sleeping when he first walked out of the tent. Whatever was out there in the dark moved again. It was getting closer.

Suzuki shook Beth and she sat bolt upright, her eyes still closed, drool trailing from the corner of her mouth. "Not tonight, Suzy, I'll fuck you tomorrow." She groaned. "I'm real busy right now. There's this cake. It's huge. Someone has to eat it. I'm gonna eat it all. You can't stop me. No one can."

Suzuki shook Beth harder until she came out of her

dream state. He didn't say anything, just pointed to the direction the noise was coming from. Now that it was closer, Suzuki could tell it sounded almost like a lawnmower, a mechanical contraption whirling to life. And it was even more obvious now that the thing was closing in on the Mundanes' camp.

"Wake up Sandy and Stew."

Beth leaned over to shake Stew and Sandy awake. Both of them opened their eyes slowly, but Beth put her finger to her lips and then pointed to the source of the noise.

In the darkness, two bright eyes opened.

They were at least twenty feet away and watched the Mundanes closely. Then they disappeared. A few seconds passed and they opened back up, the groaning of some awful thing accompanying the eerie, yellow floating eyes.

Then the noise stopped.

The eyes disappeared.

It was as if there had been nothing to begin with.

Suzuki rose slowly, pulling out his axe and the rest of the Mundanes did the same, preparing themselves for whatever was in the dark. They were at a major disadvantage. Whatever had tracked them to their fire was obviously built for the darkness. Suzuki could hardly see anything a few feet from the fire. Diana would have been able to see due to her SD card upgrade, but she was asleep, and taking the chance of exposing his back to an enemy was not something Suzuki wanted to do. They were going to have to figure this one out on their own.

Suzuki scooted close to the fire and whispered, "Get around the fire. Sandy, do you think you could cast—"

Sandy shook her head as she brushed against Suzuki, trying to get to the flames. "No, I can't cast any elemental magic," she grumbled. "Still don't know all of the how I can be useful."

Something large and fast moved overhead. Suzuki could have sworn he heard beating wings. "All right, all right, we're going to have to improvise then."

Suzuki scrolled through his inventory as he tried not to be distressed by the flapping wings above. He found exactly what he was looking for. Four torches appeared in his hands. He handed each of the Mundanes one and then plunged his torch into the fire. The four of them spread out a little bit more, casting more light in the dark. It was unnecessary, though.

A creature nearly as tall as a troll flew into the clearing. It had the head of a chicken and the torso of a lion, a snake for a tail, and chicken's feet. Its eyes were bright yellow, and it clicked as well as roared as it scratched at the ground, its snake tail rising and hissing in the direction of the Mundanes. "Oh fuck," Stew muttered. "That's a fucking big chimera."

Suzuki quickly appraised the situation, looking over the different parts of the animal's body. "Are you sure it's not a cockatrice?" Suzuki asked.

The snake tail struck at Beth, who dodged to the side and shouted, "Do you guys really think right now is the best time to be arguing about this?"

"No! I'm not arguing! It's important. You can't look a cockatrice in the eyes or it'll turn you to stone."

Stew drew one of his swords and slashed at the snake's head. "No, it's not! Cockatrices have a rooster head and they're mostly dragon. This thing is most definitely a chicken head. Look how fucking stupid it looks. Plus, it's got three different animal pieces. We're definitely in chimera territory."

The chimera didn't seem to care either way and it roared again as its chicken head came crashing down toward Beth, who was still on the ground, scrambling to get out of the way.

Suzuki ran his hand over his axe as he leapt forward, flames covering the blade. He hit the chimera in the chest, took hold of it, and tried to wrestle his way on top. As he reached over, nearly on the chimera's back, the snake head snapped and hit him in the back of the neck. Suzuki felt the snake pump venom into him, and his whole body went numb. He slumped off the chimera as Sandy dove forward and dragged him to safety.

As Sandy touched Suzuki's wound, the venom drained out, floating to Sandy's fingers, and remaining on her fingertips as she looked down at her hands.

Feeling flooded back into Suzuki's body as he sat up. "Thanks. Hey! Mundanes! That snake head is venomous. Don't get bit!"

Beth had pulled out her daggers and was circling the chimera with Stew at her side. "None of us are dumb enough to get bit by a giant fucking snake, dude!" Stew shouted as the snake head lunged for him, the chimera bounding forward almost as if it were dancing, stomping the ground with its talons.

Suzuki tossed his axe at the snake head, which narrowly moved out of the way as Suzuki recalled his axe, hoping to nail the snake on the second go. The snake still managed to get out of the way, and Suzuki realized his aim might not be good enough for such a fast-moving creature. He was going to have to risk getting up close and personal like the rest of the Mundanes. As Suzuki prepared to run off, Sandy grabbed him by the wrist. "Wait," she said. "Let me help first."

Sandy touched the side of Suzuki's face with her poison

stained fingertips. Suzuki felt the spell instantly and he didn't need to be told what had just happened. He took off toward the snake's head as Sandy followed. Suzuki wasn't sure it was the wisest decision for Sandy to be throwing herself in the middle of a fight. Last time might have been a fluke. She still didn't seem to have a good grasp on what she was capable of doing.

Suzuki leapt onto the chimera, holding onto its fur as it tried to buck him off. Below, Beth and Stew were still contending with the creature's talons. Even though they had both managed to land blows, it didn't look like they had done any damage.

The snake head lunged forward again too fast for Suzuki to do anything about and sank its fangs into Suzuki's shoulder and his whole arm was set on fire with pain. But it wasn't his axe hand, and that was all that mattered. Suzuki swung his axe, cutting halfway through the snake's head. He raised his axe again, ready to cleave the head off completely when something sharp flew through the snake's neck, severing it. A couple of other sharp objects flew through the air past Suzuki, landing in the chimera's back.

They were sharpened bones. Suzuki turned to see Sandy holding her hands up, her palms facing the chimera. A bone slowly forced itself out of her palm and flew as if fired from a gun. Suzuki leapt off the chimera, hoping to give Sandy better aim.

The chimera roared loudly as it tried to turn around and stop Sandy. Sandy levitated off the ground, bones protruding out of her skin, covering her in armor, two large goats horns pushing themselves out of her forehead as her fingers stretched, the bones cracking and the nails stretching into razor-sharp bone claws.

The chimera pounced on Sandy, who brought her arms into her chest, the bone armor fusing together. The chimera brought its beak down on her, trying to crack into her but to no avail. Sandy cackled as she reached up and slashed at the chimera, who grabbed Sandy with its talons and slammed her into the ground. Sandy shut her eyes as it prepared to slam her again, and bones shot out of her body, obliterating the chimera's talon. Sandy managed to roll away and join up with the rest of the Mundanes.

Stew stared at Sandy with a look of shock and awe. "Sandy, you're practically naked," he murmured, staring slack-jawed at her, her body almost completely covered with bones but still leaving enough to the imagination.

Sandy looked down at her new form. "Fuck, you're right. I look pretty fucking hot."

Beth tossed her daggers, bringing them back quickly and tried to circle the chimera. "Flirting later, killing now!" Beth shouted as she flung herself at the monster.

Stew cracked his knuckles, and his body began to swell as he entered into berserker mode. He roared as he ran toward the chimera, now only a little smaller than the creature, and tackled it to the ground as his shoulder cannon fired off a blast of hot plasma that tore through the chimera's side. Sandy came up from behind Stew and volleyed off his back, tucking her arms and legs in together, sharp bones bursting out of her body. Stew leapt into the air and grabbed Sandy like a baseball and flung her into the chimera's head, smashing open its eye and beak.

The chimera struggled to its feet, and Suzuki saw Beth was coming in hard from the left. Suzuki took the right, leaping onto the chimera and driving his axe deep into its neck. On the other side, Beth was hacking at the chimera's neck, blood spouting in her face, her eyes wide with blood lust. Suzuki pulled his axe out, and with all his strength, struck again.

Suzuki rolled off the chimera. The rest of the Mundanes had managed to avoid being stuck under their dead foe except for Sandy, who was knee-deep in gore, having continued to rip open the chimera with her bones. When she realized the creature was dead, she stood up, not even bothering to wipe the blood off. She went to the chimera's head and picked it up, staring at it. The chimera opened its eyes, and they locked gazes before the chimera closed them for the final time.

Suzuki looked around at the Mundanes and shook his head. "Now, that was some fucking teamwork," he congratulated them. "Glad to see we can still take care of business without Chip's and Diana's help. I was worried we were going to start getting sloppy, with such a big party."

Stew returned to his normal size and pulled out his butchering knives. "Dude, the only one who has ever been sloppy is you," he teased. "I'm glad you're finally starting to pull your own weight."

"Dude, I fucking decapitated that thing."

"With Beth's help. I was the one who tackled it and set you guys all up for a stellar finish. I'd say I definitely win MVP of the fight."

"Do you even know what 'stellar' means?"

"I know how to use it in a sentence, and that's ninety percent of communication."

Suzuki wanted to say something back, but he was stumped. Stew had out-thought him this time around. "Anyways, losers." Stew chuckled. "It's cockatrices that are poisonous, right? Chimeras are just different kinds of meats."

Sandy nodded as the bones in her body started to withdraw. She scrolled through her inventory and selected a set of robes to wear. "Yeah, cockatrices are poisonous. Fuck, I'm going to have to figure out this whole clothing thing. I don't want to shred my robes every time I get in a fight. Stew, how come your clothes never rip when you get all yoked?"

Stew motioned for Suzuki to come give him a hand. "Oh, I got them custom made. They grow with me. And you, get your ass over here. You never help with the butchering, and you eat nearly as much as me."

Suzuki groaned as he caught the knife Stew threw him. "It's fucking gross," he whined. "I don't like rolling around in animal guts."

"We're battlefield to table, dude. You gotta start lending a hand, starting right now."

While Stew and Suzuki butchered the chimera, Sandy and Beth went back over to the fire as Chip and Diana came out of their tents. "What's with all the noise and warlike sounds?" Chip yawned.

Sandy laughed as she watched Diana stumble around, still obviously mostly asleep. "Did you guys really not hear any of that?" Sandy asked.

"I mean, there were noises, and I knew there were noises. That's as close to an answer of gross negligence as you're gonna get from me. I was also having a talk, though. Myrddin finally got back to us, and we got a problem."

Suzuki, covered in chimera guts, came over and sat next to the fire. "I fucking hate meat," he grumbled. "And what's the problem?"

"Myrddin has intel that says another facility on the island is getting a delivery. Giants. The Dark One is going to see what happens when one of those angels pops out of them."

"Guess we're stopping it?"

"Yeppers. First thing in the morning. Next time something needs killing, y'all can wake us up. Maybe not Diana. She's kinda on the heavy side."

Diana was still looking around as if she were lost, murmuring to herself.

"It's okay, Dee, you can go back to sleep," Chip said as she walked Diana back to their tent.

Sandy laid down next to the fire and yawned. "You guys just wanna crash out here? It's a nice night and we'll be prepared if anything else comes for us?"

Suzuki flopped down on the ground. "That sounds like a great idea," he said. He was asleep within seconds.

19

The Mundanes rose before the sun began to make its way over the horizon. Beth and Suzuki spent the morning listening to Stew and Sandy bicker over whether or not Sandy should just rock the bone bikini or invest in something that would accommodate her new powers. Chip and Diana talked quietly over their meal, quickly cleaning up their plates and stomping out the fire when they were done.

Diana stepped forward and cleared her throat. "There's been a change of plans," Diana explained. "Chip and I were emailed this morning about a second convoy on the other side of the island. We're going to have to split up for this one. The convoy we're going after isn't too far from you and isn't as large. We should be able to take care of it and then meet up with you at the angel facility without a problem. At most, this will just be a slight delay."

Beth threw her arms up and pretended she was dismayed. "Who's going to be the unflinching voice of reason for us, though?" she kidded.

"I'll be back soon enough to suck the fun out of your

quests. And trust me, you don't want Chip on this mission with you."

"Why not?"

Diana turned to Chip and asked, "Do you still have the footage?"

Chip smiled and rubbed her hands together like a child finally getting to perform a prank they've been dreaming up. She waved her hand and digital screen appeared in front of her, projecting from her eyes. "There are certain kinds of missions Chip tends to...get carried away with," Diana said.

The video started. There was a small convoy of bandits on horses. It was hard to see what they were transporting, but it didn't matter. Within a few seconds of the video playing, Chip came barreling through the horses, riding an elephant. The last shot of the video was Chip's bright smile as she fired arrows into the bandits. "Where the hell did you get an elephant?" Stew asked, amazed.

"Trade secrets. Nothing like a good chase to get your heart a-pumping. Almost makes one a little, shall I say, interested between the legs if you get my drift, you filthy perverts. But I remind you to do as I say and not as I do. Even I got in trouble for that one. So, remember. Your little quest ain't just kill the baddies. The giants are free of the Dark One's control. Make sure you play nice with them. Any questions?"

"Elephant. How?" Stew repeated.

"Hush. I'll send you guys the coordinates. Be safe enough. Lates."

Chip and Diana mounted their battle cats and waved goodbye. Suzuki wondered in the back of his mind whether or not Chip and Diana had stayed inside during the fight to see if the younger Mundanes could handle themselves without the vets. He doubted it. The former Horsemen already had a large amount of respect for the Mundanes. He was probably just being insecure.

Stew was packing up the rest of the cooking supplies. "I can't believe she got a fucking elephant. Even if she's a little off her rocker, Chip is fucking cool," Stew said. "I wish I had that kind of knack for destruction. She's like you, Sandy, just not as creepy."

Sandy was playing with her necromantic powers a little bit by stretching her finger bone out of her skin and then pulling it out. "Oh, babe, you think I'm creepy? That's so sweet," she said, smiling.

Stew grimaced but still smiled. "Dude, you are hella creepy. Anyways, you guys ready to get started? I've never stopped a convoy before, not even in-game. Sounds kinda like a Wild, Wild West type of thing."

Beth laughed as she gave Stew a hand getting everything packed up. "Really? It just reeks of military for me," she said. "We used to stop convoys all the time. You know, an army has to eat. One of the easiest ways to force someone out of a spot they're holed up in is to take out their food supply. The Dark One's forces still need to eat and we used to regularly take out their food convoys. Glad Myrddin has the foresight to stop those giants from getting to the Dark One's research facility. Can you imagine giant angels? No fucking thank you."

The Mundanes tore down the rest of the camp and mounted their battle cats. Suzuki looked up the coordinates through his HUD. They still had a pretty hefty trek ahead of them. The coordinates Chip had sent also allowed him to look and see how far the convoy was from the research facility. As long as they didn't get distracted by anything along the way, the Mundanes would easily overtake the convoy before it was anywhere near the facility.

It was a good thing Myrddin had gotten in contact with the Mundanes. Suzuki was starting to lose faith in the old man. He didn't seem to have as strong a grasp on how the war with the Dark One was going, or he was overwhelmed with trying to keep the fight going. Either way, it was good to see that Myrddin was still invested in the fight.

The Mundanes took off toward the convoy as Suzuki let his mind wander. Beth and Stew took the lead. He was still trying to wrap his head around what it meant for the Dark One to be trying to convert all living beings to himself. It was a level of tyranny Suzuki thought might never have existed before. True, atrocities had happened throughout history, but there was something special about this—unprecedented extreme megalomania. And that ego was now part of Suzuki's genetic material.

The battle cats were running flat-out, and the wind whipped past Suzuki as they crested the hill. He checked his HUD to see how far they were from the convoy, to find that they'd be intercepting them in a little under twenty minutes. "Beth, we need to find a place where we can get a good vantage point," Suzuki shouted.

Beth pulled out her spyglass and surveyed the area. She pointed ahead a few clicks, a little out of the way from where the convoy was going. "Those hills!" she said. "We can head over there and get a better idea of what's going on."

Stew laughed as he spurred his battle cat forward, leaping ahead of the rest of the Mundanes. "Dude, this is so sick. It is going to be so Wild West. Call me Wyatt!"

"No, Stew. I am not going to call you Wyatt, or any other stupid-ass name you come up with."

"What about 'the lieutenant?'"

"Why the hell would you think I would call you that?"

"I don't know. Might as well give it a try."

The Mundanes raced toward the hill. It didn't take long before they were atop it, looking down the valley, Beth searching for the convey through the spyglass. "All right, got them," Beth said, pointing ahead and handing the spyglass to Suzuki.

Suzuki looked through the glass and saw the convoy. It was mostly orcs riding horses, but there was something that looked like a tank. The body of the vehicle was steel and shaped like a truck, but there was a cannon attached to it. That surprised Suzuki. Outside of tech at the Dark One's defense rings, Suzuki hadn't seen anything that looked like modern technology, but it really didn't matter. He was just glad the tank wasn't as sophisticated as some of the stuff he'd seen in the defense rings. That would have been a lot more trouble than he wanted to deal with.

The spyglass was passed to Stew and Sandy as well so they could see what they were up against. "Is that a fucking tank?" Stew asked.

Suzuki nodded as he took the spyglass back and handed it to Beth. "Yeah, that's what it looks like."

"So, what's the plan, dude?"

Suzuki thought it over for a few seconds. He was going to have to figure out what they were going to do fast before they lost the upper hand. If the convoy got too far, they would be stuck chasing it down, and that would put them in a shit situation. "All right," Suzuki said, thinking aloud, "that tank changes things. We don't know how much firepower it has, but it's being used to transport the giants, so there's a good chance they're not going to want to use it in combat. I say we ride straight into them and cut them off. They won't see it coming, and by the time they try to change routes, we'll be too close and won't have much of a fight on our hands. Stew and Sandy, that tank is your responsibility. I want you to take it down, make sure it's out of the fight, and then come join up with us. That sound doable?"

Sandy and Stew nodded in unison. "Yeah, we can take it down," Stew said.

Suzuki turned to Beth. "You're nimbler than I am. I'm going to need you to deal with the majority of the orcs. I'll be there to back you up, but I think you're going to be the one doing the most damage. Reasonable?"

Beth turned one of her daggers and flipped it in the air before catching it. "Suzy, that's not so much a plan as you saying something obvious," she teased.

"Yeah, well, I just wanted you to know."

"Oh, trust me, I know how good I am."

"All right, Mundanes. Let's go free us some giants."

20

The Mundanes took off over the edge of the cliff toward the convoy, the battle cats racing along the open plain. It would not take long for the Mundanes to overtake their prey. Still, Suzuki did not want to congratulate himself too quickly. Just because they looked like they were evenly matched with the orcs ahead, didn't make it true. These were the Dark One's forces. Anything could, and often did, happen.

They cut across the plain in a horizontal fashion, heading to cut off the convoy a few feet ahead of their destination, hopefully forcing the convoy to change direction and lose speed. The Mundanes split apart as they got closer.

Beth glassed the formation and pointed ahead, signaling to Suzuki she was ready to press in closer to attack. Behind Suzuki, Sandy and Stew were changing course to head straight for the tank.

Suzuki sped up. In a few moments, they would be coming over another hill, and either the tank or orcs would be within striking distance. Suzuki felt his guts up in his heart. He'd been in fights before but very few fights while riding. And even then, most of the fights had been trying to flee and avoid combat. This was the first time he'd be leading a strike on the offense. It was more than a little nerve-wracking, and he tried to control his breathing so his nervousness wouldn't get the best of him. He drew his axe and shakily stood atop his battle cat as they crested the hill.

The orcs were moving at a steady, fast speed. Their horses were huge, their nostrils flaring as if they could have snorted flames. The orcs were larger than most of the orcs Suzuki had seen. Their bodies were covered in a variety of tribal tattoos. They must have all been tribe leaders. The orcs moved along with the tank in the back with the efficiency of a machine. They hadn't taken any notice of the Mundanes.

In the back of his head, Suzuki couldn't help but feel bad for what he was about to do. The longer the Mundanes had been fighting the Dark One, the harder it was getting to do their job, every few weeks finding out just how little control any of the Dark One's forces actually had. These orcs didn't want to kill the Mundanes. They didn't want to be taking over the realm. But here they were, not even aware they no longer had a will.

Beth rode up to Suzuki's side. "Are you ready to do this?" Beth asked.

Suzuki motioned for the spyglass and glassed behind the tank to see if Sandy and Stew had gotten into position. Stew raised his hand to signal to Suzuki he was ready. "Yeah, let's do this," Suzuki finally said. He and Beth sped up, heading for the front of the convoy. As they closed in, Beth pulled off her short bow, got to her feet, and took aim. She fired a shot. The arrow landed in the head of the orc in the lead. Suzuki took aim with his axe as well and sent it flying at the next orc.

The axe hit him in the arm and sent him flying off his horse. Suzuki recalled his axe.

Beth grabbed the fur of her battle cat and kicked it in the sides. "Come on, we have to close the gap!" she shouted.

The two sped toward the convoy as the orcs snapped the reins of their steeds and increased their speed, the horses' hooves digging into the ground. The orcs leaned over, their muscles twitching together with those of their horses as they turned their course to the right, attempting to put distance between the two Mundanes coming up on them from the side.

Suzuki noted the orcs didn't turn to fight. That wasn't common for orcs, especially orcs under the Dark One's control. Getting the giants to their destination was obviously the priority, and a big enough one for the orcs to try to avoid a fight. Suzuki was curious to know what was going to happen if Sandy and Stew were able to get the tank away from the rest of the convoy. That might be enough to get the convoy to stop completely. Then they could have a stand-up fight and see if they were strong enough to best a group nearly three times their size.

Sandy and Stew were working on getting the tank separated from the rest of the convoy. It looked as if they were still trying to figure out the best way to stop the tank. Stew obviously was strong enough to tip the thing over, but he was at a disadvantage due to being restricted to his battle cat. He and Sandy still hadn't gotten close enough for him to get his hands on the tank, and it would be damn near impossible if they were still moving.

Usually Sandy would have called down lightning or hit the tank with a fireball, but that was out of the question now. She was noticeably frustrated, trying to figure out how she could stop the tank. There was the option of her recently realized bone-based attacks, but none of that seemed strong enough to take out the tank.

The tank didn't have any visible signs of entry other than the cannon, but it would be an obvious mistake to try to climb down the barrel of what was in essence a huge gun.

Suzuki and Beth raced after the head of the convey, which had managed to change their course to the right. They were moving at roughly the same speed as the Mundanes' battle cats. This was going to be fight of attrition. If the orcs lost enough of their riders, there would be a good chance they would risk a fight. *Or the horses,* Suzuki thought.

Suzuki turned to Beth and shouted, "Take out the horses!"

Beth took aim with her short bow and let loose shot after shot, her arrows hitting the legs of one of the horses toward the back of the convoy, the horse's legs going out from beneath it before pitching it forward, and tossing its rider. The rider's face slammed into the ground, and he slid across the grass, dead.

As Beth prepared to take aim again, one of the orcs turned in his seat with a plasma rifle in his hand. He fired and a large bolt of burning hot plasma arched over the plains, scorching the grass beneath it, heading straight for Suzuki and Beth.

Suzuki and Beth broke apart, Suzuki going to the right and Beth going to the left. The bolt of plasma ripped up the ground they had stood on. "We gotta close the distance!" Suzuki shouted. "We can't compete with that kind of fire-power. Get in close and do it fast."

Both Suzuki and Beth grabbed their battle cats' fur and kicked them in the sides. The cats were fast, and they could go faster still.

Ahead, the orc who fired the rifle took aim and fired again.

The bolt of plasma came straight for Suzuki. There was enough distance that Suzuki was able to dodge the attack.

That was going to be the risk.

If they remained at a distance, they would have space to maneuver around the attacks, but that would reduce them to sitting ducks. If Suzuki and Beth got closer to the convoy, it would make it easier for them to launch their own offense, but the tradeoff would be they would have much less room to maneuver away from the orc's superior firepower.

Stew and Sandy were still trying to close the gap between them and the tank. Stew turned to Sandy and asked, "Okay, so do we got anything?"

Sandy's forehead was still screwed up as she tried to figure out how she was going to get Stew and her closer. Then something clicked. She pointed her arm, reaching out toward the orc who lay dead beside its horse. Her eyes turned black and her skin paled as a row of bones protruded from her spine.

The dead orc rose slowly, picking itself up off the ground and reaching down to grab its axe as its horse rose beside him, their eyes white in death. The orc climbed onto the dead horse, and they took off toward the tank.

Sandy wasn't done yet. She grabbed one of the longer bones coming from her spine and pulled it out, screaming in pain as she ripped it from her skin and sending a trail of blood flying after her. She reached for another and ripped it out, then slammed the two pieces together, fusing them into an even longer bone, almost like a vaulting pole. She took the sharper ends and thrust it into her palm, the bone growing over her hands and fusing to her, protruding and running up her arm, then clasping down and reinforcing her strength. "Get hard, Stew," Sandy shouted.

Stew's body started to bulge as his muscles swelled and he grew. Sandy waved her bone pole in front of Stew, kicking her battle cat to increase its speed and catch up to the tank. Stew took hold of the pole and Sandy leaned back, and with all her strength, aided by Stew jumping in the same direction, swung Stew into the side of the tank. Stew tucked his body as well as he could, effectively becoming a giant wrecking ball. The bones along Sandy's arms started to crack and she screamed in pain, but the bone pole held, and Stew slammed into the side of the tank.

The force of Stew's body dented the tank and rocked it to the side. As Stew and Sandy watched, their eyes wide and hopeful, the tank slowly tipped over, fell on its side, and skidded across the ground. That was enough to get the attention of the orcs ahead, who turned to see what was happening as Stew hit the ground, looking for his cat.

Two of the orcs turned back and headed toward Stew. One of them pulled out a plasma rifle and fired. The shot hit Stew point-blank and sent him flying through the air. He hit the ground and grasped his torso. The shot had burned through part of his chest, and the skin was seared off. Stew roared in pain and rage as his eyes lost their true color and turned bright red. His body swelled again, and he grew even larger as if the pain were fueling his rage. He didn't wait for his cat. He bolted toward the two orcs who were pelting toward him.

The orc fired again and Stew dodged to the side, now on all fours, bounding toward the two orcs and connecting with one of them. They tumbled across the ground, the orc the first to his feet, pulling out his axe and slashing at Stew, who grabbed the axe mid-swing, pulled it back, and ripped the orc's arm off. Stew lifted the orc and snapped his neck, then threw the body at the other orc.

As the orc sailed through the air, the bones in his body started to pop out and the body swelled as if it were filled with poisonous gas. Once the dead orc's body hit the other orc, it exploded in a mushroom cloud of green gas.

Sandy rode up to Stew. "You need to shrink," Sandy said. "Then jump on."

Stew closed his eyes as he tried to concentrate. His body didn't return to its normal state. "Can't." Stew huffed. "Can't get small."

"Oh, shit, that's not good."

Stew waved away Sandy's concerns. "Not now. Later. Now kill. Now kill everything." Then Stew bent over on all fours, his body still swelling but now taking on a leaner, tighter look, as if the bulky muscle that had been used for strength was now being used for speed. He took off toward the rest of the convoy, which was beginning to loop back around to deal with the lost tank.

Toward the front, Suzuki and Beth had nearly closed the gap between them and the convoy. They were both trying to pick off as many orcs as they could, but they had overestimated how many of them there were.

One final push was all it was going to take.

Beth stood atop her battle cat as it got closer, and she leapt, landing on the back of one of the orc's steeds. She stabbed the orc in the sides repeatedly until he slumped over and she tossed him off the horse, now in the thick of the rest of the orcs. She flung her daggers into the crowd, still tethered to her through the alien tech, and swung them around, cutting up all the orcs in her radius. Most of the orcs managed to speed up in time to keep from getting caught in the flurry of death, but Beth was able to cut down a good chunk of them.

As the orcs rode toward the tank, Suzuki enchanted his axe and sped his battle cat up. He threw his axe into the back of one of the orcs toward the front of the convoy, hitting him in the back and killing him. The orc's body burst into flames, and as the rest of the orcs rushed past their fallen comrade, Suzuki closed his eyes and concentrated on the most recent rune he had carved into his axe: explosion.

The body of the flaming orc exploded, setting on fire two other orcs and their horses. The rest of the orcs scattered to get away from the flames.

Most of the convoy had been destroyed, and what was left was heading toward the tank. That was until Stew sailed through the air, grabbing one of the orcs off his horse, turned in mid-air, and tossed him at another orc, knocking them both over before his shoulder cannon whirled and fired, burning through both.

At that point, the rest of the orcs fled as the Mundanes converged on the only one stupid enough to have returned to the overturned tank. The orc jumped off its horse and ran toward the tank, turning suddenly and drawing its sword to face off against the four Mundanes.

The orc spat on the ground and slammed its sword against its shield. "You'll never fucking take me!" the orc shouted. "I will not give up my master's spoils."

Suzuki looked at the rest of the Mundanes. "I don't know, four on one is pretty fucked up," he said.

The rest of the Mundanes nodded. Sandy stepped forward. "You sure you don't want to just, you know, *go*?" she asked.

"I will not flee. Ever."

Sandy nodded slowly as if she understood a great truth. "You're wounded," Sandy said. "Your leg."

The orc looked down at his leg. He was in fact wounded, a large cut running up his thigh.

Sandy pointed at the orc's leg, and the joints in her hand twisted and cracked.

The orc screamed in pain as the wound in his thigh stretched all the way down to his foot. His femur pushed out of his skin, and he fell to the ground. Sandy walked over to the orc and knelt beside him. "I am not going to kill you," Sandy whispered into his ear, "but I am going to get information from you. Do you understand? You are going to talk, or you are going to hurt. Do you understand?"

"I will not talk!" the orc shouted.

Sandy stood and waved her hand over the orc. Giant bones erupted from the ground and encased the orc, hiding him from the view of the rest of the Mundanes. She walked back to her fellow MERCs. "You guys let the giants out. I need to help Stew," she said.

Suzuki pointed to where the orc was. "Sandy, what the fuck do you think you're going to do?" he asked.

Sandy looked back casually. "I'm going to torture him until he tells me what I want to hear."

"Jesus Christ, are you serious?"

"Our intel has been shit. Myrddin isn't giving us enough information."

"Sandy, we can't do that. That's not—"

"Suz, that's not you, and it doesn't have to be you. It's not Stew, and it doesn't have to be him. But it's me, so just look away, all right?"

Beth rested her hand on Suzuki's shoulder. "Come on, we need to get those giants out of there."

Suzuki nodded and followed her. He didn't want to think about what was going to happen to that orc. He wanted to push it as far from his mind as he could. But he knew, deep down, it didn't matter. It wasn't any worse than what had been done to Beth. It wasn't any worse than having just mowed down a dozen orcs. The only difference was that he didn't have to have this blood on his hands.

Still, Suzuki couldn't help looking over his shoulder at Sandy kneeling in front of Stew, who looked more like a monster than a human, his shoulders bulging with muscles, his eyes large and red and his mouth wide, covered with blood, the rest of him slumped over, supported by his massive hands. Sandy had his face in her hands and was kissing his forehead. Slowly, Stew's body began shrinking, his muscles deflating, his bones shortening, until he looked like his normal self again. Once he had returned to normal, he ran over to join Beth and Suzuki, while Sandy made her way to the bone cage she had created.

Stew leaned against the tank and pushed until he was able to flip it over. Suzuki couldn't help but note that even in his regular state, Stew's strength had nearly tripled. The tank must have weighed at least a ton. And on top of that, the tank was filled with giants. Once the tank was flipped over, Stew ripped the door off.

Inside there were at least twenty giants. They were chained together, and their hands had been pulled down to their feet and chained there as well, so they were forced into an extremely uncomfortable position. Their heads had been covered with black bags. They trembled in the sunlight.

The Mundanes were too shocked to move at first. Finally,

Suzuki climbed into the tank. He reached out for one of the giants, who screamed at the touch of Suzuki's hand. "Hey, it's going to be okay," Suzuki whispered. "We're not going to hurt you. We're here to free you."

Suzuki cut through the giant's chains, then Stew and Beth climbed into the tank and helped Suzuki free the rest of the giants. They removed the giant's head coverings and exited the tank to give the giants room to step out and stretch to their full heights.

The giants looked around, confused at first. Then the largest one turned to Suzuki and knelt so they could be eye to eye. "You freed us, little one," the giant said. "We are forever in your debt."

Suzuki smiled and extended his hand. "Don't even worry about it," he said. "We're all in this together."

The giant smiled, a sad-looking spectacle.

There was no joy in his expression.

It was the smile of one who was only hanging on by a thread. "Many of our brothers and sisters died when we were captured. We may be the last of this tribe," he said slowly. "It means a lot to us all that you did not allow us to become play-things for the Dark One. One day, we will repay you."

Stew stepped forward and unsheathed his sword. He presented it to the giant. "You could take up arms with us," Stew suggested. "Having allies as big as you would make a huge difference."

The giant shook his head as he stood up. "No, I am afraid that is the one thing we cannot do. Violence is not a part of our nature, and we wish for it never to be. There must be some on Middang3ard who remember such things. Thank you once more, and we will repay you."

The giant motioned to the rest, and they took off running

in the direction of the jungle. Stew knelt and looked at the footprints. "Shit, how the fuck can something so big be such a fucking wuss?" Stew grumbled. "Totally all right with letting everyone else fight their battles."

Suzuki crouched beside Stew. "I think he's right. Maybe everyone *shouldn't* be like us."

Beth came over to the two young men and sat down next to them. "No, he is right," Beth said. "We're soldiers. Mercenaries. Killers. It's important there are people like us, but that doesn't mean everyone should be. We do this so others don't have to."

Stew looked at Beth. "You really think so?"

Beth nodded her head. "We aren't the same kids who used to sit around and play VR," she said. "We all know it, even if we're having fun most of the time. And that probably says something else about us, that we're enjoying this. We're warriors. It's deep in us. I don't have any shame about it. We're strong enough for others. That's the way it should be."

Suzuki heard Sandy's voice from behind him. "All right, I got our intel," she said.

Sandy was covered head to toe in blood and held a sharp bone dagger in her hand. Suzuki turned to face her. "What did you—"

"I didn't kill him. Turns out necromancy goes both ways. I still can heal. I didn't know what to tell him. It's not like I could say, go enjoy the rest of your life. He doesn't have a life anymore. All that's going to happen is he's going to run back to the Dark One and get put back to work, not even knowing he doesn't even have his own fucking mind anymore. It probably would be better if he was dead. But I couldn't do it. Not like that. But he told me what I wanted."

"And what was that?"

"We got more work to do before we hit that facility."

Stew's stomach grumbled loudly, and he lay back and groaned. "I know this isn't the most appropriate time, but do you guys want to eat?" he asked. "I'm fucking starving."

Suzuki looked around the battlefield strewn with bodies, covered in blood and viscera. "Surprisingly, I could eat, dude," he said. "Let's get cleaned up."

21

During their meal, the Mundanes discussed what their next steps would be. Sandy had found out this was only one part of a larger caravan that had been split off from the first in an attempt to confuse the Mundanes.

It was, in fact, a decoy.

The orcs who had been sent were very aware they were probably going to die, but they had not expected any of the Mundanes to be willing to torture one of them for information. It sounded like the Dark One was not expecting that level of savagery from the Mundanes. Even though it turned Suzuki's stomach, he knew this was a lack of foresight on the part of his enemies he could use to his advantage.

The second part of the convoy was much larger. There were no horses, just four tanks. Unlike the tank they saw today, these were armed—heavy artillery from what Sandy had been told. "What kind of artillery, though?" Suzuki asked, irritated at the vagueness of her descriptions.

A bone blade slowly pushed out of Sandy's palm and she

pulled it out, wincing. "Do you want me to go find out?" she asked.

"The orc is still here? I thought you let him go."

"No, I said I didn't kill him, and I healed him. I didn't let him go, though. I wasn't sure if we were going to have a use for him later. Does that bother you?"

Suzuki shook his head. He'd had a lot of time to think over what Beth said. The Mundanes existed so everyone didn't have to become what they were becoming. Even their enemy didn't think they were capable of becoming what they might need to. "No," Suzuki finally said. "And I want to be there when you interrogate him this time."

Sandy shook her head as she tossed the dagger in the ground. "No, you don't, Suzuki. It's going to get really bad in there. He's a tough son of a bitch."

"I know I'm not going to like it, Sandy. That doesn't mean you should have to be the only one to do this. I'm going with you."

"All right. Don't say I didn't warn you. Probably wasn't the greatest idea to eat first but, who knows, might help out your stomach. Come on, let's get this over with."

Sandy stood and Suzuki followed her as she walked over to the bone cage. She waved her hand, and part of the bone chipped and fell away. She stepped inside, Suzuki right behind her. The bone wall sealed up behind her.

The orc sat in the middle of the cage. Bones stretched out from the ground. His arm had been broken, and the bone that jutted out was fused to the bone cage. He looked up when the two Mundanes stepped into the cage. He spat on the ground in their direction when he met their eyes. "I'm not telling you fuckers anything else!" the orc shouted.

Suzuki knelt in front of the orc and cleared his throat. "My name is Suzuki. What—"

"I know what your fucking name is, human," the orc interrupted.

Suzuki cleared his throat again and swallowed. He took a deep breath. He hadn't thought this through. Had no idea what to expect. No idea what he was going to do. At the very least, he knew it was an interrogation. Possibly torture. "I said, my name is Suzuki," he started again. "What's yours?"

"What the fuck do you want to know my name for?"

"So I know who I'm talking to."

"Does it matter who you're talking to?"

"It would be nice to have a conversation. Unless you want Sandy to keep cutting you?"

Suzuki raised his eyebrows, trying to look as if he didn't care either way. If he was honest with himself, he'd admit he would prefer not to see what Sandy was capable of doing to the orc. He knew Sandy had a thing for violence, but the callous way she had decided to torture the orc indicated a level of sadism Suzuki hadn't known Sandy had in her. He would be all right not witnessing it firsthand.

Suzuki grabbed the orc by the chin and forced him to look at him. "I'm going to ask you some questions," Suzuki informed him. "I would like you to answer those questions. We already know another convoy is coming, mostly tanks. I want to know what kind of artillery they're using."

The orc laughed harshly. "Why do you think it matters? It's more than enough to deal with four puny humans," he countered.

"Not too puny to have killed your entire troop. Right? Or were you all exceptionally weak?"

The orc's face twitched.

Suzuki had touched something. He wondered if he could get the information he wanted to get without having to hurt the orc. Maybe it was just as much of a mental game as anything else.

Suzuki let go of the orc's chin and leaned a little closer. "Is that why you got sent to be a decoy for us?" he asked. "Because you're weak and expendable? I'm assuming that's how working with the Dark One goes. The weak ones to the front to get chopped down. Anything else he feels like is superior, stronger, gets to live. But orcs like you? You're just grunts, waiting to die, right?"

"We were not weak. We knew the risk. We took the sacrifice."

"So, you knew ahead of the time this was going to be a sacrifice. You knew ahead of time you were going to die?"

The orc puffed out his chest and looked away as if he were thinking of something else. "It is an honor to know your duty and to fulfill it to your clan."

"And that was your clan? Even with the different clan markings? It looked like you might have all been chieftains of another clan. What happened to those clans?"

The orc refused to meet Suzuki's eyes.

The corners of his mouth did twitch, though. It was the first time Suzuki could recall ever seeing a break in the Dark One's indoctrination.

Somewhere, beneath all of the brainwashing, there was still an orc, one who remembered their traditions, one who perhaps remembered their family. But more importantly than any of those things, it was an orc who was beginning to remember he was an orc.

Suzuki leaned back as he rubbed his chin. "Since when is it honorable to be a sacrifice?" Suzuki asked.

The orc snapped forward, gnashing his teeth. "What the fuck do you know about sacrifice?" he shouted.

Suzuki laughed. "I've sacrificed my entire life. Everything I ever knew. The kind of person I used to be. All of it gone, and I'm never getting it back. I sacrificed it all to wipe piece-of-shit acolytes of the Dark One off the face of the realm. That's everything I've sacrificed. I might not be willing to do anything to get the information I want, but I know Sandy is."

Suzuki stood and turned, ready to leave the cage. He met Sandy's eyes. "He's all yours."

Sandy stepped forward, bone spikes starting to push out of the skin on her shoulders, up and down her spine and her arms. The orc screamed and pulled back away from Sandy as a dagger pushed its way through her palms. "All right, all right!" the orc shouted. "I'll tell you whatever the fuck you want to know. Just keep her away from me. Anything you want! Anything you want! Don't let her get close to me."

Suzuki breathed a sigh of relief.

He had been ready to let Sandy get the information, but he had hoped the orc would crack before then.

Suzuki wasn't lying.

He was willing to do whatever it took to take down the Dark One.

But there were some things he was more willing to do than others and some things he would like to avoid. He was glad he could leave it off at interrogation and not torture. Suzuki turned to meet the orc. He knelt beside Sandy, who had her dagger inside the orc's mouth, pressed against the side. "What are they packing?" Suzuki asked.

The orc looked up at Suzuki and then to Sandy as if he were thinking of changing his mind. Then he said, "All Dark One tech. The advanced shit. Not just plasma rifles. We aren't all given the same information. But they're supposed to be prototypes of new battle tech that is going to roll out. This is their practice. They've been specifically designed for you."

"Wait, what do you mean, for us?"

The orc looked uncertain about speaking again, but he went ahead anyway. "The Dark One has decided the Mundanes are enemy number one, more than any military. Even more than Myrddin. The tanks were designed specifically to counter the core aspects of your formation, specifically the mages. That's all I know. I don't know how they're supposed to, but that's what they're supposed to do."

Sandy looked up at Suzuki and smirked. "Guess that little power demotion was a blessing in disguise," she conceded. "They're probably expecting the flying, lightning bolt throwing mage I used to be. That gives us a little bit of the element of surprise. Anything else you want to know?"

Suzuki turned back to the orc. "When are they arriving?"

The orc moved his tongue around awkwardly in his mouth as he tried to avoid the dagger. "Around one in the morning. They're taking a different route, though. Closer to the facility."

"Are you going to tell us exactly where that is?"

"Yeah, yeah. Of course, I'll take you there. Swear by the gods."

"How do I know you aren't setting us up for a trap?"

"I don't fucking know. I don't fucking know how to prove that."

Suzuki leaned back and thought for a few seconds. "Oh, I know how to," he said as he looked through his HUD. He put in a requisition order to be filled ASAP, listing it as an emergency of the highest caliber. If there were any questions, they could get in contact with Myrddin.

Suddenly, Suzuki's HUD began to ring. He didn't know what the sound was at first, but it sounded vaguely like a cellphone ring. He stood up abruptly and said, "Hold on, I got to take this. Sandy, make sure he doesn't get too comfortable."

Suzuki stepped outside and answered his HUD. "Hello?" he asked tentatively.

The voice on the other end was grave, severe, and annoyed. "And when has it become custom for MERCs to throw around my name as proof their requisition orders are important?"

Suzuki almost choked as he realized he was talking to Myrddin. "Oh, shit, I'm sorry, sir. I didn't realize anyone would actually get in—"

"Do you have any idea how irritating it is to get an email in the middle of the night concerning a requisition?"

Something flared up in Suzuki, and he spoke without thinking. "Do you know how fucking irritating it is to be trying to get a requisition order filled for a mission you sent us on, only to be called up like some delinquent child for trying to get supplies to take care of said mission?"

There was a long silence, and then Myrddin started to laugh. "Oh, my, you are not the meek child I brought to Middang3ard those few months ago. How you have grown, my dear boy. Do I hear a hint of resentment?"

Suzuki took a deep breath. "No, sir. There isn't. Just irritation, and not just with this moment. I feel like we've been in the dark about so much, and when we do give you information, we don't necessarily see what is done with it."

"Much of the information we keep quiet is because it is classified, and it would be a security risk to tell every MERC party out there."

"We aren't just any MERC party, though, sir. The

Mundanes are being specifically targeted by the Dark One. We're enemy number one. They've developed tech specifically for our party."

Myrddin didn't answer at first, but Suzuki could hear him breathing over the phone. Suzuki took this as another chance to speak. "I know you share intel with Chip and Diana and not the rest of us. I think it's time we were given the same amount of respect the Dark One is giving us. It's time we stopped getting treated like children and get brought into the loop, sir. We're all here for the same thing. Help us defend Middang3ard better."

Myrddin coughed, a forced and fake sound. "You make a good point," he said. "José did well to choose you. Fine, going forth, you'll have access to confidential reports and information. Do not make me regret this. And it goes without saying, requisitions that don't need my approval. I'll push through this order, and when you return, we'll clear the Mundanes for Alpha Level access."

"Thank you, sir."

"Not a problem, MERC. Try not to die tonight. If the Dark One wants you dead this badly, we obviously need you. Good night, Suzuki. And good luck."

Myrddin hung up. Suzuki let out a deep breath. It was the first time he had ever stood up to an authority figure other than José. It felt good not to be walked over, not to be ignored. And he had said exactly what he felt. It was about time the MERC officials started treating the Mundanes like the vital piece they were.

Suzuki went back into the bone cage. The orc and Sandy were still in the same position. "You're coming with us," Suzuki said as he opened his inventory and selected his requisition order. A MERC uniform, one of the outdated ones with the massive MERC insignia on the front and back, materialized in front of the orc. The outfit came along with a helmet fit specifically for an orc. "Suit up. You're a MERC tonight."

———

The Mundanes had the orc, now dressed in MERC gear, lead them down to the path the Dark One's caravan was going to use to reach the facility. It was more than a few miles up from where the Mundanes had intercepted the orcs. The facility was visible in the distance from their vantage point. There was still about three hours before the caravan was to arrive.

Sandy looked about the road and asked, "So, what's the plan?"

Suzuki knelt, looking at the beaten path of the road. It was well-traveled. That meant whoever used this path was used to it and would most likely take it for granted. Their guard would be down. "Going head to head with tech specifically created to take us out is a shit idea," he mused. "Even if we've had enough class changes to throw them off. I think Stew and I are the only ones still rolling with what we started with. And even then, Stew's berserker mode seems like it's been changing. Got any news on that, Stew?"

Stew shrugged and looked away sheepishly. "Nothing I really understand," Stew admitted. "Last time I went berserk felt the same as any of the other times, but my body was doing weird stuff. Muscles kept changing around for different reasons, not that I'm complaining. The only problem was I couldn't just switch back like I usually do. Sandy had to calm me down before I could change. But I don't see how that's going to be too big of a problem. Just means I'll be more available to rip shit up as far as I'm concerned."

"All right, that's one less thing to worry about. So, if anything, we have the chance to catch them off guard. I think we should take another route, one we've never done before, and they'll definitely not be ready for. We're going to set up a trap."

The Mundanes looked at each other, a little uncertain of what Suzuki was suggesting. Suzuki could see their wariness and smiled. "Hey, it's not that big a jump. It's not like we'll only have that to rely on. I'm thinking we could set up some traps, take out as many of the tanks as we can; that way, we don't have something on our plate we can't handle."

Beth was the first to voice her objection. "And we all know exactly how much about traps?" she asked.

Suzuki nodded as he thought it over. "True, we don't have the most experience. But we have a rogue and a necromancer. That should be enough to get this shit going. Beth, I want you to go through your HUD and see if you can find anything that's applicable in the tutorials. Sandy, I've seen you getting creative while figuring out how to use your necromancy. Now's the time to get very creative. Chip and Diana will be here in about half an hour, and they can help us flesh out the rest. While you guys take care of that, I'm going to see if our little orc friend wants to take a walk with Stew and me and see if there was anything that's slipped his mind he might want to let us know about right now."

Beth took a seat in the high grass and started to go through her tutorials. It had been a long time since she had felt the need to refresh herself with any combat protocols, but she quickly found there were numerous sections on building traps with things that were already in her inventory. As she had slowly been changing over her class, her HUD had been compensating by changing out some of the equipment she no longer had a use for and replacing it with more rogue and assassin based equipment and tech.

Sandy, on the other hand, was walking the length of the road, occasionally stopping to press her hand to the soft dirt, then her ear, listening to what was beneath. She smiled as she worked, ideas obviously starting to pop up in her head.

Suzuki and Stew took the orc on a walk. As they walked farther down the road, Suzuki asked the orc his name again. The orc snorted and asked Suzuki why he wanted to know. "You're a party member tonight. I'd hate for you to fall in battle and for none of us to know your name."

The orc snorted and spat. "I am not a part of your pathetic party," the orc retorted.

Suzuki laughed mockingly. "It doesn't matter if you think you are or not. The caravan is going to think you are, and they're going to fire at you regardless. Unless they know specifically how many Mundanes there are supposed to be tonight."

The orc looked around as if he had a reasonable hope of getting away and then collapsed into himself, his face crushed. He was defeated. Suzuki could see it. "So, what's your name?" Suzuki asked.

"Tobin. Tobin of the winter Clans of the Hills, son of Gworm and Ethilda."

Suzuki extended his hand to Tobin. "I am Suzuki, Lover of the Great Dragon Ashegoreth, Bane of Krampus, the One Unnoticed, the Man of Many Fates, the Mundanest of the Mundane. It's nice to meet you."

The orc eyed Suzuki's hand suspiciously. "What is the game you play, human?"

"Like I said, they're going to be firing at you too, and I'm not just going to let that happen. As long as you wear those colors, you're a MERC, and as long as you're a MERC, you're a teammate. You don't turn on us, we don't turn on you. Got it?"

"But I serve the Dark One."

"How much of you does? When you talk, I still hear a little of that orc pride."

Stew stepped up next to the orc and bumped Tobin's shoulder. "If you can still call yourself an orc," he chided. "From what I knew, orcs didn't serve anyone. They definitely wouldn't be a slave to some bullshit asshole they don't even respect. Unless you respect an alien piece of shit who has to mind-control their army."

"I am not mind-controlled!"

"Then what the fuck are you doing following the Dark One instead of being a fucking orc?"

Tobin was silent. He looked down at his hands, at his long, strong claws. "I am...I am very confused..."

Suzuki circled Tobin, looking for any obvious signs of an implant. He couldn't see any. "Were you ever given an implant?" Suzuki asked.

Tobin looked at Suzuki, confused. "An implant? What do you speak of?"

"Something like a small microchip placed into your body."

Tobin shook his head. "No, I have nothing of that sort. But actually, a few years ago, I received an immunization. A plague had broken out amongst my tribe and our neighbors. We were approached by a scientist who said they had a cure and could immunize us against any more outbreaks." Tobin pulled down his pants so he was completely nude.

Stew turned away, covering his eyes. "Dude, you gotta tell

us when you're gonna pull out orc dong," he exclaimed. "No one is prepared for that. Ever."

Suzuki was too interested to be disturbed or embarrassed. There, right above the orc's cock, nestled in Tobin's pubic hair, was a microchip identical to those Suzuki had seen before. That was how the Dark One had gotten the orcs. He hadn't sent an army. He had poisoned them, then, under the guise of help, infected them with his indoctrination. Suzuki didn't ask permission. He pulled out his axe and slashed across Tobin's crotch. The orc tried to leap back, but he was too slow. Suzuki's axe hit true and cut the microchip in half.

An electric pulse rocked through Tobin's body, and he fell to his knees as he convulsed, foaming at the mouth. Finally, the convulsions left him and he knelt there, swaying like a dying tree. "What was that?" Tobin muttered.

Suzuki knelt next to Tobin and asked, "Do you remember anything? What do you remember?"

"You were asking me if I had an implant, then you swung your axe at me like a fucking madman."

"What about the Dark One? What do you think about the Dark One?"

Tobin gave Suzuki a look of immense confusion. He opened his mouth to speak but said nothing, his jaw hanging open as if someone had just snatched the words from him. He closed his mouth and then opened it again, saying, "I hate him with all of my heart for everything he's done."

A voice came from behind Suzuki. It was Chip. She was shouting something he couldn't hear.

"Come on," Suzuki said. "Time to meet the rest of the team."

Suzuki and Stew led Tobin back to the rest of the Mundanes. They had gathered around Beth, who was pacing.

Tobin removed his helmet, and Chip and Diana saw he was an orc. Neither of them reacted strongly. Diana nodded and introduced herself.

Chip extended her hand to Tobin. "I'm assuming there's news to be given to me at some point or another."

Suzuki decided it would be better to get it out of the way from the get-go. "This is Tobin," Suzuki explained. "We captured him earlier today, and we've dechipped him. So, if anyone has anything to say before we get started with what we have to do, now is the time to get it out in the open."

Sandy stepped forward, holding her head up high. "I'm sorry for what I had to do earlier," she apologized. "It must have been horrible. But you had—"

Tobin raised his hand, silencing Sandy. "There's no need to apologize," he said. "You did what you had to do. I have done worse without wanting to. If you hadn't taken me prisoner, I would not have my own mind anymore. If anything, I owe you Mundanes my thanks. I will make it up to you tonight and for as long as it takes."

Diana looked the orc up and down before sighing and chuckling. "Never thought I would have the experience of fighting alongside an orc," she said. "Should be interesting."

Suzuki stepped into the middle of the circle the Mundanes had formed. "Yeah, interesting is right. But interesting is not what we have to focus on now. We only have a little bit of time before the caravan gets here. Beth, how are those traps coming along?"

Beth pointed to two separate spots along the road. "These are the places I got picked out. But I'm a little—"

Suzuki pointed toward Chip and said, "Give Beth a hand with those traps. I want them finished as soon as possible."

Chip nodded and grabbed Beth's arm, then led her off into the darkness.

Suzuki turned to Sandy. "How are you coming along?" he asked.

Sandy walked toward the edge of the path, the place where the worn road met the soft, green grass. "I've planted trolls along the pathway. Once the tanks roll over them, they should summon the trolls we killed earlier."

"Are you all done?"

"Should be."

"Diana, check Sandy's work, and Sandy, go let Chip and Beth know they need to move their traps a little farther up the road. That way, we'll be able to catch the tanks that make it out from under the trolls."

Diana nodded and went to investigate Sandy's work as she went over to find Chip and Beth to relay the information about their traps. Suzuki turned to Stew and said, "You're going to have to find a place to hide too. Once the traps go off, I want you to take out at least one of the tanks, two if you can manage. How does that sound?"

Stew cracked his knuckles before stretching his arms. "I can definitely take out two of those," he boasted. "And I'll clean up anything else we miss."

"All right. Ideally, what I want to do is break up the caravan, take out each tank, and then sneak into the facility. The more damage we can do out here, the less we're going to have to deal with in there."

Stew left to figure out the best place for him to set up for the ambush. Suzuki turned to Tobin. "All right, Tobin, I need you to give it to me straight," he said. "Where are you at right now?"

Tobin looked down, his face crestfallen and ashamed. "I

am confused...there...it feels like there has been a huge part of my life carved out. I don't understand where it has gone because I feel like I was there the entire time. Confusion...but more than confusion...hatred. I know who took that time... who made me someone other than myself. And I want nothing more than to rid the realm of that person."

"All right. That sounds pretty solid to me. I'm going out on a limb with you here. I want you with Stew. Give him backup. And, I'm going to tell you this right now, if you hurt anyone under my watch, I will stop you. And I'll give you to Sandy. Do you understand?"

Tobin shivered as he answered. "Even if I wasn't completely on board, I would listen purely not to be alone in the same room with her ever again."

"Either way, that's good enough for me. Go figure shit out with Stew."

Tobin left and went to Stew, leaving Suzuki to watch as the Mundanes all figured out their separate pieces of the plan. Now Suzuki had to figure out how he was going to make a difference in the battle to come. He sat down, looking out into the night, the moon hanging heavy in the sky, swollen as if pregnant with possibilities.

It was a little past one in the morning when Suzuki saw the caravan approaching over the small bump of a hill in the distance. He sat up from his hiding spot, momentarily shedding the grass camo he and Beth had fashioned earlier in the night as they spoke about the plans of the evening, also talking about their other plans, the latter being vague and ambiguous, confusing and frightening them both while also planting a fire firmly in both their chests.

Suzuki raised his axe and set off his fire enchantment for a moment so the axe flashed in the night. It could have been easily mistaken for a shooting star, not that it needed to be. The flash was bright and fast and was meant for certain eyes. It was doubtful anyone else would have noticed.

The battle cats had been corralled somewhere in the darkness, watched by Diana. Suzuki thought it would be best to keep her out of the mix. If the tanks had been developed for the Mundanes, Diana's role was close enough to Sandy's old one that she could easily be compromised. Diana had reluctantly agreed. If the situation became horrid, she would rally the battle cats and bring the fight to the tanks. For the time being, she would wait and see how the ambush unfolded.

Suzuki took out Beth's spyglass and surveyed the caravan as it approached. There were five tanks, the exact same model as the one Suzuki had seen before. He wondered what it meant that these tanks had been designed for the Mundanes, and why the one they had encountered before was only a prototype. Maybe there was one tank per Mundane. Suzuki was flattered by the idea that it would take an entire tank to fell one Mundane. That flattery was short-lived as he focused on the war machines moving through the valley.

The first tank wasn't too far from Sandy's handiwork. That was the sign for the Mundanes. If everything went smoothly, they could take care of most of the tanks without a problem. And Suzuki had no lack of faith in his party members.

Suzuki heard the explosion before he saw anything; there was a loud bang but no light. Suzuki looked through the spyglass. He spied a cloud of deep green smoke rising from the ground, nearly obscuring his ability to see. He had already thought something like this might happen, so he jumped to his feet and ran to his second vantage point.

The first tank had crossed over Sandy's trap. The explosion had been her corroding bombs unleashing. As the miasma settled over the tanks, the hands of the dead trolls burst from the ground, grasping for the wheels.

The tank sped up, trying to speed past the reanimated appendages of the trolls. It was able to, flying past them, but the second tank was not so lucky. By now, the trolls had mostly pulled themselves up from the ground, their bodies still in fairly good condition, their eyes burning red in the night as they turned toward the tank closest to them, surrounding it, their massive arms slowing the tank down to a stop, tipping it over while the rest of the tanks, backed away and tried to go around the obstacle.

Up ahead, the first tank exploded in a flash of light. Suzuki glassed the area. The tank must have just gone over Beth and Chip's traps. They were simple things. Mere explosions but rigged expertly so the slightest touch would cause them to engulf in flames whatever passed over them. And there were more. That was just the first. The whole path had practically been lined with them.

The other tanks flew off the road, trying to avoid the path. That was when Stew stepped in. Even in the darkness, illuminated only by the flames of the fire, Stew's hulking presence could be seen as he leapt from the shadows like some overgrown mix between a man and a wolf and ran toward one of the tanks, his shoulder cannon firing.

The tank's cannon turned to face Stew, but he was too fast. He slammed into the side of the tank, sending it flying through the air as his shoulder cannon fired two more shots that tore the top of the tank off. It was close to where the prisoners were being held, but Suzuki trusted that Stew had his shit together enough not to make a grave mistake such as that. As the tank fell to the ground and skidded, Suzuki could see Tobin running toward the tank, holding to the darkness, so he could free the giants held within.

Suzuki looked over the entire battlefield. That was three tanks taken care of. There were only two more left. "Converge on the tank closest up the road," Suzuki commanded through his HUD as he checked the percentage of the party's success. It rested at a comfortable ninety percent. "Sandy, keep the tank in place. Stew, get in there and do damage. Beth and Chip, spread out and get ready to deal with the second one. Tobin, keep opening up those tanks."

There was a chorus of "rogers".

Suzuki watched as bones ripped out of the ground and covered one of the tanks moments before Stew, having grown larger and much less lean, barreled into the side. The tank tipped over before Stew leapt atop it and ripped the cannon off. *That means just one more*, Suzuki thought, glassing the last tank.

As Suzuki watched the last tank, he noticed it had not followed the other tanks, nor had it veered off its path. It had stopped dead in its tracks. Within seconds, it became obvious why the tank had ceased to move.

The night air filled with a siren. It sounded like the old World War II sirens Suzuki had heard in the movies.

The tank's wheels shot out from under it and four spindly legs stretched out as the top section of the tank extended into the air, arms stretching from the new upper torso as the cannon extended farther up. The arms split apart at the elbow so each had two separate appendages attached and ended in two plasma cannons each.

Suzuki leapt onto his battle cat and pulled his axe out.

He wasn't sure which of the Mundanes this tank was meant to target, but he was acutely aware it was not something any of the Mundanes had been expecting. He rode off toward the tank, his free hand gripping his battle cat's fur tightly as the rest of the Mundanes looked up, aware of the gigantic mechanical fiend that had risen up against them.

The mobile tank fired four shots, one from each of its hands, and another from the cannon atop its head. The plasma ripped through the air, leaving the scent of sulfur. The bolts hit the ground near Chip, searing away the grass and the earth as she leapt into the air, barely avoiding the blast. Diana ran toward Chip, casting a levitation spell and tossing Chip away from the burning earth.

As Suzuki rode toward the massive mechanical monster, he pulled up his HUD. Twenty-five percent chance of success. *Goddamn it,* Suzuki thought as he stood up on his battle cat. He scanned the battlefield. The rest of the Mundanes were getting into defensive positions, hiding behind the hills that enclosed the valley. It looked like Suzuki was the only one who was heading toward the machine. That was probably the best idea. The rest of the Mundanes had abilities that set them apart from each other. Suzuki didn't. He added nothing exceptional to combat other than his mind, and that was not something you could pin down and attack. At this point, it didn't make sense to try to micromanage the party. They knew what the threat was. They would be able to figure it out on their own. All he had to do was make sure he wasn't fucking it up.

Suzuki took aim at the cannon atop what looked to be a

head on the giant mechanized tank. He slowed his breathing, tried to imagine his axe flying in an arc toward its destination. Then he launched it and waited to see what would come.

The tank turned all its cannons toward Suzuki's axe and fired. Suzuki watched as his prized axe was obliterated. "Oh, that's just fucking great!" Suzuki shouted as the cannons turned in his direction. *Just my luck*, Suzuki thought. *The tank meant for me would be the one that was left over.*

Suzuki ran through his inventory until he came across the magic flares. He fired one into the air, setting the sky aflame with a streak of red. "All Mundanes on me," he shouted as he kicked his battle cat's sides, racing for the hill he had come from.

The machine fired five shots, one from its head and the others from its arms as its multiple legs scrambled in Suzuki's direction, steel and gears groaning as it raced past the rest of the Mundanes.

Sandy stretched out her palm and bones erupted from the earth, snagging the machine's legs. "Battle cats!" she shouted.

The battle cats lying in wait bounded from the darkness, each of them going toward their rider. Azrael was first amongst them, and as Sandy leapt onto him, a massive bone spear shot from her palm, nearly the size of her entire body. Blood gushed as she screamed in pain, and the spear connected with the back of the machine moving toward Suzuki.

The machine paused in its attack. It turned, swaying its cannon like some sort of eye to the rest of the Mundanes. "All right, guys," Beth said. "This is where we end it."

Suzuki patched himself into the rest of the Mundanes as he swung around on the other side, oblivious to the tank now that it had another focus. "Stew! Take the legs out with Sandy. Chip and Beth, if you can get on top of that thing, go for the cannon. Diana, come in strong. I want as much fucking wind as you can bring to topple this son of a bitch."

Diana took off from her position. She levitated into the sky, the black clouds swarming behind her, her wand outstretched. The cracks of her skin shone bright blue in the dead night, and bolts of lightning streaked through the sky, striking in a circle around the giant machine.

As the ground tore itself asunder, Stew's body pulsed and swelled. He fell forward on all fours, his jaw stretching as if he hoped to swallow the whole body of his prey, and he bounded forward as Sandy ran after him. Stew threw himself against one of the machine's legs while Sandy shot bone spear after bone spear at the other.

The machine took aim with its head plasma cannon as it began to topple, trying to fire but unable to choose a target. Its plasma beam went flying into the darkness of the night as its massive hands hit the ground, trying to hold itself up.

Suzuki was closing in atop his battle cat. He saw his opening and stood. Even if he didn't have his axe, he still had the standard weapons in the MERC inventory. He pulled down his HUD to see his percentages. Eighty percent chance of success, and that was unarmed. Fucking perfect. He leapt from the back of his battle cat, sailing through the air as, across the battlefield, Beth did the same. They both landed on the back of the machine as it stumbled to its feet in awkward movements.

Beth pulled out her daggers and slammed them into what would have been the spine of the creature. Suzuki ran toward its head cannon, pulled a broad sword from his inventory, and began hacking.

At the machine's base, Stew had set to the task of crippling it. He threw his entire body into the attempt. Sandy was beside him, pulling up bone after bone to wrap around the machine's other foot as Chip slid beneath the machine's legs, firing plasma shot after plasma shot, tearing through the machine's crotch. Above, Diana was bringing down another series of lightning bolts.

Suzuki raised his sword and drove it deep into the machine's main cannon.

There was a puff of smoke and something like a groan from the machine. Then the giant mech tank collapsed forward. Beth and Suzuki leapt off it, letting the machine crash into the ground.

The Mundanes gathered around the broken machine as Tobin rushed over and freed the giants within.

Suzuki only caught a glimpse of Tobin. His focus was elsewhere. In the distance, he saw a tank heading for the lights of the facility. *Goddamn it*, he thought to himself. *They had a backup plan.*

The Mundanes watched as the tank disappeared into the distance, the giants surrounding them and standing silently. "I'm going to assume I'm not going to be able to persuade you guys to help us."

The largest giant nodded and opened his mouth, no doubt to give the same speech the giants they had encountered earlier had given. Suzuki raised his hand and nodded quickly to show the giant he already understood their reasons for not wanting to join the fight. "No problem, don't worry about it. We understand."

Stew clicked his teeth as he looked at the giants but kept his mouth shut. Sandy was coaxing him so his muscles would return to normal.

Beth peered at the facility through her spyglass. "It's not that far away. We could get there in under half an hour."

Suzuki took the spyglass from Beth and looked through it. She was right. It wouldn't take too long to get there. The problem was not knowing what they were walking into. The fact there were giants heading to the facility meant it was probably manned, but they also weren't getting any deliveries from a sphere overhead. That meant there was a chance the facility wasn't filled with angels. It was most likely this was going to be a trap. The Dark One had already anticipated the Mundanes' decision to try to derail the caravan. It would not have been a hard guess to assume they would chase after the giants to free them.

Suzuki handed Beth the spyglass. "They're going to be waiting for us," he admitted.

Beth scoffed and pocketed the glass as she jumped onto her battle cat. "Obviously, but we're the heroes. We gotta do what we gotta do," Beth countered. "What else are we going to do? Sit on our asses and wait for them to come out and greet us?"

"We're going to have to go into this one blind."

The rest of the Mundanes climbed on their battle cats, Tobin jumping onto Diana's steed as Diana awkwardly looked around while Tobin wrapped his arms around her waist.

Suzuki pointed his new MERC axe at the facility. "All right, Mundanes. We know there are giants, probably angels, a shit ton of sprouts, and maybe the hardest fight of our lives," he shouted. "For honor!"

"For glory!" Beth, Stew, and Sandy shouted.

"For XP!" Diana and Chip joined in.

Tobin looked around confused, his eyes jumping from

Mundane to Mundane. "You guys have a fucking catch-phrase?" he asked.

Suzuki's HUD dinged. He looked down to check it. The message was from Myrddin. It said, **Most recent intel. Omega-level threat. Facility is massive. All staff is armed. Unclear how deep it runs long and down. Sending reinforcements. Do what you can. Stay alive until the cavalry arrives.**

"Tobin, I think you should head out for this one," Suzuki said. "Just heard from Myrddin. Apparently, we are in for a fucking fight. He doesn't know all of what's inside there, but whoever the hell is there is armed. We'll give you the coordinates for the Red Lion."

Tobin tried to argue but Suzuki raised his hand. "No, you're going to the Red Lion. But you are a MERC now. Get your ass out of here. All right?"

Tobin finally stopped putting up a fight and nodded. "All right, but the next one, I'm coming with."

Suzuki extended his hand and Tobin took it. "That's a fucking promise."

The Mundanes approached the facility, coming up on it slowly. Staying to the outskirts so they would not be caught in the light, the Mundanes attempted to be as quiet as possible. It felt like a useless decision. Suzuki was certain whoever was inside the facility already knew the Mundanes were coming. There was no way they didn't. Still, he wanted to avoid walking into a trap outright.

Once they were along the side of the facility, Beth and Chip separated from the main group to attempt to find a way in. It took less than ten minutes for them to find a suitable window to crack open so they and the rest of the Mundanes could sneak inside.

Suzuki was the last one to go through the window. He'd taken a moment to pull another axe from the MERC inventory, remembering Stew's endless weapons stock and drawing a new one. He stumbled onto the cool, sterile floor and picked himself up as quickly as he could. He looked around the room. None of the lights were on, and it was very dark. It had the same feeling as the last facility they had gone through, but Suzuki knew this one was not abandoned. "Find some lights," Suzuki suggested.

Chip's eyes glowed a bright white. She scanned the room, light falling wherever she cast her eyes. She found a switch and flipped it.

Once the lights were on, Suzuki could see the layout. They were in some kind of research room. There were scientific devices laid out on different tables, the likes of which Suzuki had never seen before. The tech in the room, as usual, was far beyond what Suzuki had ever seen before. The only thing Suzuki recognized was a datapad lying on the table. He grabbed it and tossed it to Chip.

Chip caught the datapad and booted it. "Might not be a good idea to go hacking in. Could mean giving away our position and a shite-ton of ghoulies coming up our asses."

"Get as much information as you can," Suzuki replied. "We're blind here. Maybe a layout, or at least the closest guess of where they would be taking the giants."

Chip looked through the datapad, groaning with irritation as she searched for the answers. She finally found what she was looking for. "Most likely going to be in the breeding room," she said as she pocketed the datapad.

Stew coughed and tried to stifle his giggling. "Is it seriously called the breeding room?" he asked.

"That's what it said."

"Sweet. I've always wanted to check out a breeding room. See how it's done."

Suzuki shook his head as he sighed and headed for the door. "Stew, can you keep the stupid jokes down until we have a better idea what the fuck we're doing?"

"Good thing we are checking out the breeding room. You

might be able to pick up some tips. Beth would probably appreciate it."

Beth walked past Stew and shoved him out of the way. "Trust me, Suzy doesn't need any pointers. Come on, douchenozzle, let's get going."

They snuck out of the room and into a well-lit hallway. It was the same layout they'd seen before, although from outside the darkened room, it was very obvious this one was running at full potential. This facility was even eerier than the other one, though. Somehow the medical pristineness was more off-putting than blood-covered walls.

Chip pointed down the hallway, looking at the datapad. "All right, we're going this way."

Beth rustled up against Suzuki as they walked down the halls. "We're blowing this place up, right?"

Suzuki nodded. "First, we find the giants and get them out. Then we blow the shit out of this place. Everyone, keep your eyes out for good spots to place detonators. I don't want to have to go on a full tour after we get the giants out."

The Mundanes moved down the hall. The doors lining the hall began to get farther apart until there were none. Suzuki wondered where all the workers were. If this facility had the same enchantment that increased its internal size, there was a good chance they weren't going to come across anyone, even if they were working.

There was a loud groaning from the rafters above the Mundanes. Suzuki held his hand up, and the party stopped. They stood in silence as Suzuki strained his ears to see if he had heard something or if it was just his mind fucking with him. After waiting for a few seconds, the Mundanes went forward.

They came to the end of the hall. There was one ominous

door, larger than all of them, and it whooshed open the moment Suzuki walked in front of it.

The room the Mundanes stepped into was huge. Not just long and wide, but also tall, the top of the room was capped with an ornate dome. In the dome was what looked like a laser. The room was also filled with tables, desks, and computers. In the middle of the room was a large tube, roughly twice as tall as Stew, which was filled with blue liquid.

Suzuki walked up to the tube to get a better look at it. He pressed his face close to the glass, and something in the water slammed against the tube. Suzuki jumped back out of instinct, surprised.

The thing that had attacked the tube was an angel, but it was not like any of the angels Suzuki had seen so far. This one was smaller, roughly the size of a gnome. Its arms were long and disjointed, looking as if they had three or four elbows. Its back legs were bent like a grasshopper's and its chest was concave and covered in spikes. Much like the angels he'd seen earlier, its back muscles were extremely enlarged, and it didn't have a face, only the line that ran from the top of its head to its chin, slowly peeling back in a snarl that showed row upon row of teeth.

Stew came up next to Suzuki and leaned close to the glass. "Looking to give it a kiss?"

Suzuki shoved Stew away and said, "Fuck off, dude."

Diana came up behind the two of them and separated them almost the way a mother would. Then she peered into the glass tube to look at the creature swimming around in it. The angel took notice of her and lunged against the glass, foiled by its container. "Hm...just as I thought," Diana murmured.

Suzuki crossed his arms as he watched the creature. "Care to illuminate us?"

"The angels change their body composition based on the host. See the markings around its hands? Those are the same markings redcap goblins are born with. This one must have had a redcap for a host. That was probably why those redcaps we saw were being attacked. They were being harvested for experiments."

Beth was walking around the room, looking into its corners alongside Chip. "This looks like a good place to start blowing shit up," she suggested.

Suzuki glanced over his shoulder at Chip and Diana. "All right, get the charges set. We'll detonate when we leave."

Chip and Beth went about to the different corners of the room, placing charges on the ground and ceiling, Beth boosting Chip up on her shoulders so she could reach higher.

As Beth and Chip worked, the door to the room opened. Four orcs wearing lab coats walked in. They dropped their coffee cups when they saw the Mundanes and instantly reached for the plasma rifles slung over their shoulders.

Suzuki reacted without thinking, pulling his new axe from his waist and launching it across the room, nailing one of the orcs in the chest. "Finish them fast!" Suzuki shouted as he sprinted toward the orcs, jumping to the side and narrowly dodging a plasma bolt.

Stew drew his sword and rushed toward the orcs, the cannon mount on his shoulder spinning around, taking aim at one and firing a blast of plasma in the orc's direction. The orc leapt out of the way of the attack and fired his rifle. The blast hit Stew square in the chest, sending him flying through the air, slamming against Diana, and knocking Diana's wand out of her hand. Diana scrambled for her wand as Sandy shot a bone spear from her palm, nailing one of the orcs to the ground.

Suzuki was the closest to the orcs, so he went for the one in the middle, hoping to break up the group. He tackled the orc to the ground and then wildly swung his axe around him, driving both of the other orcs away from him as the orc beneath him reached up and grabbed Suzuki's throat. Suzuki brought down his axe on the orc's arm and severed it clean from the orc's body before one of the other orcs grabbed Suzuki by the back of his armor and yanked him off.

Stew had gotten back onto his feet and closed the gap between himself and the orcs. He slashed the orc who held Suzuki, killing it. Sandy was right behind him, her bone daggers in hand, sailing through the air and landing on the orc who was just pinned to the ground. She drove her daggers into its chest and dragged them down, ripping its flesh, and then jumped away.

Suzuki fell atop the orc beneath him and slammed his sword into the orc's skull. He stood up as the orc twitched its final death spasms. "All right," he said as he wiped off his sword. "Stew and Diana, watch the doors until Beth and Chip are finished. It'd be nice not to have any more surprises."

Diana and Stew moved to watch the door as Beth and Chip planted the last few charges. Then the Mundanes moved the bodies of the orcs into a closet on the right side of the room. Suzuki went to look at the angel one last time before they left as Chip scrolled through the datapad, looking to see if she could find anything that would give them a heads up. "Got zilch." She sighed. "Best bet is to kill anyone who sees us."

The Mundanes exited through the door on the opposite side of the room they had first come through. The door opened up into another, larger room with a very similar setup. The only differences were many more tubes with angels in them. That and the walls were lined with glass cages with more angels.

Everyone froze when they walked into the room. After a few seconds, when the shock finally wore off, they stepped farther inside. Upon closer inspection, Suzuki saw all the angels were sleeping. Or something. They were lying on the ground, their legs in the air like a dog's, and they took no notice of the Mundanes, who casually walked through the room, stepping to the cages and looking at them.

Suzuki watched a doglike angel's chest rising and falling and wondered if the thing was dreaming. "Guess everything needs to sleep," Suzuki mused aloud. "Or maybe they're drugged. Chip, can you find us anything on this?"

Chip pulled out the datapad and scrolled through it, biting her bottom lip as she tried to find something useful. "Oh, okay, I think I got something," she chirped. "Looks like the little uglies started getting drugged a few weeks ago. Too difficult to work with, it says. Almost had a meltdown like in the first place we popped. Kills indiscriminately. That's what the note says, at least."

Suzuki looked closer at the angel in front of him. They were exactly like the first one he had seen, which meant these had come from human hosts. Even though the idea of the Dark One experimenting on anyone filled him with rage, there was a special hatred raging in him at that moment, thinking of the Dark One abducting humans and using their bodies for such abominations, all because the Dark One had some perverse idea of control. "How do we open these?" Suzuki asked.

Chip stepped back and blinked twice as she tried to

process what Suzuki was asking. "You did just hear me say they kill indiscriminately, didn't you? Or have you gone momentarily deaf?"

"No, I heard you. That's why I was asking. 'Indiscriminately' means they kill anyone, and this whole place is filled with people who could very easily be anyone. You saw how fast those orcs went down, right?"

Stew laughed to himself. "Yeah, those guys hardly put up a fight. This place is a bunch of fucking nerds. Not fighters."

Suzuki walked away from the cages and joined up with the rest of the Mundanes. "Exactly. And you know what would make a great distraction? A shit ton of angels running around and killing everyone. Might even set off an alarm."

Chip took a seat at one of the tables and rested her head in her palm. "Okay, I see your point. How you plan on keeping them from killing us?" she asked.

Suzuki pointed to his HUD. "Remember the SD I got? You said you used it to stabilize the Dark One's genes in me, right? You also said its main purpose was to control angels, so how about we give it a try?"

Diana stepped up behind Suzuki and rested her hand on his shoulder. Her face was grave. "That's a pretty huge gamble, but it would be a great distraction," she allowed. "I suggest you try it before we open the cages. I remember how much of a hassle these things were before."

"All right, I'm going to give it a shot."

Suzuki turned to the cage closest to him. He closed his eyes and focused. He didn't know if he was going to be able to get to the angel to do a command or if it was going to be more of an ambiguous situation. But now was the time to figure that out. Suzuki reached his hand out toward the closest angel and concentrated on a single thought: come to me.

Nearly instantly, the angel in the cage rolled off its back and opened its mouth in what Suzuki could have only assumed was a yawn. Then it crept toward the cage and pressed its hand against the glass. Suzuki did the same, and they stood there together, hands separated only by the thin layer of glass.

Go to sleep, Suzuki thought.

The angel pulled its hand away and laid back down.

Suzuki let out a sigh of relief. He'd done it, and that changed the entire situation. He wondered how many he could control at a time. Once again, he closed his eyes and focused. This time he imagined his thoughts stretching out through the entire room. *Come to me*, he thought.

All at once, the angels in the cages slowly rolled over. They came up to the glass, pressed their hands to it, and waited.

Sandy burst out laughing and clapped her hands as she jumped up and down. "Oh my fucking God, that is so cool," she squealed. "That's...at least fifteen you can control."

Suzuki thought-commanded the angels to lie back down, and they did as they were told. "Fuck yeah," Suzuki whispered. "Now we got a fucking plan. Chip, can you figure out how to open these remotely?"

Chip raised the datapad triumphantly. "Already on it," she exclaimed.

"Great. Now we move to the giants. We'll open this in a bit and let the angels do what they do, and I'll be able to keep them off us. Then we blow this fucking place."

They left the room and moved on through another series of meandering hallways. Chip led them in silence as the lights above them flickered in certain sections; the farther the Mundanes went into the facility, the more rundown it became. It looked like some sections had been abandoned as the facility continued to grow, the staff most likely moving to the newer sections of the building, trying to avoid the decrepit ones as if they were a plague. It reminded Suzuki of a horror movie he had seen once about a house that continued to get bigger long after the family living in it had died. This place was no different. It was just a different kind of horror taking place behind the walls.

Chip pointed up ahead to a series of three doors next to each other. The hallway had expanded to nearly the size of an airport terminal with hardly anyone taking notice. The ceiling was definitely high enough to get a group of giants through, with room to spare. "This is it. They're going to be in there."

Suzuki unsheathed his axe and tossed it into the air, catching it and smiling to himself. "All right, Mundanes. They're waiting for us. Let's not to disappoint them!"

Suzuki ran toward the door, the rest of the Mundanes sprinting behind him. He kicked it open and ran into a wall of light. Temporarily blind, he knew an attack was going to come from somewhere. He jumped over to the side and rolled while his eyes adjusted to the ludicrously bright room. As his vision came back to him, he saw plasma bolts flying through the air. He scrambled away and grabbed his axe as he stood up.

The room was the largest they had seen yet. There was hardly any equipment. The giants were all on a large white platform that reminded Suzuki of a gallows. Each giant was chained with an electronic device, and they were on their knees. Shackles were around their necks and were connected to what looked like a planting trough. Suzuki didn't have to use his imagination to know what was inside. The tips of the black and purple sprouts reached out from the trough. The giants were being prepared to be turned into hosts.

That was not all the room contained, either. Plasma had been fired by the dozens of Dark One grunts crammed in the room. Suzuki hadn't ever seen this many soldiers in one space before, and they all looked very intent on killing the Mundanes. The only difference Suzuki could see between any of the orc and goblin grunts was the reserve soldiers who stood closest to the giants as if to guard them from the Mundanes.

The orcs were firing their rifles with wild abandon as the Mundanes slipped into the room and separated. *Everyone must have already figured out we can't be all bunched up,* Suzuki thought to himself. *Good thing the room is so big. There's more than enough space to move around.*

Suzuki leapt, landing on one of the balconies that overlooked the room, almost like in an opera theater. He pulled himself up onto the balcony, only to find two orcs who jumped back in surprise. Suzuki axed one of them in the throat and then tackled the other one, bashing his skull in with the haft. Then he picked up one of the orc's plasma pistols and fired a few shots from the balcony. He knew the rifle packed more of a punch, but he also knew he was a terrible shot. This was mostly just to add more chaos to the battle below.

And there was chaos. The room was hot with plasma as the orcs whirled about, firing at whatever Mundane was closest to them. From the outset of entering the room, Diana had cast a protection spell over all the Mundanes to buff their defenses. No one had gotten hit yet, but if they did, the shot wouldn't be as debilitating as usual.

Once Diana had buffed the team, she ran straight into the

thick of the orcs, her wand raised, a lightning whip cracking from its tip. She waved it around her head and electrocuted the orcs directly around her. There were so many orcs and goblins it hardly made a difference. She jumped out of the mosh pit of screaming faces and firing guns and levitated to a better vantage point, using her wand to deflect shot after shot, her face set, grim, and determined.

Beth swung past Diana, using her daggers and chains as a form of locomotion, throwing a dagger ahead of her and connecting with the wall, the tech chains attached to her wrist pulling taut as she swung. She cast her dagger at whatever poor soul was beneath her and severing its head before yanking her dagger back and sending it forward again. Beth was moving fast. When she did drop to the ground, she dashed forward, her daggers held at her side, cutting through four orcs instantly before flipping back up into the air and swinging out of danger, plasma shots trailing her from behind.

Stew still hadn't gone berserk.

He looked like he was holding out for the right time. For now, he was backed up against the wall, casting Enrage on himself as he cut open his chest with his sword. His eyes turned deep red, and he roared with a ferocity that physically threw the closest orcs through the air. He closed his eyes and breathed in deeply, preparing to synergize the Enrage spell with his Battle Meditation. When Stew attacked, it was efficient and deadly. He lunged forward, his sword raised above his head and then, in two swift movements, decapitated the goblins in front of him. Then he raised his sword again, his eyes only half-open as he turned, cleaving a goblin in half, taking the goblin's sword and flinging it across the room, impaling an orc who was advancing toward Sandy.

Sandy was backed up against a wall. She was firing bone spears at the orcs who were accosting her, but there were too many. When she looked through her HUD to see her percentages, the HUD read at a dismal ten percent. She just wasn't strong enough to take on this many enemies at once. As she frantically tried to figure out what to do, she looked around the room and saw her party members all holding their own. Maybe this was what going to do her in.

Chip ran past Sandy and the orcs who had surrounded her, being tailed by a large troll with cybernetic implants and a plasma cannon attached to his arm that was so large it couldn't be lifted from the ground. Chip screamed loudly as she fired shot after shot over her shoulder before skidding in front of Sandy and firing a couple of shots to help take off some of the pressure. Then she shouted, "You're not a fucking mage anymore, you're a necromancer. Fight like a fucking necromancer!" before turning to see the troll. "Oh, dear," Chip murmured as the troll raised its cannon hand.

The words of encouragement were exactly what Sandy needed to hear. She wasn't a mage anymore. She wasn't going to sling lightning or fireballs or call down an ice storm, but she *was* intimately tied to death, and that had been her first love all along. This had been what she wanted.

Sandy raised her hands and bones jutted out of her body, the longest coming from her spine as her feet levitated off the ground. She opened her mouth as she began cackling, bones flying out of her body as she levitated toward the orcs, who were taken aback by the sudden change in character. As Sandy laughed, a dark green gas started to flow from her mouth. It came out thick as clouds and rolled over the orcs in front of her. Instantly, the orcs began coughing. Some of them fell over, clutching their chests as their movements slowed, others vomiting uncontrollably, and others still, their faces growing long with age, their skin turning gray and white. Sandy knelt beside one of the orcs and pressed her hand to his face. Sharp bones burst from his body, impaling all of the orcs around him.

As Sandy stood, an orc from across the room saw an opening and fired. She barely noticed the plasma coming at her in time enough to cover her body with rock hard bones. The blast sent her flying across the room, toward Suzuki's balcony. Suzuki leapt from the balcony and caught Sandy in midair, rolling across the ground, the both of them getting up as fast as possible as the orcs surrounded them.

Suzuki spun, Sandy at his back, and threw his axe at the closest orc. He pulled down his HUD and scanned the area. Fifty percent chance of success. In the back of his head, he was amazed. The Mundanes were grossly outnumbered, but there was still a fifty percent chance they were going to win. If that was the case, the HUD was a little pessimistic. "Chip!" Suzuki shouted. "Release the angels!"

Chip flipped through the air, hitting two orcs with her cannon before landing and taking off running as she flashed Suzuki a thumbs-up. The troll was still chasing her, and she yelped loudly when she saw that.

Suzuki pointed at the troll and grabbed Sandy. "Get that troll off her, all right?"

Sandy went after the troll, impaling two orcs and a goblin as she ran past them. A giant bone spear shot out of her back so she could catch it and knock over a few orcs before launching it through the air as a miasma of black death smoke flowed from her mouth in the direction of the troll. The spear sailed through the air and hit the troll in the throat, tearing a huge chunk out of its neck. The troll stumbled as it tried to stem the flow of blood, its arms swinging wildly. It fell against the wall, and its cannon went off as it hit the ground.

Down the hall, Suzuki could hear the screaming of the angels. He knocked an orc out of his way and headed toward the door the angels were running for. When he got to the door, he threw it open and raised his hand out in front of him. He could see the angels coming. They were racing as fast as they could toward him. *Hope this fucking works,* he thought before concentrating on a single thought: defend us.

The angels continued to run toward Suzuki. They showed no sign of slowing down. Suzuki had the briefest feeling they were going to swarm him. Instead, the angels ran right past. The one heading the pack leapt, its mouth hanging wide open, landing atop an orc and tearing into its face as another angel's sharpened tongue pierced the orc's crotch.

Suzuki flipped his HUD down. Ninety-five percent chance of success. Fucking perfect.

Stew was near Suzuki, and he reached out and grabbed him. "Hey, come with me! We have to get those giants free!" Suzuki shouted.

Stew nodded, and they fought their way through the growing mass of bodies, angels on top of orcs, ripping them to shreds. An orc ran at Stew, who took a step back, drew his blade, and cleaved the orc in half. By the time Suzuki and Stew got to the hosting gallows, they were covered in blood and gore.

Suzuki ran up the stairs of the gallows and peered down at the purple and black sprouts. He couldn't tell if the giants had been infected yet. Just because the sprouts were closed now didn't mean they hadn't opened earlier. There was no way to be sure. It didn't matter, though. They'd find out eventually. With that in mind, Suzuki raised his hand and concentrated on one of the few spells he knew. A jet of flame shot out of his hand, burning the sprouts to a crisp.

As Suzuki burned the plants, an odd screeching sound came from them, like the sound of water evaporating from a pan, a clear hiss as they ceased to be a part of the world. While Suzuki worked, Stew undid the bindings of the giants, chopping through anything that held them down with his axe.

By now, most of the orcs and goblins lay dead on the ground. As the giants tried to get their bearings, Suzuki grabbed one of them and pointed at Chip. "Go to her and she'll get you out of here, you understand?" Suzuki asked.

The giant sleepily nodded his head. They must have been drugged. "Did that flower open in front of you?" Suzuki asked. The giant shook his head slowly, his eyes becoming more awake. "Good! Now go to Chip!"

The giants took off in Chip's direction, staying to the sides of the room where there was less fighting. When Chip saw them, she motioned for them to follow her and took off down the hallway, the giants close behind her.

Suzuki glanced at the room and took it all in. The battle was over. The only orcs who remained were stragglers, or those who had fallen in battle and clung to death. Suzuki concentrated on sending a command to the angels: return back to your cages.

The angels stopped what they were doing and bolted back down the hallway. Suzuki hoped it wouldn't freak Chip and giants out too much when the angels went flying past them.

Sandy was walking around the room, finishing off anyone on the cusp of death. She looked as if she took the job very seriously. The rest of the Mundanes met up around the gallows. They were all covered in blood but there were no serious wounds. "Good job, Mundanes," Suzuki said. "Now we just have to blow this place, and we're out of here. Doesn't even look like we needed those reinforcements. I wonder what Myrddin was talking about in that message?"

Diana pulled up the messages on her HUD and read through them. "You received the same message as Chip and me, correct?" she asked.

"Yeah, same one."

"True, it does seem as if Myrddin anticipated much more resistance than we faced. Interesting. His intel is rarely off, even if a bit cryptic at times. Still, this is not like—"

A loud explosion went off and shook the room, causing most of the Mundanes to lose their footing. "What the hell? Why the hell is Chip setting off the detonators already?" Beth asked.

Suzuki looked at the spots where Chip had set primers and charges. "I don't think those are Chip's bombs," Suzuki murmured.

There was another explosion, this one even larger than the one before. The ground began to crumble, then there was another explosion. The Mundanes fell into the darkness of the facility as the floor gave out beneath them.

23

Suzuki woke up underground in a cavern.

Caverns like those they had found inside the volcano. It was dark and cold, almost freezing. He shuddered as he struggled to get to his feet. The back of his head was throbbing. He must have hit it pretty hard.

As he looked around in the dark, he pulled his HUD down and selected a torch. When the flames of the torch illuminated the cavern, he saw he was the only one here. The rest of the Mundanes had vanished or been taken.

How far did we fall? Suzuki thought to himself.

Walking was painful. The drop must have been pretty long. More importantly, though, Suzuki knew the floors of extremely well-developed research facilities don't just fall in on themselves. The Mundanes had been herded into that room with the giants, and the final trap had been sprung. This was too well-orchestrated for a random group of researchers to have been responsible for. Someone high up in the Dark One's forces had planned this. Maybe another Viceroy.

Suzuki leaned up against the wall to catch his breath. As he shone his light around, he saw Sandy slouched over against another wall. He limped to her as fast as he could and knelt by her side. Suzuki shook Sandy awake gently. Her eyes fluttered open and she stared up at Suzuki, confused but alert. "Where are we?" Sandy asked.

Suzuki pointed up into the darkness above. "We're underground. I'm banged up pretty bad. Are you okay?" Suzuki asked.

Sandy sat up straighter and checked her body. "Yep, looks like I'm pretty good. Here, let me heal you up," Sandy said as she reached over and rested her hand on Suzuki's forehead. "Nice thing about the class switch is that these powers don't burn through my manna so fast. I spend a lot less time waiting for my manna to recharge, and healing costs a shit-ton less. There you go, you should be good. Let's go figure out where everyone else is."

The two wandered down the tunnels for some time before they saw any light. In the distance was what looked like a tunnel with a yellow light glowing within it. Suzuki pulled his axe out, made eye contact with Sandy to see if she was ready, and headed for it. They crossed the threshold and stepped into what could have only been called an egg chamber, but there were no eggs. Instead, the area contained thousands of the black and purple sprouts.

In the middle of the room were the rest of the Mundanes. They were kneeling on a gallows, similar to the one they had seen earlier. The only difference was another smaller gallows meant for one person had been placed directly in front of theirs.

Suzuki looked around the room quickly for any obvious threats and then sprinted toward the Mundanes.

A thundering voice boomed from the air. It was in Suzuki's mind, ripping through each and every one of his thoughts, making it impossible to concentrate on anything. He was overwhelmed by the existence of the entity, a force so strong it made him feel as if he were unraveling.

Suzuki fell to his knees from the pain and held the sides of his head. As the pain subsided, he turned to see Sandy in the same situation.

The voice spoke again, but this time it was not as painful. Suzuki could understand each word as clearly as if he had thought it himself. "I advise you not to attempt to help your friends just yet, Suzuki," the Dark One said.

The Dark One stepped into the light. In person, he was only a little taller than Stew. His body was smooth and without any blemishes, and the locks of blond hair flowing over his shoulders could be called beautiful if they were not so unsettling. He wore only a black skirt that had skulls dangling from it. His chest and arms looked no less spectacular than a Greco-Roman sculpture, yet the blank face, devoid of any sign of humanity—no nose, eyes, or mouth—destroyed any possibility of beauty. All through the Dark One's nearly transparently white skin, his veins were visible, but they were not truly veins. It looked as if electrical circuitry ran through the Dark One's body like a central nervous system.

As the Dark One moved forward, he started to float in the air. He raised his hands, and all around the cavern floating flames appeared.

Behind the Dark One was an angel. It was the size of a full-grown red dragon and its huge, leathery wings spread, sending a strong wind through the cavern. The angel's face was blank as well, the familiar line running from its chin to its forehead. Each of its claws ended in a mass of black tentacles that swirled and wrapped themselves around each other. The angel opened its mouth and roared, fire spewing from its mouth.

The Dark One walked in front of the angel. "Who would have thought the Mundanes, the thorn in my side, would have been felled by something as simple as a fall?" the Dark One taunted. "I was under the impression there would be more of a fight from you."

Suzuki and Sandy stood petrified and silent. This wasn't the fight Suzuki was prepared for. He remembered the sheer terror he had felt in the place between realms, and how long Sandy had spent trying to hide from the Dark One. And now he was there in front of him.

"No brave speeches or retorts, child?" the Dark One boomed. "Has your courage finally failed you? Perhaps you have never been in the presence of a god."

Something welled up in Suzuki—disgust. Utter disgust for the being he saw standing in front of him. "Fuck you!" Suzuki shouted. "It's about time you decided to show your fucked-up face. What are you doing here? Come to get your ass kicked in person this time?"

"Your false display of fearlessness is admirable. Fighting with you is beneath me, unfortunately. I am here to make you a deal. As you can see, your friends are soon to become hosts to my beauty and order. Yet, you, Suzuki—you I want more than any others. I will give you their lives for yours. You take the position before the flowers and give me what is rightfully mine, and the rest of the Mundanes will go free."

Suzuki knew it was a trap.

Beyond a shadow of a doubt.

But he didn't know why the Dark One wanted him.

Something rang true about that statement.

He knew the Dark One was going to kill them all, but he didn't know why he wanted to infect him with an angel so badly.

Then it clicked.

Sandy and Suzuki were the only ones who hadn't been taken hostage. They were also the only two who had gone to the place between realms and seen they had the same finite possibilities as the Dark One did.

For some reason, it made them more desirable to the Dark One to have their genetic code written over. "I know what you're after," Suzuki shouted. "Why didn't you just tie us up yourself like you did them? Then you'd have what you wanted!"

The Dark One came closer, although he maintained his distance. "Old magic," the Dark One hissed. "Ancient works neither of you could understand in your infancy."

Sandy raised her hand, and a bone spear shot at the Dark One. "We don't want your fucking bullshit genes, you eugenic freak!" Sandy shouted.

The bone spear exploded a few inches in front of the Dark One. It never got close to him. "You will be put into order. I would have preferred not to kill you, but rather have you willingly chose a place within my order and beauty. But you have made your choice. Now I will erase you from existence."

The Dark One raised his hand, and Suzuki was no longer on the ground. He was floating ten feet in the air. He reached for his axe, and his entire body went numb as he rammed into the wall.

Suzuki tried to get up but felt his body lose control as he rose into the air again and was slammed into the ground.

Bones crunched, and Suzuki wanted to scream in pain, but his voice was gone. He felt the sides of his throat closing in on themselves as he gasped for breath.

As his eyes blurred, Suzuki could see Sandy on her knees, clutching her throat as the Dark One slowly walked toward them. He grabbed Sandy by her hair and dragged her over to where Suzuki lay gasping for breath.

The Dark One knelt in front of Suzuki and forced him to look at him. "You have never been anything but an inconvenience to me," the Dark One bellowed. "I could have wiped you out with a breath. The only reason you've lived this long was that I did not think you were worth my time to kill. Do you understand me? You are nothing. None of you are. And I will kill you all, and the world will be as if you never were. Then I will hunt down every version of you across all timelines and dimensions, and I will devour them. I will suck your very essence out of the multiverse. You will—"

There was a sound like a screech, and the Dark One looked in the direction of the noise.

A missile came flying down the top of the cavern.

The Dark One raised his hand, the missile exploding in his palm, the explosion somehow contained and evaporating into nothing. "Hm..." the Dark One murmured.

Suzuki felt the Dark One's grasp on him relax. He noticed that Sandy had fallen forward as well, trying to take in as much air as she could. When Suzuki looked up, the cavern ceiling was full of missiles flying toward the Dark One. Suzuki grabbed Sandy and pulled her toward the gallows. "Come on, we need to get them out right now," he shouted.

Sandy and Suzuki ran toward the gallows while the Dark One was busy stopping all the missiles, which exploded. The force of the explosions sent Suzuki and Sandy flying but they got up as fast as they could and finally reached the gallows. They chopped through the restraints holding the other Mundanes, and Suzuki torched the plants as soon as he could. Sandy touched each of the Mundanes' foreheads to rouse them from their sleep. Once they woke, she healed them, and they turned to see what was going on.

An onslaught of missiles was still being fired at the Dark One. None of them could get close. He stopped them and either blew them up or disintegrated them, but it was enough to keep him distracted.

Diana grabbed Sandy by the shoulders. "His name!" Diana shouted. "You found it, didn't you!"

Sandy shook her head as she squinted and tried to remember. "One of them. I found one of his names," she said.

"That's all we need. You need to get close enough that he can hear you, then you tell it to him. You understand?"

"Gotcha. Come on, Suz, we're up."

Suzuki followed Sandy, shouting over his shoulders, "You guys get ready for a fucking fight!"

The Dark One's back was facing Suzuki and Beth. He was thoroughly invested in the barrage of missiles being fired at him. "I'll get his attention," Suzuki told Sandy. "If he's focusing on me and missiles, he won't even notice you."

Sandy nodded and left.

Suzuki raised his axe and threw it at the Dark One, who spun and froze it in the air. He snapped his fingers and the axe turned to ash, then he raised his hand again, exploding the missiles coming for him. Suzuki didn't stop running and punched the Dark One in the face when he reached him.

The Dark One softly touched his cheek. "The insolence," he bellowed as he stopped another missile. He grabbed Suzuki by the throat.

Suzuki felt his esophagus caving in on itself. He tried to breathe but it was impossible. His eyes were swimming as the Dark One held him up and looked him in the eye. "You are nothing to me," the Dark One snarled.

Sandy leapt onto the Dark One's back. She wrapped her arms around his neck and shouted, "No one gives a shit, Bolverkr! Leave my friend the fuck alone!"

The Dark One dropped Suzuki, crouched, and grabbed his chest. "No," he whispered, "How could you—"

The Dark One let out a scream of rage as the circuitry beneath his skin started to glow. There was a massive pop and reality folded in on itself, a portal opening and a giant vacuum sucking the air out of the Dark One.

As Suzuki watched, the god collapsed into himself until there was nothing left. Nothing.

Suzuki was still rubbing his throat as Beth came over and helped him to her feet. "Well, that was anti-climactic." She laughed. "Guess the war's over."

Diana shook her head as she knelt to inspect the burn marks where the Dark One had once stood. "No, no, it is not. That was merely a name of power. The most Sandy has done is restrict him from our plane of reality for a bit of time. I don't know how long. It is a victory, but a small one."

The angel queen ran into the cavern, and a jet of fire shot past the Mundanes. They threw themselves out of the way. "Holy shit, I forgot that thing was even here," Stew shouted.

Behind the angel was the sound of scurrying feet. Suzuki could see dozens of smaller angels pouring into the cavern. He closed his eyes and tried to focus on controlling the angels. What he got instead was a loud screech of feedback in his HUD. *Guess that's a little too much,* he thought as he pulled down his HUD.

Minus twenty-seven percent chance of success.

Great. Now I guess we are fucked.

Something large fell from the top of the cavern, as large as the massive angel. From the back, Suzuki first thought it was a dragon, but when he looked closely, he could see it was not a creature but a metal construct built to look like a dragon.

Even though the mech had wings, Suzuki could see the boosters and jet propulsion built into its backside.

The dragon mech leaned forward and fired a beam of plasma at the angel queen, who leapt out of the way with a grace one would not expect from such a large monster.

Then the dragon mech turned around to face the Mundanes. The dragon mech had an elongated neck built out of steel material to resemble scales. It had a glowing orb in the middle of its chest, and its claws were razor-sharp. The wings that spread as it turned were energy-based, a glowing grid of blue energy in place of the skin of a dragon's wings. Two plasma cannons were mounted on its shoulders.

Stew gasped loudly before he practically squealed with joy. "Holy fucking shit, that is so sick!" Stew shouted.

The chest of the dragon mech opened, splitting apart to show a cockpit. An older man with dusty gray hair and a scar running down his face leaned out. His face was worn and looked like it had been carved out of stone. He wore an eyepatch, and his good eye sparkled with an almost child-like joy. "Heard y'all were waiting for a cavalry," the man said. "Come on, hop on the back, and I'll get y'all out of here. We're in for one hell of a fight."

Suzuki breathed a sigh of relief.

Help had come.

There wasn't time to waste asking for credentials, so the Mundanes scampered into the palms of the mech as they opened toward them. Then the mech took off, blasting off for the ceiling of the cavern, bursting through the narrow hole and out into the night sky. The Mech landed, and the Mundanes climbed out of its hands. The cockpit opened again and the man smiled down at the Mundanes. "Name's Roy Hunter. I'm with the Dragonriders. We're here to help you clean up this mess," he explained, pointing at the sky.

There were four medium-sized dragons flying in a circle. They were covered in steel armor and carried the same cannons that were slung over Roy's mech. Each dragon had a rider on top of it. It looked like Roy was the only Dragon Rider who was piloting a full mech.

The other dragons were covered in tech. Human tech, and other tech, too.

Suzuki opened his mouth to thank Roy but was cut off as the angel queen burst out of the ground, screeching and breathing fire into the night air. Once she had widened the hole in the cavern, hundreds of angels poured out like ants fleeing their colony.

Roy laughed and slammed the side of his mech. "All right, Suzuki, that big son of a bitch is yours. I have to take care of that roaming sphere up there. Looks like the one from the other facility has made its way over here. Time to knock that bad boy right out of the sky."

Suzuki's eyes went wide as he tried to find the words for his fear. "Wait, up to me?" he stumbled. "How the hell am I supposed to take care of—"

"Calm down, kid. Your friend just got here."

A few feet away, as quiet as death itself, Ashegoreth, the Red Death, the red dragon captured by the Dark One in the defense rings, landed. She also had been outfitted with shoulder plasma cannons and the steel armor the rest of the

Dragonriders were wearing. She nodded when she saw Suzuki. "There is no time to talk," Ashegoreth said as Suzuki ran toward her. "Let us burn through our enemies, and we shall speak in the comfort of their ashes."

Suzuki leapt atop Ashegoreth and grabbed her reins.

Roy's mech fired up its jets and took off. Suzuki watched as he flew toward what he had originally thought was the moon. "Focus!" Ashegoreth shouted.

Suzuki gripped the reins tighter and turned his focus to the angel queen, who was belching fireballs at the Mundanes. His friends were quickly being overrun by angels. Ashegoreth sprinted toward the angel queen. The Red Dragon tackled her, ending her deluge of fire and knocking the monster to the ground as her tail swiped at the dragon, trying to impale her.

The rest of the Dragonriders descended onto the battle-field, their plasma guns burning through angel after angel. Beth ran up to one of the riders and leapt onto his dragon, slid down the dragon's wing, and fell on top of two angels with her daggers, skewering them. She flipped off the angels and made her way toward Suzuki and Ashegoreth.

Sandy and Stew were cutting their way through as many angels as they could as they tried to get closer to Chip and Diana, who were pinned against one of the Dragonriders. The Rider's dragon spewed fire that burned through a couple of the angels. Diana raised her wand and levitated, the sky above her darkening. "Cover me!" she shouted at Chip.

Chip slammed her hands together, and they converted to her double plasma cannon. She dug her feet into the ground and started firing at anything that moved.

Rain started to pour as Ashegoreth and the angel queen

wrestled. Ashegoreth managed to sink her teeth into the angel, but not before she whipped the dragon across the face.

Beth slid under an angel, tearing its stomach open before rolling back to her feet and leaping atop Ashegoreth. She landed beside Suzuki and nearly fell over him. "You didn't tell me you had a whole other party of Dragonriders," Beth joked.

Suzuki laughed before being cut short by Ashegoreth getting back to her feet. "Dude, I had no fucking clue there was a dragon posse, but I am so glad there is!"

"It's kinda like a biker gang except cooler, obviously."

The angel roared and flapped her wings, taking off into the air.

Beth grabbed one of the reins as Ashegoreth spread her own wings and headed after the angel. "Sweet!" Beth shouted. "I thought I was going to miss out on this part."

Ashegoreth went racing for the angel, spewing fire at the monster. The angel was even faster in the air than on the ground. She easily dodged the stream of fire and doubled back on Ashegoreth before the dragon could turn around. "Don't worry, we got you," Suzuki shouted as he let go of the reins and ran down Ashegoreth's back, Beth following closely behind. "Give me your old sword," Suzuki demanded.

Beth unsheathed her sword and tossed it to Suzuki. They both leapt, weapons at the ready, at the angel queen.

Below the dueling fire-breathing creatures, Stew and Sandy were slowly making their way through the horde of angels. Sandy raised a bone creature from the corpses of the angels and the thing shuffled off, grabbing whatever it could get its hands on and ripping it to shreds. Stew stopped for a second to admire Sandy's handiwork. "Damn, babe, that is one gross-looking monster," he complimented.

Sandy smiled as she pressed her hand to an angel's head and shot a bone spear through it. "Thanks!" she chirped.

The angel queen crashed to the ground a few feet away from Sandy and Stew, throwing them both into the air as Suzuki and Beth tumbled off her. Ashegoreth landed directly across from the queen. She let out a jet of flame the queen leapt over and, landing on top of the dragon, started tearing into her neck. Ashegoreth screamed in pain as she scrambled to get away.

Suzuki turned to Stew and shouted, "The queen is too fast, and the other dragons are busy! We need you, Stew!"

Stew threw down his swords and screamed in rage as his eyes flashed red and his body started to contort, the bones cracking and stretching, his muscles growing long and taut as he grew to a size he had never reached before. He was larger than a troll, nearing the size of a giant, but unlike giants, he was not bulky and thick. His muscles were lean, and his arms were nearly long enough to touch the ground. His face had contorted as well, his nose sharpening almost like that of a goblin, his mouth filled with razor-sharp fangs. He roared in anger and took off toward the queen. He slammed his body into her side, and she let out a screech of pain as Stew tackled her off Ashegoreth.

The queen turned to face Stew. She still dwarfed him, but Stew was the only option they had until Hunter returned or Ashegoreth caught her second wind. This was the power of the Dark One's genes, Suzuki realized. It was like taking the strongest parts of a race and putting it on steroids.

Stew beat his chest as he roared and charged the queen. She returned the attack, leaping as Stew threw himself at her. They collided with a heavy crack, Stew biting at the queen as he pounded his fists into her back, the angel wrapping her tail around Stew's neck to strangle him.

Sandy grabbed Suzuki's hand and said, "We can't let him do this. He's going to get killed."

Suzuki looked at the sky. Diana was still charging her spell. "I know, I know," Suzuki said, trying to figure out what to do. The battlefield was still thick with angels, and Chip was too far away to reach.

"We handle this ourselves."

Suzuki charged at the queen. Beth and Sandy came running behind him. He tossed himself onto the massive angel's back. Sandy and Beth flung themselves onto her as well. They all started hacking as she flailed, releasing Stew from her grasp. Stew didn't waste any time on the ground, though. He rolled to his feet and grabbed the queen by the tail while the Dragonriders cleaned up the rest of the angels.

Stew pulled hard, and the queen lost her footing and fell on her face. The Mundanes jumped on the queen's back and hacked at her, trying to cut into her exoskeleton.

She pulled her tail out of Stew's grasp and lashed him across the chest, sinking the sharp tip of her tail deep into his torso. The berserker screamed and grasped the tip, then broke it off in his hand, blood gushing everywhere as he plunged it deep into the queen's leg.

From above, Diana shouted, "Mundanes, get clear!"

The Mundanes scattered, leaving the huge angel wounded and exposed.

Diana pointed her wand at the queen and screamed with the rage of a thousand storms. Flaming meteors came flying from the black clouds above.

Sandy raised her hands, her eyes going white. She pulled a shield of bones up over the Mundanes, who huddled underneath it, Stew's body rapidly returning to its normal size as he pressed on his wound.

Meteors peppered the battlefield as the Dragonriders took to the air to avoid the cataclysm. The queen tried to rise as well, but before she could get into the air, a lightning bolt double the size of her body struck her.

The ground trembled from the force of the bolt, and the meteors continued to fall for some time. Fire spread across the earth, scorching everything that lived. The Mundanes huddled as close together as they could while Sandy tried her best to heal Stew's wounds.

After some time, the meteors stopped. Sandy waved away the bone hut, and the Mundanes exited. The angel queen lay still on the ground, breathing heavily as she tried to stand and continue fighting. "Are you fucking kidding me?" Stew shouted. "How the hell is that thing still going?"

Ashegoreth landed and towered over the Mundanes, holding Diana, who was unconscious, in her claws. The magical strain had been too much for her. The cracks in her skin were more pronounced than usual, and the glow behind it was dull. Ashegoreth placed Diana in front of Sandy, then turned to Suzuki. "She lives because she is part dragon, fused with the Dark One's evil," she explained. "Dragons do not die easily, and neither does the Dark One, but she will not be getting up soon."

Suzuki walked over to the angel queen. It was true; she was down for the count. Her body was broken, and it was a miracle she was even breathing. "Okay, so what do we do?"

"My dragon's fire is enough to kill a dragon, but I do not know if it is enough to kill this abomination."

"What if I have the Dark One's genes too?"

Ashegoreth looked at Suzuki and huffed out a cloud of

smoke. "You who has my gift of dragon's blood as well?" she asked.

Suzuki tapped his HUD as he nodded. "Yeah, I got infected by the black petal sprouts. Chip saved my life, but the Dark One's genetic code bonded with mine."

Ashegoreth wistfully scratched her chin as she thought. "And you have the dragon's fire, so—"

"Wait, what are you talking about, dragon's fire?"

"I told you when I first gave you my boon of love. The blood is more than just being able to summon me. The blood defines you as part-dragon. Our fire is your fire. Come, let me touch you."

Ashegoreth slunk over to the queen and looked down at her broken body. Suzuki climbed the queen's body and stood on it. "To breathe fire is to speak the tongue of a dragon. It is difficult for a human, but you will learn eventually. It will burn itself into your mind as you sleep once you utter your first syllable. To breathe fire, you speak our word of life. That is all it means, for fire is life. The word is *ohm-serathka*. Repeat it."

Suzuki sucked in his breath and held it tight in his chest.

He looked down at the queen.

"*Ohm-serathka*."

As the word flowed from Suzuki's mouth, his body was consumed by flames.

Yet there was no pain.

He noticed it casually, and the flames died out as his entire body warmed as if he had just had a shot of whiskey. He opened his mouth and the flames poured out, a stream of fire too hot to behold, yet causing him no pain.

The flames struck the massive angel in the face, and she screamed as the fire covered her body.

Suzuki stood amongst the flames, unharmed.

He stood atop the angel queen as she burned.

He said the word again and again, fire pouring out of him and onto the abominable creature.

Eventually, the flames died.

All that was left were bones. Suzuki left the bones and went back to his friends. They all stared at him like they had seen the true him for the first time, which was exactly how Suzuki felt. Uttering those words had changed something in him. He did not know what it was; all he knew was things were different now.

Stew, his eyes hardly able to stay open, coughed up a little blood and said, "Dude, you can fucking breathe fire? It's about time you were able to do something cool."

Suzuki knelt next to Stew and propped him up. "You're going to be okay. You're going to fine."

Sandy rested her hand on Suzuki's shoulder. "He really will," she said. "I'm tied to his life energy right now. He can't slip away unless I do. He'll make it until we can get him healed."

Above them all, there was a massive explosion. It looked like a shooting star falling to the earth. As the star got closer, it became apparent it was the flaming wreckage of the sphere Hunter had gone to destroy. It crashed into the ground a few hundred feet away, tearing up the earth as it skidded across it in its flaming glory.

Hunter's mech landed behind the Mundanes and Ashegoreth, the Dragonriders right behind him. The mech opened and Hunter leaned out of the cockpit. "Sorry about all that." He laughed. "Didn't think it was going to take so long, but it looks like you chaps cleared this up fast enough. What'd I miss?"

The Mundanes looked at each other. Suzuki raised his hand tentatively. "Uh, I just found out I can breathe fire," he said.

"Huh, Myrddin wasn't joking. You are a pretty interesting bunch. Well, we've torched the facility, y'all destroyed the queen, and I took care of the production sphere. Looks like we've pretty much covered all our bases. Need a ride back home?"

"No, we have battle cats somewhere around here. But these two, Stew and Diana—could you take them back to the Red Lion with you?"

"Yeah, me and Red will get them back safe and sound. If you're up for it when you get back, I'll buy you a few drinks. Lord knows y'all have earned it."

"Sounds good."

The Dragonriders took off as Sandy and Chip loaded Stew and Diana into Hunter's cockpit. Then Hunter closed up and took off into the sky.

Sandy, Beth, Chip, and Suzuki stared at the flaming wreckage, the bones of the queen, and the dead bodies of the angels heaped upon each other. "Fuck, I need a drink." Suzuki finally sighed.

24

T he Red Lion was out of control that night.

The MERCs returned from their quests after hearing through the HUD network the Mundanes had blown up multiple research facilities of the Dark One. That was before they had even heard of the angels. Once news that Suzuki and the Mundanes had faced off against the Dark One in person got out, the drinks were flowing freely.

A table of honor was made up for the Mundanes, and they were all forced to wear the victory hats, old-school witches' hats covered in spider webs with a giant candles atop them. Anytime the candle went out, whoever was wearing the hat had to take a shot.

Chip had managed to get the ambrosia the Mundanes had mined to Wendy, the owner of the Red Lion, soon enough that Wendy was able to produce the drink the Mundanes had originally set out to create. The ambrosia was passed around without discrimination, and it was not long before the entirety of the MERC establishment was drunk off their asses.

The Mundanes, minus Chip and Diana, were sitting in a small corner of the bar. After the praise and glory had been heaped upon them, they decided to tuck themselves away for their own private decompression. The party could wait.

Sandy sipped her beer as she watched the flames of the candles before her. "So, this has been a pretty intense couple of days," she ventured.

Stew laughed, then grabbed his chest. He was still heavily bandaged. The medic had recommended Stew sleep and try to get as much rest as he could, but Stew had argued he was not going to miss the party. "Intense would be an understatement," he exclaimed. "This week has been fucked the fucked up."

Beth tossed back her shot of ambrosia and waved for another to be brought to her. "Yeah, I'll fucking say. First fetch quest I pull with you guys ends up being a whole 'save the world' ordeal. Is this what it's always like?"

Suzuki leaned back in his chair and nodded as he sipped his drink. "Pretty much," he admitted. "I think the only quest we had that was simple was the first one. Everything else kept getting out of control. Glad this one wrapped up nice and tidy. We can all thank José for getting us into this shit and still making life complicated when he's dead. To José!"

The Mundanes raised their glasses and toasted José. A few MERCs nearby heard the toast and joined in. Then the whole bar toasted José, and after that, they toasted the Mundanes.

Stew and Sandy were talking to each other quietly, and Beth leaned over to whisper in Suzuki's ear, "Hey, what do you think about getting out of here for a little bit? Do some of our own celebrating before we come back down?"

Suzuki blushed as he sat up straighter. "You mean, like—"

"You know exactly what I mean. I'll meet you upstairs. Go wash the dragon off first."

"Got it."

Suzuki rose from his chair and muttered some half-thought-out excuse before stumbling away from the table and heading for the stairs. He found his room easily enough, even though he felt like it was much farther down the hall than it usually was.

Once Suzuki got to his room, he collapsed on the bed. He still hadn't processed most of the week, and he knew he probably was never going to get a chance to. The most he could do was run through the different things that had happened and be glad he was still alive.

The urge to piss rose in Suzuki as he was musing about just how insane his life had become. He took off his pants and managed to make it to the bathroom, where he opted for the bathtub instead of the toilet. It was an amazing experience. He felt like he was beside himself. And Beth was going to be there in a little bit. God, could life get any better?

Suzuki turned around and screamed. José's ghost was standing in front of him, shaking his head. "Honestly, you just pissed in the bathtub?" the ghost asked.

Suzuki covered his crotch. "Jesus Christ, dude, do you ever knock or anything?" he shouted. "And yes, I piss in the bath when I'm drunk. So what? I once saw you piss in a sink, and you were completely sober."

José laughed. "Good point. You guys did good. You guys did really good."

On his shoulder sat Fred. Well, the ghost of Fred. "Human whelp, but a good soldier. And a good man."

"Fred!" Suzuki shouted.

"If not a loud one," the imp hissed. "I trust my implant works?"

Suzuki nodded, wrapping a towel around his waist as he walked through José and into the bedroom. "It is so wonderful to see you both. I'm surprised we got through all that. I thought the next time I'd see you, I'd be on the other side. You know, dead too."

Suzuki sat down on the bed, and José sat next to him. José didn't say anything for a long time. Finally, the Horseman cleared his throat and said, "I know what I'm supposed to be doing here, in the place between realms, the Netherworld. I know why I'm here. The fate of all the Nine Realms rests on this quest, and I'm going to need the Mundanes' help. And I'm going to need all the Mundanes to die."

"Wait, what the hell are you talking about?"

José turned to look at Suzuki. His eyes were sad, filled with a deep understanding Suzuki couldn't comprehend. Then he started to fade, and he was gone.

Suzuki sat on the edge of his bed, trying to understand what José had just said.

Beth opened the door and barreled into the room. She had two shots in each of her hands and placed them on the dresser as she walked over and kissed Suzuki. "You ready to show me just how much dragon we can get in me?" she asked.

Suzuki nodded, his eyes distant and confused. Beth handed him a shot and then scooted away from him. "Hey, Suzy, you okay?" she asked.

"I just saw José...and Fred. They said...they said they need our help again."

"Okay, so what's new?"

"Well, it's just that José said we're all going to have to die for it."

Beth sat in silence with Suzuki for some time, both looking at their drinks, not knowing what to say or knowing if there was anything to say. Finally, Beth sighed and took Suzuki's hand in her own. "Suzy, we lived through everything this week, didn't we?" she asked.

"Yeah, we did."

"So, how about we enjoy being alive tonight. And we'll worry about that shit tomorrow."

Beth took Suzuki's chin in her hand and kissed him. "Let tomorrow be tomorrow," she said. "Let tonight be tonight."

They both fell on the bed together, wrapped up in each other's arms, their hands exploring each other's bodies. Tonight would be tonight. Tomorrow would come when it came.

In the Red Lion, the MERCs continued to celebrate.

They drank until they were tired and they ate until they were full.

Tonight was a cause for celebration. It was another victory against the Dark One, and it was proof there was a chance they could win.

The Red Lion didn't shut down that night. The party raged on until the early morning.

Not that Suzuki would have known.

Both he and Beth slept late into the afternoon for the first time, unconcerned with the world outside of the bedroom.

There would be other days to fight.

But not right now. Not this night.

AUTHOR NOTES RAMY VANCE

DECEMBER 21, 2019

Middang3ard has endless potential.

It is a rich universe that has numerous realms and a variety of heroes who can participate in never-ending adventures.

To date, Michael and I have come up with at least 4 possible spin-off series set in Middang3ard and will have already started one of them: (Dragon Approved). It is a Dragon Riders where the dragons wear mech armor and awesome riders taking the fight to the sky.

Our tagline is: Find me a Goddamn Luke Skywalker to win this war!

That said, I wanted to assure everyone that Jose, Suzuki and the Mundanes WILL be back. The Netherverse storyline is a major plot point in the Middang3ard universe (it will be our Infinity Wars, but without all the moral posturing) and several heroes and storylines will be affected by it.

But what about the Mundanes?

The issue that Michael and I are debating is whether or

not the Mundanes series will continue or if they will play a supporting role in the other series.

Whereas the Mundanes storyline did well, it wasn't a homerun and with so many stories to tell, we knew that we could do better.

That said, if you're a Mundanes' fan and want to see more, help us get the word out there! Share, scream and nerd out on their story.

Force your friends, family, colleagues to buy and read the books (gunpoint, optional).

And if we see an uptick in sales, we'll keep writing 'em.

If not, well, their story will continue in the spin-offs.

Either way, this is not the last you'll see of the Mundanes.

AUTHOR NOTES MICHAEL ANDERLE

DECEMBER 21, 2019

Thank you for reading our stories and talking to friends and others about them. We can't do what we do without you!

YOU HAVE GONE TO HELL AND BACK...

Well, not really. I mean, it's hard to conceptualize hell when you have something similar to, but not exactly the same as, Oompa Loompas.

Now, it's time for you to move over to the new Middan-G3ard Series, which might or might not include a blind dragon rider.

(It does, it totally does!)

But before you go read that, stay a minute as I'm working to introduce people BEHIND THE SCENES here at LMBPN to you, our readers.

Today, we have Kayla Curry, Graphic and Web Designer. If you have seen ANY of our images in the last year, you have seen Kayla's work.

We are going to go through her questions and answers, and I'll >>*occasionally*<< butt in.

1. **What turns you on?**

Engaging in a conversation where thoughts, ideas, and knowledge are exchanged.

2. **What turns you off?**

Closed-mindedness.

>>*Very hard to have a two-directional conversation with someone who is closed off. I have no issues having a conversation with a non-likeminded person...but closed off? What a PITA.*<<

3. **Who do you most admire? Why?**

I have admiration for a lot of awesome people. Angelina Jolie is my role model for confidence and humility. Aaron Draplin is my role model for graphic design—our styles are very different, but our views of the industry are very similar. And finally, Ellen DeGeneres for always bringing happiness and joy into the world.

>> *I have to agree with Ellen DeGeneres for her ability to stand up for her opinion, and yet find friendships with those who might not agree. Yet, she has (to me) seemed to always rise above it. She is one very classy lady.*<<

4. **What profession other than your own would you like to attempt?**

I've been known to dabble in many interests, but lately I'm exploring app and game development. I love playing video games, so creating my own would be a fun and exciting challenge.

>>*Heavy on the challenge! I (kind of) wished I had been born later so I could have used the game creation software available now to build something of my own. However, I lack the desire to enjoy programming anymore. So, GO KAYLA GO!*<<

5. **What profession would you not like to do?**

Cooking dinner is the part of my day I least look forward

to. Anything where I have to cook for several hours straight would be torture for me.

>> *Cooking is fun... Cleaning is HORRIBLE.*<<

6. If heaven exists, what would you like to hear God say when you arrive at the Pearly Gates?

That's a tough one. I'm a pantheist, so it's hard for me to imagine this scenario...if God were the universe, and the pearly gates were a sparkling nebula or something, I'd want to know that I will still have my consciousness after death in some way.

>>*Ok, I thought Kayla was my second Pantheist to learn about in the last twenty-four hours. But, I just (researched) and found out Hinduism and Pantheism are not equivalent. Huh, learn something new every day. For those interested (as I was)* https://sites. google.com/site/sanatanhindusite/hinduism-monotheistic#TOC-13.-Is-Hinduism-Pantheistic-Panentheistic-Polytheistic-monotheistic-or-henotheistic- <<

7. What is your favorite movie?

Any movie that Angelina Jolie is in will be toward the top of my list, but *Beyond Borders* had a huge impact on me when I was a teenager. It opened my eyes to the world beyond my own. It got me started in being more active and aware of the problems others face. It was a huge turning point for me as I made the transition from a selfish teen to an altruistic human being.

>>*Man, this is poignant. I had not yet met a person (until now) who had been positively affected by these aspects of Angelina Jolie's career. This is cool.)*<<

8. Who is your favorite character and from what book by which author?

Sherlock Holmes will always be my favorite character and

the original *A Study in Scarlet* will always be my favorite story. Sir Arthur Conan Doyle is a genius.

9. What is something most people do not know about you?

I touched on this in another question, but I'm a pantheist (a scientific pantheist if you really want to narrow it down) and I don't really tell that to a lot of people. It's not a secret, however it's not something I bring up often. I haven't completely defined my exact beliefs, but I explore them anytime I have an opportunity.

10. What do you look forward to most in the new year?

I'm looking forward to growing my business, teaching my kids more about what I do, and learning more creative skills as well. I'm taking some courses on character design and learning new graphic design techniques constantly. I'm also learning more code and starting to utilize my tech knowledge to create some awesome custom web elements.

11. What's your favorite non-LMBPN series you've done? What's your favorite series inside LMBPN?

Non-LMBPN (besides Sherlock Holmes) would be S. M. Boyce's *Grimoire Saga*. Inside LMBPN would have to be a tie between all the original Oriceran series...*Leira Chronicles, Kacy Chronicles, Fairhaven Chronicles, Midwest Magic,* and *Soul Stone.* The Brownstone series are definitely up in the top favorites as well.

>> That Oriceran Universe has a lot of fans – specifically The Leira Chronicles. *I think maybe Martha Carr is paying people off ;-) <<*

Do you have a web site you'd like to promote?

https://currygraphicdesign.com/

We appreciate you spending your time reading our

stories. Now, we have to get back to the laptop and get cranking more of them out!

Ad Aeternitatem,

Michael Anderle

OTHER BOOKS BY RAMY VANCE

Mortality Bites Series
Keep Evolving Series
Fatebound Series

Other Middang3ard Books

Never Split The Party (01)
Late To the Party (02)
It's My Party (03)

Blue Hell And Alien Fire (04)

Death Of An Author: A Middang3ard Novella

BOOKS BY MICHAEL ANDERLE

For a complete list of books by Michael Anderle, please visit:

www.lmbpn.com/ma-books/

All LMBPN Audiobooks are Available at Audible.com and iTunes

To see all LMBPN audiobooks, including those written by Michael Anderle please visit:

www.lmbpn.com/audible

CONNECT WITH THE AUTHORS

Connect with Ramy

Join Ramy's Newsletter

Join Ramy's FB Group: House of the GoneGod Damned!

Connect with Michael Anderle and sign up for his email list here:

Website: http://lmbpn.com

Email List: http://lmbpn.com/email/

Facebook:
www.facebook.com/TheKurtherianGambitBooks